Ike McAli.

as he rounded the rocky ledge. A bullet whistled by his head and pinged off a boulder behind him. He dove off Ally and ducked behind the large granite outcropping, waiting for their next move. Cattle thieves weren't common in this part of South Park, but they weren't unheard of either. Some of his stock was missing, and he'd picked up these riders' trail. His partner, Buster, was on the other side of the Park searching for the same stock, so Ike was alone on the valley floor.

He peeked around the rock, gripping his gun handle. The rustlers were driving five cattle south, away from his ranch. At least they hadn't gotten either of his bulls. The drag rustler looked back occasionally, but none of them seemed to be in any hurry. Ike considered his options. He could follow and if he was lucky, scatter them with his rifle, then drive the animals back to his spread, or he could turn back now and let the bandits have the cattle.

He never was one to turn back. He'd get his stock one way or another.

Praise for Mike Torreano

THE RENEWAL is the sequel to *THE RECKONING*, released in 2016 to five-star reviews.

~*~

"*THE RECKONING* is cleverly plotted, and expertly paced."

~*~

"The storyline of *THE RECKONING* makes you want to know what's around the next page and to the next book from this author."

~*~

"Masterful combination of yarn spinning, period dialect, and highly descriptive prose."

The Renewal

by

Mike Torreano

The Renewal

Cover Art by *Kim Mendoza*

The Wild Rose Press, Inc.
PO Box 708
Adams Basin, NY 14410-0708
Visit us at www.thewildrosepress.com

Publishing History
First Mainstream Historical Edition, 2018
Print ISBN 978-1-5092-2001-4
Digital ISBN 978-1-5092-2002-1

Published in the United States of America

Dedication

This is dedicated to my two daughters, Lisa and Dina.
Lisa has done much great research
to help *The Renewal* come to pass,
and Dina is the doting mother of a passel of future
cowboys and cowgirls.

Chapter One

South Park, Colorado, Spring 1872

Ike McAlister spied three rustlers ahead as he rounded the rocky ledge. A bullet whistled by his head and pinged off a boulder behind him. He dove off Ally and ducked behind the large granite outcropping, waiting for their next move. Cattle thieves weren't common in this part of South Park, but they weren't unheard of either. Some of his stock was missing, and he'd picked up these riders' trail. His partner, Buster, was on the other side of the Park searching for the same stock, so Ike was alone on the valley floor.

He peeked around the rock, gripping his gun handle. The rustlers were driving five cattle south, away from his ranch. At least they hadn't gotten either of his bulls. The drag rustler looked back occasionally, but none of them seemed to be in any hurry. Ike considered his options. He could follow and if he was lucky, scatter them with his rifle, then drive the animals back to his spread, or he could turn back now and let the bandits have the cattle.

He never was one to turn back. He'd get his stock one way or another.

He swung his bad leg up gamely on Ally, his warhorse. She bobbed her head as if to say, 'let's go.' Ike nudged her and rode out from behind cover. He'd have to stay farther back than he wanted, as there was little to conceal him on the basin floor. He put a hand to his Winchester in the scabbard by his left leg. Then he drew his Colt .44 and checked the cylinder. He wished the day was a little further along than it was, as the bright sun overhead acted like a spotlight. On them, too, but they didn't need cover like he did.

He didn't recognize any of the rustlers—who they were or where they were from. He spent most of his time on his ranch, so he didn't know many people in the nearby town of Cottonwood. Every day brought enough to do on his spread, including shadowing cattle thieves. These three weren't hard to follow, as slow as they were riding. He told Ally to keep them in sight.

Just then a lone rider galloped toward the trio from the left.

Buster!

The rider fired at the rustlers from a distance, and they turned and fired back. Ike spurred Ally and drew the Winchester. He shot in the thieves' direction but wasn't likely to hit anything but air, bouncing in the saddle as he was. Soon, the three wheeled their horses away and vamoosed south, leaving the cattle standing blankly in the middle of the large Park basin.

Ike pulled up as he neared Buster. "What were you thinkin', ridin' in all alone? Seein' ain't your strong suit—couldn't you tell there was three of them?"

"I just heard a shot and scooted over here. With my eyesight, it looked like there was eight or nine wranglers, so I figured it was gonna be pretty near an even fight." He tried to hide a smile behind his stubbly beard flecked with gray.

Ike whacked a hat against his jeans. "Don't know

what I'm gonna do with you, Buster. I ain't payin' you enough to afford a decent burial, so I guess if you'd got killed just now, I woudda just dug a hole somewhere out here and stuck you in it."

"That works for me." Buster pointed to a small copse of pines off in the distance. "Looks like a nice spot over there."

Ike laughed. "I'll have to remember that." He turned Ally toward the cattle grazing nearby. "Let's get these doggies home." The two men drove the stock ahead of them, and a peregrine falcon screeched overhead while they talked.

Buster said, "They wasn't like any rustlers I ever saw before. They wasn't gallopin' the animals and tryin' to cover their tracks. Can't figure that."

Ike patted Ally on the neck. "I guess I won't spend a lot of time thinkin' on what they were doin', but they did seem to come apart pretty quick." He took a quick look behind. "Let's don't tell Lorraine about this, she's got enough to worry about already."

"Whatever you say, she's your wife."

When they neared his spread, Ike said, "You go on ahead and get them settled back in with the rest of the herd. I'm goin' up in the hills to the west and look for strays before it gets dark." Come springtime, his cows liked the seclusion of the low foothills when they were ready to calve.

Buster said, "Don't stay too long, Ike, Lorraine worries about you."

"Don't know why. I've never given her cause to."

Buster shook his head and grinned.

With a slight nod, Ike was off. He reached the forested foothills not long after. The sun had just slid behind the distant snowcapped summits, and the temperature was dropping. He glanced at the gentle slopes surrounding him. Patches of snow lay scattered in this sheltered part of the forest. Springtime in the Rockies was a chancy proposition at best. As he climbed, he found some recent cow sign leading up the hill. The unmistakable yowl of a mountain lion came from the draw just ahead, and he reined Ally in. It was an eerie sound that floated in the air like the tortured cry of a baby. He whispered to Ally and slid his bad right leg off the horse. His fingers wrapped around his worn gun stock. He flicked the leather loop off the hammer, then reconsidered. A rifle might be a better choice. Drawing his Winchester out of its scabbard, he crouched sideways in the piney depression and crept forward.

He thought about leaving the cow, but he couldn't afford to lose any more stock than he already had. He figured she had to be in the yawning clearing dead ahead where he'd heard the lion. The puma's low growl had a "stay away" edge to it, and as Ike inched closer, he saw why. The big cat had taken the cow's calf down and stood straddling the dead newborn, long yellow teeth bared. The cow was bawling nearby, charging the puma again and again, stopping just short of the cat's slashing claws and sharp teeth. The lion's ribs showed through a dirty, matted coat, and it made no move to abandon its prize.

Ike swung his rifle up as the cat turned and growled, ready to spring. He stepped backward, tripped on a loose rock, and fell with a thud on his bad leg. His rifle flew away. Before the lion could leap, a shot rang out from the forest. A bullet pinged off the granite ledge at the animal's feet, kicking up small shards of sharp rock and stopping the big cat. Its ears flattened and it shied away, then loped off; small red streaks on its dirty tan sides.

Ike struggled to a stand and swept up his rifle. He crouched as he scanned the forested upslope ahead, but the shooter stayed hidden. He kept an eye on his surroundings and the cow. Silence reclaimed the forest, but as he neared the distressed animal, Ike's sixth sense told him to look up the hillside again. An Indian had come out from the cover of the pines and sat motionless atop his horse not fifty feet above him.

Rain Water!

His was a face Ike would never forget. Ike swung his Winchester upward and stared at the still warrior. Rain Water held his rifle at his side, and Ike sensed the brave wasn't going to shoot him. If that's what he meant to do, he already would have. Ike lowered his weapon. There were likely several other braves still hidden nearby. A young Ute chief of his prominence never rode alone. Rain Water sat like a statue. Ike didn't know what to say. It had been almost four years since he'd seen the Indian, and that encounter hadn't ended well. It was a time in his life he'd tried to forget, but there were some things that seared a man so deeply they were never forgotten.

Ike's heart pounded. "You came silently, Rain Water. I did not see you." It wasn't much of a conversation starter, especially after several years.

Rain Water said, "You did not see me because I did not want you to."

The Indian's eyes moved over Ike's slightly-stooped form. There was a coldness there Ike could feel. No doubt Rain Water was replaying their last meeting in his head, too. Ike waited for the warrior to respond.

Another minute passed as the men stared at each other. Rain Water leaned forward on his horse. "You are still weak, stumbling when you should not. No real warrior would fall in front of puma." He raised his chin as he spoke.

Ike squinted at the Indian. Rain Water still had the upper hand, even after all this time. A flush warmed Ike's face, and he pursed his lips hard to keep his tongue in check. He limped toward the motionless cow and threw a lasso around its neck, avoiding looking at the brave who sat straight above him. He tugged the animal down the slope toward Ally. Several times he tried to mount up, but the fall aggravated his old leg injury and he failed each attempt. Anger and embarrassment coursed through him. He finally pulled himself crosswise on the saddle then swung his right leg over the horse and straightened. The leg hurt too much to get his right boot in the stirrup.

A vein in his neck pulsed.

Damn!

He held the cow's rope in one hand and gripped the saddle horn hard with the other. He wanted to turn and say something before he rode off, but the words wouldn't come. The warrior had likely just saved him from serious injury or worse, but he was at a loss how to acknowledge Rain Water's gesture. Ike sat still in the saddle for a moment then dropped the cow's rope, nudged Ally gently, and rode down the draw without looking back.

An early evening chill would soon blanket the low

hills, and he drew his thick coat tighter around his neck. He broke out onto the broad valley floor at an easy trot. His small ranch lay in this northern part of South Park near the town of Cottonwood, south of the small village of Jefferson. The ranch house was still almost an hour away—plenty of time to gather his thoughts.

In the distance to the north, he saw two, three men working on the basin. One of them looked like his brother-in-law. Made sense. Professor Hugh Walnutt married his sister Sue last year and was leading the survey team for the new railroad due to come from Denver through South Park soon. The train would take land when it came, and that likely promised a fight with nearby ranchers that Ike didn't look forward to.

The sun was just a memory when he pulled up at his barn. Buster stood by the open door and took his reins. A calico cat swished her tail atop some hay still warm from the day's sun and stared at him with droopy eyes. She was his daughter Jessie's cat for sure, but when she wasn't around, Ike's lap made for Calico's next favorite spot. The barn was a work in progress he and Buster were still expanding. It was well past the stage where it had been not much more than a tall wooden lean-to with only room for their horses.

There were several stalls inside now along with a separate tack room. The rest of the barn held hay needed to get his cattle through winter and early spring. Deer and elk couldn't poach it in here. The pile of hay had dwindled considerably over the last few months, and Ike wondered if he would run out of feed before he ran out of winter. He looked forward to when the Park meadows filled with enough new green grass and early sage to more than feed the herd.

A circular split-rail corral sat next to the barn, and a stream swollen by late spring runoff gurgled nearby. As he passed by Lorraine's small garden he smiled, thinking about the joy she got from serving her family homegrown vegetables.

He rubbed Ally down, filled her oat bucket, and released her into the small corral where she could cool off and drink from the water trough. Ike eyed his warhorse. She was getting to an age when most horses started slowing down. But Ally had never been most horses. She hadn't shown any signs of age yet, but no telling how much the war had taken out of her.

He smacked a dusty hat against his jeans and brushed back longish brown hair. A quick swipe at his short beard, and he limped toward the ranch house. Lorraine was already out the front door walking toward him, with Jessie running right behind as fast as her three-year-old legs would carry her. Lorraine hugged him hard, grabbed his chin, and stood on her toes to kiss him. She stepped back from her tall husband and hit him lightly on the shoulder.

Ike feigned a surprised look and eyed his pretty wife. Flashing gray eyes that missed nothing. Straw-colored hair pulled back in a bun. Simple smock. Wry smile. "What's that for?" He sported the smallest of smiles, as if he didn't know.

Lorraine hugged him again. "Nothin' in particular. Just somethin' to remember me by when you're away so long. And don't be comin' back here at dusk any more. You keep scarin' the chickens, and they won't lay."

Ike knew his wife well enough to know that was her way of worrying about him. Her smile couldn't mask the fear in her eyes, though. She'd told him more than once she worried about losing both her husband and the ranch in the coming fight over land for the railroad. And he was concerned about her, in her condition. Her second miscarriage a little more than a year ago put this pregnancy in doubt. They hoped summer would bring a healthy new McAlister.

He'd stayed in the hills too long today, delayed by his encounter with Rain Water. Seeing the Ute chief again after all these years had been a shock. One he kept replaying in his mind. How foolish he'd looked.

His reverie was broken by Jessie who bounced in front of him with her arms held high. He scooped her up and swung his little girl in a small circle over his head. She squealed with delight as he took her by the hands and spun her round and round with her legs straight out, brown hair flying, then gathered her to him and kissed her gently on the cheek. She'd always been able to change his face from a frown to a grin.

Lorraine broke in. "You keep tossing her around like that, and she's gonna throw up all over you. She just ate." She swept an unruly lock of hair back and put her hands on her hips in the manner Ike had become so used to.

"My little girl wouldn't do that, would you?" He tickled her ribs, and she burst into hysterical laughter, wrapping her short arms around Ike's sunburned neck.

Lorraine took his hand and led him toward the house. Ike patted his wife's growing bulge, showing more prominently at the seven-month point. She wasn't much more than five-feet tall, while Ike stood more than six.

Inside the ranch house, Buster stirred the fireplace

to life again. Round river stones blackened by countless fires lay under blazing pine logs and spread a faint warmth throughout the modest house. The McAlister cabin was not much bigger than the bunkhouse at the Emerald Valley Ranch that had dominated the large South Park basin years ago. The Park lay at about ten thousand feet, covered by wild grasses and sage and surrounded by towering mountains to the east, north, and west.

Ike and Lorraine built the ranch three years ago with the reward money Hugh Walnutt shared with them for finding the rest of the cash stolen from the stage coach line years ago. Buster threw his cut into the cause as well. At the time, he told them, "I ain't got no people closer to me than you two, so the least I can do is help you get a good start with this place." But the good start was a memory, and the ranch was barely feeding the four of them after a long hard winter. They lived off money Ike raised selling cattle in the fall and the garden vegetables Lorraine sold in Cottonwood in the summer.

Years ago when he was still drinking, Buster was Lorraine's handyman at the small boarding house she ran in town. With his grizzled features, it was hard to tell how old he was. A long stretch as a mountain man had aged him prematurely, and his drinking only hastened it. But Ike was indebted to him for leading him to his sister, Sue, when she disappeared several years ago. Buster wasn't much of a ranch hand, but it wasn't for lack of trying. As far as Ike was concerned, the man had paid his dues, and there was a place on his spread for as long as Buster wanted it.

Ike settled into his chair at the table. Dinner was warm beans, bread, and a small portion of venison. It wouldn't do to eat beef and cut into his coming profits. Lorraine flitted around the small house tonight, first sitting across from him at the wooden table then jumping up for coffee and stirring the already-roused fire.

Ike watched her scurry around the open room, which served as kitchen and dining room rolled into one. "What's the matter with you? You ain't stayed put in one place since I got home."

Lorraine slowly sat across the table from her husband. She glanced at Buster, then back at Ike. "Sue came to visit today." She said it in an offhand way, but Ike noticed she stopped short and broke eye contact with him.

Ike set his fork down. "That's a good thing, ain't it? What brought her out here? Too many boarders in that small house?" He said it half in jest, but his only sister hadn't been out to the ranch in some time. It wasn't like her to visit out of the blue.

"No, she said she just stopped by to say hello. She did ask where you were." Lorraine looked over at Buster for help.

In between forkfuls, Buster said, "I think she came out here mostly to see you, Ike. May have somethin' on her mind."

"What makes you say that?" Ike ripped off the end of a hard loaf and offered a cut piece to Lorraine. "Can't a sister pay a visit to her favorite brother?" He smiled, then noticed Lorraine bunching her napkin.

Buster said, "Well, sure, but I got the feelin'—"

Ike looked from Buster to Lorraine. "One of you spit it out. What are you gettin' at?"

Buster said, "Well, if you just let me finish, I'll tell

you. Sue looked worried, Ike, and it was clear she wasn't gonna share her worry with me or Miss Lorraine."

Ike eyed his companions then gazed in the direction of town. "Sounds like somethin' that needs followin' up on."

Lorraine laid a hand on his arm. "Maybe so, but there'll be no followin' up tonight, cowboy. There's plenty around here tomorrow to keep you busy, too. So why don't you just forget about Sue's visit and keep your eye on me. No tellin' what trouble I'm liable to get into if you don't." She smiled a tight smile, but Ike knew what she was trying to do.

****

In the morning, he sat at the breakfast table while Jessie talked his ears off.

Lorraine brought plates of flapjacks over. "Jessica, now stop your yammerin' and let your father eat his breakfast. You need to eat too."

Ike debated telling Lorraine he was going to town. Maybe he could throw her off by riding out toward his small herd, which was grazing in the opposite direction from Cottonwood, then circle back. No. That wouldn't do. They'd never lied to each other, and he wasn't going to start now. After breakfast, he got up from the table and kissed Jessie on top of her head. He put a hand under Lorraine's chin and held her gaze hard. "I'm off to town to see Sue." He steeled himself for her response.

She turned away and started clearing dishes. "I know that."

"How'd you know?"

"I ain't been married to you for the last four years

without pickin' up some of what you're thinkin' without you sayin' it." She stuck her chin out. "Go on now, go."

Ike hesitated. "Buster'll be with you while I'm gone. I'll only—"

"Buster and I will be fine. You just go about your business and get right back here."

Ike pulled her close. "There ain't nothin' that could ever keep me away from you for long." A slight nod to Buster who nodded back. The man always had Ike's back. Ike kissed Lorraine softly on the cheek then headed out the front door and disappeared into the barn.

Ally nudged the iron clasp on her stall when he walked in. She was always up for the next ride. Ike stroked her neck and spoke quietly while she bobbed her head, ready for the bridle. His eyes traveled to the scars on her hindquarters. The war seemed a long way away, but Ally carried several reminders. It had been another lifetime in some ways. A conflict that had taken his parents and a big part of his heart.

Ike led his horse out of the stable and into the yard, swung a gimpy leg over, and straightened in the saddle. Lorraine stood at the front window with a hand to her mouth. What was she worried about? It was just a visit to see his younger sister. He nodded at her and with a gentle nudge to Ally's flanks, started into an easy lope for Cottonwood.

Chapter Two

The terrain between the ranch and Cottonwood was a series of low rolling hills, covered with brown grasses that greened to life toward the end of spring. The snow-capped Rockies loomed to the west. They dominated the high valley and served as a reminder that winter still held sway over Colorado's higher reaches.

Ike slowed Ally to a walk when he reached the outskirts of town. Fresh lumber lay to the side of the skeletons of several new buildings. Main street stretched farther than when he first laid eyes on the town four years ago, but Cottonwood seemed somewhat foreign now. Town never did feel like home, even when he roomed at Lorraine's old boarding house. He'd always been more at ease at his ranch or riding the South Park basin.

"Hallo, Ike." Ned O'Toole waved from his mercantile store with his ever-present smile. "I declare, it must be a coupla months since I seen you in town. Where you been keepin' yourself?"

Ike returned the greeting. The shopkeeper had always amused him, even when he'd thrown Ike's clothes out the first time they met. "Been out ridin' around lookin' for a good place to start a real dry goods store. Somethin' to give you a little competition, Ned. Think I found just the place, too."

O'Toole's smile widened, and he gave a little

shake of his head. "For a hard-bitten cowboy, you're pretty quick with a comeback. Come on in and have a look-see when you're done with your business." With that, he waved again and went back into the store.

Ike pulled up at Sue's boarding house and threw Ally's reins over the front post. Sue and her husband, Hugh Walnutt, bought the place from Lorraine several years ago, and she was running it now. Another boarding house had recently opened, but Sue and Ike's brother Rob was still boarding with her. She and Hugh had added a couple of rooms to the ground floor to accommodate Cottonwood's growth. And now with the railroad survey team in town, the boarding house was full again.

Sue's little hostel had never looked very fancy, even when new. Several boards creaked as Ike stepped up to the front door, knocked, and pushed on in. Three fellows sat around the dining table, one calling Sue for more breakfast. Ike had never seen any of them before. but then there were a lot of people in town he hadn't seen before. Silver mining in the hills to the west was keeping local merchants busy, and it seemed like the stagecoach brought newcomers almost every week.

The boarder ignored Ike and continued to holler at Sue in the kitchen. Ike walked along the hallway and peeked in at his sister. She was scurrying around with pans, eggs, and flour all a blur. He snuck up behind her as she stood at the stove and put his hands on her waist. She turned with a spatula in her hand and readied a blow until she saw who it was.

"Ike!" She threw her arms around his neck and sank her head against his chest.

Ike held her tight, then looked at her closely. Faint

circles under her young eyes. A dull sheen to her straw-colored hair. He held back from remarking on her appearance. "How've you been, Sis? I was just in town and thought I'd stop by," he lied. Something wasn't right. Sue had always had a certain spirit, but there was only resignation in her this morning. "Why don't you let the kitchen fixin's go for a second and have a cup of coffee with me?" He filled a cup, grabbed her hand, and led her toward the parlor. Her coffee was only tolerable, but she had lots of years left to improve on it.

Just then a voice came from behind Ike. "She ain't gonna sit and have coffee with you 'til she's fixed me seconds." The man was stocky and young, maybe twenty, and spoke in such a way that he seemed used to getting what he wanted. He pointed a finger at Ike. "And you let her be. I might just be gettin' ready to lay claim to her."

Ike stiffened, and his eyes went hard. Good thing Sue's husband hadn't heard that. Hugh was the fastest draw in town.

Sue hurried into the dining room and stood between the boarder and her brother. "Ike, that's Mr. Bert Quincy, he's one of my lodgers from the railroad," she said without any enthusiasm.

The boarder looked surprised when Ike said, "From the looks of her"—he jabbed a thumb in Sue's direction—"I don't think she's ready for you to lay claim to her." Ike didn't really want to cause a ruckus in his sister's place, but he wasn't about to let anyone bully her. His light blue eyes fixed on Quincy as the boarder rose from the table and advanced toward him. Ike motioned for Sue to move away.

She took a step backward and stood wide-eyed.

Ike stared back at Quincy. He guessed if a fight was coming, might as well come now. "I figure your lack of manners means you're done eatin'." Ike was several inches taller than the man, but the young oaf had maybe thirty pounds on him. The loudmouth carried the same sidearm on his hip as Ike did—the leather loop still over the top of the hammer.

"I told you, mister. Leave her be; she's too pretty to be spendin' all her time cookin'. I got some plans for her that don't concern you."

Ike saw red. Instinct took over. Before Quincy could duck, Ike backhanded him hard across the face. He hadn't been in town more than a few minutes and already he was mixing it up. Trouble just seemed to find him even when he wasn't looking for it. The man's head snapped back, and he put a hand to his jaw. A red splotch sprang to life on his cheek. His other hand moved toward his holster, but Ike slapped him hard again before he could free his gun. This time the man staggered backward, his stumble only halted by the kitchen wall. Ike waited for him to react, left hand lightly resting on his holster.

"What was that for?" The man rubbed his reddened jaw, his eyes dropping to Ike's Colt.

Ike looked the man over. "Just gettin' your attention. Seems like this is your lucky day. My sister has decided to overlook your disrespect. Haven't you, Sis?"

Sue nodded silently.

Ike loosened his Colt in its holster. "I'd suggest you leave us alone, mister, and just finish your breakfast."

The man eyeballed Ike then wiped at the tear in his

eye. Hard slaps stung. He hesitated, then with a slight flick of his fingers the hammer loop came off. Ike rushed him and landed a solid fist to the midsection which doubled Quincy over. He grabbed the boarder by the collar and pulled him lurching toward the front door. With a final heave, Ike threw him headlong into the street and drew his sidearm. The man rolled to a stop and went for his gun but stopped when he saw Ike's Colt aimed at his forehead.

The fracas kicked up a small cloud of dust which hung in the air.

"You don't know who you're messin' with, mister."

Ike cocked his gun. The man threw his hands up, stood, and backed away down the street. Ike had cowed the boarder, but he guessed this wouldn't be the last time he ran into the fellow. He turned back to the house as the other two boarders scurried outside. Sue stood away from the door a bit, holding back tears. Ike put a hand on her shoulder. "It's okay; he won't bother you anymore."

She brushed his hand away. "I can take care of myself, Ike McAlister. You should know that by now. I don't need my big brother protecting me." Her eyes narrowed, but she wrapped her arms around him and gave him a quick hug before heading back toward the kitchen.

Ike followed, a little unsure of what to make of her reaction. He hesitated. "Uh, Buster said you stopped by the ranch yesterday, like you might have somethin' on your mind."

"It wasn't anything, really." She avoided looking at him and busied herself wiping the already-clean small table.

"Buster has known you as long as anybody around here and has always had a knack for puttin' two and two together before most people even know there's a two out there."

Sue sidestepped Ike on her way to the dining room and started clearing dishes. "Can't a girl just pay a visit to her big brother and his family?" Ike had said almost the same thing to Lorraine yesterday.

He followed her into the dining room. "This is me, Sue. Tell me what's wrong." He lowered himself into a chair.

"You mean other than you just scaring away a paying boarder?" A solitary tear trailed down each cheek. "I'm sorry. I didn't mean that. Thank you for chasing that skunk away. I still got a few more boarders, and then there's always Rob."

Ike brightened. "So, where is Hugh? Did the railroad send your husband on ahead to scout around here in the valley?" Ike was best man and Lorraine maid of honor when Sue and the Englishman married last year.

"It's just one of his usual trips surveying land for the railroad. He'll be back soon, and every time he returns, that varmint you just drove off acts real nice around me. Guess he knows my husband's reputation with a gun."

Ike put a hand on her arm as she was leaving the room. "Sue. Quit changin' the subject and tell me what's botherin' you. Please." His sister was doing a good job of talking about everything except what was bothering her.

Sue sagged into the chair next to him and pursed

her lips. "I don't know that it's anything at all. I can't be sure if I heard right, but I thought it might be something you should know anyway. Like I said, that boarder you just braced works for the railroad, the one everybody says is gonna come through the valley sometime. Him and another couple railroaders been boarding here for the past couple of weeks. It's been nice to be full up, or at least it was."

Ike patted her arm. "And?"

"And yesterday at breakfast, I heard them talking about the land the railroad's gonna take when it comes through. The young feller you jumped said they'd be confiscating ranches laying in the path. He didn't mention yours exactly, but it does lay in the general direction he said the railroad's gonna go. He was almost bragging about takin' ranchers' land, like he was a big man. Talked about damning up the streams, too. Never did cotton to an hombre with greasy hair."

Ike clenched a hand. "Is that all? Nothin' to worry about." He wondered if Sue believed what he just said, because he didn't. "No one's gonna take my ranch— that's called stealin'—and you know what happens to rustlers. There's still laws against that, even out here." But Ike wasn't so sure. Land wasn't any good without water, and frontier justice seemed to favor whoever had the most money and connections. That wasn't him. "And quit worryin' so much. I want to see that big smile of yours again." He leaned over, kissed Sue on her cheek, and headed for the sheriff's office. His brother Rob's place.

As he walked along the slightly-crooked main street, he kept an eye out for Quincy. At the sheriff's office, he jiggled the tricky door latch until it gave way.

Inside, his younger brother was seated at a small desk.

Rob looked up and smiled. "Brother Ike. Good to see you."

Ike shook Rob's outstretched hand. It had been a while since he was last in town. "Good to see you, too." He returned Rob's smile and eyed his brother up and down. "Sheriffin' must be agreein' with you. You look plumb fattened up. Can't be Margaret's cooking, though."

Rob grinned. "Now, don't you go makin' fun of her cookin'. You ain't so handy with a pot yourself, and I don't remember Lorraine winnin' any blue ribbons on May Day. But excuse my manners. Have a seat." Ike started to sit on the edge of the desk when Rob motioned to a single chair, which had seen better days.

Ike eased himself into it. "This chair looks like it's pretty well used up, Rob, just like the tired wrangler sittin' in it." He smiled and tipped his Stetson back.

"You ain't but a few years older than me, Ike. You just wear your years harder."

Ike nodded. "Reckon you're right. How's things here in town?"

"All in all, pretty quiet, except for some shenanigans on Saturday nights." He pointed to the cowboy in the single cell drowsing on a small cot. "Nothin' I can't handle. What're you doin' in town? You don't get here much."

"Just came to pay my respects to my brother and sister." He smiled broadly as if that tickled him somehow. He steepled his fingers. "Say, I heard there's railroaders in town. When's it supposed to be runnin' through here?"

"Don't know for sure, but it's some time away. The

folks the railroad sent seem real nice. Hugh's leadin' the survey crew that's plannin' the railroad's route on the way to Fairplay. I've already gone ridin' through the valley with them a few times. The boss is a man named Charlie Hawkins. Not the most likeable sort, but he's a real smart fella."

"How's that?"

"'Cause he's payin' me extra every month to keep things in hand so's people comin' through here will see Cottonwood is a nice, friendly town." Rob broke into a grin.

Ike frowned. "He's payin' part of your salary? Does that mean you're workin' for him now?" Ike stared at his younger brother until Rob broke eye contact.

"I'm still workin' for this town, Ike, and don't you ever doubt it or question me that way again. I won't have it. Understand?" Rob's grin changed into a flinty-eyed stare.

Ike softened. "Just checkin'." He scanned the room to let the tension ease. He'd always been close to Rob and didn't want to let this hang in the air between them. His brother was a good man. "Got any coffee left?"

"Over there on that table by the rifle rack. Brown pot. Margaret brings it by every morning."

Ike rolled his eyes on his way over to the small table. "Speakin' of Margaret, when are you gonna make an honest woman of her?" Ike enjoyed teasing Rob. His brother had always been popular, especially with the ladies.

Rob arched an eyebrow. "Don't be bringin' that up neither, even if you are my kin. Did Sue put you up to that? She must beat me up about that every day seems like. I'll get around to it in my own time."

Ike started to say something but let it go. Rob was more than old enough to figure out what his next move with Margaret was. He'd been hard enough on him already. Rob had never taken life very seriously, but he was the kind of person everybody liked. "Sue says she heard they've pretty much decided on the route the railroad'll be takin'." Ike peered at the sheriff. "That right?" He poured himself a cup of coffee.

Rob's answer was cut short when the door latch rattled, and a stranger strode into the jail. He was beefy and wore a dark suit with a white shirt and black string tie. The man fixed his gaze on Rob and tipped his black bowler hat back a bit. "Sheriff, there's a problem I need you to fix." The man ignored Ike as if Ike wasn't there and as if what he had to say was the most important thing at hand. "One of my men just got rousted at the boarding house by a stranger. He was minding his own business when this cowboy shows up and starts threatening him with a gun. Can't have that, Sheriff. Can't have that at all."

Rob looked uncertain. "What'd this hand look like?"

"I expect he looked like any other roughrider around here, except taller. I want you to stop by the railroad office. That way you can ask my crewman yourself. His name's Quincy."

"I'll do that, Mr. Hawkins. By the way, this here's my brother, Ike. Ike, this is Charlie Hawkins—he's in charge of gettin' the railroad through South Park. They call it the Denver, South Park, and Pacific. Grand soundin', ain't it?" Rob smiled at his brother who still cradled his full cup of coffee.

Hawkins grunted at Ike.

Ike took a sip. This was the man that the young punk who disrespected Sue worked for. There weren't many things that riled Ike, but insulting his family was at the top of the list of things that did.

The railroader narrowed his eyes. "You the drifter that jumped my man?"

Ike nodded again.

"You saw that, Sheriff; he admitted it." Hawkins was speaking to Rob, but his eyes never left Ike. "Lock him up."

Ike put his cup back on the table. "That's not gonna happen today, Mr. Hawkins. One of your lackeys just told you a tall tale, and you believed him. Let me tell you somethin'. If your man comes around the boarding house and harasses my sister again, he'll get more than a couple slaps on the cheek. And tell him to find another place to bunk." Ike was almost six inches taller than Hawkins and took full advantage of it in his exchange with him.

Ike's meaning was clear, but Hawkins didn't seem to be a man easily cowed. He looked at Ike with fire in his eyes. "Stay away from me and my men, or you'll find out how we handle people who get in our way." Hawkins looked over at Rob. "Doesn't look like you're planning to do anything about this ruffian, Sheriff, but that's all right—we got our own way of dealing with thugs. I been real nice so far, but looks like it's time to show you and everybody else how things are gonna run around here from now on. I'll be telling Mr. Hansen about our little conversation, too. You'll be hearing from me."

Rob stepped between Ike and Hawkins. "Now, no

need to get riled up, Charlie. Ike here didn't mean no harm, did you, Ike?"

Ike looked at his brother then Hawkins and put his hat back on. "Looks like we ain't got off on the right foot, Hawkins. Be seein' you again, I'm sure." He nodded his brother's way, stepped around Hawkins, and headed for the door.

Hawkins got the last word in. "Steer clear of my men if you want to stay healthy."

Ike paused for a second but didn't turn around. When Hawkins said nothing more, Ike jiggled the latch open and left. As he walked along the wooden walkway in front of the town's shops, the brisk morning air cooled him off some. A woman called his name.

"Ike. Oh, Ike."

He turned and saw Margaret Pinshaw coming toward him. She was crossing the dusty main street carrying a coffee pot and potholder.

She hurried up to him. "How are you, Ike? Haven't seen you in town in some time. Lorraine comes in now and then with your little girl for supplies, but then I don't get to talk with her much, and I was just going to the jail to…well anyway, how are you?"

"I'm fine Margaret, you're looking well, and that hat does you justice." He tipped his stained Stetson and smiled. Margaret owned the only dress shop in town, The Sew Pretty. "Off to see Rob?"

Margaret blushed. "Well, yes I was, you see his coffee pot usually needs a refill about this time of morning." She smiled and looked in the direction of the jail.

"Well, I know he appreciates your attention."

Margaret arched her eyebrows. "Do you think so?

Did he say that? I mean, he seems to, but he never says so, and I really don't know. I would think he does, but you know your brother—he'd never say so, now would he?" Margaret asked it in such a way that it was clear she wanted an answer.

The corners of Ike's mouth turned up a little. "He remarks on your food, too."

"Really? Oh, I'm so glad. I think I'm getting so much better at cooking. Made him toast and eggs this morning." She broke into a big smile.

Ike put a hand to his mouth to cover a smirk. "I've heard him talk about your toast and eggs. According to Rob, they're almost cooked to a—I mean, they look like…" Ike flushed a little and reined his wayward mouth in. He turned toward the jail. "Yes, well, I reckon I'd best let you get on with your business." He tipped his hat. "Ma'am."

Margaret beamed. "Yes, I don't want Rob's coffee to get cold."

"Then your timing's good, because the pot in there is pretty light about now. I'm sure him and his visitor will be glad to see you."

"He has a visitor? Who is it, Ike? Someone I know?"

Ike squinted at the small building. "Just someone we're likely to see more of as time goes on."

"Well, then, I'll be off…" Margaret smiled, gave a little curtsy, and hurried toward the jail, her ever-present blue parasol bouncing under an arm.

Ike continued down the wooden sidewalk in the direction of the boarding house. As he neared, he recognized the horse hitched next to Ally. He stepped up the low front stairs and hollered through the open door. "I'm comin' in, so if you two are messin' around in there, better stop."

Hugh Walnutt met him at the door with a smile. The Englishman used to work for the stage line that ran through South Park, but now he worked for Hawkins. "Well hello, Ike. Sue said you were in town. It is nice to see you; we don't have the privilege often enough."

Ike admired Hugh's steady hand and the way he treated his sister. "I ain't much of a privilege, Professor, but it's nice to see you, too. Where'd you just get back from?"

"Well, you know the railroad has me scouting a route through this part of the Park. Surveying, really. I have been gone for several days, so it is nice to be back." Ike started to reply but Hugh cut in. "Excuse me, Ike, but Sue said you ran into a little trouble here earlier. Which one of our esteemed guests was it?"

"Don't know. Didn't really take his measure, but he's a stocky one. Sue can tell you which one."

"Well, she is being rather closemouthed about it. It shook her up pretty well. I think she is afraid of what I would do to the rounder. But I have a good idea who it is."

"She was kind of mad at me for throwin' him out. Said she coudda handled it herself."

"That's my Sue. It is probably a good thing I was not here to witness the cad's behavior. I don't lose my temper often, but I would have made an exception for him. We need paying customers but not that badly."

Ike changed the subject. "So, tell me about this railroad. Where's it likely to go when it comes through? Lots of us want to know if it's gonna try to come through our spreads or not."

Hugh nodded. "You said, 'try,' Ike. I am afraid there's no 'try' to it. The railroad is going to take the land it determines it needs, including right of way for a mile on either side of the tracks. But your concern is understandable, certainly. Right now, we are just doing very preliminary surveying, and the railroad will not actually come through South Park for a time yet. Things could change, I suppose, but I really do not think you have anything to worry about. The likeliest route will miss your ranch."

Somehow, Ike didn't feel relieved.

"But the railroad will need some of your neighbors' land."

Ike shook his head. "Have you told any of them yet?"

"No—that's Mr. Hawkins' job, and there is no sense upsetting people before we know for sure. Like I said, it is not going to happen for a good while anyway."

"It ain't right the railroad can just take people's lands, especially when there's plenty of empty ground just to the north. Why can't the railroad lay track where it don't take any ranches?" Ike whacked his hat against his pant leg. "Some of these ranchers been homesteadin' for years now, lots of 'em longer than I have."

"It is not my decision, Ike. Hawkins is going to make the final call on where the track is laid." Hugh broke eye contact with Ike for a moment, then continued. "You are familiar with eminent domain, where the government has the authority to take land for the common good."

Ike had heard of it but hadn't ever heard it used in

connection with land in South Park. Yet.

"Even though we do not exactly have eminent domain here, the railroad will purchase the land needed with the governor's blessing. I have heard he's even an investor in the enterprise. But if the rail line cuts through any ranches, the railroad will pay landowners handsomely for their property."

"Handsomely, huh? I'll bet it don't feel handsome to a rancher that has to sign his land over to some company out of Denver. Wouldn't to me. Also wouldn't surprise me if some of my friends resisted turning their spreads over."

"Well, I hope it does not come to that, but it is something you will probably not have to worry about, like I said."

Ike could see his brother-in-law fidgeting a bit. He raised an eyebrow. "I'll hold you to that, but even if the railroad doesn't take my property, my friends' lands are still at risk, and no one's gonna take kindly to that when there's other routes."

"Now, Ike. Threatening these railroaders is not going to get anyone anywhere. They are well connected and powerful. And used to getting what they want."

"Ain't no threat; that's just the way folks are around here." He yelled a goodbye to Sue, headed out the door, and swung up on Ally.

He rode west along the path he thought the railroad might take based on what Hugh said. The first spread he came to was the Donaldson place several miles down the way. He knocked on the door.

Mrs. Donaldson greeted him with a big smile. "Ike, it's so nice to see you. Won't you come in? Abe is working out back in the garden, digging and planting.

I'll call him."

Ike stared out the kitchen window at the distant hills to the west. He imagined a powerful, loud locomotive pushing a cloud of gray smoke into the piercing blue sky. Donaldson interrupted his thoughts.

"Ike, what brings you our way? Please sit. Mother, would you bring our guest some tea?"

Ike stood as Mrs. Donaldson poured from a teapot into beautiful china cups. "These cups are one of the few things I have of my parents. It's little enough to remember them by, but I so enjoy using them when I can. Thank you for coming by."

Ike smiled, raised his cup, and took a sip. He placed it gently on the table. "There's trouble brewin', and I want you to know it's comin'. It's possible the railroad's gonna try to take our land, when they could take a different route that don't roust ranchers or farmers. I'm holdin' a meetin' in two days to talk about it, and I need you to spread the word, Abe. Ride on down range and tell the Spencers what I just told you, and have them tell the next ranch and so on." He looked at Mrs. Donaldson. "Is it all right if we meet here? Hawkins' men may be watchin' my house. I been makin' the most noise so far. Day after next, about five o'clock?"

She nodded. Her face wore a worried frown. "Of course."

****

The meeting didn't start off particularly well. There were almost twenty ranchers and farmers from miles around in the Donaldson barn. The first part was an airing of concerns, not the least of which was the railroad's route and whose land lay in the way.

Ike tried to bring some order. "All right, we know the railroad's a danger to many of us here. As for the miners, they're good people, but they need timber and water to work, and they're been stripping lots of the surrounding forests. The railroad needs lumber and will need water, too, which sets up a possible fight with the miners." The grumbling increased as the crowd realized they were likely smack in the middle of a struggle for the future of the Park.

There was a holler from the back of the crowd. "What about land, Ike? We've got to have open range to run our cattle on; one hundred sixty acres just ain't enough. And how can we fight the railroad if it tries to grab our property? What if the government moves in on the Park range and fences it off? I hear they been doin' that other places."

The grousing was getting louder. "What if our water gets shut off? There ain't enough of us to fight all the miners and all they gotta do is come up with a big silver or gold strike hereabouts and there'll be lots more of them."

Things weren't turning out the way Ike hoped. "This is startin' to sound like a turn-tail meetin' "—he scanned the weathered faces—"and I know we're all tougher than that, so let's figure out how we're gonna protect our places."

One of the men in front shook his head. "I ain't never run from anythin' in my life, but how can we fight the railroad, the miners, and the government?"

Ike walked over and put a hand on the man's shoulder. "We can't fight them by ourselves, but if we stay together, we can give them a go." A few heads nodded, and a loose range group was born. "Anybody runs into any trouble, just holler. We'll meet here again next month." Ike wasn't exactly sure if banding together was going to work, but it had to be better than riding solo into whatever danger lay ahead.

Chapter Three

The last Saturday of May dawned with rosy-hued streaks in a pale blue sky as the sun peeked over the eastern horizon. Tables were festooned with red, white, and blue bunting for the annual May Day festivities. The centerpiece of the day's activities was the red maypole, which stood more than fifteen feet high with a round top and multi-colored ribbons of rope dangling nearly to the ground.

Every year May Day welcomed spring to the high country, as the celebration heralded the promise of better times to come. Hundreds of people arrived on horse, buggy, wagon, and afoot. More than in the whole town of Cottonwood. A small ensemble was setting up to play in the middle of the park on a rough wooden platform resembling a gazebo. Tables and chairs were arranged in a loose circle toward the edges of the field.

Ike and family came in from the west on their wagon.

As they drew nearer, Margaret Pinshaw hailed them with the queen's wave. "It's so good to see you, Lorraine. I'm sorry I haven't been out to the ranch to visit lately, I've just been too busy what with these preparations, and time seems to get away from me." She smiled widely, as though she meant it.

Lorraine leaned toward her from the bouncy seat in front. "Don't give it a thought. We see each other about as much as we want to, I reckon, but it's good to be here." Lorraine considered thanking her for being in charge of the planning again this year, but that remark would just be an invitation for Margaret to launch into a lengthy description of the trouble and problems the planning presented. All naturally overcome, of course.

Ike pulled the dusty wagon to a stop outside the large circle of tables. Jessie sat next to him, and he folded her in his strong arms as Buster set the wagon brake and dismounted. After getting off, he reached a hand upward for Lorraine and helped her from the wagon. They'd had enough hard times lately; it was time for some fun.

Ike took Jessie by the hand as they walked toward the sounds of May Day laughter. He knew a few of the folks there, but that was all. No doubt some of the newcomers were miners who had scoured the black dust from their bodies and donned clean clothes. Most folks were dressed in their Sunday best, such as it was. The little boys looked scrubbed, with pink cheeks and their hair mostly combed, but that wouldn't last long as the May Day field was still full of wet ground that would turn into mud before the day was over.

Ike could tell Lorraine enjoyed the change of scenery. The conversations and waves she traded with neighbors reflected the ease with which she seemed to handle almost any social situation. Ike basked in her enjoyment and smiled when Jessie unwrapped her small hand from his and ran toward the tall maypole where the other children were spinning, laughing, and shouting. "Be careful, honey," he yelled after her, which didn't slow her a bit.

Buster joined Ike at the tables laden with foods of

all types; from local produce to specialty homemade dishes, and he put a little bit of everything on his plate. "I ain't had real good home cookin' for some time," he mumbled to no one in particular. Behind him, Ike said, "Don't let Lorraine hear you say that. And don't ever let her hear you compare her food to Margaret's. If I knew for sure which of these dishes were Margaret's, I'd steer clear of 'em. Not sure how Rob tolerates it. Maybe that's why he hasn't asked her to marry him yet. It's a wonder he ain't skin and bones."

Their laughter stopped when Margaret hurried up from behind. "Why gentlemen, won't you try my rhubarb pie? I made it special for today."

Buster removed his cowboy hat, revealing thin, graying hair. "Thank you kindly, ma'am, don't mind if I do. And Ike here, he was just sayin' how good it looked. Weren't you?" Buster wore a wry smile.

Ike cleared his throat. "Yes, ma'am. In fact, I was just askin' which dish was yours, wasn't I, Buster?"

"That's a fact, Miss Margaret." Buster nodded and wiped his forehead with a tattered bandana.

Margaret blushed. "Well, thank you. Let me just help you to a serving, Ike." She enthusiastically lifted a large slice onto Ike's plate, her ever-present parasol tucked out of harm's way. "Please try it while it's still warm."

Ike took a small bite and swallowed quickly. A hesitation, a hand to his mouth and a long drawn-out, "Mmm, mmm. That's mighty…tasty, Margaret. Mighty tasty indeed. Say, that reminds me, you haven't seen my wife, have you? I oughta check on her to see that she's not been whisked away by some fella better-lookin' than me. But Buster here ain't tried your pie yet, and I know he's eager to do so, so I'll leave him in your good hands." He tipped his hat to Margaret, winked at Buster, and hurried off.

He found Lorraine at the other end of the food tables, hemmed in by several women, all chattering about what a beautiful day it was to have a spring festival. He'd certainly gotten lucky when he married her. Ike stopped short for a moment, admiring how she brought life to everything and everyone she met. That wasn't his way, although she'd tried to encourage him to be more social. He just wasn't a good learner, he guessed. It made him appreciate her even more. He was about to go back for more food when one of the women standing nearby noticed him.

"Mr. Ike, how nice you could join us. Ladies, let's make a place for one of the handsomest men in town."

The compliment came from Eleanor Whitaker, the mayor's wife. Ike had never thought himself handsome, so he stammered a short reply. "Thank you. I was just thinking how you all added to the beauty of the day." Where that came from he didn't know, but it prompted giggles and broad smiles from the women.

Lorraine hurried over to him. "Now, you all just give my man a wide berth. He's so darned good looking that if you got any closer, I'm sure you'd keel over."

A flush spread up Ike's neck.

One of the women asked, "Well, seeing as Ike's not available, how about his good-looking brother? Is Rob in the men's raffle today?" She caught Lorraine's eye. "He can put his feet under my table any time."

Another lady tittered. "I sure would like to win him for a day."

Lorraine rolled her eyes. "I'm sure you would,"

then with a nod she guided Ike back to the food. "You're all mine, cowboy, so don't you go thinkin' any different. And you better stay on my good side. I already shot at you once, so don't think there couldn't be a second time." Her wide smile belied her words though and warmed Ike from the inside out. "Say, where'd you come up with that beauty thing you told the ladies anyway? I've never heard you say anything as pretty as that, except to me."

Ike smiled back. "And I won't be sayin' anything like that again, I reckon. Not if it gets me in trouble with my best girl." Ike kissed her on the cheek.

"Am I still your best girl?" Her eyes sought his. "I was beginning to think Jessie had taken my place."

Ike was in dangerous territory and knew it. He paused. "You'll always be the first girl I ever fell in love with and am still in love with. Jessie can't ever take that place, now can she?" A flood of relief coursed through him. Pretty good for spur of the moment. What's more, he meant it.

As they toured the tables, Ike heard a voice bellow his name. He turned to the sound. Hawkins. The man wore an expensive-looking black suit, with a white shirt and a red string tie this time. The bullnecked cowboy next to him was the boarder Ike tussled with. Quincy. Ike stared silently at Hawkins.

Hawkins smiled, his hands behind his back, strutting a bit. "Aren't you going to introduce me to your wife?"

Ike debated, then said, "Lorraine, this is Mr. Hawkins, of the railroad."

"The pleasure is mine, Mrs. McAlister. Nice to meet you. I've already met your husband. Perhaps he mentioned our encounter?"

Lorraine looked up at Ike. "Why, no, Mr. Hawkins, he didn't. I would have remembered that."

Ike nodded. "Perhaps you told your boss in Denver about your man harassing my sister?" Ike glanced at Quincy then looked back at the starched shirt standing in front of him.

Hawkins returned Ike's stare then turned to Lorraine. "I'm afraid I've interrupted something. Perhaps we'll have an opportunity to have a conversation some other time."

Ike cradled Lorraine by the elbow and turned her away. Lorraine said back over her shoulder, "Nice to meet you, Mr. Hawkins."

Hawkins answered as Ike guided Lorraine. "The pleasure was mine, Mrs. McAlister."

As soon as they were out of earshot, Lorraine turned on her husband. "Just what was that all about, mister? He seemed nice enough."

Ike considered his response. He'd had a bad feeling about Hawkins from the first time he laid eyes on him, and his intuition had rescued him from more than a few tight spots in the past. He debated how much to tell Lorraine about the threat Hawkins represented. "Not really sure. There's just somethin' about him that's off-puttin'. Can't put my finger on it yet." He'd say more when he knew more about Hawkins' plans for the route. "Sorry if I'm not very good company right now." He gazed in the direction of his ranch.

Lorraine placed a hand on his shoulder. "I'm not buyin' it, cowboy. Somethin's eatin' at you, and you ain't lettin' me in on it for some reason. Don't leave me out in the cold too long, or I might just freeze."

Ike picked up on her drift. Their talk was taking a dicey direction, and he needed to ratchet things back a bit. "Why don't we head over to the maypole and find out what Jessie's doin'?"

Lorraine cocked her head at him and after a pause said, "That's the smartest thing you've said today, but don't you be thinkin' you're just gonna throw me off whatever's botherin' you just like that. You think on what's goin' on and tell me somethin' true soon. But for now, let's just enjoy the rest of the day."

Ike had come to recognize when something was behind his wife's words. Whenever they argued and he wanted to leave, she forced him to stay and talk. He never liked doing that at the time, but it had smoothed out more than one argument. Ike faked a small smile. "That's a deal. Where do you suppose my best little girl is?"

They wandered through a throng of people, past tables crowded with steaming casseroles, desserts, and meats sizzling over hot coals in a fiery pit. There she was. Twirling with other children, big and small, running around the tall pole holding a red rope that draped from the top. Long sandy brown hair flying in all directions.

Ike reveled in his daughter's joy. She always brought a smile to his face, regardless of how well or badly his day had gone. His wife and his daughter were his world. He'd do anything to protect them. Ike turned toward the food tables and started fixing a plate for Lorraine. He stopped at a dish of lamb and decided to tease her. "Would you like some lamb, honey?"

"You know I ain't a lamber, cowboy, so don't be puttin' any mutton on that plate. In fact, why don't I make a plate for you, too?" She grinned sideways at him. "I'll eat what you put on my plate if you eat what I put on your plate." She broke into a laugh as she looked at him.

This time Ike didn't have to force a smile. "Why not? Deal." At first, he searched for radishes to populate her plate with but then switched to her favorite foods instead. When they traded dishes, they both chuckled. Each had gone out of their way to pick lots of what they knew the other liked.

Ike relaxed as the sun hung overhead and warmed the crowd. He spied Rob coming his way, maneuvering through the crowd with Margaret hurrying to keep up. He hadn't seen Sue yet, but she and the professor were no doubt in the crowd somewhere. He was searching for them when he saw Quincy again. There was an ugly sneer on the young railroader's face.

He narrowed his eyes at Ike from only a few yards away. "You enjoy yourself today, mister, 'cause you ain't gonna enjoy what's comin' your way soon."

Ike tensed. He was just about to answer when Hawkins appeared out of the crowd.

"I see you've run into my man again, McAlister. Seems like the two of you can't get enough of each other."

Ike had had enough of Hawkins' barbs. He asked Lorraine to get Jessie. She stayed put. He said, "Please." She left in a huff. When he was sure she couldn't hear him anymore, he turned to Hawkins. "I don't like you. And I don't like your toady there. Looks like you've made up your mind we're going to tangle, whether it's here and now, or down the road. You pick the time and place, and I'll be there." He stared at the heavyset man.

Hawkins paused. "I'll tell you what, McAlister, instead of fighting each other, why don't we have a more civilized contest? I hear there's a shoot-off here today for the men. If you're game, why don't you try your luck against me there?"

Ike considered. He didn't know anything about Hawkins' shooting skill, but he knew his way around a firearm. His upbringing and the war had taught him well on that score. Still, a man doesn't suggest doing something he's not good at, so Ike had the feeling Hawkins was probably a crack shot. Didn't matter. "You're on. Follow me." Ike led him over to the makeshift range which was nothing more than a few paper, hand-drawn targets hung on a line fifty yards away backed up to a short hillock. The targets swayed in a slight wind.

"Targets wasn't what I was talking about, McAlister. I imagine you're pretty good at hitting something that's not moving, like my man the other day. Why don't we make it more interesting? How about shooting fifty-cent pieces out of the air? With pistols instead of rifles. How would that be? Unless still targets are the only thing you can hit?" He smiled widely, but his eyes bored into Ike's. "Whoever hits the most coins wins."

Ike nodded involuntarily. His blood was up, and he would have agreed to anything Hawkins suggested. He didn't lose his temper often, because things didn't usually turn out well when he did. He was on the verge of it right now, though, and the slight ringing in his ears told him there was no turning back. Coins would do.

Hawkins called Rob over to officiate. "Your

brother and me are going to have a little contest. You just throw these coins in the air all at once. Think you can do that, Sheriff? Think you can keep it fair, this being your brother and all?"

Ike struggled to control himself. Rob had always had an easy manner about him, but Hawkins had just taken advantage of it and belittled his brother publicly. He wasn't about to let the bully get away with that. If a fight was coming, his father always said it was better to get to it sooner rather than later and on your terms. He dropped his hand to his gun. "Or we could just shoot each other and be done with the coins. How about it?" Lorraine would have had his hide if she'd heard that. Good thing she was out of earshot.

Hawkins arched his eyebrows and turned to Rob. "So, you need your big brother to stick up for you, is that it? Not man enough to stand on your own?"

Rob balled his fists as he scowled at the two combatants. After a short silence, he said, "Nobody's gonna shoot nobody else here today. Ike, you stand down now, and move your hand away from your holster." He turned to the railroader. "Mr. Hawkins, why don't you quit tryin' to provoke him and just let things be?"

Hawkins ignored Rob and turned to the crowd surrounding them. "You heard McAlister here threaten me, didn't you, boys? I just want everyone within the sound of my voice to know I didn't threaten him." He eyeballed the folks gathered to see the shoot-off. "Everybody got that?" He turned back to Ike. "I didn't hear what you said about coins, McAlister. That's better than shooting each other up, wouldn't you concur?"

Ike nodded. But only slightly better. "You supply

the coins." Money was in short supply at the McAlister household this time of year.

"I'd be happy to donate them, because when the railroad does come through here, I'm gonna be a rich man. And I'll wager you're gonna be especially interested to see the route it takes."

Ike hesitated. What did the bully mean by that? Hugh said he didn't have to worry; the route wasn't coming near his place. A flush rose upward from his neck, and there was still a faint echo in his ears. Just then, the mayor of Cottonwood called to Ike from a short distance. Henry Whitaker was not known for bold thinking or action.

He hurried up to Ike and in a whisper said, "Ike, what are you doing? You're riling Hawkins up for no good reason. We don't want him and his company to think the town of Cottonwood is inhospitable. There's lots riding on the railroad coming through here. The citizens are depending on the prosperity the train will bring. Don't do anything to make Hawkins mad. Please. We need him a lot more than he needs us." Whitaker almost trembled, he was so worked up.

Ike shook his head. "There's some things more important than money, Mayor. Like self-respect, and fightin' to hold on to land a man's put long days and lots of sweat into. Those promises the government made about bein' able to homestead our land ought to be honored too, don't you think?"

Hawkins walked up and interrupted. "You done with your little talk?" He sported a thin smile.

"I was done before it started." Ike motioned Whitaker away, and the man stepped back into the crowd.

Hawkins jangled three fifty-cent pieces in his hand. "These ought to do it, don't you think? Three coins, three shots."

Ike nodded. He was a better shot with his pistol anyway, and he'd pulled his Colt's trigger more times than he cared to remember. Its worn handle was silent testimony to that. He drew the weapon, checked the cylinder and copper caps, and spun it before placing it lightly back in his holster. When he looked up, Lorraine was striding toward him, Jessie in tow. Striding fast. Her face was a mixture of frown and fury.

"What're you doin', Ike McAlister? A man don't check his gun if he's not plannin' on usin' it. This here's a picnic; it's no time to be drawin' weapons. Especially around little children. So just forget whatever it was you were thinkin' of doin'." She pointed at Hawkins. "And there's no sense gettin' tangled up with that hombre. That's a face not even a mother could love."

The railroader stiffened.

Lorraine took Ike's hand and was walking away when Hawkins called him out.

"Well now, that was awfully convenient timing, McAlister. Just when you were gonna lose a shooting contest, your wife shows up and drags you away. Sharp tongue and all. Sounds to me like you better go, because it's clear she runs things in your family."

Before Ike could respond, Lorraine marched up to Hawkins with her chin stuck out and hands on her hips. "My man makes his own decisions, Hawkins, and I'm guessin' he just decided to put you in your place. But he can speak for himself." She turned back to Ike.

Ike's heartbeat always slowed when he faced

trouble. He tied his holster off on his left leg, cinched his belt a notch tighter, then eyed Hawkins coolly. "Anytime, railroader. And why don't we use quarters instead of fifty-cent pieces?"

"Sounds like a capital idea. Would you like to go first? Or should I show you what you have to beat?" He fished three quarters from his vest pocket.

"Any way you want."

Hawkins stood with an infuriating smirk on his face. He kept jangling the coins in his hand, trying to irritate Ike. It was working more than Ike let on.

"Lorraine, you and Jessie please step back now."

She lifted their daughter in her arms and moved toward the crowd of bystanders.

Hawkins looked at the throng gathered around the two men. "I need someone to throw these coins in the air, same time."

Buster stepped forward. He walked toward Hawkins with his hand out. "Hand me them silvers."

Hawkins closed his fist around the coins. "You ain't gonna do it, you old alky. I heard about you. You're liable to stumble and fall before you could even throw them. Go on now, get back in line."

Ike took a slight tug at his hat brim and snugged it lower on his forehead. Buster was his good friend. He glared at Hawkins, and his left hand twitched. "He don't throw for me, I don't shoot. And find someone else to throw for you."

"Fine, fine. No need to get all worked up, homesteader." Hawkins scanned the crowd. "Let's see. You there. Walnutt. Come pitch these into the air for me."

Hugh stayed put. He put a hand to his face and

rubbed a clean-shaven cheek. "You do not need my assistance to toss coins. Buster can do that just as well as I can for the both of you."

Buster tried to break the tension. "What Hawkins said about me is true. I've dropped a lot of coins in my day back when I was a drunk, but I figure I can handle these." There was a steady smile on his face as he said it, but he shot Hawkins a dark look.

The railroad man ignored it. "Here's how it'll play out." He pointed to Buster. "You count to three then toss them up. Better watch out when it's your boss's turn though, 'cause he's just as likely to hit you or me as those coins."

Ike calmed himself. Fury wasn't a friend when it came to shooting straight.

Hawkins said, "I'll go first."

Ike watched as Buster tossed the quarters high. Three shots rang out in the late spring air, and two coins spun crazily before dropping to the ground a good distance away. The third fell untouched at Buster's feet.

Hawkins broke into a wide grin. He snugged his string tie tighter and responded to the crowd's cheers by doffing his black bowler hat. He said to no one in particular, "I'd a got that third one too if my gun hadn't misfired," apparently overlooking the fact he had fired three shots. He holstered his gleaming new Colt and beamed at Ike.

Ike stared back. There wasn't any jamming. Hawkins had just missed and lied about it. Still, two out of three wasn't bad and he would have to go some to equal or best him. His hand rested lightly on his Colt's stock as he nodded to Buster. The coins flew upward, and Ike fired three shots. This time, only one quarter careened away. The other two dropped intact nearby.

Hawkins clapped his hands together, and his yellow teeth showed through a wide grin. "You lose, McAlister. But I knew you were going to end up on the short end. No one around here can match me with a pistol. And you ranchers"—he turned to the crowd—"y'all are supposed to be crack shots. I guess shooting a coyote must be a lot easier than hitting a little coin."

Lorraine moved toward Ike and hugged him. When he tried to draw away, she hugged harder. He bent and whispered, "You need to let me go, woman."

"I'll let you go if you head toward our wagon with me right now."

Just then, Hugh stepped forward and dropped three quarters in Buster's hand. Silently, he stood and waited with his feet spread slightly and a hand resting on his holstered gun. He gave Buster a quick nod, and the coins flew skyward. Three coins danced like they had a life of their own. Light gray smoke trailed from the professor's barrel as he holstered his weapon. He turned silently away while Hawkins gaped, and Sue rushed toward her husband. He had her by the hand and was walking away when Hawkins called after him.

"That don't mean nothing, Walnutt. Nobody was betting with you. You had nothing riding on that. 'Sides, you work for me and don't forget it." He raised a hand to his upper lip to wipe away beads of perspiration and stole a sideways glance at the crowd around him. Their faces mocked his bravado.

A faceless voice yelled, "You didn't know the professor could shoot, did you?" Hawkins turned to the sound. The same voice came again. "Well, you for sure know it now. Likely a good thing to remember."

Chapter Four

Rob was at his desk cleaning a rifle when Margaret sashayed into the jail. She flounced her dress and grinned. "I was just thinking, Rob, it would be so lovely to go for a picnic this weekend. Maybe at our little spot by the creek? We could spread a blanket out in a sunspot there. It would be nice and secluded and if it wasn't too cool we could—"

She'd barely gotten those last words out when Hawkins blew through the front door. "McAlister, I expect you to do something about..." Hawkins stopped and nodded to Margaret, then turned back to Rob. "I got something to get off my chest, Sheriff, and I don't need her in here when I do. Nothing personal, ma'am." He touched his hat and waited.

Margaret glared back and forth between the two men, her lips pursed. When Rob just looked at her she said, "Why, I never. Rob McAlister, are you just going to stand there and let him order me out that way?" She looked defiant, but there was a touch of pleading in her voice.

Rob came out from behind the desk and drew an arm around her waist. He whispered, "I need you to leave me with Mr. Hawkins right now. I'll just see what he wants and then come see you later. Okay?" He glanced at Hawkins and gave a shrug while he ushered Margaret out. When he'd closed the door, he turned back to Hawkins. He considered taking the man to task for his rudeness but decided to prod him instead. His whole life he'd been living in Ike's shadow but being sheriff gave him his first chance to escape it and he was going to lean into it.

"Ain't seen you around lately, Mr. Hawkins. Where do you go when you disappear out of town?"

"That ain't none of your business. You and me got other things to talk over."

Rob gestured to the small chair by his desk.

Hawkins declined with a dismissive wave of his hand. "What I got won't take long. I'm going to start visiting some of the ranchers who are likely in the direct path of the railroad. Walnutt's given me a couple names to start with. I want you to ride on out to these spreads with me while I talk with them."

Rob scratched at his stubbly beard. "Last I heard, you ain't even decided on the exact route through South Park yet. You sure you want to start stirrin' things up at this point? You ain't likely to get a good reception, but then, you ain't likely to get much of a welcome any time."

"When and where we decide on a route doesn't concern you, so leave it be. Besides, I don't care about the reception we get, but just in case, you're going with me. You keep those homesteaders on their little spreads under control. I don't want to have to make you earn your wages, Sheriff, but if we run into any trouble, do your duty. Don't kill anyone if you don't have to, but shoot anybody who threatens me. That'll bring the other ranchers in line. We leave in an hour." He turned and strode out.

Rob stared at the man's broad back as he

49

disappeared. He gazed out the jail window for several minutes, then gathered his gear. He'd always been able to talk his way out of trouble, but this was different. What had he gotten himself into? On his way to Hawkins' office, he stopped by The Sew Pretty.

Margaret met him at the door to the shop. "He was just so rude to…"

He cut her off. "I'm gonna be gone a while, not sure how long. I'll let you know when I'm back." Rob carried a rifle in one hand, his gear in the other.

Margaret put a hand out to stop him. "I've never seen you so armed up." She frowned. "What are you going to do?"

"Don't worry. I'll be back soon enough. Just a short trip." He tried maneuvering around her.

She reached up and kissed him on the cheek. "That's until tomorrow." She hesitated and broke eye contact. "I'll see you then. Come by when you're back, all right?" She turned back to her desk.

Rob met Hawkins outside the one-story wooden railroad office. The pine side boards were so new they hadn't started to gray yet. Two of his men were already mounted up. One was the kid Ike tangled with, along with another rough-looking sort. Hawkins took center stage. He straddled his large stallion and announced, "We're heading to the, uh"—he searched a scrap of paper in his hand—"the Donaldson place first. Looks like it's about forty-five minutes away. I hear there's a couple and two daughters. Ought to be easy to persuade." He drew that last word out. "Then if we have time, we'll ride over to the next ranch." He turned to his crew. "Head out. Sheriff, you take the lead."

Rob nudged his horse into an easy trot toward the

low hills to the west. A high sun beat down on the small troupe, warmer than usual for early summer. Rob knew the Donaldson spread. He'd been to almost every ranch nearby during the past three years. Some were friendly visits, some not. Most of the ranchers were homesteaders eking out an existence on spreads that barely fed them.

The miles flew by as the riders rode over the early sage sprouts of the Park basin. A rutted wagon route led out of town. As they neared the Donaldson ranch, Hawkins pulled the riders up. "You let me do the talking, got it?" He didn't get any argument. "I don't expect any trouble, but keep your eyes peeled anyway. Don't want the last thing I see to be some dirt farmer aiming a gun at my face." He gazed around the place then kicked his tan dun toward the small ranch house. They reined in at the narrow front porch.

There was no one outside, then the door opened slowly and a man cradling a rifle stood framed in the entryway. He looked at Rob. "Howdy, Sheriff." He lowered the weapon. "Wasn't gonna shoot anybody, just didn't know who you all were. Who ya got with ya?"

Rob dismounted, and the others did the same. "Abe Donaldson, this here is Charlie Hawkins. He's headin' up a crew surveying the land for the route the railroad's gonna take when it comes through here."

Donaldson glanced at Rob. "When's that?"

"Don't know for sure, probably a year or so off. They gotta decide on the course it'll take pretty soon, though. They say new rail lines take a lot of planning ahead of when they start up."

"That a fact?" Donaldson looked Hawkins up and

down. "So, what're y'all doin' here at my place?"

Hawkins said, "Yes, let's get right to things, shall we? Can we step inside? It's a mite windy out here." He walked up the front steps without waiting for a response.

"Reckon we can. Come on in."

Hawkins was already through the door.

Inside, Mrs. Donaldson stood stock-still by the stove with a wide-eyed little one clutching at her dress. Donaldson introduced Hawkins and motioned to the rickety wooden table in the middle of what passed for the kitchen. Rob, Hawkins, and Donaldson sat. "Mother, would you please bring us some coffee?"

His wife served while the child held on to her.

Donaldson stared at Hawkins.

"Mr. Donaldson, I've come here today to let you know that your ranch—and a fine place it is—is likely going to be right on the path the railroad will take through this part of South Park." Before Donaldson could reply, Hawkins continued. "As a result, the Denver, South Park, and Pacific railroad is prepared to make you a very handsome offer for your land and structures. In fact, you are in a position to command top dollar because of where your spread lies." He paused.

Donaldson's coffee sat untouched. "Don't know as I want to sell to no railroad, Mr. Hawkins."

"I can certainly understand that. Why, I look around here at your ranch house, the stable and barn outside, and the stock I saw nearby, and I'm very impressed. It's obvious you've put a lot of work into this property. That's why our offer is so generous." A Cheshire cat smile.

Donaldson looked at Rob. "You done this with

other ranchers? I ain't heard anyone else talk of it."

Rob could honestly say Abe was the first they'd talked to. He turned to Hawkins. "I think what Mr. Donaldson would like to hear is how much the railroad is prepared to pay to move him and his family off his ranch and this way of life."

Hawkins cleared his throat. "All right. The Denver, South Park, and Pacific railroad is prepared to offer you two dollars per acre for your land and buildings. That would be five hundred dollars for you and your family, which is more than you would earn from the ranch in the next couple of years. I checked. That money would allow you to get a good start in another enterprise, Mr. Donaldson, say another piece of land or perhaps a business in this soon-to-be-prosperous town." He swept an arm wide and looked satisfied with himself.

Donaldson glanced at his wife, then Rob, and back to his guest. "I'll have to talk with my family, Mr. Hawkins. You know, givin' up a ranch you've poured years of your life into ain't an easy thing, no matter how much money a man gets for it."

"Mr. Donaldson, you drive a hard bargain. I can tell you're a shrewd businessman. So, I am prepared to increase my offer to six hundred dollars, no more. I advise you to take that; you're not going to get a better offer, and we're going to get your ranch one way or the other."

Rob stiffened. What did Hawkins mean by that? This was supposed to be no more than talking, not a land grab. It was clear Hawkins meant to close this deal now and not give the Donaldsons time to consider.

Rob could almost see the rancher cave. Donaldson's shoulders slumped, and he put a hand to his forehead, then spoke to his wife. "I reckon we better take it, Mother. We been workin' this land for years and never made hardly anything. The only crop we had more of than we needed was dirt." His wife stared silently at him, her hands folded together.

Hawkins cut in. "Don't be too hasty now. Like you said, maybe you want to discuss it, just the two of you." Hawkins was prodding Donaldson now, like a coyote playing with a rabbit before he pounced.

Hawkins' false concern fell on deaf ears. Donaldson said, "No need. I make the decisions around here, and I say we sell." He got up from the table to shake Hawkins' hand. Rob looked at Mrs. Donaldson. She looked small and forlorn sitting there, silently watching her husband sell their home and their land out from underneath her.

"You sure, Donaldson?" Hawkins' eyes had a strange new light in them. "I wouldn't want you to do anything to get yourself in trouble with your pretty little wife. She doesn't look real happy. Maybe I ought to come back another time and go over that five hundred dollar offer again."

"Five hundred? You said six hundred dollars."

"I did? That was so long ago now I don't even remember saying that." He was drilling Donaldson into the ground. He squinted at the rancher. "And if I have to come back, maybe it won't even be five hundred." Jerking the man like he was on a string.

An uneasy quiet descended over the small house. Up to now, Rob had intended to keep quiet and just be along for the ride, not really sure why Hawkins had told him to be there. But as long as he was here, he decided to speak up. "Looks to me, Mr. Hawkins, like Mr.

Donaldson accepted that six hundred dollar offer you made him. That's what you just agreed on, isn't it?" For once he'd turned from spectator to actor. From 'go along to get along', which had always been his forte.

Hawkins snarled. "Sheriff, you just stick to upholding the law and let me handle business. This is a business deal, right, Donaldson? Why don't you and me settle on the five hundred dollars I offered before that figure starts to go down?"

The rancher looked pleadingly at Rob, but he didn't return the gaze. He'd decided to back off. Confrontation wasn't his strong suit. Donaldson was on his own.

The rancher nodded. "It's a deal. Five hundred dollars. Do we do the paperwork when the railroad comes through?"

"That could be years from now. I'm not waiting that long. I want you off this place come sundown tomorrow."

Donaldson looked stunned. "But I can't do that. I can't get everything packed by then."

Hawkins was unmoved. He gazed around the room. "Doesn't look like there's much here worth taking anyway." He waved dismissively. "Tomorrow sundown or the offer drops to four hundred dollars." He turned on his heel and strode out the door.

Rob spent a minute trying to reassure the dazed couple, then met up with Hawkins outside. They mounted up and trotted away.

Hawkins was in a fine mood as he rocked in the saddle. "Got the land for nothing and the water, too. Not bad." He looked quite satisfied with himself.

Rob glanced at the braggard. "I thought this was

just a neighborly call. Didn't know you were goin' out there to swipe his land. I'll not be a part of stealin'. Never have been and never will be. You're on your own with the ranchers here on out." He wheeled his mount back toward town.

"Don't do something you'll regret, Sheriff."

He could feel Hawkins' eyes boring into his back and wondered if the next thing he felt would be hot lead.

Chapter Five

Conversation died down as Ike raised a hand for quiet. The twenty or so ranchers in the Donaldson barn were in a bad mood. Ike called the spur-of-the-moment meeting after Abe Donaldson told him about Hawkins' visit. He knew Hawkins was going to move against the ranchers but hadn't expected it this soon. Word of Donaldson's predicament spread like wildfire.

"Thanks for comin' on such short notice. I figured we'd have more time, but Hawkins don't seem to carry a time piece." He forced a smile at his small joke. "Don't matter, though, 'cause we gotta figure out how to handle him. You all know he tried to steal Abe's ranch the other day, and he's likely coming for the rest of us soon. Hugh Walnutt tells me Hawkins wants to wrap his land grabs up by the end of summer."

Someone shouted from the back of the haystacks. "Your brother-in-law's workin' for the railroad. Don't know as we can trust much he says."

"Look." Ike held both hands high. "That don't matter. What matters is how we stand against Hawkins. Stop him from takin' our spreads."

Another rancher said, "How can we do that? The railroad's gonna need land to come through here."

"They don't have to come through our places, though." Ike shook his head. "There's plenty of good, empty land north of us they could run the line through.

Hawkins must be makin' money somehow by routing it our way, and I got an idea how."

Abe Donaldson spoke up. "Don't know what we can do, Ike. He says he's gonna get our property one way or t'other."

"That ain't true. No way he can just up and grab our land for next to nothin' if we don't let him. Either we band together to fight him, or we'll lose what we came out here and worked so hard for in the first place." Approving mumbles floated among the crowd. Things were going well, when there was a disturbance at the barn door.

Hawkins.

How'd he find out about the meeting?

He walked in like he owned the place. He was dressed to the nines, with a fine frock coat and white shirt, black string tie. The only thing missing was an eastern top hat. He wore a cowboy hat that sat cockeyed on his head instead. "Don't mind me, fellas. I'm just interested in hearing what Ike McAlister has to say. Not here to interrupt anything, so go ahead with what you were saying, Ike." He parked himself in the front row.

Ike burned. First, the blowhard has the gall to show up and second, he calls him Ike. Like he's a friend. He took a deep breath. "I was sayin' you're tryin' to steal our land when you could take a different route and leave us alone."

Hawkins piped up. "Not exactly true." He slowly drew himself to a stand. "I'm a reasonable man. I've had a successful life. And I'm willing to share that success with you." He swept an arm grandly about the room. "You all have worked so hard on your land, it's time now to cash in on all that labor." He stuck both thumbs into his black vest pockets.

A sugary smile. "I'm here to make you money." He glanced Ike's way. "Sounds like Ike's trying to keep you from getting it. Getting what you deserve. This will be the payoff for all your hard work. Enough to make a first-rate, new start." He strolled back and forth. "Maybe buy another ranch, or start a business. We need another saloon in town, maybe more than one. How about a laundry? And it's time someone gave Ned O'Toole some competition at his dry goods store." Hawkins shook his head and frowned, then lowered his voice. "I don't want your wives and children struggling in the cold anymore. I want them to have enough to buy a house with a fine chimney in town. With a big roaring fire."

Ike could feel the mood of the men shifting. Several were sitting up straighter, leaning forward.

Hawkins was in his element. He held up a full bottle of whiskey. "Got some extra spirits here." He walked up to a rancher who held a coffee cup. "Care for a drop?" A nod and Hawkins poured a liberal amount in the man's cup. He repeated the gesture for several more homesteaders. "And there's more where that came from. I just got a shipment of fine liquor in at the Wildfire, and you deserve your share of it. Everybody follow me over there after this. Drinks are on me."

Ike started to interrupt, but Hawkins cut him off with a wave of his hand. "Now, you all know Ike here. He seems a likeable sort, even if he does have a hair-trigger temper."

Ike flexed his fists and bit his lip as he felt a flush rise from his neck.

Hawkins flashed an insidious smile Ike's way.

"Calm down, Ike. Goodness gracious, calm down, man." Hawkins jabbed a finger in Ike's direction. "He would have you keep working dusty patches of ground that haven't paid you back a nickel." He stuck his chest out, looked toward the roof and raised a meaty fist. "I promise you money for your land. Now!" He turned back to the ranchers with a triumphant smile. "I'm on your side. Whose side is McAlister on? Ever asked what's in this for him? Ever ask yourself that?" Like a lawyer trying a condemned man, he turned toward the ranchers with a solemn expression. "I've had my say, now it's up to you to decide. Do you want McAlister, who's not gonna make you a dime, or me, who wants you to get what you deserve? What you've worked so hard for. What you've *earned*." With a slight bow and a big smile, he excused himself.

That was enough to shove Ike over the top. "You lyin' bastard. You don't care about these men. All you care about is the money you'll make when the railroad comes through." Ike's ears pounded and he raised a clenched fist. "Get out of here and don't come back. You're not welcome among hard-workin', honest folk." He jabbed a thumb toward the door. "Out!"

Hawkins extended his hands in front of him. "I didn't mean to rile you so, Ike. I was just talking about making our friends here some money." He turned to the crowd. "I guess I really got under his skin, men. Not sure why. All we're talking about is how you come out ahead, but sounds like Ike here doesn't want you to."

Ike started toward him and Hawkins raised a hand. "Whoa there, Ike. I can't understand why you're getting so worked up, but I'll be leaving now." He turned to the crowd. "And remember, gents, drinks are on me." With a wave goodbye, he said, "Keep in mind, I'm the only one here who wants to make you some money." He sauntered out the door, whistling.

Ike was shaking he was so mad. "Don't you let that snake fool you. He don't want nothin' of the sort; he's just tryin' to get rich off of you. We need to stay—"

A voice from the back interrupted him. "Is this about you, Ike, or us? I ain't lookin' to get involved in a personal feud between you and Hawkins."

Ike started to respond when another man said, "He's promisin' us money for our land now. That sounds awful good to me." Murmurs and nodding heads. Someone shouted, "I don't know, Ike. I've worked my land day and night for years, and it ain't give me and my family much in return. I'd like for my wife and kids to have that little place in town with a chimney. Lord knows she's put up with plenty out here on the basin."

Ike jammed his thumbs in his jeans. "I know it sounds good, especially at the end of a long, hard winter, but all we have to do is outlast Hawkins. The railroad can't just come in here and take our land. That's still illegal."

Another rancher said, "When I told my wife where I was goin' tonight and why, she said, 'You listen real careful.' "

For the next several minutes, a low buzz enveloped the meeting. He was losing them. Didn't they know he was on their side? Part of him wished he'd decked Hawkins right there, but the rest of him knew it would have made things even worse.

Some of the ranchers got up from their bales, talking among themselves in small groups. A few made for the door. After a few desultory conversations, Ike jammed his Stetson on and strode out the door. Seeing Ally nearby bobbing her head lifted his spirits. A little.

****

At the ranch, Ike lowered himself from Ally and laid her feed out in the corral. He was limping toward the ranch house when Buster hailed him from the barn.

"How'd it go?"

It was a simple enough question, but Ike ignored it. "Everything okay here?"

"Sure, but how 'bout the meeting?"

Ike scuffed at the ground. "Wish you'da been there. Hawkins showed up. Stole the meeting right out from under me. Had those ranchers eatin' out of his hand."

"How?"

"Promised 'em money, said he was gonna make 'em rich. Even though it's a lie, it's hard to turn your back on money that's dangled in front of your nose."

Buster said, "They oughta be able to recognize a snake when they see one. We got plenty of 'em around here."

"Dress a snake up pretty enough, and it don't look like a snake anymore."

"Is there somethin' you know about this guy you ain't sayin'?"

"Nope. Just always had a bad feeling about him, and my gut ain't let me down yet. 'Sides, this ain't about me, it's about people livin' their lives the way they want with nobody tellin' 'em what to do, or say, or think. It's about the future of this valley, and I ain't about to let no snake steal it." His heart threatened to thump out of his chest.

Buster folded his arms. "You lost your temper, didn't you?"

Ike picked up a stone and heaved it into the dark. "Hell yes, I did! He turned everything around, made it sound like I was the bad guy."

"I knew it."

"Knew what?"

"Knew you lost your temper. Every time you do that, somethin' bad tends to happen."

"Damn it all!"

"I wouldn't worry too much about it, Ike. The ranchers know you; they know you're fightin' for them. They'll come around."

"Wish I could be sure about that." With a shake of his head, he headed for the house.

****

Hawkins was holding court in the Wildfire, having Nick fill the ranchers' glasses as they emptied. He was closing deals right there at the bar, promising more than he planned to pay. The homesteaders were eager to take his offers, and the longer they stayed the more willing they were. He figured he was making about two hundred dollars per spread that went right in his pocket. Telling his bosses he bought the spreads for less than he did was going to set him up for several years.

When everyone else was gone, he raised a final shot glass. "Quincy, I just put that two-bit cowboy in his place. Cut the head off the snake. All I have to do now is take him all the way down and the rest will fall in line."

And he had just the plan in mind.

Chapter Six

Ike had gotten an earful on the way into town. Lorraine said, "Why do you have to be the one to square off against that varmint Hawkins?"

"Nobody else has stepped up to do it, and it has to be done."

Lorraine shook her head as Ike pulled the wagon up at Doc Early's office and helped her down. Lorraine had an appointment with the doctor today. She was nearly eight months pregnant, and her last two pregnancies ended in miscarriages, so Doc wanted her to stop in every month.

As they walked toward the office, Ike circled his arm around his wife, but she nudged it away. "I ain't helpless, Ike McAlister. I'm just havin' a baby, and I don't need you fussin' over me all the time."

"Woman, you can be the cussedest person. Just let me help you sometimes, will you?"

"I'm sorry, Ike, guess I'm just a little worried about what Doc's gonna say."

"Why's that?"

"I shoudda told you, but I've been havin' some pains lately and...some other things."

Doc Early moved toward them from his small desk as they came in. "I heard that, Lorraine, come and sit here with me, please. Ike, why don't you go occupy yourself getting some supplies on down at O'Toole's?"

"That's okay, Doc. I'd rather stay here."

Doc turned to him with a firm stare. "And I'm telling you I don't want you here right now. You'd think you'd have picked up on my drift without me having to hit you over the head with it."

"Oh…okay Doc, I'll just be down the street if you need me." He stood looking at the doctor.

"Fine, Ike. Now go."

"Sure thing, I'll go ahead and leave now, okay?"

Lorraine chimed in. "Shoo!"

Ike nodded and left. Outside, he stared up and down the street and looked back, but Doc had already closed the door behind him. Might as well stroll over to the mercantile and look around. When he came in, Ned O'Toole hailed him like a long lost rich relative.

"Why, Ike McAlister, this is a special day, indeed. You have sure picked the right time to visit. I just got some new shirts and pants with your name written all over them."

Ike glanced at his worn cotton pants and faded bib shirt. He brushed a hand across the front. "Don't guess I need anything new. Just came in to pass the time."

"Why, that's even better. Come over here and sit and catch me up on things. Coffee's only a day old." Ned poured a couple of mugs, and they sat on either side of an upright oak barrel which made for a perfect table. Ike was finishing his cup when one of his neighbors, Jeff Ferguson, shuffled in with his wife, Harriet. Ferguson's spread was several miles from his, and Ike hadn't seen him for a while.

Ferguson raised a hand in brief greeting. "Howdy, Ike." It was a hello without any enthusiasm.

O'Toole was up and off his seat as they gazed

around the store. "What can I do for you, Jeff?"

"Me and the missus are shoppin' for some goin'-away goods." His wife was already over by some of the stocked shelves.

"Where you goin'?"

"Bein' run out is more like it. Had a visit from Hawkins the other day, and he bought my place."

From across the store, Mrs. Ferguson yelled, "Stole is more like it."

Ferguson's chin sank toward his chest. "Didn't have much choice. After that meeting we had the other night at Donaldson's, I figured it was just a matter of time."

Ike rose and tipped his hat toward Harriet, then squared up on Ferguson. "Why'd you let him do it? You've worked that land as hard as I've worked mine, and our cattle drink from the same streams. Why'd you give in? We talked about this, about stickin' together."

"Didn't want to, Ike, but he has a persuasive way about him when you're lookin' down a gun barrel. He offered me about half of what it's worth. Said the sheriff—your brother—would run me off if I didn't sell."

"None of that's true. Rob wouldn't be involved in doin' somethin' like that, and Hawkins can't just come rob you and call it legal. It ain't. There's no reason we have to give up our places when there's other routes they can follow." Ike whacked his hat against his pants. "Did you already sell? Did you take his money?"

"No. He told me I had to be off my place by today, and I told him I couldn't be off until tomorrow."

"That ain't true either, Jeff. You don't have to sell. You go on back home and I'll be out your way tomorrow and we'll face Hawkins together. The railroad can't just steal our places."

"I'd be obliged, Ike."

Ike nodded, then gathered up a small circular mirror he'd been eyeing for Lorraine for some time and paid O'Toole. He stormed out without a wave.

As soon as he hit the street, he heard, "Hey McAlister, what are you doing in town? I thought all you did was ride the Park riling up the ranchers against me."

Hawkins was striding toward him in the middle of the street. Stout features that seemed to be held together by the tight button on the collar that made the man's neck bulge. He steeled himself and slowed his breathing. "Don't know that that's any of your business. Just leave me be, and we'll both be the better for it."

"I'll leave you be if you leave me and the railroad be. How's that? There's no stopping progress, McAlister; the railroad's gonna come right through here whether you like it or not." Hawkins balled his hands and thrust his chin out.

There was no avoiding the bully. Ike lifted his hat and swept a hand through his hair. "I ain't against progress, but it's easy to see you don't have to take anyone's ranch. Just leave us alone. But I guess I know why you're doin' this. You stand to make a lot of money. Maybe your bosses would be interested in knowin' about that."

Hawkins pointed a pudgy finger at Ike. "You stay out of this, or there'll be a reckoning 'tween you and me."

Ike smiled inwardly. He knew all about reckonings, and if one was coming, he wouldn't go out of his way to avoid it. "As long as you're stealin' land you don't need to steal, I'll be your shadow, so figure out if you want to see more of me or less. It's gonna come down to one or the other. Frankly, I'd rather see less of you, and I'm bettin' you feel the same way."

Hawkins' face reddened, and his cheeks puffed out even more. "Don't mess with me, McAlister. I know about you. I heard what my fellow brethren did to your folks back in Kansas." The shadow of a smile crossed his face.

Ike squinted and his ears rang. A man didn't gloat about another man's parents being murdered. That was something even the most wicked of men didn't do. He spit at Hawkins' feet. So the blowhard was a Confederate, like those bastards who had slaughtered his folks back in Lawrence. Ike forced his temper to take a step back. Self-control wasn't usually his long suit, but Lorraine was already bound to hear about this argument in the middle of the street and Ike didn't want to raise the stakes any more than Hawkins already had. He started moving past Hawkins when he saw his brother.

****

"Now what are you two doin', arguin' out here at the top of your lungs? Can't you see you're scarin' people?" The easy manner he said it with was typical of Rob. He ambled toward them and took a position in-between the two as townspeople gawked on the wooden sidewalks. "My guess is this can be settled without either one of you losin' any sleep over it. Why don't you both be on your way before the heat of the day makes you even hotter? Myself, I could go for a cool one right about now; how 'bout it?" He eyed both men with a smile. He put a hand on Hawkins' shoulder and nudged him away toward the Wildfire. Back over his shoulder he said, "Come on Ike, I'm buyin' and that don't happen very often." The same wide grin.

Ike shook his head and started to turn away when Hawkins shouted.

"Watch yourself, McAlister, or that railroad could take a turn and head right through your place."

Ike forced himself not to answer, but Hawkins' threat worried him. Was it an idle boast, or was Hawkins enough of a villain to do something like that? He better talk to his brother-in-law. If anyone knew the route it was Hugh. Ike stole a glance back. He and Hawkins were likely going to lock horns again. And soon.

He set his sights on Doc's office. Lorraine hadn't come out yet, so she hadn't seen the scene in the street. That was a good thing. He frowned. She hadn't come out yet—what did that mean? He pushed through the door and was relieved to see a smiling Lorraine sitting and chatting with Doc. He helped her back up in the wagon, and they started home. Ike played the quarrel again in his head. Hawkins was Hawkins, but where did Rob's loyalties lie? Their father had always taught them family comes first, but now Ike wasn't too sure where his brother stood. And that didn't sit well.

****

Later that evening, Rob grabbed his Spencer from the rifle rack behind his desk. He chambered several rounds and turned his attention to his Colt .44. A spin of the cylinder showed five of the six chambers full. He always kept one empty. Copper caps on as well. He swept his hat up and grabbed his coat off a hook.

Evening rounds still got chilly this time of year. First stop was the Wildfire, where most trouble happened if there was any. On Saturdays, noise from the saloon blanketed the town until the wee hours, but since tonight was Wednesday, this would likely be one of the quieter evenings in the gambling hall.

As he walked up, Rob peered into the smoky room and surveyed the people inside. Poker players, cowboys at the bar, a few miners, dance hall girls. One in particular caught his attention. She was new, and pretty, but young. Her hair was longer than most ladies'—a lengthy mass of jet black. She didn't have much rouge on, but at her age she didn't need much. After watching her work the room for a while, Rob stepped into the saloon and headed for the bar. His gaze met hers partway there, and before he could lean his rifle against the counter, she'd sidled up next to him.

"Hello, Sheriff. My name's Hannah. Just got into town and already I like what I see." She looked him up and down. "How about you?"

Rob hesitated. "Welcome to Cottonwood. It's always nice to have a new face around."

"My face wasn't what I was talkin' about." She motioned to Nick, the bartender, and turned back to Rob. "Why don't you join me? It's cold out tonight, and a whiskey would do some of the warmin' you look like you need."

Nick set two whiskeys on the bar.

Rob had been around enough to know how to handle himself in most situations, but he was at a bit of a loss with this woman. He'd never met one as direct as her. She kept him there for a long time, and he hadn't gotten more than a word in edgewise. In due course, he extricated himself. "Nice to meet you, Miss Hannah. I'll be gettin' along now on my rounds." He doffed his hat, suddenly aware of the eyes in the place staring at the two of them. He started for the swinging doors.

"What about our drink, Sheriff?"

Rob looked back. "I don't drink much on duty, so it's yours." A tip of the hat again and he was gone into the night. Even in the cool of the evening, a small rivulet wound its way down his back. But it wasn't his heavy coat that was causing him to sweat.

****

The next night he pulled his rifle from the rack and headed out on rounds a little earlier than usual. When he got to the saloon, it looked like Hannah was waiting for him. She stood at the bar, facing toward the door with a drink in her hand. Rob's heartbeat quickened just a touch, and he walked into the place. He looked around like he didn't know she was there at first, then let his gaze fall on her.

He nodded. "Ma'am."

"You knew I'd be here, didn't you, Sheriff? Were you lookin' forward to seeing me again?"

Rob's eyes widened a bit. Truth be told, he had been thinking about her. "Just out on my rounds as usual."

"Your eyes are givin' you away, lawman. That smile in them says different." She flashed a coy grin.

A flush ran up his neck. He hoped the blush wouldn't spread to his face.

"Mind if I ask you a question?" Without pausing, she said, "I hear the railroad's payin' your salary. Is that right?"

Rob pulled back. "Who told you that?"

"Just part of the regular gossip that works its way through any saloon. So, are they?"

Rob narrowed his eyes. "That ain't somethin' you or anybody else ought to be botherin' with." He picked his rifle up, strode to the front doors, and disappeared.

Over the next few nights, he made a point of intentionally avoiding the Wildfire. What Hannah said bothered him more than he wanted to admit. He'd also heard that some of the regulars noticed his interest in the new girl. Besides, she was probably too young for him. Back at the boarding house one night, he studied himself in the wavy mirror and wondered if he'd look younger without his dark beard.

Staying away from Hannah didn't last long. He ventured into the Wildfire again several nights later. She walked over with a wide-eyed look on her face and apologized. "I shouldn't have said anything; it wasn't my place."

"I shouldn't have been so touchy. I guess everybody knows about it anyway."

"Let me buy you a drink." That had become a joke between them, and it lightened the mood. She waved to Nick. "A whiskey and a lemonade please, barkeep."

Her little tease made him smile. They moved to a table off to the side. Hannah whispered, "Maybe everybody knows about it, but all the same, how'd it come about?"

Rob tapped his fingers on the table for a moment. "Hawkins is payin' me to keep the peace around here so when the railroad comes through, the town's got a good reputation."

"I've heard talk about Hawkins. What do you know about him?"

Rob hesitated, but it wasn't any secret what Hawkins was doing in Cottonwood. "He's been here for a while now, ramroddin' a survey crew that's layin' out the railroad's route through South Park."

"Where'd he come from? Denver?"

"I reckon so. That's where the railroad company is."

"What did he do before here?"

"Don't know and don't think I care to know. I just hope we get rid of him soon and get back to normal. He's a bad one. Steer clear of him."

Hannah leaned closer. "A bad one? What do you mean? I've seen him in here a few times but don't know anything about him."

"That's just as well. Not sure he wouldn't knife his own mother if she had something he wanted."

Hannah sat back in her chair, a distant look on her face. "I think you're right." She paused. "I mean, sounds like you know him pretty well. Good advice."

Hannah was the most interesting person he'd ever met. She came from back east—she wouldn't say exactly where, and she had a fire in her belly he couldn't put his finger on. Something was driving her, and he guessed he'd have fun finding out just what it was.

As they sat at what had become their table in the Wildfire one evening, she said, "You don't know why I came to Cottonwood, do you?" She eyed him in the saloon's dim light. "You don't have any idea. No reason you should, I guess."

"Didn't know a person had to have a special reason to be here. Most people don't have a purpose for bein' where they are—they're just there." He could tell she was toying with him, but he was intrigued nonetheless.

Hannah smoothed a hand over her hair then clasped her hands together. Her eyes bored into his. "If I tell you a secret, will you promise to keep it to yourself?" She pulled his face nearly to hers. Her tone changed from lighthearted to earnest, and she had an intensity he hadn't seen before.

"Is it something I need to know? If not, I'd just as soon not hear it." He turned and studied her.

She loosened her hold, and her gaze darted around the room. "I want to tell you; I need to tell someone. It's burnin' a hole inside me." Her eyes were ablaze.

"Then tell me."

"I didn't just come here by accident. I planned it, been plannin' it for some time as soon as I knew. It just took me a while to work up the courage to come." She was almost breathless. "And now that I'm here, I'm not sure what to do anymore."

Rob broke in. "About what?"

Either she didn't hear him or she decided to ignore him. "I've thought about what I'd say to him. I even thought about what I'd do to him, but now that I see him, he scares me even more than I thought he would."

Rob raised his voice. "Who are you talking about?"

"Will you keep it to yourself?"

Rob nodded.

She brushed a hand over her eyes. She leaned toward him and as she whispered in his ear, Rob's eyes widened.

As the days turned to nights, Rob was drawn further and further into Hannah's web. They began meeting outside the Wildfire. Rob would steal away on the back trail that led out of town. His pulse always quickened when the cottonwood grove down by a small stream came into view. There was a secluded glen there they started taking advantage of on a regular basis. He didn't know where their relationship was going, but he was enjoying the journey.

Hannah began talking about their future and pressing him to end it with Margaret.

****

One morning Rob stopped into The Sew Pretty. He hadn't been by in a few days. The shop was always like entering a foreign world. The low wooden tables were laden with multi-colored bolts of cloth, ready to be cut and sewn into dresses and such. While her clientele were primarily the women of Cottonwood, Margaret also stocked blue denim to make jeans for Cottonwood's men and the nearby miners. Her hats, always her favorite items, hung on small hooks spaced evenly around the shop's four walls.

Margaret looked up as the little bell on the door ting-a-linged. Even in the flickering light of an oil lamp, Rob could see the disapproving look on her face.

"Hello, Margaret. I just wanted to stop—"

She cut him off. "Forget it, Rob. I'm not really interested in what you have to say." Her face grew even angrier as she mended a pant leg at her sewing table. She kept her eyes on her work.

Fearing he already knew what she'd say, he asked, "Why are you actin' this way?"

With a ferocity he'd never seen before, Margaret said, "Because you're acting the way you are! Don't think I don't hear things. Why, Eleanor Whitaker just delights in spreading rumors, and there's no getting around who she's talking about, even though she never mentions you by name. You've made me into a laughingstock. Thank you very much. Now go on, I have work to do that doesn't involve you. I'm sure you can find someone else to occupy your time with." She dismissed him with a wave of her hand.

He backed out of the shop, carefully closing the door behind him. The shop felt even more distant. He headed down Main Street with no idea how he was going to deal with this latest dustup. He jangled the broken latch on the jail's door and wandered in, lost in thought and unaware of his visitor.

"About time you tended to your duties, Sheriff, and stopped your playin' around." A disagreeable Hawkins sat at his desk, leaning back in his chair.

The man got under Rob's skin just sitting there. He was in no mood. He ignored the railroader's barbs and placed his Spencer in the rifle rack, his back to Hawkins. He didn't relish even looking at the bully.

"You got some explaining to do, McAlister. I pay you to do what I say, but you're not as smart as you think you are. You're playing both sides of the fence by not helping roust those homesteaders off their land. That's not the way it works. Sooner or later, that barbed wire fence you're sittin' on is gonna grab you right 'tween your legs." He got up from the chair and pointed a rigid finger at Rob. "I got a legal right to take those homesteaders' property. And while I'm at it, that brother of yours is interfering with railroad business. He's got the ranchers hereabouts riled up against me, and I won't have it. Tell him to back off or else. It's past time to choose a side, Sheriff."

Rob had had enough. He turned on his antagonist. He could feel the flush on his face, and he tried to talk calmly, but his voice rose as he spoke. "Better steer clear of my brother, Hawkins. He's not a man you want to rile. And now that you mention it, let me see somethin' that says you got a legal right. Where's the paperwork that gives you the right to take a man's land for some high rollers back in Denver who don't care nothin' about the people who live and work this valley. Show me some proof, Hawkins!" He couldn't tell if he was madder at this arrogant bastard or himself. His words seemed to echo off the walls of the small office.

For the first time, Rob saw Hawkins fumble for a moment. The bully reached into both pants pockets and then his vest. He produced a piece of paper he held out to Hawkins.

"Take a look at this, McAlister. It's signed by the governor."

Rob took a moment to study it. "Yeah, it's signed by the governor all right, but that still don't give you the right to steal land. There's nothin' in here that says you can rob men. This ain't worth the paper it's writ on. And eminent domain don't hold out here. Yet." He flung it back at Hawkins, and it floated to the floor.

Hawkins picked the paper up, folded it, and put it in his vest pocket again. "You're making a big mistake, a big mistake." He glared at the sheriff, his chin thrust out, nodded, and left.

Rob had one more thing to take care of. Margaret or Hannah. It had taken a while, but he'd made a decision. He jammed his hat on and headed out onto the street. Across the way piano music was tinkling out of the Wildfire. He rubbed his beard hard and strode in that direction. Now was as good a time as any and better than most. As long as he was digging a hole for himself with Margaret and Hawkins, he might as well make it deeper.

Rob put a hand on the swinging half doors and looked around the room. There were more empty tables than full ones. Then he saw Hannah—she was leaning over a cowboy who'd had too much to drink. Rob moved straight for her and reached for an arm before she even turned around.

"Come with me, please." He hoped no one would notice, but how could they not?

She said, "What are you doing?" as he propelled her toward the back room.

He closed the door to the little room behind them and paced back and forth.

She stared at him wide-eyed. "Whatever's gotten into you, Rob?"

"I don't know how to say this, Hannah, other than to just say it."

"Say what?"

"I can't be with you anymore." There, he'd said it. He reached a hand up to his cheek and scratched at a phantom itch.

"What? You can't see me? Where's this coming from—Margaret?"

"It's not Margaret; it's me," he lied. Truth was, he didn't know where it was coming from, either—Hannah, Margaret, or Hawkins, or himself—or maybe all of them.

"So, Mr. Sheriff—I share my innermost secret and my favors with you, and you turn around and tell me you're out of my life?" She picked up a book laying on a table nearby and hurled it at him. He ducked, and the book grazed his shoulder as it flew by. "Get out! Get out you...you monster!" She ran toward him, fists balled.

He backed away, holding her off with one hand as he opened the door behind him with the other. He quick-stepped through the saloon as she ran after him, yelling at the top of her lungs. Customers stared. He pushed the front doors open just as a whiskey glass exploded against the doorframe inches from his head.

Things weren't going well. It was time to call it a day.

Chapter Seven

Bert Quincy almost bounded out of the small railroad office mid-morning. He had just come from a meeting with Hawkins, who laid out a plan to sidetrack Ike McAlister, and he was going to be the one to carry it out.

He angled toward the stable, where the owner was outside working as he walked up. "What can I do for you, Mr. Quincy?"

"So you know my name, old man?"

"Sure, I'm always on the lookout for new customers." Red Crawford looked worn by time, and his full head of white hair stood in stark contrast to his dark, leathery skin. He pointed to the stable. "That last horse there must be yours, right? Good-lookin' animal, must have cost you a pretty penny." Without waiting for an answer, he said, "I reckoned the owner would show up sometime. Nice to meet you." He gripped a large hammer over a small fiery forge.

"I ain't got time for you, old codger. You'll get paid in due time." He moved toward the stalls.

"Pardon my manners, young fella. I guess I should've introduced myself. Name's Red Crawford and I run this place." He moved from the forge and stuck a hand out. Quincy ignored it and tried to brush by. Red jabbed his hand directly in Quincy's gut, and a whoosh escaped the young man's lips. "Don't seem neighborly to refuse a handshake, mister. And we try to be neighborly around here." He offered his hand again, and Quincy took it. Red gradually squeezed the young man's hand harder until Quincy let out a muffled groan. The old man's handshake was iron. The grizzled owner was full of surprises.

Quincy covered his sore hand with his other one. "It's my mistake, mister." He flexed his fingers and reached in his pocket for a couple of silvers. "Is that enough to cover the board?"

Without looking at the coins, Red said, "That'll be fine, son."

Red turned to go back to his blacksmithing but stopped when Quincy said, "I'll be needin' another horse as well." Quincy noticed the question on Red's face. "I'm just provisionin' up for the railroad crew up the way yonder." He pointed west. "I should be back tomorrow."

Red nodded. "Take the roan in the next to last stall. She's old, but reliable and knows the terrain hereabouts. Just don't load her too heavy. Neither the mare or me will like it if you do. You're welcome to board here again when you get back." With that, he picked up a horseshoe with iron pincers out of the blazing fire and lowered it into a tub of water. The sizzle said their conversation was over.

****

Before he left, Quincy visited the general store. His long shopping list was making Ned O'Toole's day. The mercantile owner beamed. "Why, you railroaders comin' to town has been one of the best things to happen to this place." O'Toole was leading his customer around the store, picking up items that Quincy had and hadn't asked for. "Now, you'll need some of these as well. I know they ain't on your list, but you'd kick yourself out on the Park if you didn't have 'em." He dropped a couple of iron spurs into the peach basket he carried. "And these." An extra pair of jeans suddenly became essential. "Best you not go without an axe, too."

Quincy held up a hand. "That's enough, shopkeeper. Just stick to the list."

The smile never left O'Toole's face. "Just helpin' out. I know you and your boys ain't never been out this way before, so you might not be used to—"

"Like I said, just stick to what you see writ, and we won't have no trouble." He rested his hand on his holster.

"No trouble, no trouble at all. Say, ain't you a little young to be outfittin'? How old are you, anyway?"

Qunicy didn't know how to answer that. "I'm old enough...to do stuff...things like this. Just get my provisions and stick to sellin' wares."

O'Toole smiled and put everything else on the list in a large galvanized tub. "Here now, you take the other side, and I'll help you out to your wagon with this."

"Ain't got a wagon, just a pack horse, so get me some burlap bags to throw this stuff in. And put it on the railroad's tab." After loading up, Quincy rode south toward the McAlister place. He skirted the main road and stayed inside tree lines where they existed. From a slight rise, he surveyed the ranch in the distance. There wasn't much cover, so he sat back, observing.

Soon, Ike McAlister and another man came out of the ranch house, saddled up, and headed down range. When they were out of sight, Quincy pulled the packhorse along and rode the slope down toward the small home. A little girl was playing outside with a calico cat. She twirled a small branch in the air with long strands of brown grass wrapped around it. The cat lunged every time the twig swooshed by, swatting at the trailing grass. Quincy broke the stillness. "Hello, little girl. My name's Quincy, what's yours?"

She shielded her eyes from the bright sun and looked up at him. "Why, I'm Jessie, of course. Everybody knows that."

"That explains why I don't know you. I'm not from around here. Just been in Cottonwood a little while."

Jessie petted the calico with long strokes the cat pushed into. "I been there with my momma. It's fun."

"Yes, it is. Say, is your mother inside?" He cast a glance at the log ranch house. No sign of activity.

"Yep." Jessie skipped toward the porch and waved for him to follow. She burst into the house, loudly proclaiming, "Momma!"

****

Lorraine looked up just as a young man came through the front door. She wiped her hands on her apron and stepped away from the breakfast dishes she'd been washing. She managed to say, "Welcome, mister. Just passin' through?" He looked vaguely familiar, but she couldn't place him. "Have we met?"

"No, ma'am, we ain't, and yes, I am just passin' through. But this valley looks so nice I'm thinkin' of stayin' and maybe gettin' a place of my own."

Lorraine paused for a moment before responding. Strange that someone would just appear at her door. "What brings you out our way?"

"That's what I wanted to talk with you about." He

turned to Jessie. "Jessie, would you mind checkin' on my horses?"

Jessie grinned, and before Lorraine could stop her, she dashed out the front door.

The intruder stepped in front of Lorraine and backed her into a corner of the kitchen. "Now, don't make no noise, and I won't hurt you." He drew his pistol and held it at his side. "I know your man ain't here and ain't likely to be back for some time, so let's do this easy."

Lorraine looked for something to fend him off with. She grabbed a dirty knife from the sink and swung it back and forth in front of her.

He grabbed her arm, which forced her to drop the knife. "I told you, don't do nothin' stupid and you won't get hurt."

Lorraine extended both hands in front of her. "What do you want?"

"You're comin' with me. Now. You and me are gonna go out that door together, and you're gonna tell your little girl you'll just be gone a little while and for her to stay right by the house."

"I'm not leaving my daughter, and I'm not going anywhere with you." She narrowed her eyes and eased her hand toward another kitchen knife.

With two quick steps, the man swatted it away. "I don't want to hurt either of you, but I will if you don't do what I say. Got it? Now, let's go."

Her mind raced, and her heart thumped. "Go? Go where? Why?"

"It don't matter why. All you have to know is that if you don't make a fuss, I won't hurt Jessie."

"You stay away from her!" She quickly lowered

her voice. "How do you know her name?"

"I just do—now let's get a move on." He put a hand on his gun and nodded toward the door. "You better get a jacket. You won't be needin' nothin' else."

"Where are you taking me?"

He motioned silently toward the door.

She pulled her only coat off a hook. It wasn't likely heavy enough to take the chill off cool mountain nights, but it was all she had. She glanced around the cabin and walked outside. Jessie stood holding the cat, and Lorraine quickly brushed away tears from her cheeks. With a slight crack in her voice, she said, "Jessie, I'm going with—what's your name?"

"Quincy, just Quincy."

"I'm going with Mr. Quincy for a minute. You stay right here by the house and wait for me to get back, hear?" A wan smile appeared as she said it.

Jessie looked at her mother and beamed. "Want me to come with you?"

"No!" said Lorraine, more forcefully than she intended. "I mean, I'll be back soon, honey, so just stay here and keep playing with Calico."

Quincy motioned for her to mount up. "You get the pack horse." He smiled at Jessie. "Nice meeting you and that's a nice cat you got there."

Jessie drew her arms around the calico. "She can do tricks."

Quincy turned his horse south while pulling Lorraine's reins.

Down range they angled toward the western slopes that surrounded the Park basin. As they climbed into the foothills, Lorraine gazed back. No one was following them. It would be difficult for anyone to track them in this forested terrain that mostly hid from the sun. A carpet of green made most of their sign vanish. Soon, they broke into a clearing and rode over crumbled granite debris that lay everywhere in these mountains.

Suddenly, Lorraine kicked her horse into a dead run down the hill. Her rein broke loose from Quincy's grip and danced crazily in the air behind her. Quincy spurred his mount and overtook the packhorse just as they broke out onto the valley floor. He grabbed the laden horse's dangling leather and yanked her to a stop, almost throwing Lorraine off. When she looked at him, his Colt was aimed right at her face. Her heart raced, and fear coursed through her like electricity.

He yelled, "Don't you *never* do that again, hear? I told you once if you try escapin' what I'd do to your little girl. Maybe I wouldn't go after her right away, or maybe I would, but you'd always be looking over your shoulder wonderin' when I was comin'. In fact, maybe I'll go get her right now. Yeah, think I'll go back and take care of her now."

Lorraine screamed at him. "Don't you dare! I won't ever try to escape again, just leave her alone. Will you promise me? If I stay with you, will you promise me you won't go after my daughter?" It wasn't much of a bargaining card. Suddenly, pain shot through her, and she doubled over on the horse.

"What's the matter with you?"

"I'm gonna have a baby, and I've got cramps. That's what's wrong with me."

"Not right now, are you?" He wore a stupid look.

"Maybe, maybe not, but you keep ridin' me around these mountains and it might be soon." She pressed a hand to her belly and mumbled under her breath. That wasn't the smartest thing she'd ever done.

"Sure… I'll promise you, but I ain't never been too good at keepin' my promises." He grinned. "But I'll promise if you want me to."

They rode for several more miles deeper into the mountains. The earliest hint of summer had just come to these hills, and tiny purple wildflowers dotted the landscape. A gentle breeze swept through the trees and set the light green aspen leaves fluttering. The two rode in silence as they crested ridgelines that led to more alpine heights. Soft, cushiony ground cover hid whatever tracked over it. Lorraine alternated between looking back and toward the summits ahead.

It was mid-afternoon when the line shack came into view. After several wrong turns, Quincy had found the right valley. A dilapidated structure backed up to where the mountains began their steepest ascents. The solitary building looked small, dwarfed by the towering peaks behind. Weeds and brambles had taken the small log hut hostage. Old, dirty bottles littered the tiny front porch, which sagged where a couple of wooden steps were attached to it.

The shack was only about twenty feet wide and fifteen feet deep, topped by a slanted roof with several holes that rain likely found every time. The ramshackle top looked like it couldn't keep anything out or in. A tin pipe with holes in it stuck upward through the roof at an odd angle. Weathered logs were missing whole sections of mud chinks, giving the mountain winds free rein. The plank wooden door hung slightly askew, and a grimy front window probably wasn't letting much light in.

As they neared, Quincy reached for his pistol.

Drawing it out, he held the gun out in front of him. "You in there, come on out, I got you covered." He waggled the gun back and forth. Silence greeted them. He dismounted and began a slow, crouching walk toward the front. He pushed the creaking door farther open with his barrel and waited. A quick peek inside, and he inched through the door frame. The hut was empty.

Lorraine dismounted and followed him into the shack. She shook her head. "Come on out, I got you covered? Is that the best you could come up with?"

Quincy spun toward her, and his face reddened, even in the spotty light. "It worked…sort of."

Lorraine put her hands on her hips. "What are we doing here, anyway?"

"I don't have to tell you nothin'."

Lorraine looked around the small enclosure. Jammed up against the far wall was a single little cot. A cobwebbed black stove with a rusted sheet metal pipe extending through the roof sat to one side. Old iron pots hung from nails driven into the wooden walls. A grimy black kettle rested on the stove.

"Get used to it. This is where we're hidin' out for a while."

Lorraine stared at him. "You're holed up with a pregnant woman who's mad and achy." She scowled. "I'm bettin' you just bit off more than you can chew."

Chapter Eight

Ike and Buster rode back to the ranch after a long day on the range. Ike eased Ally into the small corral. His bad leg always tightened up on him after a lengthy ride, and he winced as he dismounted. He glanced toward the house, undid Ally's reins, and patted her neck. Lorraine usually kept an eye out for them this time of day when the afternoon sun started sliding behind the snow-capped peaks. She'd stand with Jessie in the open door, sometimes with a bowl in her arms, mixing up dinner. Today, the doorway was empty. The cat lay curled in a small sunspot on the front porch, soaking up the last rays of the day.

The front door creaked slightly, and a small face peeked out. Jessie! She ran to her father, arms straight out, bawling like he'd never seen her cry before.

"Jessie! What's the matter, honey? Where's your mother?" Ike glanced at the farmhouse's surroundings for any sign of her. He looked at a small face streaked with dusty trails of tears.

"She left, Daddy. A man came, and Momma went with him and said she'd be back soon." Her little body shook with sobs, and she rubbed her eyes. "But she didn't come back, and I been here alone all day." She wrapped her arms around one of his long legs.

Ike gave Buster a silent look. "It's okay, honey. Mommy's fine. She'll be back soon; don't you worry none." But worry was the one thing Ike could count on these days. "Let's go on inside and cook us up a grand dinner, okay?" As he picked her up, he heard a shout behind him.

"Ike! Hold up!" It was Abe Donaldson, his nearest neighbor. Donaldson rode straight for Ike before pulling up in front of the ranch house. He leaned toward Ike. "I saw your missus ridin' out this afternoon with someone I didn't recognize. Looked awful strange, so I thought I better come by and let you know."

Ike turned to Buster. "Take Jessie inside, willya?" He waited until she was in the house before he turned back to Donaldson. "Where'd you see them?"

"They rode hard past my place goin' south, so I saddled up and followed them for a bit. After several miles they angled off to the east, but when they disappeared behind a hogback ridge in the distance, I decided to turn around and ride here to tell you. Just didn't look right."

Ike considered, then looked back at Donaldson. "Thanks for lettin' me know." With a quick wave of a hand, he disappeared inside the house and scanned the dwelling. There wasn't anything that looked out of place, nothing that would indicate a struggle. Jessie sat in a chair at the kitchen table, sniffling. Ike wrapped a thick blanket around her, then placed Calico in her lap. Soon, the cat's hindquarters rose in time with her strokes.

Ike dragged a skillet off a shelf and huddled with Buster over the stove. He looked back to make sure his daughter didn't overhear him. In a quiet voice, he said, "Nothin' we can do tonight. We'll head out in the morning and see if we can track them. But first, you take Jessie to Sue's in town, then double back and catch up to me on the trail. If they kept to the basin, they should be easy to track. If they went up in the foothills it'll be harder, but we still oughta be able to follow 'em."

Dinner that night was a somber affair, although Ike did his best to lighten the mood even as terrible visions flew around in his head. Ike and Jessie sometimes liked to play an 'I see something' game, which she always managed to win somehow. Ike tried to sound off-handed as he suggested it. "Honey, let's play 'I see something', okay? Can you tell me what this man looked like?"

Jessie broke into a smile. She loved playing games. "He was a little tall but not as tall as you, Daddy."

"Did he have a beard?"

"Uh huh. He had brown hair on his face."

"How old do you think he was?"

"He was really old. Like Aunt Sue." Her mouth turned up at the corners.

"Do you remember which way they went?"

"That way." She pointed south toward the Park basin.

"Thanks, honey. You are really good at games, you know that?"

She nearly bounced in her seat with happiness. "I know. You're good too, Daddy."

That would be all the questioning for tonight. After dinner, Ike tucked her into bed and sat on the edge. He told her a story about a beautiful princess who lost a slipper, but after a big search, found it and was glad again.

"I like that, Daddy. I bet she was really happy to

find her shoe. Did she have a mother?"

Ike paused. "Yes, she had a beautiful mother who loved her very much, just like your mother loves you. And she's gonna be back real soon, 'cause she misses her little girl." Ike tried to end the evening on an up note, but it was not to be.

"I miss my momma." Jessie started crying again. She turned away and pulled the covers over her head.

Ike rubbed her back until her sobs stopped, and she drifted off to sleep.

The morning dawned darkly. A low-hanging ceiling hung halfway up the hillsides and looked like it was in no hurry to leave. Gray clouds brought a chill with them that didn't bode well for what Ike needed to do.

Ike headed out to the stable after a cold breakfast, followed by Buster. Jessie was still sleeping. Ally bobbed her head in her stall when Ike came in. She knew when there was work to do. Ike stroked her neck and spoke to her in a low voice as he led her outside. Her large brown eyes never left his as he told her what they were up against in trying to follow Lorraine's trail. No one could tell him she didn't know what he was saying.

After tying his bedroll back of the saddle, he loaded his saddlebags with dry jerky and cold weather gear—poncho, gloves, heavy blanket. He had no idea how long he'd be gone. Didn't matter. He'd search as long as needed to find his wife and bring her back home. He mounted up and cast a wary eye on the gathering storm clouds to the west.

"Buster, I'm headin' south, then turnin' east. Don't know where that'll take me but shouldn't be no trouble for you to figure out where I went. You're a better tracker than me anyway. If we don't meet in two days, I'll see you at Buffalo Point." It was a prominent granite outcropping miles away on the eastern side of the valley.

Buster returned Ike's hat tap. "Don't you worry about your little one, none. I'll get her all cozied up at Sue's and let Rob know. I'll be along after a bit." Buster glanced at the Winchester that sat snug in the scabbard at Ally's side. "Glad to see you're takin' your Winchester."

"Yeah, I'm takin' it, but you know I ain't never been very good with a rifle. Prefer my Colt, which just means I have to get a little closer to do business." But Ike had always been able to get close enough to do what needed to be done. "Tell Rob to stay in town and look after Jessie while I'm gone. I don't want him ridin' out here. I need to know she's all right."

Buster nodded and went inside to fetch Jessie.

Ike let Ally's reins fall loosely on the side of her neck. She stepped off at a walk south toward the heart of the Park floor. The clouds seemed to drop even lower as Ike rode out of sight of the ranch. An ominous bank of gray looked to be moving his way. It was hung up on the mountaintops, but the wind would soon lift it off, likely whipping it and whatever it held right toward him. He drew his wool collar tighter as the whistling wind bent trees and shrubs to its will. Unusual to have a storm this time of day. Weather mostly stayed on the other side of the mountaintops at least until early afternoon, when all bets were off. This one didn't seem to be able to tell time, but it had the wind-whipping part down pat.

The first splatters of rain smacked into him not more than five miles into the trek. The track Lorraine and the kidnapper left had been easy enough to follow up to this point. Now, wind and rain were threatening to keep him from seeing the trail clearly—tracks that were quickly disappearing into dust squalls. Ike squinted in the distance to try to determine the general direction the hoof prints took. As he studied the land, the wind died down, but he'd lived on this Colorado plateau long enough to know that wasn't necessarily good. The meanest part of the storm was about to hit. Even darker clouds scudded from the west now, and he had an idea what was coming.

Hail.

It swept in as if someone opened the heavens. Small pieces at first gave way to the storm's angry core. Large, solid stones of ice pelted him, Ally, and the surrounding landscape. He spurred hard for a copse of pines to his right and took cover. The pine branches whipped left and right so hard that what cover they would have provided had nearly vanished. As the hail stung his arms and back, he pulled Ally down and tried to cover them both with his small bedroll blanket. The incessant hammering filled his ears and tore at his flimsy covering. After what seemed like an eternity, the hail finally stopped its drumbeat pounding. Next came a violent rain. As he huddled with Ally, pummeled and soaked to the skin, Ike waited for the clouds to empty. When the storm finally abated, he scanned his shredded surroundings. The basin floor was white as far as he could see, as if someone had painted it. Low clouds still hung menacingly above, but the wind was in check. In the dim morning air, a slow-moving river of hail coursed through a low spot in the basin. Ike had no illusions about the trail still being there. He tipped his hat to drain water and remounted an unfazed Ally. She had every right to be skittish, but they'd both been through worse during the war.

Where to look now that the trail had been washed away? He'd keep heading south in the direction Donaldson said, but he wondered if Lorraine's captor had left the more easily-followed valley floor and taken her up in the hills that framed the Park to the east. That's what Ike would do. He turned Ally in that direction and started a systematic sweep of those low slopes.

Chapter Nine

Hawkins strode across the street toward his office. A large breakfast at his boarding house caused him to try to hold his growing paunch in as he walked. Wouldn't do to have townspeople think he was soft. He stepped into the small railroad building where one of the survey crew loafed in a wooden chair.

"Get your backside up! I won't have any idlers in my employ. Go get Walnutt and Rob McAlister. And do it now!" The youth scurried out of the building, but it wasn't until mid-morning when the professor and Rob showed up. "About time you two got here. Sit. We got lots to talk about."

Rob stood. "Yeah, we do have plenty to talk about. Did you know my sister-in-law is missing?"

Hawkins leaned back in his chair behind a large mahogany desk that was too big for his office. "Seems like I did hear something about that, yes, but it doesn't have anything to do with why I wanted to talk with you this morning."

Rob wasn't about to let it go. "Roustin' ranchers is one thing, roustin' family is another." He glowered at Hawkins.

Hawkins didn't rise to Rob's challenge. "Now, here's what's going to happen. Sheriff, I need you to accompany me on some more rancher visits. Word's gettin' around about Donaldson by now, so it should be easy to clear the rest of the homesteaders out. Looks like we have the route pretty well planned out, so no reason to wait. Right, Walnutt?"

The professor shifted in his chair. "The survey is close to being done. But I was wondering why we do not lay the track farther north so we miss the ranches the present route would confiscate. We still have the option of doing that."

"That's not your worry, Walnutt. You just do what I say, and you'll stay on my good—"

Rob interrupted, "Where's Quincy? That fool kid doesn't ever stray from your side."

Hawkins sneered. "The no-good just up and left. Said he was going to San Francisco or something. Good riddance, I say."

The professor cut in. "That is somewhat surprising. When he was at the boarding house, I never heard him talk about leaving town. In fact, he seemed to rather like it here."

Hawkins shifted his gaze to Rob. "Maybe when your brother jumped him, he changed his mind. But we have more important things to take care of."

Rob leaned toward Hawkins. "My brother said a young man took Lorraine. Too big a coincidence to not think it was Quincy."

"Like I said, Quincy doesn't matter. We—"

A flush spread across Rob's face. "You ain't plannin' on handlin' other ranchers the same way you did Donaldson, are you?"

"Why not? It worked on him, didn't it? Like I said, by now word's spread to the other farmers in the valley, so they should be ready to sell. You just tell your brother to stay out of things from here on out. He had another meeting the other day that I busted up, but if he keeps riling those homesteaders, we're gonna lock horns, and I got bigger horns than he does." Hawkins looked confident he'd made his point.

"I told you before. I won't be part of that. You'll have to find yourself another flunky." Rob glanced in the youth's direction. "Maybe a fine, upstanding citizen like your toady there." He jabbed a finger toward Hawkins. "I'm gonna find out about Lorraine if it kills me. Or maybe it'll kill you. You and me are done." He grabbed his hat, and the door slammed behind him.

Hawkins smiled at the professor, his bottom lip beading. "We're better off without him anyway. It's just you and me now, Walnutt."

Hugh maintained steady eye contact but said nothing.

"You still with me?"

Hugh deflected the question. "The other day I noticed you made a new notation on our route map. You circled an area outside of town that is not on the railroad's planned course. It looked like you wanted to seize that property, too."

Hawkins scanned the valley map on his desk for a moment. "Yes, that's a fine piece of land I think would make a wonderful building site. Its location makes it ideal for use as a supply dump or even something like a getaway."

The professor glared. "You and I both know whose land that is, and we both know why you want it. It is Ike McAlister's ranch, and you want to seize it to force him to leave the valley and away from the ranchers he has been uniting against you."

Hawkins sprang from his seat, as well as someone

his weight could spring. Veins bulged in his neck. "You listen to me, Walnutt. Don't ever cross swords with me again. As long as you work for the railroad, you do what I say."

Hugh reached into his front pants pocket. "I'm glad you put it that way. No one tells me to do something I don't want to. You could not pay me enough to do your dirty deeds." He plopped a sheaf of papers on the man's desk. "Here are my calculations and notes on the route. These tell you the true course you should follow. Just to the north. Anything else and you will be off track, and off track is not a good place for a railroad to be."

"Don't lecture me, Professor." Hawkins came out from behind his desk, fists balled.

"And what if I do?" Hugh placed his hand on his gun stock.

Hawkins stopped in his tracks. He pointed to the door, finger shaking. "Get out, you turncoat. Get out and stay clear of me from now on."

"My pleasure." Hugh backed out of the office, his hand still atop his gun. He didn't bother to close the door as he left.

****

Sweat popped out on Hawkins' forehead. He wiped at his face and slammed both hands on his desk. His chest pounded. But the split with Rob McAlister and the professor wasn't his only worry. He fingered the telegram he'd gotten from Denver that morning. His bosses wanted to know about his progress, but losing most of his survey crew just now likely wasn't the kind of progress they were looking for.

He sent a vague reply, which he crafted as he trudged to the telegraph office.

Good progress on the route through South Park to Fairplay. Send another head surveyor. End.

That should hold them for a while, although the last part of the message probably made them wonder. The truth was, the route wasn't going to go to Fairplay like he said, but by the time the company found out its real direction, he'd be a rich man and gone. His travels over the past few months hadn't been for nothing. Just as well the professor quit. He'd have been a handful once he found out the truth.

He hadn't heard from Quincy since he'd sent him after Lorraine. In this case, no news was good news. Ike McAlister was no doubt down range, searching for his wife and out of the way. Perhaps it was better that he'd parted ways with Walnutt and the sheriff. The gun hand he'd hired would be coming in on the stage tomorrow. The path was open for him to acquire the nearby homesteads at giveaway prices, especially with a gunman tagging along. A different gunman than Rob, but he could no doubt make do with the new one.

Late the next afternoon, Hawkins waited in front of the mercantile. The stage would be arriving soon, on its way west from Denver. A cloud of dust rose in the distance and gradually grew bigger as the coach neared. Wouldn't be long before the railroad replaced it and the sooner the better. The coach pulled to a stop in front of the small crowd. A smallish man with a cane stepped down from the carriage and helped an older woman do the same. There was no one else inside.

Hawkins beaded up again. He yelled to the man on the bouncy seat in front holding the reins. "Driver!"

The dusty teamster ignored Hawkins. The guard hefted a double-barreled shotgun and scanned the surroundings. Neither got down right away. The driver said to the guard quietly, "Not sure why the sheriff's not here to greet us. He knows we got a big load of silver in the strongbox." He yelled to no one in particular, "Go get the sheriff." A little boy scooted away and ran straight for the jail. Rob McAlister was just coming out when the boy pointed toward the stage. "You better come, Sheriff. They asked for you particular."

Rob strode to the coach. The driver was dismounting. As Rob walked up, the man whispered, "Watch the stage while I'm gone, Sheriff. There's a valuable payload on board."

Hawkins hung back and observed the scene. He was still looking for the gunman he hired when the short male passenger tipped his bowler hat to the woman then caught his eye. "You Hawkins?"

"Yes, I'm—" He stopped. Could this be the shootist? The man looked like a bank clerk. Hawkins had hoped for someone tall, dark, and menacing. "Are you Mr. Slade?"

"J. Slade, that's my name. You look surprised, Hawkins. Are you thinkin' I might not be up to what you have in mind?" The man was a little shorter than Hawkins, who wasn't all that tall to begin with. The glasses didn't help the would-be gunman look imposing either. Slade was wearing a pistol but didn't look the sort to use it well. He twirled the wooden cane and stared at Hawkins. "Tell me what you have in mind."

"Let's go somewhere private." Hawkins reached out to grab Slade by the arm and steer him to his office, when Slade's eyes went cold, and he jabbed Hawkins in the chest with his cane. "Don't ever touch me again,

Hawkins. Ever. Got it?"

Hawkins was taken up short. "Just showing you the way." He narrowed his eyes. "Come with me, please." They walked down Main Street to the railroad office. Inside, Hawkins closed the door and shut out the outside world. "Have a seat, Mr. Slade."

Slade looked at the small chair Hawkins indicated with contempt written on his face. "I'll take your desk chair."

Hawkins couldn't reconcile the soft appearance of the man with his harsh manner, but he eased into the smaller chair.

Slade leaned forward. "What do you want done?" His eyes bore into the railroader.

"Uh, I need you to ride with me when I buy up some homesteaders' land for the railroad that's coming through here."

"What do you need me for? Sounds pretty straightforward." Slade folded his hands on the desk.

"Well, they don't know we're gonna take their ranches yet, and they're likely not gonna take it kindly when I tell them." Hawkins shifted in the too-small chair.

"But you're paying them for the land, right? And maybe a little more as an incentive?"

"Not exactly. I'm going to pay them less than their property's worth."

"So, that's why a cheat like you needs me, right?"

Hawkins sat up straight. No one had every called him that and gotten away with it. He started to get up from his chair.

Slade said, "Sit, Hawkins. My guess is I'm the only friend you got, right?"

Hawkins didn't know how to answer that. He decided to ignore the insult and respond to Slade's question. "Yes, that's why I need...someone. To persuade them." But with every minute that passed, he was less sure Slade was the right man.

Slade eyed him closely for a minute. "I got a hankerin' for poker. Where's there a game around here?"

Hawkins' doubts multiplied when he heard that. Why did the man want to play poker when he was being paid to back him up?

"A poker game. Where is one?" This time Slade raised his voice.

Hawkins pointed diagonally across the street. "The Wildfire Saloon."

Slade was quickly up and out the door walking in that direction, Hawkins hurrying after him. Strange little man. Slade pushed through the swinging saloon doors and stopped just inside. No one seemed to notice him. He turned to Hawkins. "Who's the toughest hombre in here?"

"That would be One-Eyed Jack, at that table over there, dealing." He pointed to where six men sat playing cards.

Slade walked toward the table. He spoke to the player seated directly across from One-Eyed Jack. "I'd like to play; would you mind if I took your place?"

The man didn't even look up at Slade. "Go to hell."

Without batting an eye, Slade rapped him viciously atop his head with his cane, and the man fell unconscious at Slade's feet. One-eyed Jack started to rise and draw his pistol, but before he could clear leather, Slade whizzed a bullet past one of his ears, nicking it slightly.

"I'd sit if I were you. Got it?"

Jack stood motionless, holding a hand up to the wound.

Slade holstered his gun. "Why don't you invite me to join your game?"

Jack cupped his hand behind the bloody ear. "What?"

Slade still had his hand on his sidearm. "Invite me to play."

A dazed-looking One Eyed Jack said, "Uh, sure. Why don't you join us?"

The gunman said, "What did you say? I couldn't hear you."

One-eyed Jack repeated himself. "I asked if you would like to join us." Blood dripped between the fingers of the hand he still held to the ear.

Slade smiled. "Thanks. Don't mind if I do. I'm obliged."

Rob strode into the saloon and confronted Slade. "Heard some shootin' goin' on in here. We don't put up with that in Cottonwood."

Slade brushed his coat back with a hand near his holster.

Rob paused. "Better leave your hand right where it is, Mister. Saw you just gettin' off the stage. You bein' new here, I'll let it go this time, but keep your finger off your trigger around here."

Slade stood motionless until Rob turned and walked out. He sat and motioned for One-Eyed Jack to do the same. Red trails wound down the tough's neck. After winning several hands, Slade rose and walked toward the other poker table. Before he got there, though, four men stood and offered their seats. In the meantime, the players at his first table made for the door.

Hawkins didn't need any more convincing.

Chapter Ten

Sleep eluded Lorraine her first night in the line shack. Quincy slept on what passed for a bedroll on the floor. He let her have the shabby cot, such as it was. She'd gotten up to try to sneak the pistol away from him during the night. The creaky, wooden floorboards gave her away though, and it was too dark to see anything well, so she crept back to bed. As daylight seeped in through the two small windows, she saw the pistol's stock peeking out from underneath his leg. Could she get it before he reacted? She inched forward with one hand extended. She lunged and grabbed it and pointed it directly at his chest. "Get up, you varmint."

Quincy blinked his eyes open and looked at her. "No."

She cocked the hammer. "I ain't gonna tell you twice. Get up, or I'll shoot you."

He rolled over to go back to sleep. "Go ahead."

Lorraine decided to fire a round just over his head. She pulled the trigger, but nothing happened. She checked the gun's cylinder and sighed.

Quincy turned toward her with a hand full of bullets. "Lookin' for these? I ain't as dumb as I look. Now it ain't likely I can get back to sleep again thanks to you." He threw off the thin wool blanket and stood, stretching his arms high overhead.

She leaned back against the small iron stove.

"Can't be all that comfortable sleepin' on your firearm, but I guess if you're young enough, you can sleep through almost anything."

"I've slept in worse places. Let me have the pistol."

Lorraine handed it back and considered her options. Quincy had already threatened to hurt Jessie sometime, somehow, if she tried to escape again. She thought about braining him in his sleep with an iron skillet, but she'd have to kill him to be sure he didn't make good on his promise. She didn't think she could do that. She sighed and studied the inside of the small cabin. It would take some doing to clean it up enough to be habitable. How long would she be there?

She said, "Set a fire in the stove while I get some fixin's ready. You do know how to set a fire, don't you?"

"I set plenty in my time. Had to learn how 'cause I been on my own most of my life."

Lorraine sensed an opening. "Where are you from?"

Quincy dodged the question. "Ain't important. Just cook us up some breakfast."

He'd turned her questions aside, but she'd watch for another opportunity to get him to open up.

****

Ike rode south along the edges of the forested foothills rising to the east of the basin. Any track left after the storm would probably stand a better chance of still being visible on the hillsides rather than the drenched valley floor. He'd ridden Ally for several hours when he thought he heard something off to his left. He sensed he was being watched. He scanned the surrounding upslopes but couldn't see anything in the shaded light. Still, he'd lived in these mountains long enough to know when to rely on his intuition. Was it Lorraine's captor? Was it anyone, or was he just jumpy? He slipped behind an imposing granite outcropping and slid off Ally. As he drew his old Colt, he crouched and waited. He didn't need to check to see if the gun was loaded. He kept it that way, with a full cylinder in his saddlebag in case he ran into real trouble. Silence ruled the forest except for the piercing screech of a jay in a nearby pine and the wind rustling through the treetops. After half an hour, he holstered his gun and remounted Ally. The feeling of being followed had passed. Still, he glanced around at the green landscape from time to time as he looked for tracks.

He worked his way south for the rest of that day and the next, winding for miles up and down the low mountainsides. He saw bear scat and some elk droppings, but no horse track. Since he'd been able to see animal prints on the hillsides, he figured there might still be horse sign if Lorraine and her kidnapper had ridden this way. But so far this search looked like a dead end. As the afternoon waned, he broke off and rode for Buffalo Point. Soon, the imposing granite formation rose in the distance. Buster wasn't there, so Ike guessed he was still behind him. Ike unsaddled Ally and let her drink from a little stream that gurgled nearby.

As he searched his surroundings, Ike tried to push his fear away and focus on the problem at hand. What if he couldn't find—he stopped mid-thought. That kind of thinking wouldn't do any good. Buster should be along soon. A fire would help his partner locate him and take his mind off Lorraine at the same time. There was plenty of downed timber on the hillsides, so it didn't take long to gather enough for a big bonfire. The burning dead wood produced a large column of curling gray smoke that rose lazily skyward in the early dusk. The odds were good Buster would see it, but it was likely the kidnapper would too, if he was nearby. Ike set to figuring as he waited. He hadn't seen any places that could serve as hideaways as he scouted these hills, so the chances captor and captive were anywhere near were slim. Still, Donaldson said Lorraine came this way...

Ike spread some grain out for Ally and unwrapped a slab of dried jerky from his saddlebag. He fed the fire until it roared, just like *he* wanted to. To shout to the hillsides and let his worry and anger disappear into the forest once and for all. But that wasn't his way. The night was going to be cold, so he spread his blanket near the flames. He lay awake most of the night staring at the clouds hiding the moon. In the cool morning, he sat sipping a lukewarm cup of coffee when Buster broke out of the trees and rode toward him at an easy trot. He'd never been so glad to see his friend before.

Buster unsaddled his mount, fed him, then let the horse loose to graze nearby with Ally. He smiled at Ike and squatted next to the fire. "You're a sight for sore eyes."

Ike shook his hand. "I was gonna say the same about you. You have any luck?"

"No, all I saw were Ally's tracks and some mountain lions', mostly."

Ike gazed in the distance. He picked up several loose rocks and tumbled them in his hand. "This is feelin' more and more like a dead end. If they came this way. we should've seen some sign—somethin'—by now."

Buster nodded. He was an experienced tracker from his years as a mountain man. "I was thinkin' the same thing."

Ike threw one of the rocks skyward, and flung the rest away. "I ain't stayin' here any longer. If they're still farther south, then so be it, but I don't think they are. I'll circle back to the ranch and reprovision, then try the slopes on the west side of the valley. But first, I'm gonna pay Donaldson a little visit." Ike gathered up his few belongings, tied them on Ally, and swung up in the saddle.

Buster gulped his coffee and followed.

****

The days dragged on for Lorraine. The foodstuffs Quincy packed were obviously chosen by a man. Mostly beans, bacon, and jerky. A small amount of flour and almost no eggs, lots of coffee. Their moods were deteriorating. Nothing to do but stare out the caked window or sit on the saggy porch. The horses were hobbled so they wouldn't drift off. Lorraine had taken a liking to her packhorse and spent time rubbing him down with pine needles and hand-feeding him grain. Quincy had also shorted them on oats. They would run out soon, depending on how long they stayed. Which led Lorraine to an opening.

"How long you figure we're gonna be here, Bert? What's the plan?"

"How'd you know my name was Bert? You call me Quincy—nobody but my mama ever called me Bert."

"You forget I used to run that boarding house

you're stayin' in. I know everyone's name there, yours included. But I didn't know you by sight until you decided to rob me of my family and my freedom."

Quincy said, "It weren't me, it—" He looked like a kid ready to burst. He heaved a stone at the surrounding trees. "I didn't want to do it; I just had to."

He went back inside. Lorraine followed, her eyes boring into him. "I'm not buyin' it, mister. A man does what he wants to do and is accountable for what he does. He knows the difference between right and wrong. Did your mama raise you this way?" That seemed to hit home.

"Don't talk about my mama. She never did nothin' bad her whole life and look where it got her. An early grave stood over by two people when she went." Quincy pounded the table hard with a fist. "She deserved better than that! She deserved better than me." He sat and put his head on folded arms.

Lorraine knew this was a good time to keep quiet.

After a while, he looked up. "I'm done talkin'; don't talk to me no more."

Lorraine backed off. She hoped her comments would seep into Quincy like water into a teabag. Maybe they would in time, but time wasn't on her side. She would look for another opening soon.

****

It was going on dusk when Ike reached the Donaldson place. He didn't have to practice what he'd say, it was going to come from deep inside. As he pulled up in front of the little ranch house, Mrs. Donaldson stared from the small front porch. Ike swung his bad leg off Ally before the horse even stopped. He touched a couple of fingers to his hat brim and handed

111

Ally's reins to Buster.

"Ma'am. Is Abe about?"

She stared soundlessly at Ike for a moment. "Um, he rode into Cottonwood sometime this morning. That's where he still is. Either that or he's riding back here now."

"Let him know I was asking for him, will you?" His eyes burned into hers.

She white-knuckled her dirty apron. "Yes, I will, Ike." She put a hand to her mouth, then said, "He's been under a strain lately…" She stopped. "I know why you're here. I told him not to lead you astray, that there's no amount of money that's worth turnin' on your friends. Hawkins came by again and spooked him, and he lost his head." She looked down at the ground. "Your wife never passed by here."

Ike hadn't expected a confession, but that's what he'd just gotten. He steeled himself not to take his anger out on her. "Mrs. Donaldson, I been ridin' for days south of here, straining to find track of the man who kidnapped my wife. Can you even imagine how hard that's been? How scared I been?"

She smoothed at her dress. "No, I can't… I mean, yes, I think I can. I've been so worried about the whole thing, what with us having to leave this place and your wife disappearing and all. Abe's just been eaten up."

Ike mounted Ally and held her hard with a stare. "You let Abe know he has a reckoning coming with me. I'll attend to him later." He tipped his hat and whirled Ally east toward his ranch.

Mrs. Donaldson called after him. "Just don't kill him, Ike. Please. He ain't much, but he's all I got."

Ike spurred Ally hard—as hard as he ever had. So

much time had been wasted. His insides were burning up, almost like he had a fever. Damn Donaldson! If Lorraine was harmed—or worse—his head pulsed and his mind raced. Where to look now? South and east were out, and it was unlikely they'd gone north because the original track headed south from his spread. He'd resupply at the ranch, then turn southwest. A chance to see Jessie tempted him to ride to town first, but he decided otherwise. No telling how much time Lorraine had left. If any.

In the morning, Ike told Buster they would split up and meet again at sundown, figuring they could cover more territory that way. They were up and out of the ranch house at first light. Buster hurried to catch Ike at the stable, where Ally was already pawing at her stall. Ike fitted her with bulging saddlebags, and a tight bedroll. His Winchester filled the scabbard. He swung up and reined Ally south at a fast gallop. After a few miles, he pulled up and yelled to Buster, "I'm gonna take off directly west. Keep ridin' south, then head west up into the hills. There's a small mountain meadow just short of that ridgeline there that juts into the sky." Ike pointed to a gray granite rim in the distance.

Buster nodded, even though the promontory was a blur in the distance.

"We'll meet up there tonight." And he was off, letting Ally pick a path up into the foothills ahead. The skies looked promising this morning, but no telling what the afternoon would bring when the wind usually picked up. The black clouds from a few days ago flashed through his head, but that image was quickly replaced by a vision of Lorraine missing from the front porch at day's end.

****

The line shack was starting to get to Quincy. The impatience of youth was on full display as he took to pacing inside the little shack, then carrying his restlessness outside to wander some more. He was growing sullen and withdrawn. Lorraine was afraid he was coming apart, something she couldn't predict, prevent, or control. Their world was unchanging.

One morning Lorraine decided to act before Quincy completely lost it. As she cleared their meager breakfast away, she said, "Come sit at the table with me. I've got little pieces of kindling here we can use to play cards. You do play cards, don't you?"

Quincy rubbed his forehead and sat across from Lorraine. "Sure, I play cards, but poker, mostly. At the Wildfire. Do you even—"

"You don't suppose I know how to play? My daddy taught me, and I grew up on poker. There wasn't much else to do in Julesburg in between cattle drives coming into town. I learned how to play with the men, and sometimes beat them at their own game. How about it?"

The deal passed back and forth between them over the next couple of hours. Their 'cards' were notched sticks. The wagers were small, with each player up a few sticks or down a little at any given time. Lorraine took the opportunity to try to get Quincy to open up. "You play pretty good, young man. Where'd you learn?"

"Wasn't at home. The only thing I learned there was how to defend myself. Nights, I'd go searchin' for my pa in town to make sure somebody hadn't shot him or to see if he was chokin' on his own vomit." He blinked rapidly. "How about more playin' and less talkin'?"

Lorraine backed off. She let him win several hands she had him beat on, but his mood stayed dark. The small opening had closed.

****

Ike bushwhacked through the underbrush on the western hillsides. It was slow going. He didn't want to miss any sign, no matter how small, so he took his time. He made enough noise so any animals nearby would have fair warning. The last thing he wanted was to be knocked off Ally by a predator. He alternated between glancing at the ground and at his surroundings. Scattered pine needles covered the terrain except where wind had swept the exposed granite clean. There were spots where needles had been disturbed, but Ike couldn't tell if that was track made by horses or animals.

The last downpour had been several days ago, and what prints there were had grown faint. Ike dismounted several times to study possible sign and rest Ally. By the time he'd refilled his canteen twice, the sun was threatening to disappear behind the mountaintops. He found a ridgeline that led toward the meadow he'd mentioned to Buster. When he got there, Buster already had a small fire started close to the tree line. Ike rode in and slid off Ally. His back, leg, and neck all protested. They'd been in strange positions the last couple of days, and they let him know it. He fished a cloth bag of oats out of his saddlebag and laid it on the ground. The extra calories in oats would do Ally good. When she was finished, he held out a handful of salt which she quickly licked clean.

Buster had picked a spot by a little stream downwind from anyone or anything above them.

"See any sign, Buster?" It was a terse question, as if Ike already knew the answer.

"Some bear track, but I also saw some Indian sign. My guess is it's the Utes, hunting around here now that winter's relaxed its grip."

Ike considered. "Utes, huh? Maybe our friend Rain Water." There was something unsettling about sharing the wilderness with a man who could track more skillfully, move quieter, and fight better than he could. The idea that Rain Water might have him in his sights without him even knowing it also gave him pause. "Well, if we leave them alone, maybe they'll leave us alone."

Buster poked at the fire with a small branch. He knew Ute ways, having been on good terms with them in years past, but he couldn't count on their goodwill now. "I ain't so sure, Ike. They got no reason to leave us alone to roam these hills. They're liable to look at it like we're invading their hunting ground. They don't know why we're here, and they don't like not knowin', so why don't we double up tomorrow? It'll give us a little more edge if we run into trouble."

Ike stared at coals just beginning to glow in the growing fire. "No. We'll stay split up. We'll be able to cover more ground that way, which is what we're here to do. If they want to kill us, they could dispatch both of us just as easy as one of us. We stay separate. Just keep your eyes peeled." He sounded more confident than he felt.

Night was falling, bringing an uneasy end to a fruitless day. After another meal of jerky and lousy coffee, Ike laid his bedroll out and eased his sore body down on it. How many more days would pass before they caught wind of Lorraine's whereabouts? The longer it took, the less likely it was there would be a good outcome. It had been a long time since he prayed, but he clasped his hands together and looked at the night sky. He searched for the right words. "Lord, please bring my Lorraine back to me safely. And...well, that's about it. Thank you." As the night passed, he tossed and turned under his light blanket. He'd be sure to visit O'Toole's for a heavier one when he got back.

The stars overhead pierced the heavens in random patterns, as if to relieve the blackness of the sky. He gazed at them, wondering if Lorraine was looking at the same night lights—wondering if she was looking up at all. An image of Jessie's tear-stained face drifted through his mind as he lay there, his head crosswise on his saddle. He should have taken the time to see her in town before riding back out.

Sleep would come hard again tonight.

****

Lorraine stared at the star-studded evening sky. She sat on the shack's dilapidated front steps, looking northeast toward where she imagined her home was. The Park was blanketed in darkness, but in her mind she pictured lights shining bright inside the ranch house. Jessie would be begging her father to stay up longer right about now, bargaining with him because he was such a pushover. Lorraine would interrupt them in the midst of Jessie's pleas and take Ike off the hook. She'd lay her only child down on her small bed, the softest in the house, and draw the covers over her.

Calico would already be there, curled in the blankets, waiting for her best friend. As she sat alone in the midst of the wilderness, Lorraine ran a hand over her expanding middle and smiled, then wiped at tears that wound down her cheeks.

The next morning, she vaguely heard her name being called as she stirred.

"Miss Lorraine, Miss Lorraine."

She usually didn't sleep in long enough to have to be awakened. She awoke to find her captor making an unexpected attempt at cooking breakfast. An agreeable aroma filled the small house. She rose off the bed and surveyed the result. "Somebody's taught you how to cook, Bert. I'm guessing it was your mother. Doesn't sound like your father was much of a hand at anything."

"I told you. Don't call me Bert."

Lorraine was undeterred. "What do you have against your own name?"

"That was my father's name, too." Quincy grabbed the metal bowl he was mixing eggs in and hurled it against the log wall behind the stove. The runny contents ran down the wood and dripped onto the floorboard below.

The young man broke down before Lorraine's eyes. He ran out the front door and disappeared into the woods above the shack. With a worried expression, she turned back to the stove where some bacon still spattered in a pan. She grabbed a couple of hot strips and put the rest on a plate for him for whenever he came back. Just as it wasn't possible for her to escape without putting Jessie at risk, it was also impossible for Quincy to escape what he'd done in kidnapping her. Something that's been done can't be undone, but this looked to her like another opening, if he ever returned.

It was mid-morning when she heard his boot steps on the porch. She stood at the small stove as he walked through the door. He offered no explanation for his flight but sat at the table staring at nothing. She let him be.

Finally, he clasped his hands together on the tabletop. "I'm sorry for what I done, ma'am. I didn't mean it personal. You was just somethin' I had to do." Lorraine brought the remnants of breakfast over and sat opposite him. He ate silently and avoided looking at her.

"I can tell this is tearin' you up, Bert. I don't believe you meant me any harm, did you?"

Quincy sat ramrod straight and didn't answer, but he also didn't upbraid her for using his name again. His continued silence confirmed what she had suspected.

She placed her hand on his. He drew it back.

"Tell me how this came about, Bert."

He chewed his food until there was nothing left to do but answer. "I didn't know what he meant at first." He halted and finally looked at Lorraine. "Then he said that takin' you for a while would help a lot of people in the valley. That he'd let me know when I could bring you back, but I ain't heard nothin' from nobody since we been up here. Seems like he forgot what he said he'd do."

"Hawkins?"

Quincy nodded.

Lorraine got up and cleared his plate. "Maybe that's what he planned all along. To hang this on you, and deny he put you up to it. It would be his word against yours, and this town wants and needs that railroad, so you were gonna be the guilty one, and he goes scot free."

Quincy lowered his head toward the table. "My momma would tan my hide if she was here now."

"My guess is she knows what you did and is hoping you'll turn around and make it right."

Quincy pushed away from the table and stood. His bottom lip quivered. "I need to make it right. For myself, and to show I ain't like my pa." He walked out to the front stoop and gazed into the distance.

Lorraine was ready for this to end. "I'll make you a deal, Bert. Let's you and me go back to town and give this foolishness up. You walk away and I walk away and none's the worse."

Quincy grimaced. "I can't go back to town. Hawkins would probably shoot me on sight to keep me quiet. I got nothin' and nobody to go back to. Damn!" He hurled a small piece of firewood into the air and watched it fall, forever lost in a forest of trees.

****

Buster always rose early. He stirred the faint embers from last night's fire to life with dead pine branches that created a smoky start to the morning. The sleep that eluded Ike last night now held him fast, and he lay unmoving. Buster fixed a hasty breakfast of flour mixed with water, then stirred and baked the dough over the still-warm embers. Baked hardtack biscuits, along with strong coffee, made for a welcome meal.

The smell of coffee finally roused Ike. Buster padded over with a steaming mug, which Ike sat up for. Buster broke the still mountain silence. "I still think we ought to stick together."

Ike was not having any of it. "We already talked

about this, Buster. I'll head toward the top of the ridgelines today, and you take the lower hillsides. Keep goin' south, but when you see a way west, take it and double back to find me if you have to." He tossed the coffee grounds away, gathered his gear, and limped to Ally. He patted her neck. She was one of the few constants in his life he could count on. Ike searched the distant hills for a suitable rendezvous for tonight, but the forest blocked his sight. "Don't know where exactly to meet up later on, but when the sun starts to slip behind the heights, I'll be ridin' for the hilltops. Start a smoky fire for me to see, willya?"

Buster doused their little campfire. "Still think it's a bad idea, Ike."

"Heard you the first time."

The mountain man was one of the people Ike usually listened to. Not today. There was no talking him out of what he was going to do. When he made up his mind, there was no changing it.

****

Buster watched Ike mount up and disappear into the pines. He shook his head, brushed the campsite clean with a pine branch, and mounted up as well. He nudged his horse with his heels and moved along the hillside.

Winter still held some sway this high in the mountains. Blotches of snow lay scattered on the forested slopes, which would make tracking Lorraine somewhat easier if she had come this way. Buster's sight wasn't what it used to be, but his hearing was excellent, and his intuition even better. Years as a mountain man had given him a sixth sense about the high country. Not much escaped him. After several hours of squinting at the terrain, he sensed something or someone to his left. Without looking in that direction, he continued upward until he came to level ground that would be more to his advantage. He drew his rifle out and cocked the hammer as he turned and pointed it left. He caught a flicker of movement among the trees. A horse? He sat motionless, staring at the spot.

Finally, Buster put his rifle away, then looked back to the left. "Rain Water. Mighty chief. I am honored by your presence. I have not seen you for many moons. Why do you follow me?"

Rain Water's horse moved out of the pine shadows, and the young chief appeared not more than thirty feet away. He wore lightweight hunting clothes. Leather leggings with a buckskin shirt. Buster wondered how long he'd been following him. Five more braves materialized out of the trees behind the Indian.

Rain Water stepped his horse toward Buster then pulled up. The same horse Buster had seen the Indian ride years ago. The chief was higher than Buster on the hillside and looked down at him. "You are old, Bus-ter. Too old for these mountains. Why do you not find a rocking chair? Why do you enter our hunting grounds?"

The chief was taunting him, just like when Buster tried to rescue Sue from the Ute village years ago. "It's true I'm old, Rain Water, but I'm not ready for a rocking chair. I'm not here hunting, except for a woman, and when we find her we will leave. I have never lied to you."

"You are here with the lame man who came into my camp years ago. Mc-Alister. He was foolish then, and he is foolish now for almost getting killed by puma. Why do you ride with such a man?"

"He is my friend, Rain Water. A man don't have many friends in this life, so when he finds a good one, that friend is worth keeping. He's a good man."

Rain Water grunted. He jammed his rifle into the blankets covering his horse. "I know why you are here, and who you look for. I will tell you where she is." He flung a tomahawk at a nearby tree. It imbedded several inches. "Ride there, free her, then leave this land so I do not have to kill you."

Buster nodded. It wasn't a hard thing to agree to.

"She is in the hills there." He pointed to the southwest. "Two ridges away. Little house. Go."

Buster knew he meant it. He'd already been spared by Rain Water once. He didn't want to push his luck. There was no negotiating with the Indian. That he had let Buster and Ike live was only due to the Indian's sense of honor. But that sense of honor had limits. Buster kicked his horse into a quick stride up the mountainside. When he looked back, Rain Water and his braves were nowhere to be seen. He debated whether to alert Ike now about Lorraine or ride ahead by himself to find the hideout. He decided to signal Ike. Better to meet up with him still at a distance from the house than to find it and not be able to signal from there. He dismounted in a little clearing, cut off a pile of red needle boughs from nearby pines, and lit a fire under them. The needles and pitch caught immediately. Old, fallen timber encouraged the fire from below. A wandering pillar of white smoke rose upward from the meadow. That should catch Ike's attention. Buster decided against firing a shot as he didn't know how far away Lorraine was. If the wind was swirling in the wrong direction, a gunshot could alert her captor.

The fire crackled while Buster paced. He worried that Lorraine's captor would see the smoke but hoped Ike would. Even if he did, would there be enough daylight left for them to reach the captor's hideout today? Buster scanned the direction Ike would likely come from. If he came. After another half hour of worry, Buster fetched his rifle and fired a shot. Better to risk the kidnapper hearing it than Ike not knowing he needed to come now.

Another half hour passed before Ike broke through the trees lining the little meadow. Buster was already mounted. He waved Ike forward and took off west. Ike caught up to him as they hurried over slightly rising, open terrain.

"Buster! Slow down, what's happened?"

Buster yelled back. "I found out where Lorraine is!" He didn't break stride. "Hurry. We need to cover some ground before the sun disappears."

****

Lorraine put a hand on the young man's shoulder as they stood on the front steps to the small cabin. "Nothing's ever quite as bad as it seems, and nothing's ever quite as good as it seems. You'll get through this, Bert—now let's head on out of this rathole and get back to livin'."

He shook his head. "I can't go back to Cottonwood. Nothin' but trouble for me there. I'll see you to the valley floor, then head my own way. You won't have to worry about me no more."

Lorraine didn't have an answer for that.

They quickly gathered their meager belongings and loaded the horses. Quincy strode to the side of the shanty where a stack of old wood lay rotting and reached in. He immediately screamed and pulled his hand back. "Rattler! Damn!"

Lorraine turned to the sound. "What in the world are you doing, Bert?" She rushed to him as well as she could. He stood there holding one hand in the other.

"I was gettin' my rifle. I hid it there early on 'cause I didn't want to keep sleepin' on it, and you knew where the bullets was. Didn't see the snake."

She took his hand in hers. Two round puncture wounds on the back of it were already surrounded by small red circles. "Come inside and let's get some of the poison out." She pulled him back into the shack and sat him at the small table. "Where'd you hide the knives?"

"In the wood by the stove."

She grabbed a knife and wiped it on her dress, then cut an X into the wounds. Putting her mouth over each one, she sucked as hard as she could. Then spit. Again and again.

"Damn it! That hurts!" The back of Quincy's hand was already swelling. "I can't feel my hand anymore! Let's get out of here."

Lorraine shuffled to the little stream outside and dipped several cloths in. She squeezed them together and hurried back inside, cleaning Quincy's hand and wrapping it tightly. She pulled his belt off and wrapped it around his arm just below the elbow. "You keep this tight, hear? Let it loose every now and then, but mostly keep it tight. Now get on your horse and let's light out for town." She helped him up into the saddle, struggled up herself, grabbed his horse's reins, and pulled them behind her as she descended the slope.

The sun would set soon and riding at night was a

risky proposition, but Quincy didn't have time to wait until morning. He might not make it anyway, but she wanted to give him the best chance she could.

****

Ike hurried to keep up with Buster as they rode up and down slopes that seemed to blend into one another. Always west.

Buster yelled back over his shoulder. "Should be comin' on it soon. Rain Water said—"

"Rain Water! You ran into Rain Water? What'd he say?" It was hard to hear over their pounding hooves.

"He said Lorraine was bein' kept in a small house up in the hills to the west. We're ridin' in the direction he pointed. He said he'd kill us if we didn't get her and leave."

After a half hour, Buster raised a hand. In the distance lay a small meadow with a line shack that had seen better days. Ike suspected it was one of the Emerald Valley Ranch's cabins that had been deserted several years ago. The two riders pulled up downhill and dismounted. They split up, Ike to the left and Buster to the right. Each moved slowly upward among fluttering aspen, crouching with guns drawn. As they neared the shanty, Ike motioned to Buster to stop. The front door was ajar, and there was no sound from inside. A waggle of Ike's gun and both crept forward until Ike flattened himself against the log wall next to the door. A smoky smell drifted from the shack. He poked his head inside for a second and scanned what he could of the interior. Buster hurried to the other side of the door, his gun held high.

Ike whirled through the door, his sidearm sweeping across the one-room structure from right to left. He spoke to Buster in a low voice. "It's empty but someone's been here real recent."

Buster walked in and lowered his weapon. "Did they somehow know we were comin'? There's no way they could have. But it looks like they lit out of here pretty quick—everything's scattered around."

Ike walked over to the small bed and picked up something red. He stared at it, then closed his hand around it.

"What's that, Ike?"

"It's a scarf I bought Lorraine some time back." He strode out of the shack and scanned the ground outside. The two men spread out. There was lots of recent horse sign. The hills were mostly cloaked in brown ground cover just starting to green up, but there were still bare areas this high.

Buster found one and yelled to Ike. "Lookee here. Fresh track from two horses, and it leads down the hill that way." He pointed in the distance.

Ike was already limping over to Ally. He grabbed her reins, swung a leg up, and yanked her toward the new sign. He hurried Ally on, careening downhill faster than he should. The sun had already dipped behind the mountaintops. Daylight was fading and riding in the dark would bring new danger.

Chapter Eleven

Lorraine led her horse in and out of the foothills' dense underbrush, navigating the slopes in the dark. She settled on a downhill route and tugged Quincy's horse behind her. The sun was gone, and a thick blackness lay over the land. A low, early moon cast eerie shadows on their dim path as the wind played with treetops. She kept looking back to make sure Quincy was still upright on his horse. If not upright, at least still in the saddle.

She went slowly, owing to her condition and the faint moonlight. She was a good rider, but this was unfamiliar terrain and it wouldn't do to have either of them take a spill. After an hour of slow going, she pulled up near a little clearing. She wanted to get off the horse to stretch but wasn't sure she could get back up. She drew Quincy's horse forward and held a canteen out to him. She pulled the youth closer and held the water against his mouth, but most dribbled down his chin. He was slumped forward, almost on top of the horse's neck. Quincy mumbled something, and she leaned close to try to hear but couldn't make sense of what he was saying. She needed to hurry and get him to Doc's. Her maternal instincts were working overtime.

She nudged her horse down the slope and hadn't gone more than twenty feet when she heard a thud behind her. She knew what had happened before she even looked back. Coming to a stop, she eased herself to the ground and hurried back to where Quincy lay sprawled on his back. He was conscious—barely—and slurring nonsense. She couldn't lift him; he'd have to help her some to get back on his horse.

"Bert!" She drew her face close to his. "Bert!" He roused slightly, and his eyes fluttered open. "You've got to get up if you want to live." The truth was Lorraine knew there was no way either of them was going to be able to mount up again. She was at a loss. She slapped him on the cheek, hard. "Get up!" A second slap. She was afraid she was hurting him, so she stopped as a crimson blotch appeared on his cheek, even in the ghostlike light.

He gazed at her with unfocused eyes. They were in a small, sloped clearing. Lorraine trickled some water on his lips and took a swig herself, then got right in Quincy's face again. "You have to walk over there!" She pointed to a group of pine trees that would give them some shelter and be warmer than being in the open. "Let's go. Lean on me." He pushed to his knees, and she wrapped an arm around his waist. "Walk if you want to see the sun come up!" He worked himself to a stand, and they stumbled their way slowly toward the dark recess. She eased Quincy to the ground. He rolled onto his back and lay still, splayed on the loose pine needles. Lorraine surveyed her surroundings as well as she could in the dark.

Staying warm was a must. They would freeze without a fire. She had no idea what was in the saddlebags; she only hoped one of them held matches. Finally, in the last bag she searched, she fished out a couple. She unsheathed the large knife Quincy kept stuck in his belt and hacked at low pine branches, stopping to catch her breath. A good quantity of dead wood lay scattered on the forest floor. When she'd arranged the small pieces of wood and green pitch branches just so, she eyed the matches. They had two chances to live.

****

Buster yelled to Ike as they sped down the hillside. "Ike! Hold up, you're gonna get yourself killed in this dark. And what's worse, you're gonna kill Ally!" That was about the only thing Buster could have said to slow Ike down. Ike reined in his old warhorse and waited for Buster to catch up.

His friend said, "And you ain't takin' the lead on this hill."

There was no arguing with Buster when his dander was up. Just like someone else Ike knew who usually waited for him back at the ranch house.

Buster moved his horse in front of Ally. "Besides, you know you ain't a tracker. You'd probably just get us lost, and we'd never get found 'til someone saw the buzzards swirlin' over our dead bodies. What's more, Lorraine can do without me, she can't do without you. Now, draw back willya, and let me do the trackin'."

Buster was right. Ike took a deep breath and pulled Ally back. It had always been hard for him to wait on anything. And with Lorraine missing, waiting was nearly impossible. But they had a better chance of following her trail with Buster leading, so he gave way.

Silvery moonlight danced through the pines as the two trackers descended the mountainside. The moon played hide and seek with the two riders and created broken patterns on the ground. Buster picked his way forward. Ike let Ally choose her own path behind

Buster's horse. Trees weren't hard to avoid, but underbrush was another matter. Scrub oak and prickly bushes reached out and grabbed at Ally's legs, and more than once Ike felt her falter for a second, but she steadied herself, then suddenly moved to the left instead of behind Buster. Ike tried to rein her back in line but couldn't. She kept drifting to the left. He yelled to Buster. "Somethin's gotten into this horse of mine. All of a sudden, she's got a mind of her own. Rein your horse back up here with me."

Ike let Ally have her way, and it wasn't long before he heard something off to his left. In the dark, he couldn't tell exactly where the sound was coming from, so he dismounted with a hand on his bad leg. Ally took off ahead without him, and he had to hurry to keep up. The horse was quick-stepping toward the sound he'd heard. Ike caught up with Ally just as she broke into a little clearing, and he saw an unlikely sight. There, in the pines just ahead, Lorraine was singing softly, with an unconscious young man lying next to her.

She was sitting on the ground shivering and holding the young man's head in her lap. Neither one was dressed for the cold night air that had a special bite this high up. Moonlight shone faintly on her, but her expression was still shrouded in shadows.

"Lorraine! My God, you're here! Are you all right?" He rushed to her and bent over his still wife. "I've never been so glad to see a body as I am right now to see you." She looked at him stiffly, moved Quincy's head off her lap and reached out to Ike who helped her to an unsteady stand. "Are you okay, honey? Is the baby okay?"

Lorraine nodded and slowly drew her arms around

Ike who folded her gently against his chest. She cried softly into his coat and held tightly. Ike stepped back for a second, doffed his jacket, and wrapped it around her. "I should have made you get a warmer coat."

"Never thought I'd be out in the mountains needin' one, cowboy. Couldn't get a fire goin'. Sorry, but you're going to have to hold me up, my legs ain't workin' so well right now."

Ike looked at the mumbling young man. "Who's this, and why's he here?"

"That's the fella who kidnapped me, and he's been bit by a rattlesnake. Name's Quincy."

Ike drew his Colt, pointed it at the kidnapper, and cocked the hammer, but then hesitated. He'd been involved in more killing than he cared to remember, but this would be murder. He holstered the gun. "Just as well. Looks like that snake already did him in."

"We've got to help him, Ike. He'll die if we don't."

"Then I reckon he'll die." He drew an arm around Lorraine's waist and helped her to where her horse was nibbling grass nearby.

Lorraine twisted free and staggered back to Quincy. "Ike, we can't just desert him!"

"Desert him? I'd say he'd only be gettin' what's coming to him. Why not leave him here for the crows? Did he give you any consideration while he was holdin' you captive?"

"Not at first, but that don't give us the right to leave him here to die."

Ike threw his arms in the air. "I don't get you, woman. The boy kidnaps you, a pregnant woman, keeps you captive in the hills, and you want to save him?" He kicked at the ground, holstered his gun, and spoke to the unconscious young man. "She just saved your life, for now, mister. Why, I don't know, 'cause it's clear to me you ain't worth it." Ike spit near Quincy. He had nowhere to let his anger out. He turned away from Lorraine and stood stroking Ally's neck. He'd never handled his feelings well, good or bad.

Lorraine teetered on the hillside. "Ike. Don't shut me out, please. He did a bad thing but was gonna let me go when he got bit. He's just a kid who made a big mistake, but it wasn't his idea. Hawkins put him up to it to get you out of the way."

"Out of the way? Whaddya mean?" It made sense that Hawkins had something to do with the kidnapping, which made him even madder.

"Hawkins set this whole thing up so you'd come searchin' for me out in the Park instead of rilin' the local ranchers up against him and the railroad. He's been ridin' around to the others and browbeatin' 'em into selling, and he's brought a gun hand in to do his dirty work."

Ike turned back to his wife. "I ain't never been as mad at anyone or anything as I am right now at this kid. Even when Quantrill killed my folks. I was so scared I'd never find you again." His stern face gave way to a quivering bottom lip that even the dim light couldn't hide.

Lorraine hobbled over and wrapped her arms around him. "I'd never leave you, cowboy. No way you could ever get rid of me that easy." She kissed him hard. "Let's saddle up and get back to town and see if we can save this kid's life."

"Hold on there. Tell me about this gun hand."

"Don't know anything about him, but Quincy said

Hawkins hired a shootist. Might be from back east somewhere. Would you get the boy back up on his horse, please?"

Buster and Ike hoisted the limp body crosswise on the pack horse's saddle.

Lorraine said, "Can't you hold him with you, Ike?"

"Don't push it, Lorraine. I'd like to toss him off this horse." Ike tied the man's hands and feet together under the animal. "But it don't really matter. If he lives, makes no difference whether he's layin' across that saddle or sittin' up in it. As long as we're goin', let's get a move on." He boosted Lorraine carefully up on her horse and whistled for Ally. When they were all mounted up, Buster led, walking his horse in the general direction of the ranch, weaving through silhouetted dark pines.

The dim light made traveling difficult. As the small troupe continued down the slope, the underbrush was alive with scurrying sounds. Buster held a hand up. "Make some noise so we don't surprise anything we don't want to."

Lorraine started singing a lullaby that drifted with the wind.

> *Sleep my darling, on my bosom,*
> *Harm will never come to you;*
> *Mother's arms enfold you safely,*
> *Mother's heart is ever true.*

> ~*~

> *As you sleep there's naught to scare you,*
> *Naught to wake you from your rest;*
> *Close those eyelids, little angel,*
> *Sleep upon your mother's breast.*

Her voice faltered as she sang the last words, and

the song faded into the night air. Sniffles gave her away, and she blew her nose. Ike wiped at his eyes, and Buster cleared his throat. "What song was that, Miss Lorraine? It sounds awful familiar."

"That's a lullaby my momma sang to me when I was growin' up. I don't remember much about her, but I do remember her singing me to sleep. I sing it to Jessie now." More sniffles.

Silence grabbed hold of them. Ike struggled as he sat in the saddle. He wanted to say something soothing to Lorraine, to reassure her that things were going to be okay, that he was sorry he was so hard at times, but the words wouldn't come. He was good at a lot of things, but comforting loved ones wasn't at the top of the list. He'd rest a lot easier when his wife and daughter were home, safe and sound again. It couldn't come too soon.

The hours piled up as they snaked their way toward the valley floor. When they broke out of the forest, the land leveled out, and the first rays of a pink dawn lit their way. Ike gazed northeast and spied several familiar low ridges in the distance. There were still several hours of steady riding ahead of them, but at least they'd be in sight of their destination before long.

Ike turned to Buster. "Ride on ahead into town and fetch Doc Early, will you? Tell him about Lorraine and the boy and have him meet us at the ranch."

Buster nodded and spurred his mount forward. Soon, he was a small figure galloping in the distance as a rising sun began to bathe the Park.

After half an hour, Ike dismounted and reached up to help his wife off her horse. He walked her to a granite ledge that jutted from a hogback. It made a perfect seat, and he eased her down. Time to give the boy a look. Ike checked for a pulse. Weak but steady. He untied Quincy, pulled him off the horse, and set him on the ground by a small stream that gurgled nearby. Lorraine started to get up, but Ike waved her off. "I'll check him, you just sit there and look pretty."

The boy's hand didn't look good. The back of it was dark and the plump, bitten finger looked even darker. There had been no way to keep a belt tight around his arm on the ride and red streaks shot upward toward a discolored and swollen shoulder.

After watering the horses, Ike helped Lorraine mount up. She was about done in. He tied the unconscious Quincy back on and swung up on Ally. He rode slowly with his wife. She'd been through a lot and no telling how hard it had been on her; she wasn't one to say. Ahead were familiar landmarks that made Ike want to break into a gallop, but that wasn't possible with his two passengers and horses that were nearly done in.

When he finally spied the ranch, Ike heaved a sigh of relief. Now he could get Lorraine settled in and rested. He drew up at the ranch house hitching post, then eased her off the packhorse. He wrapped an arm around her waist, helped her into the house, and had her lie on their bed. Drawing the covers over her, he kissed her as she closed her eyes. Outside, he untied Quincy and carried him to Jessie's small bed, where his feet dangled over the end of the soft horsehair mattress. The boy's chalky white face stood in stark contrast to Jessie's colorful red bedcovers.

Ike put a hand to Quincy's forehead. "Fever." The boy's face was red and swollen as well.

Ike busied himself making a pot of strong coffee.

He stood over their bed holding a warm cup and studied the face of the woman he loved. She had creases that weren't there four years ago when they married. He put those there, he thought. She deserved better than him, but at least he'd helped produce Jessie.

As he watched her, Lorraine stirred and opened her eyes. She reached out with both arms. Ike bent and hugged his face to hers, her tears soaking his cheek. She gave him a light kiss and closed her eyes again, asleep almost as soon as she did. He wiped a wet trail off his face and stood. He walked out of the bedroom and glared at Quincy. That damn kid better live—for Lorraine's sake.

The sound of hoof beats drowned out his thoughts. Ike looked out the window to see Buster swing down from his horse before he'd even come to a stop. He burst into the ranch house. "Doc's on his way, drivin' his buggy. Should be here shortly. I stopped at Miss Sue's too and saw Jessie. She's doin' just fine. Sue said she'll keep her a while longer until Lorraine gets her legs back under her. How is Miss Lorraine anyway?"

"Exhausted, but sleeping, thankfully. I'm gonna make sure she don't get up for a week." He meant it. "And thanks for checkin' on Jessie."

Buster nodded and looked at the still form on Jessie's bed. "Is he alive?"

"Hangin' on. Got the strength of youth, so my guess is he'll make it. Not sure if he'll come through with every body part the Good Lord started him with, but most of them, likely."

The two men sat at the small kitchen table absently drinking coffee, listening for the clip clop of the buggy's horses. Worries and anger swirled through

Ike's head. Lorraine. Hawkins. Donaldson. The kid. Jessie. The gunman. His somber thoughts were interrupted by Doc Early's arrival. His buggy stopped outside, and Ike swung the door wide for him.

"Tell me what happened, Ike."

"Lorraine seems okay, but she's plumb wore out and I ain't gonna wake her up. I don't know what happened to the kid. I just know he got bit."

Doc bent over Lorraine and took her pulse. "Good, strong, steady." He put a hand on her forehead. "There's no fever, so she and the baby will likely be fine. She's a strong woman, but make sure she stays in bed for a while." He leaned over Jessie's bed to examine Quincy. After checking the boy's vitals and his hand, he said, "Wish I could have seen him lots earlier than this. That hand doesn't look good... I don't know...his arm is swelled something awful, too." He stood and glanced around the room. "I got some sharp instruments I'd like to sterilize on that stove over there. Get that fire going hotter."

Ike added more wood to the stove and bellowed air into it. When the fire was glowing, Doc put a pan of water on top. Soon, bubbles covered the water's surface, and he dipped several scalpels in it. The hand cutting only took a short time, but Doc perspired heavily and Buster wiped his forehead more than once. Quincy groaned as Doc opened up two of his fingers, then made several lengthy cuts on the back of his hand, and a couple up his forearm. Angry-looking fluid oozed from all the purplish cuts.

Doc shook his head. "I oughta take that finger off right now, but I'm just stubborn enough to see if we can save it. No need to put a tourniquet on his arm anymore, the poison's in his system by now and will do what it will." He cleaned the cuts up with the hot water from the stove and bandaged them, drawing moans from the semi-conscious patient. "I'll come by tomorrow to check on him, but you let me know if he takes a turn for the worse. Check on him every couple of hours or so. I've done all I can right now." He cleaned his instruments and put them back in his bag. "Till tomorrow." And he was off clip-clopping toward town.

Ike paced the room afterward until Buster reassured him. "Ike, go to bed, please. Lorraine is going to be fine, the baby too. You need to get some rest. I'll stand first watch."

Ike started to protest but without any conviction and lurched toward the bedroom. He gazed at Quincy as he passed. He'd have his time with the kid yet.

Chapter Twelve

Hawkins was still scheming. He squired his hireling Slade around town, stopping in most of the shops along Main Street for effect. He didn't introduce the gunman to anyone, but let Slade's presence speak for itself. He was confident word of the man's occupation had already spread far and wide, all of which would make his work easier.

Rob had never backed away from a fight and wasn't about to now. Plenty of townspeople told him about Slade's gunplay in the Wildfire, and the sheriff knew he had to act. Hawkins was a danger not only to him, but to the town and its reputation. A local gunman could scare many a newcomer away, especially one as trigger-happy as Slade seemed to be. Hawkins was showing Slade off in The Sew Pretty when he caught up with them. As Rob walked in, Slade stood silently to the side with his hands crossed in front of him. Margaret stood behind her desk, stiff and wide-eyed as Hawkins moved around her shop. Dread showed on the faces of two women customers as they hurried out the front door. Rob spied Hawkins as soon as he entered.

"Why, hello, Sheriff. Nice day to take a stroll, isn't it? You've met Mr. Slade, haven't you? I thought so. You two should spend some time together. Perhaps there'll be an opportunity to do that."

Rob strode past Hawkins to where Margaret hung

back. "Are you all right?"

Margaret made a face at him. "As if you care. Where's that little girl? Did her momma tell her she had to go right home after school?"

A flush spread over Rob's face. "I asked if you're all right, but I can see by how sharp your tongue is workin' that you are." He turned and looked at Slade. "By the way, about your shootin' up the Wildfire. Do that again, and I'll throw you in jail." He kept a hand on his holster. "Don't spend any more time here, Hawkins, unless you want people to think you're looking for a new hat. I'll escort the both of you out." He gestured to the front door.

Hawkins wore a thin smile. "Say, I heard your brother's back. Where was it he went again? Did he have a good trip?"

Rob's hand curled around his gun's stock, but he stopped when Slade drew his coat back, revealing a new-looking Colt. "You know damn well where he was, Hawkins. You sent him on a wild goose chase, searchin' after his wife. But you're right. He is back and lookin' to get even." He took his time moving toward the door and left without looking back.

****

Satisfied he'd had the impact around town he wanted, Hawkins walked back to the railroad office. A mangy dog lay blocking his path near the door. Hawkins kicked at the animal, which slunk slowly away. Slade stepped in front of Hawkins and poked a finger in his chest. "You ever do that again, I'll pistol whip you. Understand?"

Hawkins tried to sidestep the gunman.

Slade drew his Colt and replaced his pointed finger

with the gun's barrel. "I want you to say you understand." He cocked the piece.

Hawkins threw his hands up in disgust. He didn't know who was a bigger danger to him, Slade or McAlister. "All right, I understand. Now can we go in?" Inside, he placed his expensive ten-gallon on a wall hook and hurried to his desk chair and sat. Slade stood impassively.

"I'm going to visit more ranchers today. When we get there, let me do the talking, although I don't think that'll be a problem. Talking doesn't seem to be your strong suit." He unrolled a scroll and showed Slade a rough map of this northern part of South Park. He preened as he pointed to a spot on the map. "I've already taken care of this ranch, the Donaldson place. By now the other homesteaders nearby have no doubt heard he's sold out, so we shouldn't run into any problems. But if we do, you need to be persuasive. Don't kill anybody, unless they shoot first."

Slade broke his silence. "Nobody I ever shot had the chance to shoot first."

Hawkins looked at him sideways. "We'll start with the Spencer spread. But first, I got something to take care of."

He strode to the Wildfire. A half hour later, he and Slade headed for the stables.

When Hawkins came in, Red Crawford eased up off a pile of clean hay and straightened to greet his guests. "Just grabbin' a little shuteye. I don't sleep so good anymore, so I like to take advantage of it when I can." He eyed Slade. "Name's Crawford, Red Crawford. Who might you be, young fella?"

"Just somebody driftin' through, who's not gonna

be here long, so it don't matter, does it?" Slade adjusted his black string tie.

"Reckon it don't, now that you put it that way." He turned to Hawkins. "What can I do for you, Mr. Hawkins?"

"Get my mount ready. And Mr. Slade's as well. That one there. We'll be getting a cup of coffee at the boarding house. Just let us know."

"Won't take me more'n a minute to do. Why don't you just wait here?"

"Might as well. The coffee there is the worst in town, even worse than Margaret Pinshaw's."

Red soon had them in the saddle. They headed almost due west and crossed a couple of fast-moving, late-spring streams. Hawkins wasn't from these parts, but he'd been on enough solo rides over this terrain recently that he'd come to know the land and its occupants well. The Spencer ranch lay straight ahead, and the railroad would likely cut through the heart of their spread. Hawkins smiled. He'd have all the land the railroad needed in South Park locked up soon enough. At a nice profit for him. The next domino to fall after the Donaldson's was squarely in his crosshairs.

The two riders pulled up in front of the small, but tidy ranch house. Sam Spencer was by the barn, bent over with a horse's hoof in his lap, nailing a shoe in place. The *whack whack whack* of his hammer reverberated in the high country air. He glanced up as the two men tied their horses at the hitching rail.

Hawkins walked over. "Spencer, good to see you. I believe we met once in town, if I remember correctly. I'm Charlie Hawkins, in charge of the railroad project through South Park." He didn't bother to introduce

143

Slade—no introduction was necessary. "I'd like to talk with you for a minute. Mind if we go inside? I could use a drink of water, thanks."

Spencer straightened with the hammer in one hand. "I reckon I know why you're here, Hawkins, so you can say what you have to say to me standin' right here. This is as good a place as any to tell you 'no'."

Hawkins narrowed his eyes. Spencer was bigger than both him and Slade, but size had never mattered to Hawkins in a fight. "That's not a very friendly attitude, Spencer. I thought we'd be able to work out a fair offer for your land—more than it's worth, in fact. How about you listen to what I have to say? I'm sure Mr. Slade would like you to." The implication hung in the air between them. Hawkins wore a forced smile, but felt the familiar vein pulsing in his forehead when he got angry. Slade stared at Spencer and tugged his gloves on. He dropped a hand toward his holster.

Spencer held both hands up in the air. "I ain't heeled, Hawkins. Shootin' an unarmed man is still murder, even out here. We ain't got nothin' else to talk about. Now clear out and don't come back."

Slade stepped in front of Hawkins and stared at the homesteader. "Then I suggest you get heeled. Hawkins, why don't you throw him your gun?" His face broke into the smallest of smiles.

Spencer kept his hands high. "Ain't gonna be no gunplay here, unless you murder me." The rancher paused. "But my pappy always said when somethin' bad's comin' your way, you might as well get it over with, so…" Spencer coiled and threw a powerful right hook that smashed into Slade's cheek. The man stumbled before falling backward and hitting the ground on his backside. Spencer pointed a finger at Hawkins, but before he could say anything, Slade drew his gun and shot him in the leg.

Spencer collapsed, howling. "You bastard!"

Slade righted himself, rubbed his jaw, and stood with gun drawn over Spencer, who held a hand against his bloody wound. Mrs. Spencer scurried out of the house past the two intruders and knelt by her husband, then looked at Hawkins with tears in her eyes. "Don't listen to him; we'll do what you want."

"Now there's a woman who's got your best interest at heart, Spencer. She makes a lot of sense; you should listen to her." Hawkins stepped on the man's wounded leg, and Spencer screamed. "I was just gonna ask where she was and where your kids were too. But I can see that someone in this family is finally thinking clearly." Hawkins walked back to his horse and mounted up. "You aren't in any position to say no. I'll be back in a couple of days with the paperwork. Be ready to sign." He grunted at the homesteader. "Oh, and you better get that leg checked. I'll let the doc know you accidentally shot yourself." He looked at Mrs. Spencer and nodded. "Ma'am."

The two riders headed in the direction of Cottonwood. When they were out of earshot, Hawkins upbraided Slade. "I told you I didn't want any shooting."

Slade glanced at him. "I shoot what I want, when I want." As they crested a rise and put the Spencer place behind them, Slade said, "Sheriff's likely to hear about this. I may need to set aside some special time with him."

"I don't care what you do with Rob McAlister. Just

make sure it's self-defense."

They rode the rest of the way to town in silence, which only heightened Hawkins' growing sense of unease about his hired gun. Was the man someone he couldn't control?

****

Back in Cottonwood, Hawkins dismissed Slade and settled into his office, uncertainty swirling inside him. One of those uncertainties was the safe across the room.

The safe sat against the far wall, almost mocking him. It had been there since he came to town. He didn't know what was in it and didn't know the combination. It was a medium-size Cincinnati safe, squat with a black lacquer front and silver tumbler. He'd never paid much attention to it until recently. Because his office was on the smallish side, the safe appeared larger than it would have otherwise. He'd been trying to open it for weeks using different combinations, his curiosity up. What good is a safe you can't open? He couldn't let it go; he couldn't abide it sitting there staring at him.

He'd been told the safe occupied a prominent space in a local renegade rancher's study years ago. After Ike McAlister's wife shot the rancher dead, Rob McAlister moved the safe to town and the stagecoach company had a safecracker open it. Inside was the rest of the Reynolds Gang money the coach line originally sent Hugh Walnutt to find. After that, the combination faded from memory and the safe gathered dust in the jail. When he came to town, Rob McAlister offered it to him, which is how it came to sit in the railroad office now.

Hawkins got up and stood in front of the claw-footed object. Long-settled dust clung to its top. He reached over and forced the dial to turn. It always moved grudgingly, as if unwilling to reveal its secret. He drew a chair over and sat in front of the painted golden eagle with spread wings that adorned the face. He tried to imagine what might have been running through the rancher's mind when he initially set the combination. Did it have anything to do with him being a Quantrill's raider, a band of confederate guerrillas during the War? Was there a connection there? He'd already tried changing words like 'raiders' into numbers as they appeared in the alphabet, but to no avail. After another hour, he was ready to give up when the date of Quantrill's shocking raid on Lawrence, Kansas popped into his head. When was it…1863? He considered the numbers for a moment, then rotated the tumbler to 18 right, 6 left, 3 right, and tried the silver metal handle next to the tumbler. The door swung open easily, revealing a locked inner compartment, hand painted with an arrangement of decorative flowers.

A sturdy brass keyhole guarded the inner section. He thought of the key he found soldered to the bottom metal plate when he first received the safe. Rummaging through his top desk drawer, he located the key and inserted it into the interior cover's lock. The door popped open. This innermost compartment consisted of a series of inlaid rosewood-decorated cubbyholes, most of them empty. One contained several pieces of paper, however, which he drew out. There were old ledgers and notes about stagecoach freight loads and schedules, along with a folded paper on stagecoach letterhead. It told of a rancher on the western side of South Park who'd thrown in with the Reynolds Gang during the Civil War when the gang was robbing coaches and freight wagons in South Park. A Hank Waverly. That set his mind to figuring a way to make a payday out of this information. If Waverly was still around, there might be a way he could use this to his advantage.

It took Hawkins a couple rides west, but he eventually found the sprawling Waverly ranch that lay miles south of the mining town of Fairplay. He flattered the rancher by saying that his reputation spread far and wide, and that's how Hawkins became aware of him. He didn't fish the letter out. Yet.

He laid out a proposal where he would route the railroad west then re-route it south to Waverly's place, instead of to Fairplay as he'd told his bosses. Waverly would have more business loading cattle and feed than he could handle. All Hawkins wanted was a cut of the profits. Sounded reasonable to him, and if necessary, perhaps Slade could convince Waverly it was reasonable. The letter in his pocket made it sound like no one else knew Waverly had befriended Reynolds during the war, so he figured he had leverage on the rancher.

Chapter Thirteen

"It's the sheriff! It's the sheriff!" A little boy came running out from behind the Wildfire, pointing to the back of the building. "Somebody shot him! He ain't movin'!"

A crowd started to gather around the boy, who was babbling on, all the while still pointing. "I was playin'. I didn't do nothin'. I just found him, there's blood—"

Hugh Walnutt pushed through the gathering throng and rushed in the direction the boy pointed. He slowed as he got to the alley behind the saloon. Peering around the corner, he saw Rob McAlister laying on the ground face up, arms spread to the side, hat flipped upside down in the dirt a few feet away. A dark reddish-brown blotch stained the dirt around his upper body. The bullet punched a hole in his leather vest on its way through his chest. Rob's gun lay a few feet away.

It was early morning, and the sun had just peeked over the eastern ramparts, lending scattered shadows to the scene. The image of Rob staring sightlessly upward in the dirt seared itself in his mind. He turned back to the crowd. "Someone go get Doc Early! Go get the doc!"

A few minutes later, Doc Early struggled through the mob and knelt by the fallen sheriff. He placed two fingers on Rob's neck and shook his head. "Hugh, pick someone to help you get Rob to my office. Lay him out

149

on my table in the back, and don't let anyone in." He turned to the crowd. "And don't anyone go telling Sue about her brother yet 'til I clean him up some at my place. Same with Margaret Pinshaw."

But Margaret had just arrived and stood in the crowd surrounding her beau. She started shrieking and turning in a small circle. Doc rose and put an arm around her and guided her away from the scene. Early handed Margaret off to the mayor's wife, Eleanor Whitaker. "Keep her occupied for a while, okay? Maybe a cup of coffee at her shop." He turned to the gathering as Hugh and another man lifted Rob. "I need someone to ride out to Ike's place and let him know. Who'll do that?"

As he carried his friend away, Hugh yelled back, "I will take care of that—and I will break the news to Sue." After leaving Doc's office, he began a wooden walk toward the rooming house near the end of Main Street. He glanced back at the plain little building where his friend lay.

On the way, he stopped by the stable, where the horses were outside eating their morning grain. Red was inside mucking stalls when the professor hailed him. "Red!" The old man looked up. "I need you to do me a favor. I hate to be the one to break bad news, but someone has shot and killed Rob McAlister. They found him behind the Wildfire this morning." He paused to gather himself. "Could you ride out to Ike's place and let him know? I have things to attend to here in town."

Red's face drained. "Shot him? Who'd do that?" He paused. "That just don't seem right, him bein' dead so sudden. One minute you're here and the next you ain't. Not right. Who did it?"

Hugh tugged at his thin mustache. "I don't know at this point, but my guess is it was someone he knew."

"What makes you say that?"

He hesitated. "That is just a guess on my part." He wasn't ready to share his hunch with anyone yet. Since Rob was shot from the front it was likely someone he recognized. That's the only explanation he could figure for how the killer would have gotten the drop on Rob, who was a fair hand with a gun. "Would you mind heading out?"

"Why, sure. Of course. I'll leave right now. This will strike Ike a heavy blow."

"It is striking us all a heavy blow. Tell Ike to be watchful. The killer has just taken down one McAlister brother, and might have the other in his sights as well." His heart thumped as he thought about how he was going to protect his wife, the only McAlister sister.

Red rubbed at his white beard. "*His* sights? So a man did the killin'?"

That stopped Hugh cold for a second. "That is just an assumption on my part. I have not seen very many ladies locally who sport sidearms, so I—" He stopped. No sense carrying on a conversation regarding something he knew nothing about. He turned his attention back to Red. "Tell Ike I will be out there soon." He wasn't sure why he said that, as riding to Ike's ranch right now didn't make much sense when he needed to stay near Sue. He waved goodbye. "Keep your eyes open, Red."

"I surely will. I ain't ready to trade this skin in yet."

Hugh walked into the boarding house where Sue

was serving breakfast. He asked her to come sit with him in the parlor. When he told her, she started to get up, but fainted and hit her head on the table next to the divan before he could reach her. He yelled to one of the other boarders. "Go get a wet towel and some cold water!" It was several minutes before she regained her senses. Tears flooded her eyes as her husband helped her sit on the small couch.

"What happened?"

"You fainted."

"I didn't mean me—what happened to Rob? How did he die?"

Hugh didn't want to describe Rob's wound in any detail, so he just said, "Someone shot him. We don't know who it was or why."

"Where was he shot?"

"He was found behind the Wildfire with a wound to his chest. He is in the doctor's office now."

"Who did you say shot him?"

"That we don't know, but we will find the killer, I promise you." He already had a prime suspect in mind. He and Rob hadn't left Hawkins' office recently on the best of terms. He walked back into the dining room. The three boarders at the breakfast table all worked for Hawkins. Suddenly, he quick-drew his pistol. Pointing it at them, he motioned toward the front door and told them to get out. They protested, but he was not in a frame of mind to be disobeyed. "Get out now!" His barrel aimed at their chests made for a persuasive argument. "You can collect your gear out on the street later. Move!" He escorted them out of the house and watched them skulk away. He turned his attention back to Sue, who was both teary and wobbly, holding onto the arm of the couch.

"You need to lie down and rest." She started to protest, but he stood firm. "Not just because of Rob, but also because of that bump you got." He led her upstairs to their bedroom, and helped her to bed. "Will you stay here if I leave?"

"No. My brother's down the way, laying on a table, dead. As soon as my head clears, I'll go and—" She swooned before finishing the thought.

The one window in the room overlooked Main Street. He made sure it was closed securely, then went downstairs and locked the front door behind him as he left. He'd be back as soon as he could.

****

Lorraine heard the approaching hoof beats and looked out the ranch house window. Red Crawford was tying his horse at the front rail. She met him out on the porch. "Why, Red. What brings you here? Can't remember the last time you visited out this way. Come in, please." Something was wrong. Her stomach jumped, and she worked to sound calmer than she felt. Jessie walked in with her, followed by Red.

Dirty clothes, saddlebags, and a lone rifle lay scattered around the house. "Don't mind the mess, Red. I'm home from a short trip and haven't had time to clean the place up yet."

Red took his hat off. "Didn't notice a thing. Glad you're back from your…trip."

Lorraine ushered Red to the small kitchen table, but he didn't sit. For a second, he stared at Quincy, who lay semi-conscious on a small bed to the side, one hand wrapped inside a large white bandage.

Lorraine answered the question on Red's face. "His

name's Quincy, and I'm takin' care of him until he recovers from a rattler bite. Doc took one finger off so far. May need to take the hand. But he's young, looks like he'll live." She turned back to Red. "Ike's not here right now. Is there something I can do for you?"

"Is he downrange?"

"I expect so. Why?" She didn't know exactly where he was.

"I have bad news." He looked Jessie's way.

Lorraine's throat tightened and she turned toward her daughter. "Honey, why don't you go play in the other room?" She looked back at her visitor. "What is it, Red?" It had to be bad to bring the stable owner out here.

Red twisted his hat in his hands. "His brother's been shot and killed."

Lorraine stumbled slightly and steadied herself with a hand to the back of a chair. She put her other hand to her mouth and stared silently at Red for a moment. "Oh my God. How did it happen?" She sat heavily.

"No one knows. They found him behind the Wildfire early this morning with a gunshot wound. That's all I know."

Lorraine still held a hand over her mouth.

"I better ride on over to the Park basin and find Ike."

Lorraine nodded. "I don't know where to tell you to look, Red. He's somewhere with the herd." All of which was true. "You go find him, but if he gets back here before you tell him, I'll let him know." As Red left, his unbelievable news swirled in her head. "Damnation!" Ike wasn't due back for several more hours.

****

Light green grass and early sage sprouts covered the Park basin floor. The cows calved a couple of weeks ago, and Ike and Buster had branded them with Ike's slanted M iron. The sun was already well over the low range to the east and lent an intense shimmer to the surroundings. As the two partners rode the landscape, Buster said he'd heard in town that Hawkins' gunman shot Sam Spencer.

Ike pursed his lips. The stakes were getting higher—how was this going to end? He was mulling that over when, in the distance, a man galloped toward him swinging his hat back and forth over his head.

Ike recognized the rider as he pulled up. "What're you doin' out here, Red?"

"I have bad news. Your brother was shot and killed in town this morning."

At first, Ike didn't react. He sat immobile with his hands crossed over the saddle horn. He stared at Red for a long while, then shook his head. "That can't be. Can't be." He rubbed a hand over his eyes and fell silent. Part of him couldn't make sense of it, but a bigger part of him knew it must be true. He rubbed the back of his neck hard, then white-knuckled the saddle horn again. "Does Sue know?"

"The professor said he was going to tell her."

"Does Lorraine know?"

"Yes, I just told her."

"Margaret?"

"Not sure about her."

"How'd it happen?"

"Not sure. All I know is they found him behind the

155

saloon this morning."

"They have the killer?"

"Don't think so."

"Was it Hawkins?"

"Don't know. Sorry, Ike."

Ike wheeled Ally toward the ranch, followed closely by Buster and Red.

When they reached the barn, Ike swung off Ally mid-stride and limped to the house. Lorraine was waiting on the front porch and rushed into his arms. "Ike! I'm so sorry about Rob—"

Ike shushed her with a finger to her lips and wiped a trail of tears from her cheeks. "It don't seem possible." He pulled her close and leaned down to kiss her. "I'll be gone for a while. Buster will take care of you in the meantime." Ike looked over, and Buster nodded.

Lorraine held onto Ike's shirt tighter. "What are you going to do?"

"I'm going to see my brother." His eyes narrowed, and he wiped away a tear. "I'll figure the rest out after that. Stay inside and see to Jessie please." Then he was up on Ally and off, dust flying behind the warhorse's hooves.

His mind raced as he stormed over the land. What had happened? Hawkins. The man's face filled Ike's vision as he neared town. When he reached Main Street, there was no lack of townspeople who yelled to him as he galloped by.

"Doc's place!"

He pulled Ally up in front of the doctor's office and rushed inside. He brushed past Early and strode to the table where Rob lay on his back. He placed his hat against his chest and stared at the still form of his younger brother. Rob looked so peaceful. Like he was asleep. Like Ike could shake him awake as he'd done countless times growing up. He bent over the body and traced a finger around the bullet hole in Rob's vest. His hand traveled to his brother's ghost-white face, and he rested it on Rob's cheek, then whispered in his brother's ear. He stood motionless for a moment, shoved his hat on, and turned to leave. He'd track the killer to the end of the earth if need be. He'd done it when his parents were murdered and he'd do it again now.

Doc moved to block his way. "We're all sure sorry, Ike. We know this is about as hard a thing as there is, short of losing a child." Ike looked past Early with unseeing eyes and silently stepped around him. Right into the path of the professor.

"Ike, hold on a moment. Please. Don't go off half-cocked." Ike moved to get by, but Hugh blocked him again. "I know what you are thinking, but there is no proof Hawkins did this. In fact, he sent one of his men here to tell me he did not do it."

Ike's eyes focused on his brother-in-law. "Hugh, you and I are friends, but you better get out of my way or I'll have to hurt you."

Hugh stood his ground. "Then you are going to have to do that."

Ike balled his fists and readied a punch. Hugh stood with his feet spread, prepared to take a blow. Instead, Ike turned and smashed a fist into the office's plaster wall, breaking off several pieces that crumbled onto the floor. He shook his hand then held it against his midsection.

"I wish you hadn't done that, Ike." The doctor took hold of Ike's hand, and Ike grimaced. "Good thing you did it here, though, so I don't have to go anywhere to tend to you."

He pulled his hand back. "I'm not stayin' here doin' nothin', with my brother lyin' right over there. If it's broke, it's broke."

"At least you had the good sense to use your off hand to hit a plaster wall, which isn't as hard as that head of yours." His small attempt at humor fell flat. "Please let me look at it." Without waiting for an answer, the doctor manipulated the back of the hand while Ike silently fidgeted. "Feels okay, likely just bruised. I'm going to bind the hand tight. Leave it like that for a few days, then take it off and have a look. If the back of the hand's gone dark at all, you're in trouble. Come back and see me. In the meantime, keep your hands to yourself." After wrapping the hand, he paused. "I'll take good care of Rob. You go on and go home now."

Ike shook his head as if there were cobwebs in it. "Who would Rob have been meeting that late? And why behind the saloon?"

The doctor said, "I don't have an answer for that. No one knows why yet."

Ike turned and strode silently away.

Hugh followed Ike back to the boarding house where he went upstairs to see Sue. She was asleep when he came into the bedroom, but her eyes fluttered open as the two men talked in hushed tones. Hugh told him about the blow to her head. Ike hadn't taken his eyes off his sister since he came in. When he noticed she was awake, he knelt by the bed with his bad leg straight out and held her hand. Her eyes were red as she reached an arm over and pulled him close. His head lay next to hers, cheek to cheek. Tears streamed down Ike's face, and Sue's sniffles gave way to sobs that wracked her body.

Their tears dripped into the sheets, and Ike swallowed hard. He squeezed her hand gently and brushed hair off her face with his swollen hand. A kiss on her forehead and he stood, unsure what to do next. There was a knock on the front door, which Hugh went downstairs to answer.

He called up, "Ike, can you come here for a moment?"

Ike went down to find Mayor Whitaker waiting for him, hat in hand.

"I'm very sorry about your brother, Ike. He was a good sheriff and a good man. We'll find the killer and bring him to justice."

"Why are you here, Mayor? You sided with Hawkins and the railroad when Rob was alive, and now he's gone. We don't need your help. We don't want it. Hawkins is the one who's gonna need all the help he can get. Soon. So just stay out of my way!"

Whitaker protested as the professor led him outside. He said back over his shoulder, "That's not fair, Ike. I've already been in touch with the territorial governor about this and am awaiting a reply. They'll send someone to straighten this all out."

Ike burst through the open door. "Straighten it out? Like this is some damn argument? My brother was just murdered! I'll straighten it out all right." He drew his Colt and aimed it toward the railroad office. "And right there's where I'll do the straightenin'."

Hugh grabbed Ike by the arm and pulled him back to the boarding house.

Upstairs, Sue was sitting up in bed when Ike came back in. "I heard what you said, Ike. Don't do anything foolish. Please. I couldn't bear to lose both my brothers. Promise me you won't go hunting the killer. Let the law handle it."

"You know I can't do that, Sis." He kissed her on the cheek, strode out of the house, and whistled for Ally.

Chapter Fourteen

Hawkins had more on his mind than just trying to strike a deal with Waverly. When they found the sheriff dead that morning, he reckoned he was the prime suspect, and Ike McAlister would come gunning for him soon. Two things pointed the finger at him—the falling out he'd recently had with Rob McAlister, and the fact that he'd recently brought in a gunman. He wasn't ready for a showdown with the dead sheriff's brother. Yet. With the town in an uproar, Hawkins figured it was a good time for him and Slade to disappear and finalize the arrangement with Waverly. As he and Slade rode out that morning, the citizens of Cottonwood milled in the streets. Lots of stares his way. He spurred his stallion, and soon the town was a faint mirage. It took most of the rest of the day to reach Waverly's ranch.

The missus met them as they dismounted. "Hello, Mr. Hawkins, what brings you our way again?"

"I'm just here to see your husband about some business, ma'am. Is he around?"

"He's inside, resting. Hasn't been feeling well lately, but I'm sure he'll shake it soon."

Hawkins motioned toward the ranch house. "May I?" Without waiting for her response, he strolled into the sizeable ranch house. Hank Waverly was reclining in an imposing brown leather chair in the middle of a

161

neat living room. Like the ranch, the house itself was large by South Park standards. "Good to see you, Waverly. I hear—"

Waverly struggled to a stand. His still-powerful build belied his gray hair. "I didn't expect you, Hawkins. Why are you here?"

"There's been a change of plans I thought you should know about. Why don't we sit and discuss them? By the way, this is Mr. J. Slade, an associate of mine."

Waverly shuffled to his desk without looking Slade's way.

The two visitors sat across from the rancher. Hawkins said, "I've been thinking about our arrangement—"

Waverly held up a hand. "Hold on there. We don't have an 'arrangement', yet. Just my 'proposal' so far. Not sure having the railroad runnin' through my place is worth what you say it is."

Hawkins burned inside. The man was an idiot if he couldn't see the value of being a major stopover on the only railroad running through South Park. A stop with a water tank at that. How had this fool managed to build a large operation by thinking so small? But he needed Waverly and his money, so Hawkins calmed himself. Maybe flattery would work. "You've done an admirable job of building this cattle ranch. Why, your thousand acres will likely be ten times that in the coming years. With the railroad, you'll be able to triple the size of your herd and move more cows to Denver and still feed the miners around here. I hear you're supplying them with a lot of hay for their stock, too. You'll be makin' so much money you could paper this room with it."

Waverly slowly rose and poured himself a brandy. "Either of you care for one?" Slade sat impassively. The rancher poured a second one and held out a crystal glass to Hawkins. He took a big swallow, lit a cigar, offered one to Hawkins, and leaned back in his overstuffed chair. "What you said is likely true." He put his snifter down. "So, since you've had some time to think on it, what do you think of my proposal?"

Hawkins took a sip and lit up as well. He paused and ran a hand over his vest pocket that held the incriminating letter about Waverly and Reynolds. "You're going to have to do a lot better than that. Routing the railroad through your ranch is worth plenty more than ten percent of profits. You're going to double your money when it first comes through, and then double again over time. This ranch will be two thousand acres soon, then five. Your herd will stretch from here all the way to the South Platte. Ranchers from all over the valley will drive their cattle to your place for loading, and you'll charge them a pretty penny to do it. You'll have to build a big way station to feed and house all the travelers, and larger corrals for horses and cattle. And hire more people."

He studied Waverly for a minute. "So, let's talk about who needs who more. If I don't route that railroad through your ranch, another rancher around here will be getting that business instead of you and making all that money. He'll make your thousand acres look like a hundred compared to his spread." He blew a perfect smoke ring that traveled across the room and caught on a large bronze sculpture before disappearing. "But if I do run it through your property, then you'll control this whole northern part of the Park, water and all." He paused to let that sink into the old rancher's head. "But that's all right if you don't want to be involved. Why, I got just the rancher in mind to take your place." He got up and started for the door, Slade in tow.

Waverly held up a meaty hand. "Wait a second. Just wait. I didn't say I wasn't willing to dicker. I'm a reasonable man. How about I double your take—twenty percent?"

"You're wasting my time, Waverly, I want fifty percent. That still gives you half of a big pie, instead of what you got now—all of a small one you could swallow in a single bite."

"You're not taking into account all the money and sweat I have invested in my stock. Feed and all. That's gotta count for something. It's only right you reduce your take by that amount."

Hawkins chuckled. Waverly had just told him in so many words he was going to take the deal. "What you got invested in your herd is done and gone." He was about to lower the hammer. "How do you think the good folks around here would take it if they knew you threw in with the Reynolds gang that terrorized this area during the War?"

"I never did no such thing." But Hawkins saw Waverly blanch as he said it.

Hawkins took a piece of paper out of his inside coat pocket and held it up. "This says different. It's a letter I found in my office safe the stage line wrote up. See? Even got their stamp on it." He clasped his other hand behind his back grandly. "Seems the Reynolds gang piled up a lot of money robbing coaches running between here and Denver. Ruined plenty of people along the way. I don't think the local citizens would take kindly to someone who helped those bandits. So, it's fifty-fifty or no deal." He took a long draw on his cigar. "Take it or leave it." He paused. "I recommend you take it though, 'cause you're still going to be a wealthy man, even after my cut."

"That's a big payday for doin' nothin', Hawkins."

"That's a big payday for being smart, is what it is."

"How do you think the railroad would like it if I told them you were blackmailing me?"

"You got no proof."

Waverly uttered a hollow laugh. "My guess is your bosses would believe me before they'd take your word about it. Maybe they don't like you as much as you think they do. Why don't I just send them a telegram?"

Slade started for Waverly, but Hawkins put a hand out to stop him. "And why don't I let *The Rocky Mountain News* print this letter? Don't play games with me. Looks like we're stuck with each other. Let's just get this deal done." He stuck out his hand. Waverly hesitated for a long moment, then shook on it. No more talk was needed. A man's handshake in these parts was as good as his bond, crooks included.

Waverly plopped back in his chair. "So, how's this gonna work?"

Hawkins smiled. This arrangement would set him up for life. No more table scraps, he'd be eating the choicest cuts and drinking the finest wines from here on out. And more women than he could shake a stick at on top of that. He broke into a wider grin. "Here's the deal. Every time you load cattle, or hay, or anything else in the railroad cars, you give me half of what you make.

And I'll know if you short me, so don't. I got an extra set of eyes right here." He looked Slade's way. "And you keep this to yourself."

Waverly lit another cigar. "Like I said, that's a pretty good deal for you. I do all the work and you get half of everything."

Hawkins blew another smoke ring and stubbed his cigar out. "That does sound pretty good, doesn't it?"

Chapter Fifteen

The day of the funeral dawned brilliantly. Bad weather in the form of early summer sleet and heavy winds had plagued the Park for the past few days, but today's dawn colored the sky a vibrant rose pink as if it were a special show of favor for Rob. Ike gathered family and friends together in the boarding house before the somber walk to the cemetery. Speaking wasn't his strong suit, but as head of the family, he knew it was his place to pay last respects to his only brother.

The group crowded into Sue's parlor and flowed out the front door. Ike cleared his throat in the near-silent room. "I don't have the right words to say about my brother. Words that are fine enough to make clear how much Sue and I will miss him. Him and me shared that tight bond between brothers that don't get spoken of often. A family bond we shared with our sister that death can't break. Rob will live in our hearts forever, and Sue and I will miss him greatly." He barely got the last words out before he choked up and put his hat on. "Let's go render him our final regards."

The procession wound along muddy Main Street to the cemetery north of town. An old, rusted iron gate hung ajar at the entrance. It wasn't quite off its hinges but was headed in that direction. The cortege skirted a row of headstones until they came to an open grave. Ike took his hat off and stared at the closed pine box next to the yawning opening. Lorraine stood next to him holding Jessie's hand, his sister on the other side. The undertaker whispered to several gravediggers, who dropped straps that wound underneath the casket on both sides.

Ike turned to Sue and kissed her on the cheek. He white-knuckled his hat and motioned to the town minister. "Pastor, if you would, please." Ike had never been a churchgoer, but every Sunday growing up his mother read to him from the Bible. He had always felt God's presence in his life, especially during his darkest times. When the minister finished a short homily, Ike moved to Rob's coffin and silently placed his hand on the rough wooden top for a moment.

"Lord, you know my brother was a good man. The Good Book says you knew him before he was born. You and your angels must be rejoicing that one of your long-awaited best has joined you in heaven. We are torn up about that here on your Earth, but we take comfort in knowing he's in your loving hands." Ike brushed at his cheek, put his hat on, and nodded to the undertaker. He grabbed a handful of dirt and cast it into the grave, where small pebbles skittered away on the wooden top. Soon, his brother's coffin disappeared under a brown mound.

Ike and his family remained at the grave while townspeople paid their respects with whispers or gentle touches as they left. Sue looked ghastly white as she stood near the freshly-turned dirt. Hawkins was nowhere to be seen. The dancehall girl, Hannah, had been there but was gone. Margaret and Buster remained as well. A modest headstone with a cross carved into it told of a life cut far too short. The women cried as they hugged each other, while the men tried to bear up short of sniffling. It was hard to believe Rob was gone forever. He'd been such a kind soul. Ike stood a long time with his head bowed.

Lorraine reached up and kissed him. "Those were wonderful words you said over Rob. Just the right way to honor a good man and a good brother." Ike nodded and kissed her back. As he turned to leave, she caught him by the arm.

"Look at me, please. I know what you're thinking, and we all want you to leave it be. The law will bring justice to Rob's killer."

Ike whacked his hat against his pants. In a quiet, clenched voice, he said, "The law? What are you talking about, woman? The law around here just got bushwhacked. There's no law in Cottonwood. But there is retribution. There is that." He looked at his wife and his sister. "Why don't you two stay with Jessie at the boarding house for a while 'til I get back?" He caught the professor's eye, and he nodded. Ike gently removed Lorraine's grip on his arm and headed for the railroad office.

Without knocking, he burst through the front door, gun drawn. Empty. There was an open safe on one side of the room. A half-full cup of cold coffee sat on Hawkins' desk. Ike turned and stormed out of the building, only to find Buster and the professor waiting for him. He brushed past them and headed for the Wildfire. Someone there would know of Hawkins' whereabouts. He hit the swinging doors hard and stormed inside, followed by his friends. The piano player hurried from his stool in mid-tune. A table of poker players looked up as Ike strode toward them and glared.

One of Hawkins' men edged away from the card table. Ike drew on him. The railroader threw up his hands. "I ain't heeled. Don't shoot."

Ike scowled at the man, then backhanded him across the face, sending him tumbling to the floor. Ike stood over him. "Where's your boss? I'm only gonna ask once, so if you want to walk out of here in one piece, tell me."

The surveyor cringed beneath Ike. "I swear I don't know. He never tells me where he's goin', and I don't ask."

"Maybe you should've asked him, because right now it's your bad luck that you don't know."

Ike scanned the room. A young dance hall girl was leaning against the bar, staring at him.

Another of the railroad crew standing to the side slid his hand toward his holster. The professor drew and put a bullet through his hand. Everyone else backed away toward the walls, hands in full view as the wounded man writhed in agony.

Mayor Whitaker sat wide-eyed at one of the card tables. Someone in the crowd yelled out, "Do something, Whitaker. He's liable to shoot us all if someone doesn't stop him."

The mayor stood mute with his hands half-raised also, perhaps still smarting from the dressing down Ike gave him a few days ago.

Ike marched over to the man the professor shot. He took hold of his hand and squeezed until the railroader turned white as a sheet. He released his grip. "I'll ask just once, and then I put a hole in your other hand." Ike drew his sidearm and cocked the hammer. He jammed the man's good hand on a table and held it fast with his gun barrel. "Where's Hawkins?" When the man didn't answer, Ike said, "One, two—"

"Wait!" The word came out like a wail. "I saw him head west the other morning, the same day they found your brother."

"Was Slade with him?"

"Yes."

"Have you heard from him since?"

"No. Nothing."

"Where'd he go?" He pressed the barrel into the man's hand harder.

"I don't know! All I know is he's been talkin' to some rancher west of here about the railroad. That's all I know, I swear! Please don't shoot me."

Ike figured that was all he was going to get from him. He wanted to crash the stock down on the man's good hand, but held up. He'd gotten what he wanted. He turned and his voice boomed through the saloon. "Anybody else know anything about where Hawkins is?" He glared at the man he'd backhanded then scanned the customers. The saloon girl still stared at him. "No? Well, when you see him, tell him I'm gunnin' for him, and anybody else who rides with him from here on out." He eyed the two railroaders. "This is your lucky day, 'cause you're still alive. But if I ever see either of you again, I'll drill you both. Clear out." The two men scurried out the front.

Nothing more to do but wait for word of Hawkins' whereabouts to surface. The coward wouldn't leave Cottonwood for good, there was too much money to be had for him to disappear for long. And Ike would be there when he showed up again.

He headed out of the Wildfire without looking back. Time to focus on his family. What was left of it.

Chapter Sixteen

Ike came out of the saloon with his Colt drawn. He glanced around as he made his way toward Sue's place in a slight crouch. He eased the front door open, walked into the parlor, and hugged his wife. "Where's Sue?"

"She's upstairs resting. The funeral took a lot out of her, and she's not well yet."

"Think I'll go up and see her." He was determined to keep tabs on his sister, even though he knew that was impossible. Being the oldest was hard sometimes. He'd failed his only brother. He couldn't fail his only sister. Worrying about his family was an obligation he'd never been able to lay aside.

Ike cradled Jessie in an arm as he and Lorraine made their way up the stairs. Hugh sat in a chair near Sue's bed. He got up and offered the seat to Lorraine, but she shook her head. Sue seemed to be somewhere in between awake and asleep as she tossed and turned and mumbled. Lorraine leaned toward Hugh. "How's she doing?"

"Doc thinks she will be all right, but with that bump on her head she is not making much sense right now."

Ike leaned over the bed and pulled her blanket up a little higher. "I appreciate you bein' here, takin' care of things, Hugh. It—"

"In your parlance, 'don't mention it.' She is not

only your sister, she is my dear wife."

Ike shook Hugh's hand. Lorraine snaked an arm through his as they went back down to the parlor. He started to give Jessie to Lorraine, but she stopped him. "You hold onto our little girl for a while. That way I know you're not gettin' in any trouble. Think I'll go over to The Sew Pretty and sit with Margaret. She's all alone, and I'm sure she's distraught about losing Rob."

"Reckon you're right. I kind of forgot about how she might be feelin', what with all the attention on Rob. Good idea to spend some time with her. Take it easy, though. You ain't fully healed yet yourself, okay?"

Lorraine nodded and studied herself in the hall mirror. Sandy hair that curled wildly with a mind of its own. Sensible, full-waisted cotton dress that had seen better days. She moved a hand over her nearly eight-months-along big belly. She thought about her plain bonnet and almost left the house without it, but tied it around her head as she stepped into the street.

As she neared The Sew Pretty, Lorraine heard angry yells coming from inside. It was muffled, but there was no mistaking whose voice it was. Margaret was screaming, "Damn you, Rob!" over and over, followed by thumps of some sort.

Lorraine peeked in the smallish front window. Margaret was at the back of the store, throwing things. She'd never seen the shopkeeper so upset, even when the woman's husband was ambushed years ago. No sense in standing outside—either go in and see what's the matter or turn back to the boarding house. But Lorraine had never backed off from anything in her life, so she opened the door and walked into the messy shop. "Margaret! Whatever is the matter? What in the world's got you so upset? Is it Rob?"

"Of course it's Rob! What else do you think it would be? I don't have anything or anyone else in my life anymore; so yes, it's Rob. He's left me all alone, and that's a situation I'm entirely too familiar with."

The shrillness in her voice startled Lorraine. She had expected her to be more sorrowful than angry.

Margaret picked up some of the clutter she'd thrown around the place. "Damn him! If he'd only...why didn't he..." Her voice dropped, and she slumped into her little desk chair. "What am I going to do now?" She lay her head on the wooden desktop.

Lorraine came over and patted her on the back. "I know we ain't ever been real close, but I want you to know that you can call on me if you need anything. I'm just sorry to see you so torn up inside."

"Well, that's all well and good, but you've got Ike. I just never knew where I stood with Rob. Three years of courting, and now he's gone and left me high and dry. Why did he have to go and..." Her chin trembled, and her eyes filled.

Lorraine hesitated as she stood near Margaret's desk. "Maybe I should come back another time."

Margaret put an arm out. "No, please. I could use the company. I'm tired of being alone. Will you sit and stay for a spell?"

"Sure, I will." She sat in the brocade upholstered guest chair and eyed the shopkeeper. Margaret's grief was understandable, and so was the edge it had. She would just listen and let the woman get everything out.

"Tea?"

Lorraine nodded. "Thank you."

Margaret put an old teapot on the cast iron stove

near the back of her shop and lit a fire underneath.

Lorraine had never seen Margaret use the stove. It normally sat unlit, even on the coldest of days. On the few occasions Lorraine visited the shop during the winter, Margaret threw off blankets and a shawl when she came in.

"This'll just be another minute."

When the teapot whistled, she prepared two small china cups and brought them back to the desk.

Lorraine took one. "Thank you. I've heard your tea is some of the best in town."

"Unlike my cooking."

Lorraine held up a hand. "I never—"

Margaret stopped her. She fluffed her black dress and sat. "I know what people say about my cooking. Rob made fun of it, too. But no matter. From now on, it'll just be me that has to put up with it." She stared at her guest through red eyes. A cloth napkin was crumpled in her hand.

Lorraine heard the sadness in Margaret's voice and saw it in her face as well. There was something else there, but she couldn't put a finger on it. Grief was one thing, Margaret's manner seemed to be that and more.

"Have you heard anything about who did it? About who killed Rob?" Margaret stared wide-eyed at Lorraine, while she pressed a hand to her forehead.

"Charlie Hawkins is the leading suspect. He hightailed it out of town as soon as they found Rob, and no one's seen him since. Ike's searchin' for him, and I'm scared he might find him." Lorraine placed her teacup carefully on the desk. "There's somethin' about that gun hand Hawkins brought in, too. He's a dangerous, strange character."

"Slade? Do you think he could have killed Rob?" Margaret dabbed at her eyes with a hanky. One eye twitched until she put a finger up to stop it.

"I suppose. Hawkins could have easily arranged that."

Margaret leaned forward in her chair. "I heard Hawkins put that boy up to kidnapping you, so it stands to reason he could have put Slade up to shooting Rob. Someone said the young man got bitten. How is he, anyway?"

Lorraine was glad to shift the conversation away from Rob. "He's healin'. Lost a finger, but looks like he'll keep the rest."

"I suppose that's good."

That was an unusual thing to say. Margaret seemed off somehow. Distracted, even agitated. Her hair was mussed, and her hair was never mussed. Lorraine cut her visit short. She'd paid the woman a courtesy visit, but Margaret made her uncomfortable from the moment she walked into the shop. "I must be getting back to Ike and Jessie. Thank you for the tea and...well, thank you."

Margaret's mood changed in an instant when Lorraine stood and reached for her modest hat. There was a spark in her eyes that hadn't been there a second ago. "Why, I've got some real nice hats just in. Would you like to see them?"

Lorraine put a hand to her own rather dowdy bonnet and felt her face redden. "No, thank you. This one is just fine, and I couldn't afford one of yours anyway."

Margaret broke into a big smile. "Why, I could let you buy one over time. You'd look marvelous. That one over there, the red with the beige feather. Perfect."

Lorraine said, "I ain't ever had anything I couldn't pay for when I bought it, so I'll not be taking you up on your kind offer." She moved toward the front of the shop trailed by Margaret, who drew a lingering hand over her collection of fashionable hats as she walked.

In an animated voice, she said, "Thank you for stopping by, Lorraine. Your gesture is appreciated. We must get together again soon." As she said it, she nearly pushed Lorraine out the door.

"Yes, we must. Please let me know if you need anything, will you?"

Margaret grinned, then closed the door, and Lorraine watched her disappear into her dim shop.

She mulled things over on the way to the boarding house. What an odd conversation that was. The woman's mood swings made no sense. Grieving at first, then spirited. Almost giddy.

As she walked, her thoughts returned to Ike. He didn't talk about it, but Rob's death had hit him hard. As hard a blow as anything she'd ever see him bear. He had a tendency to clam up when his emotions were raw, and that's what he was doing right now.

****

Back at Sue's, Lorraine supervised Ike and Buster as they organized the ranch wagon for the return trip home. Buster had taken a shopping list to O'Toole's after the funeral service and returned with a nearly-full wagon bed. When all was loaded and accounted for, they started for the ranch. Lorraine held Jessie and swayed back and forth to the rhythm of the wagon as it rolled. Her mind drifted to her recent captivity and Quincy. She half-hoped the boy would be gone when they returned. Another part of her wanted to try to rehabilitate him, body and soul, but she wouldn't have been surprised to see he'd ransacked their place and left while they were at Rob's service.

When they pulled up in front of the ranch house, Quincy stood swaying slightly on the porch. The bandage on his hand was missing, along with the finger Doc had taken. So he'd stayed when he'd had a chance to leave. Now what was she going to do with him? And what was Ike going to do to him? Ike helped her down first, then swung Jessie high in the air off the wagon bed as she squealed in great delight. Lorraine hurried over to where Quincy stood and kept herself between Ike and him. The strain of keeping the peace was wearing on her.

****

Ike saw his wife's maneuver and stood stock still by the wagon for a moment, then shouted at Quincy. "I'll have my time with you, boy. You ain't near clear of this yet." He forced himself to turn away, unhitched the work horse, and led the animal to the corral by the stable. He turned back toward the house, but Buster put a hand out to stop him.

"Why don't you let it be for a while, Ike? This here stable could use some tidyin' up; how 'bout you and me tacklin' it?" He pulled Ike by the arm in that direction.

Ike let himself be led away. Hard work would likely do him some good. He was even a little relieved he wouldn't be tangling with Quincy right away. He was afraid of what he'd do to the kidnapper. He grabbed a shovel and heaved dirty hay out of stalls like a madman until he couldn't throw any more. He slumped to the ground as exhaustion overtook anger.

Buster roused him from a half-sleep at dinnertime. They cleaned up outside at the well and came in to a neatly set table. Quincy stood ramrod straight nearby. Lorraine wore a worried look by the stove.

Ike glared at Quincy. "You ain't sittin' at my table." He jerked a thumb toward the door. "Go on and get. Outside!"

Jessie stared wide-eyed at her father.

Ike saw Lorraine start to say something, but she stopped. She fixed a plate for Quincy, which he quickly took outside. Buster stood looking at his plate. Ike moved a chair out for Lorraine, and the two men sat after she did. She dished up a plateful of Ike's favorite beef stew from a big pot on the table and handed it to him. He stared at the plate, unmoving. Images of Rob laying on Doc's table flashed through his mind. When he looked at Lorraine, he imagined her a captive in that high mountain cabin. He thought of Jessie all alone at the ranch that day. His heart raced and sweat soaked his brow. He clasped both hands to his forehead and sat with his head bowed and meal untouched. He was torn between honoring Lorraine's request to leave Quincy alone and wanting to pulverize him.

A restless sleep that night brought no solace. Morning couldn't come soon enough. Ike was up and out of the house early. He started for the barn but turned back when he remembered Quincy was sleeping in one of the stalls. Better to stay away from him and not upset Lorraine. Halfway back to the house, he changed his mind and went straight for Ally's stall. He grasped her reins and led her out of the barn, past the stall where Quincy lay staring wide-eyed at him.

Soon, he was up in the saddle and galloping south.

He let Ally have her way. She flew over the basin's new grasses as if she understood Ike's need to get away. After half an hour, he patted her on the neck, and she slowed to a trot. He angled toward the Donaldson place. At the modest ranch house, he dismounted and told Ally to stay.

Ike pounded on the front door. It opened slowly, and he stood face to face with a pale Abe Donaldson. The smell of sausage cooking floated in the morning air. The rancher quick-stepped out on the small porch and closed the door behind him. Mrs. Donaldson looked out wide-eyed from the little front window. Donaldson started to say something, but Ike cut him off.

"I'm gonna kill you, Donaldson. You almost cost my wife her life." He drew his Colt and pointed it at him.

"I don't have no gun, Ike."

He ignored that. "You lied to me. I was your friend, damn you!" He jammed the barrel up under the man's chin and held it there. "You threw in with Hawkins. For what? Money?" He spit at the man's boots.

Fear clouded Donaldson's face. "It weren't money at all. It weren't like that, Ike. Hawkins came out here again and kept talkin' about my wife and kids. I knew they was in danger. And he told me if I fooled you, we wouldn't have to leave the ranch until the railroad came through, instead of right away. I needed to protect my family." He teared up, and the fear on his face was replaced by a look of shame. His shoulders slumped. "I'm sorry, Ike. I never meant to hurt you or Lorraine. Especially in her condition. If you're gonna shoot me, do it out of sight of my wife, willya? I'll ride out with you wherever you want, and you can kill me there."

Ike cocked the hammer and pressed it harder into Donaldson's neck. "We ain't ridin' anywhere. It's gonna happen right here." He tried to squeeze the trigger, but his hand shook so badly he couldn't pull it. He lowered the gun and wiped at his face. Images of Rob haunted him as he pressed it against Donaldson's chest and strained to pull the trigger again. The gun shook as if it had a life of its own. Suddenly, all the starch went out of him, and he stood on wobbly legs. Donaldson reached out to steady him, and Ike pushed him away. "Get away from me!" He dropped the gun to his side and gazed around with unfocused eyes.

Imaginary shells went off in his head, and he ducked. Sweat poured down his face and drenched his shirt. He heard his name being called faintly and swung around with his gun at the ready.

"Ike. Ike!" Donaldson was shaking him. "Ike, what's the matter? You want to come inside and sit?"

Ike stared at him as if he was a stranger. He stumbled off the porch and grabbed at Ally's saddle horn. After several attempts, he was up in the saddle, and Ally was off at a gallop. Behind him, Donaldson shouted, "Ike! Come back. Where you goin'? I'm sorry! Ike!"

Ally carried Ike all the way to Tarryall Creek. He sat streamside in the saddle, motionless for a long time. Finally, Ally swung her chestnut head toward him and nickered. Ike wiped a hand over his eyes and dismounted. He wet a handkerchief in the cold mountain river, pressed it against his face, and held it there. The sun warmed him as he collapsed on a gentle grassy slope beside the stream. The sounds of battle grew faint, and he lay back and fell asleep.

The next thing he knew, Buster was shaking him awake. "Thought I'd find you out here. Mind if I sit?"

Ike shook the cobwebs away and sat up. He clasped his arms around his legs and stared at the creek's swift current. "What time is it?"

"Later'n you think. You musta been out for quite a while. The sun ain't goin' down yet, but it's startin' to think about it. Lorraine's worried sick about you." He didn't ask Ike any questions, just sat next to his friend.

Ike picked up small stones nearby and tossed them in the flowing water one after the other. "Back when I was a kid, me and Rob would race to the river in Lawrence, the Kansas River. Come springtime, we'd see how far we could 'ride' rotten tree limbs before the current washed us off." He threw the rocks harder. "One day the river was flowin' real high. The current was fast, and it knocked me off my log and carried me underwater. I was only twelve, Rob ten. Rob was always a better swimmer than me. He jumped in and got me back on top of the water, and we dragged ourselves free of the current. I woudda died if Rob hadn't gotten me clear."

Buster didn't say anything.

"I'm his big brother... I was...his big brother." Ike's voice shook. "I was supposed to protect him. Keep him safe. My folks always expected me to do that. I always expected me to do that. And I didn't. And I couldn't keep Lorraine safe either. You'd do well to keep better company than me, Buster. I ain't worth much of anything to nobody." He dropped his gaze to the ground, and tears disappeared in the patchy ground.

Buster coughed. "You're worth more than all of us

put together, Ike. 'Ceptin' maybe Jessie." He smiled and put a hand on his friend's shoulder.

That brought a short laugh. "That's for sure, there." Ike picked his head up and spied Ally next to him. He labored to a stand and patted his horse. "Let's go home."

Chapter Seventeen

Sue was struggling to get out of bed when her husband came into the room. He put the tray of food down and hurried over to help her. "Are you sure you are feeling well enough to get up?"

"I'm fine, thank you."

"Not sick to your stomach anymore?"

"No, not since yesterday. I feel better today. Head's clearer. I'd like to go downstairs and see how much of a mess you've made." She lifted her arms, and he helped her up. She leaned into him and gave him a little kiss, then held onto his arm as they went. At the dining room table, she asked him to stay and sit with her.

He said, "Let me get you another tray. You need to eat. Please."

"No, not right now." She looked up at her husband with tears in her eyes. "Honey, who did this to Rob?" She never was one to beat around the bush. "Who killed my brother?"

He shook his head. "We don't know yet, but Hawkins is the most likely culprit."

"I know you and Rob never liked him, but even so, why would he kill Rob?"

"We did not leave his employ on the best of terms." The question on her face prompted him to continue. "Rob was never comfortable with the way

Hawkins was dealing with local ranchers. His plan was to offer them a lot less than their land was worth and then inform them he was going to get the land one way or the other anyway. His terms were that they leave immediately, even though the railroad won't come through for some time. Rob could not countenance that kind of bullying. I don't think Hawkins' bosses in Denver knew of his methods, but perhaps they did. I have a suspicion that after he bought the ranches, he was planning to tell his bosses he bought them at a lower price and keep the difference."

"Then why are you working for such a man?"

Hugh hesitated. "It appears I should have told you before that... I am not working for him any longer." He readied himself for what he expected would be an unpleasant reaction from his wife.

Sue raised her voice. "You're not? When did that happen? And just when were you planning on telling me?"

"Uh...I should have told you before, but it just happened a little while ago."

"Well, I noticed you hadn't been on any surveying trips recently, and I did wonder why."

Hugh drew in a deep breath. "Hawkins could not afford to have the sheriff of Cottonwood actively oppose him in acquiring lands around the area. But Rob's killer could also have been his gun hand, Slade, so Hawkins would not have to get his hands dirty. Either one of them could have done it, but likely it was Hawkins. He has always been ready to pick a fight with Ike."

Sue's demeanor changed. Her eyes grew cold. "Then let's go get him."

"What do you mean by, 'Go get him'?"

"You know what I mean, Hugh. Get Hawkins."

The professor paused. "There is a problem with that. No one knows where he is. Ike has been looking for him all over town. I believe he will show up again soon, though. There is too much money involved with his land grabs for him to be gone forever." He got up and brought a tray in to his wife.

Sue turned her attention to her plate and picked at her food. Without looking up, she said, "Then we'll be here when he returns."

****

Dance hall Hannah looked around the Wildfire coolly. She didn't mingle with the customers as much since Rob's death. This was the second night in a row she hadn't seen Hawkins in here. Where was he? She'd overheard talk that he was the lead suspect in Rob's death. Good. That would take any attention off her, but she still had something she wanted to pry out of Hawkins with a few drinks. Especially since he didn't know who she was. She'd need to do it soon, as it was hard to keep secrets for long in a small town like Cottonwood.

She talked Hawkins up as the killer with everyone she spent time with. She'd always had a sixth sense, so there were times in her life when she 'knew' things she hadn't been told. Even as a child, she'd known instinctively what adults around her were talking about when they didn't think she understood. When she first met Hawkins, something screamed at her about him. Right then, she decided what she'd suspected was true. She had more than enough reasons to want to take the man down. She missed Rob, even though he'd

187

distanced himself from her at the end. He'd never really said why at the time, but her best guess was that it had something to do with Margaret Pinshaw.

She didn't know the woman at all, just from hearsay, but she knew Rob had carried on with her the past few years. What was it he'd seen in her? If she was going to stay in town, it would be a good idea to get to know the shopkeeper. The Sew Pretty might be her way out of the saloon life, but a visit to Rob's old flame was fraught with uncertainty.

Noon the next day she called on Margaret.

As soon as she entered The Sew Pretty, she 'knew' the visit wasn't going to go well. Margaret was alone in the shop, toward the back, hunched over some material. She didn't look up. Maybe she'd already seen who it was. Hannah strolled silently around, lightly touching a bolt of cloth here, admiring a hat there, always staying toward the front of the store.

Hannah cleared her throat. "You have some lovely things here, Mrs. Pinshaw."

Margaret didn't lift her head. "So you know my name, do you? I'm certain you know more about me than I do you. Why are you even here? The nerve of you. Just leave." The cold, brittle tone of Margaret's voice made Hannah recoil a bit.

"People say you have the nicest millinery for miles around here."

"You must also know I'm the only millinery for miles around. What is it you really want?"

Hannah took a deep breath. "I wanted to offer my condolences most of all. I know you and the sheriff…" she stopped and let the sentence hang in the air, unable to think of an appropriate ending.

"And I know about you, you harlot."

The viciousness of the word made Hannah fume. A warm flush spread from her neck to her face. She looked out the front window for a moment and thought about leaving, then stopped, turned back, and raised her chin. "I may be a lot of things, some of which I'm not proud of, but I've never been a whore. I don't know what was going on between the two of you, but it wasn't me that made him drift. He did that all on his own. I can understand how that would have happened if you took the same sharp tone with him that you just did with me."

Margaret stood immobile, clutching a pair of scissors in her hand. She pierced Hannah at a distance with her eyes, then sat, head held high. "I'll not let you sully Rob's reputation to me or anyone else, and I'll not rise to your lying gossip." She resumed her needling, with what Hannah noticed was a shaking hand.

Hannah decided to back off. She continued walking around the shop. "You must hate me for what you think I've done."

No response.

"Do you mind if I look around a little more?"

Margaret didn't respond, but her needle and silver thimble flew faster.

The shop's hats were what drew Hannah's attention the most. There were so many, and they were so pretty. She'd heard they were Margaret's specialty, and she had seen several local ladies with one of her distinctive hats on. Hannah thought about what it would be like to wear one of those creations. She ran her fingers lightly over a gorgeous blue one with a beige hatband until Margaret yelled at her. "Don't you touch that one!" The shopkeeper hurried over from her table, swept the brocade up in one hand, and swooshed it behind her back.

Hannah's eyes widened. She stammered, "I'm s-sorry, I didn't mean to upset you."

"You upset me just by being here. Why don't you leave?"

Hannah had enough. She straightened up and squinted at her adversary. "I don't think it's me you're mad at. I think it's Rob, and I won't stand for your browbeating anymore. Whatever was wrong between the two of you didn't involve me, and I think deep down you know that." Hannah spread her feet slightly, prepared for the verbal, perhaps physical, onslaught she expected in reply.

Instead, Margaret wilted. Her shoulders slumped, and she seemed to shrink before Hannah's very eyes. An inexpressible sadness permeated the woman's countenance. She lowered her gaze to the floor and stood motionless in front of Hannah. Solitary tears ran down each cheek, and she placed her hands on a chair to steady herself. Her eyes seemed unfocused, and she stood as if in a trance.

Hannah reached out and touched her on the shoulder. "Are you all right, Mrs. Pinshaw?" She got no response, just a faraway look in return. "Margaret?"

Hannah put an arm around Margaret's waist and led her to the back of the shop, where a door to the woman's small quarters stood cracked open. As tidy as Margaret's shop was, her bedroom was that messy. Hannah guided Margaret to her modest bed and helped her lie down. Margaret didn't utter a word while Hannah made her comfortable. She lay with her head on a dirty pillow, motionless, looking toward the ceiling. Hannah closed the door quietly and walked to the front of the shop. She turned the sign inside the window to 'closed' and shut the door behind her on the way out.

In the morning, she stood on the wooden sidewalk a discreet distance away from the shop until the sign turned to 'open.' She opened the front door and stepped in to a ting-a-ling. Margaret was walking to her small desk and turned toward her visitor. She looked haggard, and her dress was noticeably wrinkled, not like her usual perfectly appointed appearance.

She said somewhat dully, "Yes?"

For a minute, from the blank look on Margaret's face, Hannah wondered if she'd already forgotten who she was. Like their scene yesterday never happened. She said, "I'm—"

"I know who you are, I'm just tired of seeing you here."

Hannah said, "I'm sorry if I offended you yesterday, that was not my intent. I just came by this morning to see how you were."

"Why would you be concerned with how I was?"

"I thought—"

But before she could finish, Margaret's manner suddenly changed. "Is there something I can do for you? Perhaps a nice hat, or some mending you need done?"

An altogether strange response, totally unrelated to their conversation. Hannah mumbled, "Yes, there is, actually. I'd like to leave the Wildfire, but I have to have another job to do that, so I was wondering if you needed any help here?"

Margaret didn't respond. She turned her attention to a bolt of cloth and acted like she hadn't heard Hannah.

As Hannah turned and walked toward the front of the shop, Margaret called out. "Thank you and goodbye. Come again."

Chapter Eighteen

Ike looked toward the ranch house as he worked in the barn's rustic tack room with Buster. Lorraine said she needed Quincy's help inside the house, doing what, Ike didn't know. That didn't fool him, though. She was trying to keep him away from the kidnapper.

When he finished repairing Ally's bridle, he and Buster mounted up and headed south in the morning light to keep an eye on their herd. They'd be counting the number of head with Ike's brand, a capital M slanted with one leg shorter than the other. It would take most of the day as Ike's herd mingled freely with other ranchers' stock on the open range. A beautiful sunrise against a clear blue sky promised a warm day on the Park basin even this early in the summer. At ten thousand feet, the land heated quickly, and animals and cowboys sought shade whenever they could.

Ike took a break about midday, climbing off Ally with a hand signal to stay. Buster followed and his horse nuzzled Ally nearby. He dropped next to his friend in the shade of a small copse of pines. The cattle were restless this morning, almost edgy. Ally seemed to notice it too, as she stood and bobbed her head whinnying—a sign Ike knew as her 'let's get to work' signal.

"Buster, I know we ain't seen all of 'em yet, but it seems like there might be some head missin'. Not sure if the herd's just that spread out on the valley floor, or if some really are gone astray."

"I was thinkin' the same thing. Somethin' don't seem right out here today. My bones are barkin', and that's never a good sign." Buster scanned the low rolling landscape. "Good grazin' though, they oughta be likin' things more'n they seem to be."

Just then, the crack of several gunshots split the basin's quiet. Three, four. The gunfire echoed sharply through the valley and brought a hasty end to Ike and Buster's rest. The cattle nearby responded to the gunfire as well, but in a way Ike feared. They changed from a loose, spread out herd to one that looked like an imaginary funnel was at work around them. A lead cow set to bellowing and lurched forward, north toward the ranches in this section of the Park. More than two hundred head stampeded at the gunshots. Ike swung up on Ally faster than he had in years to avoid being trampled by cattle rushing his way. Buster hopped a leg up into his stirrup and yanked his horse's reins as the front part of the stampede neared.

Ike rode hard to get to the front of the cattle to turn them back to the Park. He didn't need to use spurs on Ally to get her headed in the right direction fast. She had a full head of steam up and was gaining on the lead cow as the cattle's hooves thundered like an earthquake. He hurried Ally forward even faster as the charging cattle veered toward the Donaldson place.

Ike drew abreast of the first beast and fired several shots in the air over the cow's head. The front of the pack began a wide arcing turn away from him, and the exhausted beeves soon slowed and drew to a stop. Ike pulled Ally up, took off his hat, and swung it in a wide arc to see through the choking cloud of dust that enveloped the land. He pulled the bandana away from his mouth and wiped sweat from his forehead. He looked back for Buster, but he was nowhere to be seen.

Ike trotted toward the spot where the stampede first started. Along the way, several cows were down with what looked like broken legs. Ike shot two to put an end to their misery. He searched the land and saw his friend's horse hobbling away in the distance. Ike hurried Ally in that direction and saw what he hoped he wouldn't.

Buster was face down on the ground and wasn't moving as Ike swung off Ally and rushed over. He lay with his arms spread wide, hat knocked off, and one leg splayed out. Dirt and dust covered him from head to toe.

"Buster!" Ike knelt and rolled him over. There wasn't any blood he could see, but that didn't mean much. Ike put his face next to Buster's and felt his breath. There was spittle around his mouth, but he was still alive. He slapped Buster lightly on the face several times but got no response in return. Gathering his friend in his arms, Ike carried him to Ally and told her to stay. Adrenalin kicked in, and he muscled Buster up into the saddle. He mounted up behind him and galloped back to the ranch.

Lorraine was on the porch, waiting, when he pulled up. He yelled, "Go get a bed ready and some clean wet cloths!" He eased Buster off Ally carefully, carried him inside, and laid him on their bed. "Clean him up the best you can and try to wake him up. I'm ridin' to town to get the doc." A flick of the reins and Ally flew over the dirt road. Ike leaned forward so far his chin almost touched Ally's neck as he rode.

When Doc Early arrived at the ranch, Ike rushed him in. Buster lay motionless, eyes closed, but breathing steady. Doc bent over Buster and took most of his clothes off to examine him. After a few minutes, he said, "Some nasty bruising on his torso, probably several broken ribs." He traced a hand along the right leg. "Leg is real bruised about halfway down the shinbone. Not sure, but doesn't look like it's broken. Everything else looks all right except for those cuts on his neck and face, but I'm most worried about the blow he must have taken to his head when he got run over."

"When do you think he'll wake up, Doc?" Ike's stomach churned.

"Don't know. That's pretty much up to Buster, but from the looks of him, he's survived some serious injuries before. He's a strong one for his age—we'll just have to wait and see if that'll carry him through this time too."

Ike flashed back to the vicious stoning Buster endured at the Ute village years ago. "What you're sayin' is he might not...wake up."

Doc nodded and started to clean Buster's wounds and apply dressings.

Lorraine reached over and led Ike out of the bedroom. "Why don't you come tell me what happened out there? I saw all that dust flyin' way in the distance, and that's never a good thing." She took him by the arm and sat him in the kitchen.

Ike sat dazed. "I don't exactly know what happened. Me and Buster were sittin' out on the basin, and all of a sudden someone fired a couple of shots, maybe more, and the cattle were off and runnin'." He gathered himself. "I lit out after the lead cow and thought Buster was right behind me. Wasn't 'til after I got 'em turned and stopped that I saw he was down. Must've happened right when the stampede began 'cause he was lyin' real near where we started off after the cows."

He grew silent. His world seemed to be coming apart. First his brother, now Buster. Lorraine's kidnapping. His feud with Hawkins. He'd been trying to hold everything together for a long time. He'd only had one other friend like Buster. His best friend growing up had enlisted in the army with him, but only Ike returned from the war. He'd always been close to Rob, but he was his brother, that was different. As he peeked into the bedroom, he hoped Buster hadn't closed his eyes for the last time.

Chapter Nineteen

Sue brought two plates into the dining room. Dinner was quieter these days since her husband threw all her renters out. Hugh sat next to her. She said, "We're gonna need to find some new boarders, and soon, or we'll have to shut the place up."

Hugh sat silently for a moment. "You know why I did it. You know why I ran them off. Are you saying I should not have?"

Sue wiped her mouth with one of her homespun napkins. "That's not what I'm saying. I know we couldn't have Hawkins' men staying here after Rob was killed. That doesn't make having no money any easier, though."

Hugh reached over and put his hand on Sue's. "Look. This town is growing—we will have more boarders soon when word spreads that we have rooms again. I am sure of it." His tone was confident, but his eyes told another story. It could also be that Hawkins would warn people away from the place now, just to get even. The other boarding house was full though, so perhaps that would work in their favor. "How are you holding up, dear?"

Sue's eyes glistened. "I'm not holding up. I'm just holding on. Who did this, Hugh? And why? Rob never had an enemy, everyone always liked him."

"Yes, they did. But sometimes a man gains

enemies he is not even aware of. I did not think Hawkins was capable of murder, but Rob was standing in his way."

"His way? You mean his way of cheating people out of their land?"

"Yes. Stealing land the railroad needs."

"So land is worth killing for? Surely something else besides murder could have been worked out."

"Evil isn't worked out—it just is."

Sue wiped at her eyes. "Still no Hawkins?"

"Still no Hawkins. The coward has disappeared. Maybe he is hiding behind his bosses in Denver. That will not do him any good though. Justice has a long memory and a longer reach." He got up from the table and kissed Sue on the cheek. "I am going to get a drink. I won't be long." Before she could say anything, he was out the front door.

****

Hugh Walnutt headed directly for the Wildfire. Hawkins' trail had gone stone cold since the murder, but if there was any place it could be picked up again, it would be in the town's only saloon. He gripped the swinging doors for a moment as he looked inside and sized up the crowd. He pushed through and walked over to the bar.

Nick, the bartender, was talking with a cowboy down the way. He looked up. "Well, Professor. We don't see you in here much, usually with…" He left the sentence unfinished.

Walnutt motioned Nick over. "Help me find Rob's killer, Nick. Have any idea where Hawkins is?"

Nick glanced left then right and said in a whisper, "No, I don't."

"Has anyone in here been talking about him?"

Just then, the girl he'd come to know as Hannah moved close. "I couldn't help but hearing you're interested in where Hawkins is, Professor. Maybe we can help each other."

Walnutt didn't know her well, just through Rob and the few times he'd accompanied his friend into the saloon. He'd leave Rob in her company and talk with Nick at the bar. There had been a mutual attraction between her and Rob, and now Walnutt wanted to trade on that. "People don't talk as easily to me as they do you. Perhaps you have heard something about his whereabouts."

Hannah held up two fingers and nodded to Nick. She turned her attention back to Walnutt. "Word is he headed west out of town with Slade the day they found Rob."

"I already heard that, Hannah. Maybe they went west to throw anyone who wanted to follow them off the track." An image of Ike flashed through his mind. "Then maybe they headed back to Denver."

"I wouldn't put it past him, but I heard Hawkins has some business with a rancher west of here. He could be there now."

Walnutt glanced sideways at her. She was young and pretty, too young for Rob, which Rob had admitted. As she stood there, he couldn't figure her out. "What is your interest in Hawkins? Rob said you asked about him often."

"Yes, I did." She drank one of the whiskeys Nick put in front of them. "The man stole something from me." She held Walnutt's gaze hard. "My childhood." Her bottom lip quivered.

"What does that mean?"

"It means…it's a secret, but it's been burning a hole in me."

"What is?" His interest was up.

She glanced around then lowered her voice. "Rob's the only one I intend to tell. The secret may have gotten him killed." She finished with, "I want to hurt that man so bad, make him pay for what he did."

Walnutt raised his eyebrows. "Who?"

"You don't need to know. That died with Rob."

"It sounds like you are withholding information in a murder case and I wonder why. Did you tell anyone else?"

She hesitated. "No. Only Rob, but he wouldn't have told anyone else, unless…"

"Margaret? Are you thinking he might have told her?"

"No, no. It wouldn't have been the kind of thing he would have told her. Certainly not anything that involved me."

Walnutt squinted at her. "I am sorry, but that doesn't leave you in the clear. You had as good a reason to kill Rob as Hawkins did. And I'm guessing your secret is about Hawkins."

Hannah raised a hand to slap him, but he lifted an arm and blocked her. He ignored her anger. "Rob told me about the scene in here the other day when you threw a glass at his head. That is the action of a woman scorned and gives you reason enough to want to get back at him, just like it sounds like you want to get back at Hawkins."

Hannah pushed away from the bar and straightened up. She didn't deny anything, all she said was, "He had it coming." She turned and sashayed her way over to a lone miner at the bar.

The professor shook his head. Rob didn't have it coming, and the comment only raised more doubt in his mind about her. He took a quick sip of whiskey, placed a dime on the bar, and headed into the night. The evening air chilled him as he walked back to the boarding house in the dark, glancing first over one shoulder then the other.

****

In the morning, Sue and Hugh were clearing breakfast dishes when a knock came at the door. Sue gave him a puzzled look. "Who could that be this early?" She opened the door to see Mayor Whitaker standing on the front porch, rubbing his hands together with a silly smile on his face.

"It's a mite cold out here, Sue, can I come in?"

Sue stepped back and pulled the door fully open. "Morning Mr. Mayor, can I get you some hot coffee?"

"Why, that would be most appreciated." The mayor had a manner that fluctuated between polite and mincing. Mincing was taking front and center right now as he stepped into the parlor.

Hugh walked in and shook the mayor's hand. "Awfully early to be handling the town's business, is it not, Henry? Won't you have a seat? What can we do for you this morning?" He sat across from Whitaker and sipped his coffee as Sue brought the mayor a steaming cup and saucer.

Whitaker took a short drink followed by a wrinkled expression. "That's pretty warm, Sue. I think I'll let it sit for a bit. But it's good, it's good. Yup, it's good." The mayor's face changed into a frozen smile. He looked around the room, and conversation came to a halt.

Hugh eyed his visitor coolly. "Why are we sitting here exchanging pleasantries, Henry? What have you got on your mind?"

"Yes, well, getting to that. As you know...of course you do...what with the recent loss of our esteemed sheriff..." He nodded to Sue who had taken a seat next to her husband. "It seems to be the consensus of just about all the town's leaders, well most anyway, that we would be wise to find a replacement for Rob quickly." Whitaker coughed and took a sip of coffee. He breathed in deeply. "And in discussing this amongst ourselves, everyone agreed that would be a good idea." The mayor wiped at a glistening forehead.

Hugh put his cup down and leaned forward. "Mayor, I have heard some fine beating around the bush in my time, but what you are doing right now is among the finest I have ever heard. What are you talking about? Speak plainly man."

Whitaker took another quick gulp of coffee and glanced at Sue. He cleared his throat. "The town fathers think you would be a good replacement for sheriff."

Hugh sprang to his feet. "Me? Sheriff? What makes you think I would ever do that? I certainly would not, and that's all there is to it." He paced, glancing sideways at Whitaker all the while.

Sue also stood, silently at first, a look of shock on her face. "Hugh would never even consider such a thing." The daggers in her eyes would have killed Whitaker if they could have. "We just buried my brother—his best friend—who was murdered doing that job. No! He would never do that." She turned and glared at her husband.

Whitaker stood as well. "I didn't mean to upset you, Miss Sue. Nor you, Professor. It was just the feeling of all of us that you would be the best person to bring peace back to Cottonwood and justice to Rob. Your prowess with weapons is well-known, but I can understand your reluctance. Miss Sue and you are fine cit—"

Before he could finish, Sue raised her voice. "Reluctance? Is that what you call it? How about damn refusal?" She folded her arms across her chest, a tear winding down each cheek.

Whitaker stood ramrod straight. "I am sorry to distress you, and I will remove myself from your presence at once." He picked up his black felt hat, bowed to Sue, and nodded to Hugh.

Sue was already moving toward the front door and with a sweep of her arm ushered the mayor out of the house. She slammed the door behind him and turned back to her husband. "For the life of me, I can't think what would have possessed him to come into our house and even suggest such a thing. Surely he must have known there is no way you would even consider that." She eyed her husband who stood in stony silence at the front window, rubbing his jaw and watching the mayor retreat down the street.

Suddenly, the railroad office disintegrated in a huge explosion that littered the air with debris.

Chapter Twenty

Hawkins was laying low at Waverly's ranch. The deal with the rancher was done, and he'd taken his host up on his offer to remain for a few days. He couldn't stay longer than that, but he wasn't particularly eager to get back to Cottonwood either. He was sure people were convinced he killed the sheriff, especially after he rode out of town the morning Rob's body was discovered. Ike McAlister for certain would be gunning for him, which was fine—he looked forward to facing the meddlesome rancher. He could take McAlister. Hugh Walnutt was another matter. Maybe the professor would decide this wasn't his fight. Didn't make any difference, though. Slade was his ace in the hole.

Waverly strode into the dining room while Hawkins was eating breakfast one morning. "You still here? I'da thought you knew I wasn't askin' you to stay on forever. Time you cleared out, Hawkins. Not that you aren't welcome here, but there's got to be things you could be doin' to get that railroad routed my way."

Hawkins nodded as he soaked up egg yolk with a piece of toast. He leaned back in his chair. "Why, I was just wondering where you were, Waverly. Was gonna say my thank you's and goodbyes." He gave a short chuckle. "You've been a mighty nice host; made me feel so welcome I thought about staying here for a couple more months. But you're right; there are things I need to get back to." Ike McAlister was at the top of that list.

Slade sipped a cup of coffee and sat silently across from Waverly, his eyes never leaving the rancher.

"Time's a wasting. Let's get packed up and back to Cottonwood, Slade." Hawkins rose from the table and shook Waverly's hand. "I'll keep you posted about the railroad's progress. Should be comin' through here sometime in the next year." Even as he said that, Hawkins had his doubts. The telegrams he'd been getting from Denver recently hinted at some delays on the company's end. Sounded like financial hard times might be brewing. "In the meantime, you can be spreading the word among the ranchers hereabouts to get used to driving their cattle to your place for transport in the future." On his way out, Hawkins bowed slightly to Mrs. Waverly and the two guests saddled up for Cottonwood and uncertainty.

Early summer had a special look in the Park. The land wasn't in full bloom yet, but as the two riders headed east, they traveled through a landscape that was hinting at its beauty to come. Small, multi-colored late spring flowers nodded as they passed, and new, light green grasses waved as well. By the time they reached the outskirts of town, afternoon was giving way to dusk.

Hawkins reined his horse to a walk. "Not sure what we'll find when we ride in. Just keep your eyes peeled. McAlister is likely still out at his ranch with that fool Buster, but I'd watch out for Walnutt—him and the sheriff were pretty close. No telling what his reaction is gonna be when he hears we're back. I expect the funeral's come and gone by now, so maybe things will have settled some."

Hawkins glanced left and right as they rode down Main Street. Slade stared straight ahead. When they reached the railroad office, Hawkins pulled up. Debris lay all around the charred exterior of the building. "What the hell? I'm gonna check things out here. You go on to the boarding house and make sure everything's okay there, and bring me back something to eat." He hoped he said it in such a way as to let the gunman know who was working for who. Hawkins dismounted and tied his horse at the hitching post as Slade moseyed away.

He shook his head. The building looked destroyed. The front window was broken, and the door to the small, single-story building was slightly ajar. Damn! He struggled to shove the door open and inside found mayhem. An acrid smell like rotten eggs hung in the air. His desk sat at an odd angle, pockmarked and torn up, papers were strewn everywhere, chairs upended and broken. He surveyed the wreckage and turned and tried to close the door, but was only able to get it shut partway. "Damn McAlister!" He drew his gun, moved in a crouch to the front window, and scanned the street to see if the despised rancher was anywhere around, hoping he'd see Slade coming back first.

Nothing. He turned back to the destruction. The safe was blown apart, and the front door of the blackened box hung open at a strange angle on one hinge, its decorative painting a fiery memory. The blast wrecked everything nearby, blowing out the back window as well. There must have been more than one stick of dynamite in play to cause this amount of damage. Wooden shards pierced the plaster walls, imbedded deeply in silent testimony to the force of the explosion. Hawkins moved to the shattered front window again with his fingers wrapped tight around his Colt.

Townspeople walked back and forth past the office, mostly on the other side of the street. Some stared his way as they passed, others hurried on by with only a glance at the distinctive dun horse tied up outside. Hawkins backed into the middle of the room and sized up the damage. He didn't know how long ago this happened, but he had no doubt who had done it.

****

When Slade returned, he grasped a wrapped cloth holding two plates in one hand. He forced the door open farther, his eyes widened and a small smile appeared on his face as he scanned the destruction. "Looks like you're not gonna win citizen of the year around here anytime soon." He chuckled and laid the bundle on Hawkins' three-legged, tilted desk. He spied the two splintered chairs. "Guess we're standin' up for dinner." Hawkins' scowl made him laugh. "This here's a plate of roast beef and potatoes, the other's chicken and something. You get the chicken and something. I had to encourage the cook to serve us, but he soon saw the wisdom in that." Slade scanned the mess then gazed out the busted window at the Wildfire. "I couldn't carry drinks from the boarding house, so I think I'll rustle up something over at the saloon. You gonna join me, or maybe you want to stay out of sight?" He broke into a broad grin.

Hawkins glared.

Slade maintained that self-satisfied smile. "No? Have it your way. I'll be back in a little while. Why don't you try cleaning up this mess? No tellin' when we might have visitors." A hearty laugh and he was out the door, kicking at debris as he went.

People stared as he crossed the street. He smiled and with several short tips of the hat closed on the saloon. With a hand on his gun, he pushed the swinging doors open and strode into the place. A hush fell over the patrons, some playing poker, some sitting, others talking and drinking, some all over female companions. All eyes turned toward him in silence. In a cheery voice, he said, "Don't mind me folks, I'm just here to wash away a dusty ride." He walked over to the bar and ordered a whiskey.

Nick hurried to pour one. "Nice to see you, Mr. Slade."

Slade held the shot glass up to the crowd, then downed it. He looked at Nick, a man who was several inches taller than him. His boss's office had just been destroyed, and Slade felt the need to send the town a message. "You don't mean that, Nick. You're just being nice, aren't you?"

"No, really. It's good to see you," he said, in a high-pitched voice. He looked at an old sot standing to the left of the gunman for help. "It's good to see him, ain't it, Rufus?"

Rufus looked at Slade with a bleary glance. "Ain't so good to see him when you're lookin' through these eyes." The drunk went back to swirling his shot glass, which was one of several in front of him on the bar.

Slade considered for a moment, then pulled his gun and fired a bullet into the floor next to the drunk's boot. Rufus hopped at the sound and put his glass down. "I ain't lookin' for a fight, mister, I'm just lookin' to get drunker. Good to see you, yes, it is."

Slade smiled, downed a second whiskey with his Colt still at the ready, and threw a quarter on the bar. He looked around the room and grabbed the bottle off the counter. No one moved or talked. "Thanks for the hospitality, Nick. Keep the change." He holstered his sidearm and disappeared out the swinging doors into the early evening air.

****

Hawkins was fretting when Slade drifted back to the railroad office. There was no cleaning up this mess, and no hiding it from his bosses. He couldn't fix the place up without telling them about the break-in, and they'd surely want to know why someone would go to such lengths to destroy his office. The company was already pushing him hard to get the route wrapped up. The walls were closing in and no doubt McAlister would be by soon for a visit. In his frustration, he turned on Slade.

"What the hell am I paying you for? I got one, maybe two men who want me dead. What are you gonna do about it? And look at this place. You haven't done nothing since you got here." Sweat dripped off his round cheeks and funneled down his back.

Slade uncovered the beef plate on the leaning desk and snapped a cloth napkin open. He jabbed Hawkins with, "You went ahead and ate your chicken already without waiting for me?" He tucked the cloth under his shirt collar and sat on the edge of the ruined desk. "You ain't dead yet, Hawkins. That's somethin', ain't it?" He started to cut a piece of meat, and Hawkins screamed at him.

"Do something! Kill them before they kill me!"

Slade pointed the knife at Hawkins. They were not more than three feet apart. "Don't ever yell at me again, or I'll cheat McAlister out of killin' you." He forked a piece of beef into his mouth, the knife still handy. "What's got you so worried anyway? So what if McAlister's after you? You're faster than him."

"It's not him I'm worried about. Walnutt's likely on my trail too! And he might be a better gunhand than you! And maybe that old drunk, Buster. He and McAlister are a pair. Never did cotton to any of 'em."

When Slade was finished with dinner, he reached into his coat pocket and pulled out an expensive Havana, snipped the end, and rolled it between his fingers before lighting it. Hawkins knew it was expensive because he'd smoked the same brand back at the company's sumptuous headquarters in Denver. That was before they'd sent him out here. They'd probably hide the cigars from him now. The gunman blew smoky oval rings in the air. At least the cigar smoke masked the burnt smell of gunpowder.

"How am I gonna get this mess cleaned up without them knowing about it?"

Slade's sly smile reappeared. "You're smart, Hawkins. I didn't say honest, just smart. You'll figure something out. But you might be a little too smart for your own good."

"What's that mean?" He squinted at the gunman, then backed off. Maybe he should just fire Slade and be done with it. Then there'd be no more back and forth with a gun hand he didn't trust. He didn't have many choices, but right then he decided he didn't need Slade anymore after all. He was smarter and faster than McAlister. He'd kill him next time he saw him, then claim self-defense when Walnutt challenged him on it. McAlister's next trip to town would be his last. He turned to Slade with what he intended to be some authority. "You go back to my boarding house and sleep in my room tonight. I'll stay here. On the way, take my horse over to Crawford's and find the rest of my surveying crew. Come back in the morning."

****

At Hawkins' boarding house, the landlady greeted Slade when he strode in, but he ignored her and swept on past to the last room on the left, ground floor. He swung the door open to find three young men laying on the floor with gear strewn about the room. Slade drew his weapon and pointed it at the railroaders who stared wide-eyed at him.

"What're you all doin' here in Hawkins' room?"

The men sprang up, and the one in the middle said, "We didn't know what was goin' on—where you and Hawkins was, so we was stayin' at the railroad office up until it blew up in the middle of the night."

Slade holstered his weapon. "When was that?"

"A couple nights ago."

"Who did it?" He was sure he knew the answer already.

The middle one looked to his companions, then back at Slade. "Don't rightly know, just know it was someone we didn't want to meet. Don't know if there was more than one. Never showed his face. The only thing I saw was the barrel of a gun in the dark and a voice tellin' me if I wanted to live to get out now."

"What kind of gun?"

"Looked like the workin' end of a Colt, but couldn't be sure."

Slade pulled his Colt, cocked the hammer, and pointed it at the young surveyor. "Did it look like this?"

The man hesitated. "Why, yes it did, now that you put it that way. It was a Colt. I seen enough of 'em in my time."

"How tall was the coward?"

"Pretty tall…uh, a little taller than you."

"Well then, that ain't tall 'cause I'm short, wouldn't you say?"

Silence as the three stood mute.

Slade walked up to the one in the middle. "Wouldn't you say I'm short?"

The surveyor looked down at Slade. "You look pretty tall from here."

Slade rubbed his clean-shaven chin. "Good answer. Now listen up." He grabbed the middle youth by the shirt. "You. You're gonna sleep in this bed tonight, got it?"

He nodded.

Slade turned to the others. "You two stand guard outside the boarding house and watch for any trouble. A shooter comes, you take care of him before he gets inside. Be on the lookout for Ike McAlister, got it?"

They looked at each other like they'd just drawn the short straw, and the one in the middle said in a small voice, "Sure thing, Mr. Slade."

Slade squinted at them. "If any of you try to skip out on me, I'll shoot all of you before you can count to three. First, I'll hit you in places that just hurt. Then, when you're beggin' for your life, crawlin' away in the dirt, holdin' a hand up, I'll shoot you a second time somewhere where you'll wish you were dead. After that, I'll get mean, get my drift?"

The three nodded wide-eyed.

"Get goin'." Slade holstered his gun, left the room, and climbed the boarding house's stairs to the second level. He picked a bedroom door, barged in, and drew on a man and woman sleeping in bed. "Get up."

The man said in a husky voice, "Who are you and what do you want? We don't have much money."

"I ain't after your money or your woman. I'll give you to the count of three to get out of this room." He cocked the gun's hammer. The distinctive sound motivated the couple. "One."

They grabbed some clothes and ran out into the street half-naked as Slade stood grinning.

The gunman kicked his boots off and fell on the still-warm bed, gun at the ready. "Two, three."

****

Hawkins tried to clear a spot in the railroad office to sleep on without much success. The sour stench of gunpowder still hung in the air. McAlister wasn't likely to look for him in here, not when Hawkins had a clean room he could stay in across the way. That clean room looked awful good to him right now, but he'd be an easy target there. He took his gun belt off so it didn't dig into him and laid down amid the rubble with his head on his heavy wool coat. Too cold. He put the jacket back on and let his gun belt serve as a pillow, pistol in hand as he drifted off.

In the early morning, Hawkins rose and relieved himself behind the ruined building. He hurried back inside and took up a post at the Main Street window. As the sun rose, he heard his name called from outside.

"Hawkins, it's Slade. I'm comin' in, so don't shoot me." Slade carried a covered plate in one hand and held a steaming cup in the other. Inside, he sized Hawkins up. "You ain't froze, I see. I was half expectin' to have to drag you into the sun to thaw you out." He laughed at his shivering employer.

"Gimme that coffee!" Hawkins cradled it like it was gold and gulped the hot contents. Not even his burning tongue could slow him. When he finished, he looked up. "Why'd you call my name out just now? Were you trying to let everybody in town know I was here?"

Slade grinned. "Not a bad idea, but I was just makin' sure you didn't shoot me, thinkin' I was McAlister comin' for you already." He chuckled and looked for a place to sit while Hawkins attacked the hotcake breakfast. "He knows you're here by now anyway."

Hawkins stopped eating. "That's just as well, but how do you figure?"

"Think, Hawkins. That horse of yours is hard to miss. Lots of people know you're back. I reckon someone in town already told McAlister or his sidekick. I'd guess you'll be gettin' a visit anytime now."

Hawkins put the plate down and drew his pistol. The cylinder was full, and he checked his gun belt for bullets. "You got a rifle?"

Slade shook his head. "Got one, but don't usually use it. I always done my killin' close up. Made it more personal that way. I like watchin' a man's eyes who's about to die. And I like bein' the last person they ever see."

"Then you make sure I'm the last person McAlister sees. You haven't done anything to earn your keep yet. Hell, you don't even look scary."

"Looks ain't everything."

Hawkins let that go, then laid out a plan for when McAlister came into town. Slade would meet him head-on in the street, with Hawkins doing him in from a hiding spot off to the side. He wanted to be the one to kill the troublesome fool. None of the ranchers were selling anymore, and he only had to look at his demolished surroundings to see McAlister's handiwork firsthand. Hawkins looked out the front window. "What if he doesn't come this morning?"

Slade grunted. "He'll come. He knows you're quicker than him, but he'll still come. You can see it in his eyes. There's more to killin' somebody than just bein' faster than the other guy. Takes a cool head to keep your wits about you and put a shooter down when bullets are flyin'. He looks to me like he's the kind that gets calmer under fire."

"Is that supposed to make me feel better?"

"No, just somethin' I always been able to tell about a man. The easiest gents I ever killed always lost their steady when they were starin' at the barrel of my gun."

Hawkins looked at Slade like he was crazy. "Just get ready to do what I said." He grabbed the front doorknob, forced the door's bent hinges open, and moved in a semi-crouch down the sidewalk with his back against the street's buildings. He picked out two large wooden water barrels outside O'Toole's shop and hunkered down behind them. He had a clear view to the south between the two casks—the direction McAlister would be coming from.

Chapter Twenty-One

Ike sat at the dinner table with Lorraine and Jessie, Buster, and their new lodger, Quincy. This was the first meal Ike let Lorraine include the boy at the table. After the prayer, he eyed Buster who sat slightly off kilter in his chair. Earlier that morning, Ike breathed a sigh of relief when his friend opened his eyes again. As he passed the potatoes, he said, "Welcome back, pardner. You know those two days you were out? Well, I was hopin' for at least a third 'cause it's the first time I ever got any work done around here."

Buster returned Ike's smile. "I was hopin' for at least a third, too, 'cause then maybe everything but my eyeballs wouldn't still be hurtin'."

"Well, the bad news is Doc says you're gonna be as good as you ever were." They both laughed, and Buster grabbed at his side.

"Quit makin' me laugh. My achin' body can't take much more of your funnin'."

"How are you feelin', anyway?"

"Okay. Won't take long for me to start feelin' like my old self. You ever figure out who started that stampede?"

"No. Don't know as we ever will, either. My guess is it was Hawkins' handiwork though, puttin' some of his men up to it, or he could've hired some down and out miners too. He probably figured we'd get trampled, and he wouldn't have to be lookin' over his shoulder anymore, but he didn't count on how tough you were and how fast I was." Ike let loose a hearty chuckle.

Buster said, "The only reason I hung back was to hold the cattle up some so's you could get away. And it worked."

"Well, now you're makin' about the same amount of sense as you ever did. I'd hoped those steers would have kicked some more brains into you though, as long as you were gonna get trampled anyway." Ike grinned across the table. There hadn't been much to smile about lately, so the chance to have some fun with Buster tonight felt good, now that his sidekick was going to be all right. Times had been hard, and laughing took a bit of the edge off things. He grew serious. "Abe Donaldson stopped by to say he saw Hawkins' horse tied up outside the railroad office this afternoon. Guess he's tryin' to make amends."

Lorraine drew in a deep breath and stared at her husband.

Buster said, "Can't mistake that stallion, prettiest horse around."

Ike peered at him. "Now I *know* your head's not workin' right."

"No offense to Ally, Ike. She's still the finest horse around. I was just remarkin' on his horse's looks."

"Looks ain't everything, Buster, and that pretty horse ain't gonna help Hawkins tomorrow none."

Lorraine placed her napkin on the table and squinted at her husband. "Is that what you have in mind? To go stormin' into town tomorrow and get in a shootout with Hawkins and his gunhand?" She shook a finger at him. "You ever think that's exactly what he hopes you'll do?"

"I reckon he does."

Lorraine said, "He's just waitin' for you, Ike, ready to gun you down. You know that, and you gettin' killed tomorrow ain't much of a plan."

Jessie's eyes widened, and she started crying.

The last thing he wanted to do was upset his daughter. He lifted her out of her chair and hugged her to him and glanced at Lorraine. "No more talk like that tonight." He kissed Jessie on the cheek. "No one's gonna hurt your Daddy," then rubbed her back until she stopped sniffling.

After putting her to bed, Ike and Lorraine whispered long into the night. He tried calming her fears, but he had plenty of his own to deal with.

Before the sun came up, Ike eased from the bedroom and tiptoed out the front door with his boots, hat, and coat in hand. Buster was already in the stable when he came in. "What are you doin', Buster? You thinkin' of goin' with me? You can hardly stand, much less ride."

Buster didn't glance Ike's way. He had already saddled his horse and had the bridle on Ally. He grimaced as he checked her strap underneath. "I can ride."

Quincy stood mute to the side.

"I need you to stay here with Lorraine and Jessie, Buster. No sense you gettin' killed, too." A wry smile framed his mouth.

Buster silently handed Ally's reins to Ike and started checking his horse's saddlebags.

Lorraine burst into the stable and strode over to Ally. She grabbed the horse's bridle and held on.

"Don't do this, Ike. Let the law handle Hawkins. And there's Slade to account for too."

"Rob *was* the law, Lorraine. There's no law in Cottonwood now. No one to bring Hawkins to justice anytime soon. He's got to pay for Rob. You and I both know it."

She looked at Buster as he stood next to his saddled horse. "You too? Can't you talk him out of this?"

Buster jammed his hat on. "You know he goes deaf when his mind's made up. I don't think he can hear either one of us right now."

Lorraine rushed to Ike and held him tightly. He ran a hand up and down her back, then backed out of her grasp. She stood wide-eyed with a hand to her mouth in silent prayer as Ike mounted up and galloped away, early morning dew flying from Ally's hooves, Buster trailing.

By the time Ike neared Cottonwood, the sun was peeking over the eastern ramparts. He slowed to let Buster catch up. Even in the cool morning, he was dripping sweat. He wiped at his eyes, and as he closed them, a vision of Lorraine and Jessie standing on the ranch house porch flashed through his mind.

"How do you want to play this, Ike?" Buster was slightly slumped in his saddle, but he reached for his Sharps rifle and chambered a round.

"Thought I'd ride in and draw their fire." His face changed from a frown to the start of a grin.

Buster sported a small smile as well. "Well, then I'll follow you and get 'em in my sights while they're reloadin' after shootin' you off Ally. So, what do you want me to do with Ally after you get killed?"

Ike patted his horse's chestnut neck. "Ally'll be fine. We've been in tighter scrapes than this, ain't we girl? But if I don't come back, just don't let Hawkins have her."

Buster's smile faded. "Ike, stop foolin' around." He whacked his hat against his leg. "How about this? I go in first and you circle around back of the storefronts and we'll see if we can't flush 'em out between us."

"Nah. That won't work."

"Why not?"

Ike said, "'Cause I'm goin' first. So, you do the ridin' around back of the buildings and get behind Hawkins and Slade."

Buster looked down the street. "Think they're in the railroad office? The one that got tore apart the other night?"

"Don't know, but we're about to find out."

"Any idea how that happened?"

Ike paused for a moment, then glanced sideways at his friend. "Only thing I can think of is it must have been an act of God."

Buster nodded. "Must have been. Can't think of anyone around here who might have done it."

As the two friends drew abreast of Sue's boarding house at the near end of Main Street, Ike was glad the professor wasn't in the street waiting to join them. Buster risking his life was bad enough; Ike didn't want his brother-in-law in harm's way, too. Ike nodded and Buster rode off to the left, angling behind the town's stores. Ike dismounted, told Ally to stay, and continued down the middle of the street at a slow walk, glancing left and right, left hand on his holster.

****

The professor stood at the boarding house window. He'd been waiting for Ike to show. When he heard Hawkins was back in town, he knew he'd see his brother-in-law ride in this morning. He watched Buster split off from Ike, and his hand went reflexively to his gun. He slipped out the front door and walked under cover along the wooden plank sidewalks until he came up even across from Ike. Earlier, he'd seen Hawkins hide behind O'Toole's big water barrels. He drew his sidearm.

He gave a soft whistle, and even though Ike didn't respond, Hugh was sure he'd heard it. The two of them were coming up on the mercantile on the left where Hawkins lay hidden and the devastated railroad office on the right where Slade was probably still holed up. From the looks of it, Slade and Hawkins had a killing crossfire set up between them, and Ike was walking right into it.

Just then a woman's scream broke the deadly silence. Margaret came running out of The Sew Pretty on the left, whipping a shotgun wildly around in the air. "You all go on and get! There's not going to be any killing this morning. No killing this morning!" She fired one of her two barrels into the blue sky, then turned the gun on Ike. He threw his hands up, and she turned and fired the second barrel at Hawkins' hiding place. "You come out now, you devil!" She carried the gun like a club over to the large casks of water and smashed the stock on one of them. She dropped the shotgun, and as if by magic, reached under her dress and produced a pistol. Another scream at the top of her lungs, and she pointed the gun at the ruined railroad building. "Come out, Mr. Slade. Everybody get out here in the open. You too, Professor. Throw your guns down and your hands up." Hawkins and Slade joined Ike in the street, all with their guns on the ground and arms reaching skyward.

The four combatants stared at each other incredulously, while Buster watched from a short distance. Margaret shouted. "Now step back, and keep doing that 'til I can't see you anymore!" She waved the pistol crazily again.

Ike backed away, still facing his brother's killer. "Guess you live another day, Hawkins. You oughta thank Margaret."

All of a sudden, Margaret threw the pistol away and rushed back into her shop, hands holding her hoop skirt off the dirt street. The men stood gaping at her, then each eyed the others to see what they were going to do.

Slade spoke up. "Why don't you try me instead, McAlister, 'cause there ain't nobody here I can't beat in a gunfight, fair or otherwise. But then, looks like you're too scared to find out." He waited for Ike's response. When he got none, Slade looked at Walnutt. "Or maybe you and me could settle this between ourselves, Professor? That is your name, isn't it? I hear you're a fair hand with a gun."

"That's what my friends call me, but you can call me Mr. Walnutt." Hugh stood with feet slightly spread.

Buster came up behind Hawkins and Slade with his rifle leveled at their backs. "Like the lady said, ain't gonna be no gunfight today, 'less you can grab your gun faster than I can fire this Sharps." As Buster neared, Hawkins said, "I can't see you, alky, but I bet you're wobbling something pitiful on your feet. You even know which end of that rifle is the business end?"

As Buster moved past Hawkins, he reached back and jammed his rifle butt into the man's stomach, then smashed his toes, and the railroader went down howling in a heap. "Guess I ain't the one who's wobblin' now. I reckon I do know which is the workin' end of this rifle, and you're lucky I didn't use it or you wouldn't even be wobblin' now."

Ike hurried to his Colt while Buster covered him. He cocked the hammer and aimed at Hawkins' forehead. It made for a big target as the man was nearly bald and had a head better made for hair.

Hugh picked Hawkins' gun up. "Ike, wait! You cannot just shoot him this way—that would be murder and would make you just as bad as him." He drew his voice to a whisper. "Besides, right now there is no actual evidence he killed Rob. We know he did but cannot prove it. Yet."

Ike's arm shook as he pointed the gun at Hawkins, but he couldn't pull the trigger. "The bastard don't deserve to draw another breath, and I'm here to give him what he deserves." What was wrong with him? He had his brother's killer dead to rights but couldn't finish him off.

"Not today, please, Ike. Not yet. Give me some more time to tie him to Rob's murder. I have a stake in this too." He laid a hand on his brother-in-law's outstretched arm and pressed it down.

Ike let him, but said, "Clock's ticked too long already, Hugh."

"I'll work on this night and day if you leave here with me and Buster now."

Ike took a long look at his two enemies, one

sprawled in the dirt, the other with a small smile on his face. He turned and started to walk away.

Hugh said, "I don't think we should turn our back on these rogues, they are not to be trusted."

Ike grunted. "Let's go before I change my mind."

Buster trailed behind his friends, trusting the Sharps resting on his arm rather than the two men he'd just braced, eyes alert as he backed away.

Sue met them at the boarding house. She stood on the small porch, a palm pressed to her heart. She reached out and hugged the three men. "I was so worried, Hugh. I saw you leave, then I saw Ike walking down Main Street. And then Margaret came out screaming, and I didn't know if any of you would be coming back."

Ike drew his sister to him. "I'm just like a bad penny that keeps turning up, Sis." She was the only sibling he had left. It was up to him to make sure she outlived him. Considering his bad blood with Hawkins, that seemed more and more likely.

Chapter Twenty-Two

"Ma'am?" Sue turned to the voice. A dance hall girl stood in front of her. Young, pretty, with a worried look on her face. They were the only customers in the mercantile that morning.

"Yes? May I help you?"

"You're Sue McAl—I mean... Mrs. Walnutt, aren't you?"

"Yes, and you are?"

"Nobody. Name's Hannah. I work at the Wildfire." She paused. "I knew your brother, I'm sorry—" Her voice drifted off into nothing, and her gaze dropped to the store's worn wooden floor.

Sue's eyes widened. "You must be the one...the one people say—"

Hannah pursed her lips and nodded. "Yes, I guess I am that one...the one they say was carrying on with your brother." Her voice was almost brittle, as if it would break if she spoke any louder.

Sue stiffened. "What do you want?"

"I don't rightly know. I just wanted to tell you how sorry I was about him being shot. That's all." She bowed her head, turned away, and started for the door.

Sue watched her walk away. Young woman in a fine dress, hair done up, just a touch of rouge. Long black hair that cascaded over her shoulders. She'd never dressed as well in her life, and she smoothed at her worn, faded dress. "Wait. Just wait a minute." She walked toward her. "It took a lot of courage for you to come speak with me directly. I don't know why you did, but I know it wasn't easy. Can you stay and talk for a minute?" Sue was desperate for any morsel of information about Rob and his death. Spending a few more minutes with this woman would likely be time well spent.

She said, "Yes ma'am," almost in a whisper.

There was obvious pain under the makeup. Sue hadn't noticed the red eyes before, either. "What was my brother to you?"

Hannah brushed at a cheek. "He was—" Her voice trailed off. "He was a real gentleman." She took a deep breath. "And I'm not a whore, either. I'm a saloon girl, but I don't have anything to do with what goes on in the rooms upstairs." She paused, and tears cascaded down her cheeks.

"Oh dear. Come sit over here with me. I can see this has torn you up." Sue's vision blurred as she considered the young girl sitting next to her. A fleeting vision of how Rob must have looked lying face up on the ground flashed through her mind. She shook her head and cleared her throat. She held eye contact with Hannah. "Did you have anything to do with my brother's death?"

Hannah straightened up. "No ma'am. The last time I saw him was in the saloon when he told me he couldn't spend any more time with me. I was so mad I threw a whiskey glass at him. I knew it wasn't gonna hit him 'cause I can't throw for nothing. It scared him, though, and made me feel better."

"So you liked him?"

"Yes. I...liked him. He was one of the only ones around here who was kind to me. Most of the men who buy me drinks aren't really nice. They're mainly drunks with roaming hands. Rob wasn't like that. We talked about things. About the world outside of Cottonwood and what I wanted to do. And the future." She stopped. "He listened to me. I would never have hurt him."

Sue wondered about the girl. Either she was telling the truth, or she had missed a calling as an actress. Right now, it could have been either. "Have you heard any talk around the Wildfire? Anything about who may have shot Rob?"

"No, and I've been listening real hard. If anyone knows anything, they aren't talking. From what I hear though, Hawkins is the prime suspect."

Sue broke in. "You are, too. Everyone saw you throw that glass at him. They say you were furious, mad enough to kill."

"That's true. I was furious, but kill him? That's something I never could have done. I guess that's what I really wanted to say—I didn't do it."

"Do you know anything that might help me find who did? I hear you been asking around about Hawkins some."

"Yes, but that's for a different reason." She paused and changed the subject. "I got no right to ask, but I want to leave the saloon and get a decent job here in town. Do you need any help at the boarding house?"

Sue didn't know how to respond. The young girl standing in front of her had been somehow involved with her dead brother, and now she was asking for a job? Hannah was obviously upset by Rob's death, but Sue didn't know exactly why. Was there something she wasn't sharing?

"I can't give you a job. I don't need any help because we don't have any boarders right now, and I'm surprised you even asked me for one. I'll be honest. I just met you and don't know how much of what you said I believe."

Hannah nodded. "I understand. I'm not sure I'd believe me either if I was you." She blinked several times and whispered, "Thank you anyway." As Hannah got up and left the store, Sue watched her walk away. That was one of the strangest encounters she'd ever had. She picked up a few dry goods from O'Toole's and walked back to the boarding house.

Hugh met her in the entryway. She started to say something, but he interrupted. "Sue, I need to talk with you. Please sit." He led her to the parlor and sat next to her on the divan. "That showdown Ike and I had this morning has caused me to rethink my position."

"Your position? Your position on what?"

"On the mayor's offer."

"You mean about being sheriff?"

"Yes, exactly."

Sue squinted at her husband. "If you think you're gonna take over from Rob, you got another think coming, Hugh Walnutt. Let Whitaker find some lawman from Denver or somewhere else. You aren't gonna do that." Rob's death was a wound that hadn't even started to heal yet and right now didn't feel like it ever would.

Hugh put an arm around his wife. "Let me tell you why I want to do this and then you make the final decision." He paused. "This morning, it became clear that Ike is determined to face Hawkins, one way or another, even though we have no hard evidence yet that he killed Rob. If Ike does face Hawkins, Hawkins will kill him; he is just a better gunman. I think in the back of his head Ike knows that, too, but knowing him, that does not matter. I have concluded the only thing that will stop him from confronting Hawkins is if I become sheriff and promise to pursue the case against Hawkins hard." He paused. "Rest assured, Hawkins will not draw on me because he knows I would kill him."

Somehow, that didn't comfort Sue. She'd just lost one of her big brothers, and now suddenly faced the prospect of losing her only other brother, or her husband, or both.

Hugh reached over and gently cupped Sue's chin and made her look at him. "So it is in your hands. What would you like me to do?"

"That isn't fair, Hugh, asking me to choose—it isn't right."

"What is right, dear, is that Ike stands a better chance of living if I am sheriff."

Sue buried her head against her husband's shoulder. "I can't choose; don't make me." Tears cascaded from her cheeks, then she gathered herself. "If this is what you think this is best, well then, I'll trust you to take care of yourself and my brother." She looked skyward. "Lord, please continue to protect what's left of this McAlister family." She wiped at her face, and he put his arm in hers as they walked to the front door. He kissed her lightly on the lips and was out the door, headed for the saloon.

As she watched her husband walk away, a picture of Rob as a young boy flashed through her head.

****

Hugh stood outside the Wildfire for a minute. Inside was where Mayor Whitaker held court, doing the town's business in between throwing whiskeys back. He pushed the doors open and let his eyes adjust to the dim interior. He nodded to Nick as he walked past the bar to where Whitaker sat with a tableful of cronies.

Whitaker smiled. "Reconsider, did you, Professor? Join us." He indicated a lowback chair opposite him. "You know most of these gentlemen already"—his hand swept around the table—"and the ones you don't know, don't matter." He laughed at his little joke.

Hugh held Whitaker's gaze as he sat. He didn't like the mayor much and the thought of working for him almost made him get up and leave, but there was more in play here than just a job. "What's the pay and when would I start?"

"The pay? Same as what Rob was getting, sixty dollars a month and you'd start as soon as you put this star on." Whitaker fumbled in a vest pocket and produced a six-pronged silver badge. He pushed it across the table.

Hugh let it lay there. "Not good enough. Rob was getting ninety a month between you and Hawkins. This is a dangerous job, and I want one hundred and twenty dollars. What with miners, drifters, and drovers coming through here and the trouble with Hawkins, it ought to be worth at least that much to this town. I will pick out a horse of my choosing from Red. And if I come to you and say I need a deputy, you will say 'yes.' You will not interfere with my duties, and you will give me at least six months before you consider firing me. Do we have a deal?"

The mayor frowned for a second, looked around at

the men seated at the table, then smiled. "Of course! Pick it up, Hugh, and welcome, Sheriff." They shook hands across the table, and Whitaker called for drinks for the house. He was part owner of the Wildfire, so he could afford to be generous.

Hugh stood, tipped his bowler, and turned to leave. Whitaker called after him, "And get yourself a cowboy hat!"

Laughter erupted behind him as he pushed through the swinging doors. The jail was a couple of storefronts away, and he stopped in to take a look. A single cell adjoined a small main room with a battered desk, a desk Rob spent a lot of time sitting at over the last few years. He would make some changes. Likely a second cell at the least. The town was growing, and crime would grow right along with it. Cottonwood could afford to put some money into fixing the place up.

He hesitated going back to the boarding house. It would be easy to leave the badge off, but he kept it on. Sue probably already knew what he was going to do anyway. As he walked home, he hoped pinning that badge on his coat wouldn't be the biggest mistake he ever made.

Chapter Twenty-Three

Sue's stomach jumped, and she stared at her husband as he walked in. "I guess I knew you were gonna do it, but seeing you wearing that star throws me some. What's your plan now?"

He unbuckled his gun belt and set it aside. "I guess I will have to figure that out. What I am going to do first is find out more about Rob—who he was with last, when and where."

She didn't know whether to celebrate his new job or curse it, but she retrieved their one bottle of wine and poured two glasses. She had prepared a sturdy meal as well. She was a fair cook, and her husband had been teaching her some of the rudiments of English cooking, bland as she thought it was. Shepherd's pie was on the menu today. Truth be told, she was beginning to like certain of Hugh's favorite dishes. She had Americanized this one with beef instead of mutton.

Hugh said, "My, you are going all out, I think is the term. This is indeed a fine dinner. Thank you, dear."

"You just take care and make sure this isn't your last supper," she said, with a small twinkle in her eye. They raised glasses and toasted to a new adventure, one they both hoped would end well.

As they finished and Sue started clearing dishes, there came a knock at the door. She opened it to find Margaret Pinshaw standing on the front porch. "Why, hello Margaret, to what do we owe the honor of your visit?" When she got no more than a blank stare in return, Sue ushered their guest into the parlor. "Come and sit." She indicated a small upholstered chair.

"I'm sorry to intrude. I see you are just finishing supper. I can come back."

Sue waved a hand. "Those dishes will wait; it's not often enough that you come visit. Can I get you some coffee?"

"No, thank you. I'll just stay a moment. I had a strange encounter the other day. A young girl from the Wildfire stopped by my shop. It became clear after talking with her that she was the one sweet on Rob."

Sue cocked her head. Hannah. "What did she want?"

"I'm not sure, but I couldn't believe her gall, visiting me in my own shop after chasing my Rob."

"What did she have to say?"

"She said that if she had contributed to Rob's death in some way she was sorry. Can you believe that? Thinking Rob's dalliance with her was important enough that it might have somehow gotten him killed. For all we know, she might have killed him." Margaret smoothed at her fine satin dress and cast an eye at Sue's worn, cotton one.

Heat rose upward from Sue's neck, and she raised her chin as she sat across from her guest. Pretty dresses weren't everything. Margaret had apparently hurried out of her shop as her ever-present blue parasol was missing, but not so quickly that she forgot to don one of her signature hats.

Sue watched her guest fidget as she sat. "Was that all she said?"

"No. She wanted to know if I would hire her. Apparently, she wants to put her dance hall days behind her." Margaret sniffed. "Can you believe that? I was shocked!"

Sue wasn't. The woman had asked her the same thing. "What did you say?"

She paused. "I told her… I said…actually, I didn't say anything." She turned to Sue with a worried look. "What do you think I should do? Ever since you left, I've needed more help. You know how the town is growing, but people are saying some terrible things about her."

Sue didn't mention that Hannah had also approached her. She didn't want to poison the well if the girl was telling the truth. Let Margaret deal with her, and she would just watch.

"I don't suppose you need to worry about what other people are saying, Margaret. You've always been a strong woman who's charted her own course." She paused and searched Margaret's face. "You seem anxious, what's wrong? Is there something you're not saying?"

Margaret brushed the question off and sat up a little straighter. "You're right. I'll make up my own mind; thank you, Sue." She looked around at the tired parlor. "I really like what you've done with the place since you bought it from Lorraine."

Sue considered that for a moment. It was either a dig, because she hadn't had the money to do much to the house, or it was meant to be nice, and that wasn't Margaret's strong suit. And to think, she might have been her sister-in-law. "Well, I won't keep you any longer, Margaret. Please do stop by again soon." She moved toward the front door, which forced Margaret up off the chair. After thanking her for stopping by, she ushered her out. As she watched Margaret swish toward The Sew Pretty without her parasol, she wondered why the woman had really stopped by.

She found her husband in the kitchen washing dishes. "An Englishman in the American West, up to his neck in dirty soapy water. If only your family could see you now." She chuckled as Hugh sported a grin and flicked water at her.

"Yes, well, do not inform them of my present state or I will be disinherited and we will be penniless."

"I didn't know your family had money. If I had known that, I would have married you sooner."

"Alas, dear damsel, we don't have money, we just act like we came from it. A good front and all that, don't you know. Bye the bye, what was Margaret's visit all about? I could not help overhearing a bit."

"It was strange. I'm not even sure what to make of it. She's always been one to make up her own mind, never asked me for advice on anything before. She said Hannah asked her for a job. I'll be interested to see if she hires her or not." She picked up a cotton cloth to dry herself off, puzzled.

****

The next day Sue was in the kitchen when she heard a knock at the front door. She opened it to find a young woman standing on the porch, looking somewhat timid. Sue paused a moment. "Hannah...right?"

"Yes, ma'am."

"What can I do for you, Hannah?"

"I wanted to thank you for speaking with me the other day and to tell you I just got a job at The Sew

Pretty."

Sue tried to hide her surprise. "I'm happy for you."

Hannah followed an awkward pause with, "That means I won't have to work at the saloon anymore. I'll be making a little money and learning how to sew and all."

Sue studied her. "Certainly a good skill." There was something about Hannah that made Sue pause. The girl's eyes were almost welling with tears as she spoke. Sue said, "Anything else I can do for you, Hannah?"

The young girl almost looked startled and blurted, "No ma'am, I suppose not." She curtsied and turned to leave.

She'd only taken a few steps when Sue called out, "Thanks for stopping by."

The smile on Hannah's face when she looked back was enormous. She gave a quick wave and hurried away. Something was drawing Hannah to Sue and vice versa, and the next day Sue stopped by The Sew Pretty to see how Hannah handled a work environment.

Margaret looked up from her desk at the sound of the familiar ting-a-ling bell above her door. "Why, Sue, what brings you here? Can I fix you a cup of tea?"

The early summer sun shining through the front window had warmed the interior of the shop. No tea for her, but she would have taken a cup of coffee. "No thanks, Margaret, I just stopped by to visit you and your new helper."

"Hannah? How did you know I'd hired her?"

Sue ignored the question. "How is she getting along?"

Margaret answered Sue's unasked question. "I just thought, why not? She seems smart and wants to work.

I thought I'd give her a chance—that's just the kind of person I am. She's getting along fine. I have such a backlog now, you know, what with the miners, the local ladies, and the stagecoaches coming through with new folks, it's quite a task for me to keep up with. But I try, heaven knows I try. My clothes are in such demand." Margaret had managed to turn Sue's inquiry about Hannah into an opportunity to talk about herself.

"I'm sure everyone appreciates how hard you work, Margaret. Is Hannah here?"

Disapproval showed on Margaret's face. The focus was no longer on her. "Yes, she works in the back. Where you used to." She pointed to a little door at the rear of the shop.

When Sue peeked into the cozy anteroom, Hannah sprang up from her table, and her face flushed. "Miss Sue, I wasn't expecting you, I don't…why don't you sit here on this chair?" Hannah stepped aside and offered Sue her seat.

"No, that won't be necessary, I just wanted to say hello and see how you were getting on."

Hannah spoke so quickly that Sue could hardly understand her. "Thank you, Miss Sue, thank you for stopping by. I would have straightened things up here if I'd known." She stood stiffly beside her small sewing desk.

"No matter. Is Margaret treating you well?" Sue said it loud enough that the shopkeeper would hear it.

"Why, yes she is. She's very…nice…and fair."

The way Hannah said it didn't sound like a ringing endorsement, and Sue silently filed the impression away. The wide smile she'd seen yesterday was nowhere to be found. A large pile of mending. "Good.

I'll let you get back to your work then. Good day." She nodded slightly and turned back to the shop. On her way out she said, "Thank you, Margaret, for your hospitality."

"Can you stay for a moment?"

"I'm sure you have better things to do than jabber with me." Sue was irritated that Margaret might already be taking advantage of Hannah. "Thank you again."

"You're welcome. I'm sure." Margaret's tone was sullen. "Thank you for stopping by. Come again, won't you?"

As Sue opened the door, she turned back to Margaret. She glanced around the small store, tempted to make a snide comment in return for the one Margaret made about her boarding house, but pasted a false smile on instead and was gone.

Over the next several days, Hannah stopped by the boarding house every now and then to spend a few minutes with Sue. She was like the little sister Sue never had, and Hannah's diversions helped take her mind off the loss of her brother. On one visit, Sue asked where she was staying.

"I bed down right next to my work table at the back of the shop." The anteroom Hannah worked in wasn't big enough to hold more than a small cot. "It's fine for me."

Sue pondered that, then at breakfast the next morning, said, "Hugh, what would you think about that young girl, Hannah, boarding here?"

"Why? We've just gotten one new boarder with more to come, certainly."

"I know, but she's sleeping on a small cot at The Sew Pretty that can't be too comfortable, and I think

Margaret's taking advantage of her."

"Did Hannah say that?"

"No, but she doesn't have to. A woman knows these things, and I know Margaret. She had more in mind when she hired Hannah than just being a good Samaritan."

"Well, I am not sure about this. Have you spoken with her yet?"

"No, I wanted to talk with you first. You're always so sensible and see things so clearly." Long ago, Sue had learned to lean on her husband's robust ego to get what she wanted.

"Well then, perhaps…if you think…it would work. Why don't you make the necessary arrangements and so forth?"

"Thank you, dear. You have such a clear head about these things." Sue had already determined to charge Hannah half rent. She was looking forward to getting to know more about the young woman who had charmed her brother. "I'll take care of it tomorrow."

Chapter Twenty-Four

Ike rattled the well-worn latch on the jail door until it finally gave in to his efforts. Inside, the new sheriff looked up from behind Rob's old desk. "It is good to see you, Ike. Please come in and sit for a moment." He indicated a chair near the desk. "Can I get you some coffee?"

"Sure, but I'll get it myself, don't want to interrupt official sheriffin' business." He looked around the small room where his brother spent so much time. His first unpleasantness with Hawkins had been right here, too. He poured a cup and sat. All the things that still needed to be done with the herd this time of year had left him short-tempered. "How're you settlin' in?" Hugh had been sheriff short of a week.

"I am getting used to the routine, and I think people are getting used to me. But I know you well enough to know you did not come here to...how do you say...palaver. What can I do for you, Ike?"

Ike put the cup on the desk and leaned forward. "I was just wonderin' what you've found out about Rob's killer."

"The truth is, nothing yet. I have been making inquiries about Rob's last movements—who he was with, and who saw him when, but I have not been able to uncover much in the way of new information." He sipped his coffee. "It appears Rob left the Wildfire earlier that evening and had started on his evening rounds. Nick saw him leave the saloon at about his usual time. Then, Margaret said he stopped by to see her after that but left around ten o'clock."

"Who was he with in the saloon?"

"He talked briefly with the young lady, Hannah. They had not been seen together since she flung that shot glass at him. I have not been able to find anyone who overheard what they were talking about. Mayor Whitaker was also there, according to Nick."

"Well, someone had to see or hear something after that. Maybe you ain't spoken to the right people yet."

"You may be right, Ike. I have not spoken with everyone who was in the saloon that night. I am still trying to locate some of the poker players who were at the table with the mayor. I have already spoken with the young lady, Hannah."

"She's staying at your boarding house now, isn't she?"

Hugh nodded.

"Somehow that seems odd, Hugh." When he got no response, he said, "What did she have to say?"

"She said Rob told her he was sorry how things ended between them. The mayor said she raised her voice during their conversation."

"Any idea what they were talking about?"

"She apparently said she never wanted to see him again. According to Whitaker, she was still very angry."

"Angry enough to kill?"

Hugh let that pass. He didn't know the answer to that.

"Have you cornered Hawkins yet?"

"He is the first person I tracked down when I took the job. He is still trying to clean up the mess someone made at his office." He squinted at Ike. "Would you know anything about what happened to that building?"

Ike changed the subject. "What did Hawkins have to say?"

"He said he was just as surprised as everyone else when he came out of his boarding house early that morning and saw the crowd gathered around the saloon. He said he had a trip planned to take care of railroad business west of here, and that's why he disappeared so quickly. He said he did not kill Rob."

"I expected as much. Not that I believe anything he says anyway." He grabbed his hat and started for the door.

Hugh called after him. "Ike, I am trying to solve this, but I am just getting my feet on the ground here. I have other things—" He stopped short of saying he had other duties to attend to as well. He rubbed at his face with a hand. "Let me handle this. Please don't get involved."

Without turning around, Ike said, "But you ain't handling it, Hugh, and I am involved." It was the first time he'd ever had a cross word with his brother-in-law, and it didn't feel good. He was out the flimsy door before Hugh could respond. He cooled off some on the ride back to the ranch, thinking about how to take Hawkins out.

Buster greeted him when he pulled up at the corral. "Find out anything new about Rob's killer?"

"What makes you think I was sniffin' on that trail?" He dismounted slowly and drew his hand along Ally's chestnut neck, then smoothed the white blaze on her head.

"I know your moods, Ike, just like I can tell when weather's brewin' up in the mountains. When you're off track, there's a certain feel I get, and I'm gettin' it now."

Ike shook his head. "No. No news."

Lorraine walked over from the porch, reached up, and circled her arms around his chest. "Hello, Ike McAlister, your family's been waitin' to see you. Glad you're back because there's somethin' I want to talk to you about." She drew her arm through his and led him to the house. Inside, she poured him a cup of coffee and sat next to him.

"You know Bert is pretty much—"

"You mean Quincy."

"No, I mean Bert."

Ike pursed his lips. This was probably going to be something he didn't want to hear.

Lorraine brushed at the wayward curl that always hung down. "I want to talk to you about him stayin' on with us, now that he's healed."

He sat back. "Why would you want him to stay on, woman?"

Lorraine placed her hand on his. "Why not? He's apologized time and again for what he did, and he doesn't have any place to go. Plus, Hawkins will probably kill him if he goes back to town."

"Not our problem. Maybe he shoudda thought about that before he kidnapped you."

"Ike, he could have killed me, or left me to die up there in the mountains. He's a kid, and kids do foolish things. He's never had a break in his life."

"Maybe he doesn't deserve one."

Lorraine pursed her lips. "Think back to the war for a minute. Were there times when you didn't get killed because the Good Lord cut you a break?"

That stopped him. There had been times like that, times when he lived and others didn't. He'd often reflected on that over the years. Why was he spared? He was no better than anyone else. It was one of many things he'd never been able to make sense of. And now he was considering housing his wife's kidnapper, when he'd thought it strange his sister was housing a suspect in their brother's murder. Sometimes life didn't make sense. He nodded slightly.

"Then how about we return the favor? How about we let him stay and just see how things go?"

He gave up. "If that's what you want." He stood abruptly and started out of the kitchen for the stable, when Lorraine stopped him. "Now don't shut me out, Ike. I know that look, and I want to know what you're thinkin'."

He took a deep breath. He wasn't used to sharing his feelings, although Lorraine was good at getting him to talk when he didn't want to. But those times somehow felt like he was being backed into a corner, and the only way out was agreeing with his wife. "I'm thinkin' you're not listening to me."

She circled her arms around his broad frame and laid her head on his chest. "I don't mean to do that, Ike. Tell me what you're thinkin'. Please."

"Where's the sense in puttin' your kidnapper up at our place?"

"I guess it don't make much sense, I just feel bad for him. He don't have anyone in his corner. Told me his father used to beat him regular. Part of me wants him to be around you to see how a real man treats his family. Maybe some of you will rub off on him before he gets in real trouble."

Ike stared off into the distance.

"Think about your father. He was someone you looked up to. Admired. What if he hadn't been in your life? Would you be the man you are today? Maybe together we can help Bert still make something of himself. It's not too late."

An image of his parents flashed through his mind. There wasn't a day that went by when he didn't think of them, especially the times his father should have whupped him but didn't. Maybe Lorraine was right, maybe it was time to pass on some of his good fortune. He drew a hand across his cheek and looked at her with a small smile. "Just don't be messin' up my tack room while you're fixin' up a place for him out there."

She pulled his face toward her with both hands and gave him a long, hard kiss. "Thank you, Ike."

He kissed her back. "My pleasure, ma'am." He tipped his hat and headed for the barn.

Buster met him there. "You look all straightened out, Ike. I guess that's what a good woman can do to a man when he's off-track."

"I ain't off track anymore, Buster. And you're right. I hit the jackpot when Lorraine said she'd marry me. As for Quincy"—he didn't think he could ever call him Bert—"he's gonna be stayin' with us for a while. Help him get settled in, willya?"

Buster looked at him sideways. "He is? Then all's forgiven?"

"The fact I'm lettin' him stay don't change what he did to Lorraine."

"Think we should start takin' him down range with us?"

"That might be a good idea sometime, but not yet. He don't know nothin' about wranglin'. Lorraine will keep him busy workin' around the place. I ain't ready to forgive and forget yet."

****

A couple days later, Buster sidled up to Ike by the corral. "Beautiful early summer day, ain't it?" He smiled up at his friend. Either he was getting shorter or Ike taller. He guessed the former.

Ike spoke without looking over at Buster. "What's on your mind, Buster? I know that look on your face well enough to know you ain't standin' there just to admire the scenery. Let's have it."

"Well now, can't a feller just keep a friend company?" Buster was drawing this out, which he knew would spin Ike up a bit.

"Company's one thing, that look of yours is another. Am I gonna have to get my bullwhip to pry it out of you?"

"You know a bullwhip couldn't make me talk if I had a mind not to, but it just so happens there is somethin' on my mind." He waited, enjoying testing Ike's patience. Finally, he said, "It's about Bert."

Ike pivoted toward Buster. "You mean Quincy? What about him? If I'm gonna have to drag somethin' about him out of you, I'd just as soon not." A flush rose from his neck to his face.

"Just thought you ought to know he's a real good worker. Lorraine says he does everything she asks him to do and does it right the first time. Doin' good work for me, too. Kind of reminds me of another little boy I heard did the same thing growin' up."

"You comparin' me and him? That's too thin, Buster."

"He's just a kid tryin' to find his way in rough country. He's scared as the dickens of you, too."

"I ain't out to scare him, just tryin' to figure out if he'll fit in." Ike took his hat off, swept a hand through his hair, and strode toward the house, his boots making a little deeper print in the ground than usual.

The next morning, he met Buster in the small tack room, where Buster and Quincy slept. In a voice loud enough for Quincy to hear, Ike said, "I'm headin' out on the Park floor today, Buster. Want to go with me?"

"You know I do, but what about Bert?"

"If he's as good a worker as you say he is, and as smart as he better be, then he won't get in any trouble here by himself." Ike didn't look at Quincy as he said it, but Buster did.

Buster held Quincy's gaze for a long moment. "Work on bustin' that new bronc today and muck the stalls, okay?" He turned and followed Ike to the stable.

As Ike approached, Ally bobbed her head, snorted, and pawed at the hay in her stall. He fed her an apple and led her out toward the corral. When the two friends were mounted, Ike nudged his warhorse, and they made fresh tracks in the morning dew that sparkled over the wide basin where the herd grazed.

Buster was the first to spot the other horse prints near the cattle. "Look here, Ike." He pointed to marks that had pierced the moisture that lay on top of the low grasses. "That's horse prints. And unshod ones, too." He glanced at the foothills to the west. "I'm guessin' the Utes, on account of where the tracks lead. They were here not more'n an hour or so ago by the look of things. May be watchin' us right now."

Ike scanned the valley floor. "Can't tell for sure, but it don't look like any of our beeves are missin'. Guess some of them could be up in the far timber there." He pointed toward the western hills.

"If it's the Utes, there wouldn't be any gone. Rain Water wouldn't raid your herd. Even though he don't like you, I think he respects you 'cause of how you handled yourself trying to rescue Sue. And he wouldn't steal from someone he respects."

Ike rubbed at his stubbly beard. "Well, even if he don't respect me, I respect him. I'm beholden to him, too, for lettin' Sue go. I left him a cow earlier this spring, maybe he remembers my brand from there."

Buster eyed the hills with a faraway look. "You can be sure he does. Rain Water has a long memory."

They finished getting a rough count of the herd as the sun peaked high overhead. Lorraine packed them a lunch of jerky, biscuits, and coffee that they sat down to in the shade of their horses. A little stream gurgled nearby, and a slight wind made the new grasses bend as they ate. The basin had its own stark beauty, framed on three sides by pine-covered hills.

Ike three-skipped a stone in the water. "Are we ever gonna make a go of this place, Buster?"

Buster sat up straighter. "Don't know what you mean. Seems to me we're makin' a good go of it now."

Ike picked a delicate, small purple wildflower and examined it up close. "Maybe, but I ain't providin' like I want to for my family."

"Maybe you ought to put a 'yet' at the end of that thought. Think how far you've come in a short time.

You didn't have nothin' when you got here from Kansas four years ago, and now you got a wife, a child, and another on the way. You've got a workin' ranch and friends, Ike. Not to mention Ally. You even got a cat. Seems to me life's been pretty good to you."

Ike stared at the broad South Park expanse that was donning its summer garb. "I know you're right, Buster. Sometimes I lose sight of all those things."

"That's okay, too. Likely you got to know what patience is before you recognize when it's gone. All those years in the mountains taught me a few things, and one of 'em is that impatience can be good in a man if it's aimed right. And from what I see, you've got good aim." The two men started to get up. "Of course, your aim ain't near as good as mine. I've seen you shoot."

They laughed as they mounted back up. The sun was teasing the mountaintops to the west by the time they left the basin. When they reached the corral, they unsaddled the horses and let them loose. In the ranch house, Lorraine was fixing dinner. Ike made her squirm with a kiss on the back of her neck. Jessie ran to her father and he caught her in his big arms, then acted like he was struggling to lift her. "I can't do it, Jessie. You're gettin' so big I can hardly lift you up anymore." With a few more pretend grunts, he finally raised her to where she could wrap her arms around his neck. Her big smile told Ike how much she loved their little game. His smile said the same thing.

He set her at the table as Lorraine stirred the night's venison stew in a large black pot. Buster settled into his chair next to Jessie. Suddenly, the youngster sprang up from the table wide-eyed and waited next to her mother. "Can I take it to Mr. Bert, Momma? Please?"

"How about you and me take it out to the tack room together? Come on."

Jessie fairly skipped her way out the door, causing Ike to watch in wonder. "What was that all about?"

Buster watched as well. "Not sure, but from the looks of it, she's taken a shine to Quincy for some reason."

They waited on eating for Lorraine and Jessie to return. Ike pushed himself up out of his chair when they came back in. He whispered to Lorraine as she took command of the stove again. "Why's Jessie interested in Quincy all of a sudden?"

"Likely it's because of what happened in the corral today." That's all she said as she gave him a perfectly-toasted piece of bread and sat.

He paused and forced himself to control his tone. "Are you gonna tell me what happened?"

She smiled her sugary smile, the one that always irritated him. "Why, I thought you'd never ask." She folded her napkin in her lap. "When Bert was getting ready to break that new horse, he threw a blanket on her, and she started buckin'. About then, Calico decided she wanted to see what was going on so she strolled into the corral under the bottom fence rail. Jessie ran after the cat, but she tripped on the rail and fell flat on her face just inside the corral. The horse was rearin' and pawin' the air near her—that's when Bert got between Jessie and the horse's hooves. He took a couple hits himself, one that got him pretty good on the shoulder, but he scooped Jessie up and away from the horse and out of the corral."

Ike looked over at his daughter whose face broke into a big grin. "And Calico's okay too, Daddy." With a child's nonchalance, she went back to eating her dinner.

Ike continued to stare at her, his mind racing with fear and relief. No way could he stand to have Lorraine or Jessie hurt. He sat back in his chair and said a silent prayer of thanks. Lorraine maintained eye contact with him. He nodded, got up, and walked out.

When he got to the tack room, Quincy was sitting on his small cot leaning over his food in the dim light of a solitary oil lamp. He was balancing his plate in his lap and eating with his off hand. One shoulder had a torn white sheet wrapped around it spotted with splotches of red. He popped off the bed when Ike came in and squirmed like a skittish colt.

"Sit, son." Ike lowered his long frame onto Buster's bunk nearby, and both men looked at each other for a moment. Ike shook his head. "I'm obliged to you for what you did to protect Jessie today." He stopped and pursed his lips hard. After a long pause, he cleared his throat. "I—thank you." As Ike rose from the cot, Quincy sprang up as well, nearly knocking his meal off the bed.

"Yes, sir."

A nod and Ike was out the door back to the house. Inside, Lorraine stood in front of him, hands on her hips. That always meant trouble. "Ike McAlister, you go back out there and invite Bert to sit dinner with us, and I mean it."

He looked at his wife in wonder. She always knew the exact right thing to do and say. He'd been working on accepting Quincy but hadn't gotten there yet. He didn't like to be pushed, but Lorraine was right. He walked slowly back to the stable. Quincy popped up again.

"Son, you keep jumpin' up like that, you're liable to never finish your dinner. Instead of springin' up and down out here, why don't you come inside and eat? That way, you'll only have to get up once." It was Ike's backhanded way of saying thanks again.

When Quincy came in, Lorraine had shifted everyone slightly so there was a narrow space for him at the small table. "Looks like you're gonna need to make a bigger table, Ike." This time her sugary smile had been replaced by a real one. She put Quincy opposite from Ike. No sense trying to push her husband too fast, too soon. That's when he dug his heels in. He was moving in the right direction, and that was good enough for now.

Chapter Twenty-Five

Hannah was getting the hang of the work at The Sew Pretty. In the short while she'd been there, Margaret's moods changed moment to moment from abrupt and distant, to domineering and miserable, but the woman was a good teacher. The shopkeeper taught her about the quality of different cloths, various weaves, color matching, and how to sew the most common stitches. Hannah had taken over some of the mending, allowing Margaret more personal time with her customers. All except the men. For some reason, she had Hannah deal with them.

The majority of customers were women though, mostly interested in the latest fashions and styles. Hannah wasn't permitted to sew for them yet, nor was she to touch the hats arrayed around the shop that were Margaret's calling card. She'd gotten used to Margaret's mumblings and outbursts if she'd done something to displease her. Which seemed to be most of the time.

Hannah withstood this daily tension well. She was well-acquainted with the raw underside of life but was determined to learn a trade and escape her past. Someday she might even own a shop like this, and not be at the beck and call of anyone else for her livelihood. She'd never work in a saloon again, unless she owned it.

She didn't get lunch breaks, so she looked forward to the end of the day. Lately, when Hannah left at closing time, Margaret didn't even return her cheery goodbyes. The shop keeper was becoming more and more withdrawn. Every day after work, Hannah made a beeline to Sue's boarding house, deliberately not even glancing at the Wildfire as she passed. Her nights in the saloon seemed like a lifetime ago, but still, not long enough. She tried to block her time there from her mind—the insults, the rude men, the drinking, and the groping, but the experience always teetered on the ragged edge of her consciousness.

Sue had given her a discounted rate for a small room in the back of the boarding house, which she adored. She finally had a place of her own, and the time spent talking with Sue about life and the future was priceless.

****

Sue was nobody's fool when it came to Hannah, though. She knew the girl could have easily been Rob's killer but still rented her a room. She and Hugh had more than one hushed argument upstairs about a prime murder suspect boarding below them. But she'd always trusted her instincts, and they hadn't failed her. So far.

Sue had a couple of reasons why she wanted to stay close to Hannah. If the girl did kill Rob, then perhaps she could get her to reveal that by appearing to be her confidant. Even though Sue was only a few years older than her boarder, there was no question Hannah looked up to her. The other reason was that if Hannah were innocent, then perhaps she could offer her some hope. From what she knew, the girl's life seemed a sad mixture of disappointments and crushed dreams.

When they sat and chatted, Sue usually knitted to set her boarder at ease and asked questions that encouraged Hannah to open up. One morning at breakfast Hannah was in a talkative mood. As she sipped coffee, she said, "Miss Margaret—she seems unhappy, has she always been that way?"

Sue put more eggs on the young girl's plate, unsure where this was leading. "What makes you ask that?"

"It's just that she's always on edge. There doesn't seem to be anything I do that's right."

Sue sat across from her at the table. "Likely it doesn't have anything to do with you, Hannah. She's still grieving about Rob in her own way, and you're just the closest target."

"Do you think so? That would make sense. All of a sudden, she'll shout something and follow that with tears. She mumbles to herself a lot, too. She's a hard one to figure out all right." In between mouthfuls she asked, "Has your husband found out any more about who the killer might be?"

Sue's antennae went up. The girl's eyes were fixed on her plate. "I don't know. He doesn't tell me much about what he's found out, if anything, for fear it'll upset me, I suppose." She wasn't ready to reveal more to Hannah until she knew the young woman's heart. "He did say he's uncovered some new information that may lead to the killer." It was a lie, but she glanced in Hannah's direction to gauge her reaction.

Small crow's feet appeared around the girl's eyes as they narrowed at that news, but they disappeared just as quickly. "Well, that sounds like a good thing." She folded her cloth napkin, placed it next to her plate, then stood and excused herself. "I must be going. Miss

Margaret will be wondering where I am."

Sue tensed. "It's still early, dear, you have time."

"Thank you for the fine breakfast, ma'am, but I best be getting on," she said with a wan smile and turned back toward her room.

Sue watched her disappear—an unsettling feeling forming in her stomach. Hannah had definitely reacted just then. Was she involved in Rob's death, or was she just an interested bystander? She ached to know.

****

Hugh's own investigation had been ongoing. He'd talked with all the regulars in the Wildfire but hadn't uncovered anything new of importance. Rob was on his evening rounds when he was killed. The saloon was still in full swing then, but he hadn't been able to find any eyewitnesses to the shooting. Surely someone would have stepped forward by now if they'd seen anything. He didn't know if someone was hiding information or even if he was conducting a proper search. He'd done investigations for the railroad, but he'd never hunted a killer. Hawkins was still his main suspect, but the railroader wasn't his only one. There was Hannah, too. She'd had a serious enough dustup with Rob that she couldn't be counted out.

Hugh expressed his displeasure to Sue about the girl's boarding with them again one morning. He whispered, "It does not seem proper that one of the main suspects should sleep under our roof while I am investigating Rob's murder. I may be new at this, but I am sure that is not standard procedure."

Sue was adamant, though. "While you're searching for the killer, we may have her right here. I'm going to keep her close in case I can pry something out of her that a scary sheriff can't. I don't know if she's friend or foe at this point, but I bet I find out before you do."

Hugh was taken aback at his wife's intensity and reasoning. Why a potential killer would open up to her landlady was beyond him, but he knew when to give in, however puzzling the logic. "Would you please tell Hannah I would like to spend a few minutes with her? At the jail."

Later, as Sue served Hannah breakfast, she said, "Stop by and see my husband sometime this morning, will you?"

Hannah's eyes widened. "Certainly…yes, I will. Do you know what he wants?"

Sue put a plate of hotcakes in front of her. "No. He didn't say, and I didn't ask."

****

Hugh had been waiting for her at the jail. It was past noon when she came in. He calmed himself and motioned to a chair. "Did my wife mention I wanted to see you this morning?"

"Yes, sir, she did." She kept eye contact with him but shifted slightly in her seat.

"Well, then, why…" He stopped. Starting off by haranguing her wouldn't put her in the best mood to answer his questions. He sat behind his desk and steepled his fingers in front of him. "I just have a few more questions about the night Rob was killed. What do you remember?"

"Well, I was working the floor that night, like I usually did, getting the regulars to buy me drinks. I'd go fetch them from Nick at the bar. He'd water mine down so I could keep up with the men. Some of them can really throw 'em back." She smiled, but her eyes didn't.

"Did you stay on the floor all night?"

"Yes. I never spent time in the rooms upstairs, if that's what you're asking. Not that I had anything against the ladies who did or what they did…"

"The mayor said you and Rob had a loud conversation. What was that all about?"

"It wasn't much. I told him I never wanted to see him again."

"So, you were angry." He let the inference lay there between them.

Hannah didn't rise to it, only saying, "Yes, I was."

"How long were you there?"

"For my usual hours. I got off at midnight."

The sheriff nodded. "Did you leave the Wildfire then?"

"Yes, but I was real careful. It's dangerous that time of night. Lots of men who'd just stumbled out of the saloon."

"Was anyone else with you?"

"No, not that I recall."

"So no one else who can corroborate your whereabouts?" It wasn't a friendly question.

"No, sir."

"When you went outside, did you hear anything? Shots?"

"No, our piano player plays good and loud, mostly loud, so there's probably no way I could have heard anything right outside."

"Anything else you can tell me?"

"No, I don't think so."

"Anything else you want to tell me?" He held her captive with a hard stare.

"I didn't kill him, if that's what you think. He was the only one around here who treated me good. Up until..." She left the sentence hanging in the air.

"Would you like to finish that thought?" When Hannah shook her head, he rose and stood stiffly in front of her. "Thank you for your time."

Hannah stood, curtsied slightly, and turned to leave. As she grasped the door handle, he said, "Do not leave Cottonwood, Hannah. I may have other questions." She paused, then was out the door.

When he got back to the boarding house that night, Hannah wasn't there. He kissed Sue, then looked around. "Have you seen Hannah?"

"Not since this morning. Why?"

"Isn't she usually back from the dress shop by now?"

Sue scrunched her eyebrows. "Yes, normally. She could still be at the shop though. Sometimes Margaret works her later than usual."

Hugh put his hat on. "I will be back momentarily, but no need to wait up for me if I'm not." As he walked toward The Sew Pretty, he looked for a light within. At the front window, he glimpsed a faint glow at the rear of the shop. There, hunched over a piece of cloth, was Hannah. Satisfied, he returned to the boarding house.

Sue was waiting on the front porch. "Is she still there?"

He nodded. "Yes, working away."

"Why did you ask about her?"

"I questioned her today but did not uncover anything new. She denied shooting Rob. I have the feeling I will not get much more than that, either." He hesitated to tell Sue Hannah had a secret she shared with Rob. As he glanced at his wife, he wasn't sure why.

Sue said, "I'd like you to please steer clear of her now and give me a chance to get her to open up. I'm probably the only person around here she considers a friend. Likely there's things she wants to get off her chest, and I'm gonna let her." She maintained strong eye contact, a sign he knew well.

****

Ike passed Buster on his way to the tack room.

"Ike, we're done for the day, and I tidied things up already. Come set with me and play some checkers."

"I got other things on my mind, but thanks."

Just then, Lorraine came into the barn. "Buster, you tell him there ain't no sense goin' into town this late. Nothin' good can come of it."

"Goin' to town? What's got into you, Ike?"

"Nothin'."

"I seen that look on your face before, and I didn't like it then and I don't like it now. Lorraine's right. Ain't nothin' in town can't wait 'til morning."

"I'll not be put off any longer. There's been no findin' out who shot Rob yet. Time that debt was paid. It's overdue."

"Hasn't been that long since Rob was shot, Ike, why—" As soon as he said it, he stopped and rubbed a hand over his mouth. "I'm sorry, I..." His voice faded into nothing.

Ike felt a flush run up his neck. Not that long? It seemed like an eternity. Rob was probably looking down at him right now, wondering why he hadn't caught his killer yet since he knew who it was. He turned away. Better to say nothing than something he'd regret later. He bridled Ally and led her out into the coming dusk. The sun had disappeared some time ago in a blazing ball behind the mountains, and a faint orange tinge still stretched like fingers across the darkening sky.

Lost in thought, he gave Ally loose rein as he rode. The next thing he knew he was approaching the outskirts of Cottonwood. He had a good idea where he'd find Hawkins. After a labored dismount, he tied Ally off on a rail outside the Wildfire. The noise inside almost drowned out the piano. He swung the saloon doors apart and surveyed the place. Hawkins was holding court at a nearby table, with Slade looking over his shoulder. One or both cheating for sure.

The piano player stopped, and the room fell silent. Hawkins looked up just about the time Ike knocked his chair over with him in it. Ike aimed his Colt at Slade's chest before the gunman could draw on him. "Drop your gun belt and move away. This don't have nothin' to do with you." For effect, he fired a shot that whizzed past Slade's ear. Ike motioned with his gun again, and Slade unbuckled his belt and stepped aside. Ike kicked it away.

Hawkins was on the floor, his gun some distance away, with Ike aimed at his head. Hammer cocked. "Get up and get your hands high. Move!"

Hawkins cast a sinister glance at Slade, who stood with his arms folded and gun ten feet away. "Do something! What the hell am I paying you for?"

Slade stood motionless. "I did something."

"You didn't do anything!"

"I did what he told me. It's hard to be a hero with no gun. Like you right now."

Ike motioned to a cowboy standing next to Slade. "Toss his gun to Nick at the bar." He waved his weapon at the men near Slade. "The rest of you, move or get shot."

Men hurried to the door and disappeared. Others stood where they were to see the spectacle. Slade still stood with his arms folded across his chest.

Ike motioned to Hawkins again to get up.

"I don't have a gun, McAlister. Even you wouldn't shoot an unarmed man."

"Somebody throw him a gun so he won't be beggin' anymore. Never did cotton to a beggar." He glanced at a nearby miner with dirty overalls and blackened hands. "You. Give him your gun."

The man moved toward Hawkins but stopped when someone yelled, "Ike!"

Ike knew the voice. The sheriff stood in the saloon doorway, gun drawn. "Put your gun away, Ike. Hawkins, move away. Slade, pretend you are a statue." He eased toward the three combatants and gathered Hawkins' and Slade's guns. "Ike, back away and come outside with me."

"No. I'm gonna settle this now."

The sheriff moved between Ike and Hawkins and stood with his chest hard against Ike's barrel. "This is not the way to do this. Come with me, please, before you do something you will regret."

Ike hesitated, and Hawkins took the opportunity to back away. The sheriff took Ike by the arm and led him toward the front doors. Ike kept his pistol trained on Hawkins as he stepped away. "You don't need to cheat to win at cards tonight, Hawkins, 'cause this is your lucky day." The doors swung apart, and the two disappeared into the evening. Piano music tinkled again in the smoky air.

Ike stared straight ahead as they walked down the darkened street.

Hugh said, "What the hell were you thinking?"

Ike's expression hardened. "Don't take that tone with me, Hugh. It's been time enough, and you're no closer to catchin' Rob's killer than when he was first gunned down. I figured to stir the pot some 'cause it looked like it needed stirrin'."

"Sorry. I should have come and told you I questioned Hawkins yesterday."

Ike wasn't ready to let his anger go yet. "You talked with Hawkins and didn't tell me?" Fire rose in his neck in the darkness. "I was gonna kill him in there. Likely I still will."

"I know. I heard a shot and came running."

Brisk evening air was beginning to cool Ike as they neared Sue's. "From now on, you keep me posted on things, all right?" He took a deep breath, and his voice took on a calmer tone. "Sorry I yelled at you, but what did Hawkins say?"

The tension in the sheriff's voice also dropped a notch. "Nothing new, but he did deny killing Rob."

"Not a surprise. Anything else?"

"There might have been. He made a sideways remark about the women in Rob's life, but it was not clear what he meant."

"Doesn't surprise me he would try to pin the murder on someone else." Ike paused. "Just a friendly warning; find somethin' that ties Hawkins to the murder soon, or you won't have to worry about investigating him anymore." At the boarding house, Ike untied Ally and mounted up.

"Now Ike, leave Hawkins to me and the law. I mean it. Stay out of this."

With a hand to his hat, Ike swung Ally south and faded into the dark.

Hugh yelled after his friend. "Ike! Ike! Damn it!"

Chapter Twenty-Six

Hannah was late for work again. She always meant to be on time, but she wasn't a morning person. Never mind the many evenings she worked late into the night after Margaret retired, she always faced an irritable employer in the morning. She was usually at the shop only a few minutes after eight, but Margaret made it sound like she'd missed half the day.

"I was beginning to think something had happened to you. I stopped by the sheriff's office and notified him of your disappearance."

Hannah knew she really hadn't. Margaret was just trying to irritate her. It was working. She didn't know how much longer she could put up with Margaret's odd behavior—her barbs that often turned into mumblings, followed by sniffles. The woman couldn't seem to make up her mind if she was happy, sad, or neither. Hannah just tried to stay out of her way.

She liked learning a new craft. The sewing was fine, but the best part was working with customers and designing clothes. Little chance she got at that. Margaret always swept in when a female customer came into The Sew Pretty, as if Hannah wasn't there. Sometimes Hannah dreamed, imagining this was her own shop. She felt like she'd found a calling, as different as it was from the Wildfire. Strange that Rob's death had been the catalyst for her to leave those days behind.

During one of Hannah's daydreams, Margaret interrupted with a sharp question. "Whatever are you doing? You sit there all day, never saying much, and I can't tell what you're thinking. It's enough to unnerve a body. Speak up, child. Say something."

Hannah steeled herself for one of Margaret's ill-tempered moods. "Yes, ma'am. I was just thinking how pretty the shop looks. You've done such a good job decorating."

Margaret raised an eyebrow. "I don't know if you're making fun of me or not. Why would you say such a thing?"

Hannah didn't want to egg Margaret on, so she fell silent. She finally felt like she was mastering some of the mending. When miners came in, Hannah did their work. Mostly simple patch work on torn clothes, sometimes making new shirts or pants, which she hadn't quite mastered yet. She fashioned some lopsided articles of clothing early on, but the miners didn't seem to mind. Most were eyeing her, rather than her work. Some were very good looking. They usually came to town on the weekends and dropped items off then. She made sure she was there on Saturdays to greet them. Whatever they were mining was taking a toll on their clothing though, especially their cotton pants. When the clothes were too far gone, she made jeans for them instead.

"Hannah! I asked you a question." Margaret's shout broke her reverie.

"I'm sorry, ma'am. What was it?" Part of Hannah liked irritating Margaret, and as she became more comfortable with her work, Hannah enjoyed it more.

Maybe she'd open a competing shop some day. The town was growing so fast it could probably support it.

"Oh, you are so annoying at times. Honestly!" Margaret strode to the front of the store where her best hats hung. She traced a shaking finger around the brim of her favorite, a blue creation from Paris. Mumbles followed, then little unintelligible chirps. Sniffles.

Hannah stopped her sewing. She had other things to worry about besides Margaret. She was still one of two prime suspects in Rob's death. Her talk with the sheriff confirmed that. There was more that pointed to her other than Rob dumping her and the shattered whiskey glass. The uncomfortable fact was she didn't have an alibi. She really didn't have much of anything going for her. At least Sue was her friend. She'd been so nice in renting her a small room for so little. Then a different thought occurred to her.

Why had Sue been so nice? She had no cause to be. She'd just lost her brother, perhaps at Hannah's hand. Did Sue have another reason for befriending her? She did ask Hannah lots of questions and let her ramble on. Was she scheming against her? No, she wouldn't do that; she was far too nice. But Hannah had been around enough to know when someone wanted something from her. Or did she? She'd have to be more careful.

****

In the morning, Sue was up before the sun. She was always first to wake, even before her lawman husband. His late rounds had something to do with that. She was busy preparing breakfast when Hugh came in.

"Morning, dear. Looks like it is going to be a lovely day in the Park." He filled his coffee cup.

"Always is," she said. The smell of bacon sizzling

on the stove filled the kitchen. "How's your investigation going?"

Hugh hushed his wife. "Quiet, please. We cannot be talking about that with Hannah just down the hall."

"Don't worry, she always sleeps in. Early on, I tried to get her up so she'd be at work on time, but I've given up on that."

"Still, I am not comfortable—"

"Hugh." She said it a little louder than she intended. "Sorry." She lowered her voice. "Just tell me something. Anything."

Hugh glanced down the hall, then spoke in a whisper. "Well, I didn't want to worry you, but I had a confrontation with your brother in town yesterday. He cornered Hawkins and Slade in the Wildfire, ready to shoot one or both. Fortunately, I got there in time to head it off, but Ike seems determined to face Hawkins one way or the other." He eased into a chair at the table.

Sue's eyes widened. "You can't let that happen. You can't let me lose both my brothers. You've said Hawkins is faster on the draw than Ike." She placed a full plate of eggs, bacon, and toast in front of him. Topped off his coffee.

"I am not sure how to stop Ike. You know what he is like when he sets his mind to something. I also spent some time with our boarder, questioning her about where she was when Rob was shot. She does not have a good alibi, but that does not mean she is the killer." He turned his attention to his food which was still steaming.

In between bites, Sue said, "I've been trying to get her to open up to me, but so far there's not been much." An ever-so-slight sound came from the back of the house, which halted their conversation. Sue whispered, "Did you hear that?"

"Not sure it was anything other than the noise an old house makes waking up in the morning."

"Well, I got better things to do than to listen to this place groan." She cleared their dishes. "Think I'll call on the town seamstress."

Chapter Twenty-Seven

Ike and Buster were on the Park floor herding cattle when Ike caught sight of them. He turned to Buster with a low whistle and jerked his head toward the western foothills. Five Indians sat mounted in a tight semi-circle just this side of the pine forest. Ike couldn't tell from this distance if Rain Water was among them, but their leather leggings said they were Utes, that much he did know.

"Don't know what they're sittin' there for." Buster squinted at the braves. "That's not like them, their huntin' style calls for hit and run, not hit and sit."

Ike broke into a small grin. "You must not be too worried if you're makin' bad jokes with those warriors that close." Ike glanced at the setting sun. "About time to be headin' back, Buster, but I don't like the looks of those Indians. Somethin's not right about them just showin' up and sittin' there."

"They're there for a reason. I been around 'em long enough to know that. Don't look like a war party, no paint I can see from here, but they don't do what they're doin' for nothin'. I'd almost say we should ride on out of here, but—"

Ike broke in. "But your curiosity's up, too, isn't it?"

"That it is."

"Let's ride their way. Slow. I'm gonna rest my rifle

271

upward on my leg, like they're doin'."

Buster nodded and the two men nudged their horses into a walk toward the Indians. The braves didn't move as the two drew near. "Dunno if it's good or bad that they're still just sittin' there. Never seen Utes act like that."

"Well, you should know. You spent enough time with 'em over the years." Ike kept his eyes on the brave in the middle.

Buster said, "Those days are distant memories now."

Ike drew Ally up about twenty feet in front of the warriors. He raised a hand. "Why do you sit here?"

None of the Indians moved, but the one in the middle swept an arm in a wide arc. "Ute land."

Buster squinted at him. The brave was older and looked like one of the Indians he knew years ago, but then again, his eyes weren't as sharp as they used to be. He ignored the brave's claim. "What do you want?"

The middle brave stared silently at him.

Buster's eyes widened. "You are...Dark...Wolf... friend of Rain Water."

The Indian didn't say no. He only said, "Kiska dies," then waited.

"Kiska?" Buster turned to Ike. "Wasn't that the name of the Ute squaw who nursed Sue when she was wounded? Saved her life."

"I remember." Ike's gaze was fixed on the middle warrior. The Indian had pronounced sun-browned cheekbones and wore a tan buckskin shirt that his long black hair lay on. The other braves kept their eyes on him.

The riders stared across from each other for a

moment, then Dark Wolf spoke. "Yellow-hair woman."

Ike tilted in his saddle toward Buster. "What does that mean?"

Buster said in a low voice, "It means just what you think it means. Kiska has asked to see Sue."

Ike leaned well forward in the saddle. "Well, it don't matter if it does mean that. Sue's not goin' anywhere near Rain Water's camp."

"Wait just a minute; don't rule that out yet. This is an important thing Kiska asked. Since the warriors are here, Rain Water must have agreed to it. Very rare. White women are not allowed in a Ute camp, and yet Kiska asks for Sue. Must not have been an easy thing for Rain Water to agree to."

"Don't care, that ain't happenin', so just forget it." Ike wasn't going to let his only sister ride into what could turn out to be a death trap. Ever since Rob died, he'd doubled down on what he felt was his obligation to watch over her.

"Now Ike, think on this for a second. The chief sent these braves to bring Sue to camp. She'd be under their protection the whole time."

"She's got all the protection she needs right here." He fingered his Colt. The braves stirred and lowered their rifles at Ike.

Buster raised a hand and nodded toward Dark Wolf. "We will meet you here tomorrow when the sun climbs over those mountains." He pointed to the east. The brave sat motionless. Buster turned his horse toward Ike. "Let's go before we get an answer we don't like, or you get us both killed!"

As they set off for the ranch, Ike slowed Ally to a walk. He didn't want Dark Wolf to think he was running from them.

Buster broke the silence as they rode. "I know you're tryin' to keep Sue safe, but ain't this her decision?"

"No, it ain't, and neither of us are gonna tell her about Kiska—this is between me and her."

"That's as it may be, Ike, but this ain't your decision either."

"It is if I make it mine, and I don't want you sayin' any more about it, hear?" His heart pounded in his ears, and his mouth felt cottony.

They rode the rest of the way in silence. When they dismounted and released the horses in the corral, they still weren't speaking to each other. Dinner that night was chilly as well. Ike held tight to his secret, but it had started to burn inside him, almost like it was struggling to get out.

Finally, Lorraine sat back in her chair and looked at him. "What's eatin' you, husband? Speakin' of eatin', your plate's still near full, and that ain't like you. My cookin' ain't that bad. And you, Buster, you ain't said a word since you came in." She put her fork down and told Jessie to go play with her dolly. "Now out with it, Ike. What's gnawin' at you?"

"I'm fine; nothin's wrong."

Lorraine swiveled to Buster. "Tell me true, Buster, what happened out there today?" She pointed toward the Park basin as she spoke. When Buster kept his eyes fixed on his plate, she stood up. "You two are startin' to scare me. What's happened that's thrown you off your feed? Out with it, Ike. Please."

Ike tossed his napkin on the table and got up to leave, but Lorraine's next words gave him pause.

"Don't leave this table right now, Ike McAlister. Don't you dare leave this table, or you'll regret it." Her voice was hard, but her eyes were moist.

Ike stopped and dropped his gaze to the floor. Buster rose as well, followed by Lorraine. The three of them stood like figurines, all unwilling to speak. Finally, the words tumbled out of Ike in rapid-fire fashion. "Rain Water sent five braves to tell us the Ute woman Kiska is dying and asked to see Sue. There, that's about the size of it." His hands had gone clammy.

Lorraine brought a hand to her mouth. "Oh, Lord." She sagged into her chair. "Lordy. What are you going to do, Ike?"

Ike drew in a long breath. "Well, I ain't gonna tell her, that's for sure." He didn't look at Lorraine or Buster—he didn't want to see their reactions. But then he stared their way and waggled a finger at them. "And nobody here is gonna tell her either, got it?"

Lorraine came and put an arm around his waist. "You know that ain't the right thing to do. I can tell you're torn up because you know it, too." She held him gently and laid her head on his chest. She put his hand on her stomach. "Family is family, and secrets will tear a family apart. I know your heart, and I know this would rip your insides out after a while if you didn't tell Sue. And she'd find out, sometime, somehow, anyway. You know she would; she's *your* sister."

Ike wrapped an arm around his wife. He tried to hold them off, but tears escaped his tall, lean frame. The thought of Sue in danger terrified him.

Buster looked away.

Ike couldn't speak. His lips quivered, and he nodded at Lorraine, then held her for a moment longer.

He shook his head and kissed her on the cheek, then picked Jessie up and held her tightly. After he put her down, he picked up his hat, whacked it against his jeans, and headed silently out the front door.

Lorraine hurried after him. "You ride careful now, Ike McAlister, 'cause I'll be lookin' out this window for you until you get back."

Buster followed Ike to the corral. They saddled up silently, and Ike headed Ally toward town. He was going to see this through before he changed his mind. He'd never set out to do something he dreaded as much as this in his whole life. Even fighting during the war was easier than this.

The ride flew by with Ike lost in thought. Soon, the early evening lamps of Cottonwood glittered softly before them. The wind picked up and blew small dust devils along Main Street as they rode in. Ike pulled Ally up at the boarding house and limped up the front steps. He pulled the door open without knocking and strode into the dining room, where Sue was serving a young woman and two other boarders. Hugh sat at the head of the table.

Sue's eyes flew wide. "Ike, what are you doing here this late?"

Ike reached out for her hand. "I need to talk to you. Will you come into the parlor?"

"Sure, but—"

The young woman spoke up. "I can finish feeding everyone, Sue. You go on now."

Ike led her into the front room. "Please sit, Sis."

"You're scaring me. Whatever is the matter?"

His stomach jumped. "Me and Buster had visitors today out on the range. Five Utes appeared out of nowhere, waitin' until we rode over to them." Ike wiped at his mouth and licked his lips. "Buster knew one of 'em from years back. He said Rain Water sent them." He broke eye contact with his sister and stared at the wall.

Sue cut in. "What for?"

"The Indian said Kiska is dying and asked for you." His heart leapt in his chest, and his ears pounded. He wanted to clench his teeth so he couldn't say more.

"What?" Sue dropped heavily on the divan. "She's dying? What's wrong with her?"

"I don't know; they didn't say." Ike dreaded what he guessed Sue was going to say next. By this time, Hugh and Buster had come into the room, too.

Sue said, "I'll start out first thing in the morning."

She began to leave for the dining room, but Ike held her arm as she went past. "You can't go, Sue. It's too dangerous; you almost died last time you were in that camp."

"I did not! The only reason I survived that gunshot wound was because of Kiska, and I'm going and you know I mean it, Ike, so we'll have no more talk about that."

Ike slapped his thigh. "Damn! I knew it. I *knew* you'd say that. You're so stubborn! Always have been, but this time I'm askin' you to listen to your big brother for once."

Hugh broke in. "I'm with Ike on this, dear. If she is dying, you are not going to be able to change that by going to see her."

Sue stuck her chin out. "You stay out of this as well. I'm not going to save her. I'm going to say my goodbyes. Now help me figure out what I'm gonna need to take."

Hugh said, "Then I'll go with you. We'll—"

Sue waved him off. "That don't make any sense. Kiska didn't ask for you; she asked for me. Besides, you got sheriffing as well as this house to tend to while I'm gone."

"I'll take you there, Sue." Buster stood slightly stooped to one side.

"No, you won't. Remember, Rain Water said he'd kill you on sight if you ever came to his camp again, even if he was your friend once."

"Sorry, I don't remember that," Buster lied, "and if he ever said it, he's probably forgotten it by now anyway."

Ike broke in. "Enough of this. I'll be the one to go with her. That's all there is. We'll have no more discussion about it."

Sue started to argue but hadn't gotten more than two words out when Ike wrapped his arms around her. He whispered, "Don't try to talk me out of it, Sis. I'm goin' with you, and that's that. I could never let you go alone. And I know Ma and Pa are lookin' down right now, agreein' about me goin' with you, so you have to say yes."

There was no getting around that for Sue. She looked at her big brother and nodded. Morning would see them both on the trail.

Chapter Twenty-Eight

Ike didn't sleep well that night. He tossed and turned until the first glimmers of dawn stole through the ranch house's bedroom window. That was long enough. He tiptoed out of the room holding his pants, shoes, boots, and gun belt. In the kitchen, he packed a sizeable bag of jerky and ground coffee. Flour and a couple of hard boiled eggs filled out his kit. He'd water up and grab his bedroll in the tack room.

A cool fog hung low on the Park floor. The early morning mist would be scattered as soon as the sun woke up, but for now Ike made swirls in it as he strode to the barn. Inside, Buster was arranging their saddlebags. Ike stuck his thumbs in his jeans. "Buster, I don't want to fight with you. You know I'm the one to go. She's my sister."

Buster looked over at his friend. "I should go, not you. I'm old and wore out. Losin' me won't make nobody any difference and besides, I used to count Rain Water as a friend, and him me. He wouldn't really hurt me."

Ike knew what he was trying to do but wasn't in the mood for it. "He didn't just hurt you last time, he almost killed you. If Sue hadn't nursed you, you wouldn't be here right now, losin' an argument with me."

"You just said it yourself, Ike. She saved my life. I

owe her, so I'm the one ought to be goin'."

Ike knew he could spark a big fight that ended with Buster not going and their friendship damaged. For once though, he'd back off bluster and try leaning on that friendship. "I'm askin' you as a friend not to go. I need you here to watch the place and look after Lorraine and Jessie. I'd take it kindly if you'd do me the favor of stayin'. I need to know my family's okay. Please."

That was about the only thing that could have kept Buster from going, hearing his friend's heartfelt appeal. He pursed his lips and slowly nodded. "All right. I'll let you trade on our friendship this one time, but I will ride to the edge of the foothills with you and Sue."

Sue and Hugh's horses were outside by the time Ike and Buster settled things. Sue held her brother's gaze hard. "You can't go, Ike. Rain Water said he'd kill you if you ever came back."

Ike kept saddling Ally. "Last night you said you're goin', and that was all there was to it. Well, just like you, I'm goin', and that's all there is to it." The two McAlisters stared at each other until Sue's shoulders slumped. "All right. Let's get going then." She turned to Buster. "By the looks of your face, I can tell you're not goin'."

"Partway."

Lorraine came out of the house to send Ike and Sue off. Jessie skipped behind her, trailing a piece of string which Calico chased. Lorraine put her hands on her hips in her familiar way. "Time's a wastin'. If you're goin', best get to it 'cause you're burnin' daylight." She reached up to Ike and gave him a long, teary hug.

"Ain't you gonna punch me on the arm?" His smile

made her do the same. "Give me a goodbye whack for luck?"

She struck him lightly on the shoulder. "There, that should keep you safe."

His smile widened, and he kissed her gently. He swung Jessie into the air, and she dissolved into giggles and he set her down. "Buster will be back directly, dear. Keep the home fires burnin', I'll see you in a few days."

Everyone knew that was likely a lie.

The three mounted up and struck out for the place the Indians appeared yesterday, Ike in the lead. After a hard ride, a warming sun was well over the eastern horizon when they drew near the foothills. Ike slowed and asked Buster to stay behind. Ike and Sue rode slowly toward the pines, the fresh smell of new sage floating in the air. Would the Utes be there? It likely wasn't a hoax as Ike had never met an Indian with a sense of humor.

Before long, Dark Wolf appeared out of the forest shadows, flanked by four braves. His eyes narrowed, and he aimed a painted lance at Ike. "Go."

Ike straightened in the saddle. "I mean you no harm, Dark Wolf, I only want to ride with my sister as she visits Kiska. Rain Water knows I am a man of my word."

"Go!"

Ike sat straighter in the saddle. "I will not!" He jabbed a finger at Dark Wolf. "I challenge you to a fight for the right to ride with my sister. You would not shun a fight, would you?" His gestures made plain what his words meant.

Uncertainty appeared on Dark Wolf's face, as the

four braves behind him shifted on their ponies and mumbled. The Indian raised his lance. He pointed to a young warrior to his right, who leaped off his horse. The muscled youth brandished a tomahawk high in the air. Dark Wolf turned toward Ike. "Fight."

Sue screamed at Dark Wolf. "Do not hurt him, or I will not go!"

Dark Wolf silently turned his horse toward the foothills.

"Wait!" she pleaded. "I'll go with you, alone." She turned to her brother. "Please don't try to follow me. Rain Water's not gonna have me escorted to his village to harm me."

Ike felt his cheeks flush, but he kept his temper in check and backed off. He stared at Sue for a moment, then Dark Wolf, before he eased Ally away from the young brave in front of him. Sue looked back as she disappeared into the pines. Ike rode Ally back and forth gesturing at the lone Indian Dark Wolf left behind to block his way. The Indian was getting agitated, and Ike taunted him some more, then swung Ally in the direction of the ranch at a dead gallop, rifle waving in the air. He looked back to see the Indian start to mount up. By then, he had a good head start and after several minutes, pulled up behind a low hogback where Buster was hiding. He shouted, "Keep ridin' toward the ranch like you're me. Hopefully, that'll throw him off my trail. While he's chasin' after you, I'll circle back and catch up with Sue."

Buster nodded. "Just stay out of sight. Dark Wolf will kill you if he finds you trailin' him."

"I'll hang back far enough so that won't happen. Go on now. Thanks."

Buster lit out for the ranch just as the Indian crested a hillock in the distance behind them. Ike hoped they were far enough away so the brave would think Buster was him. Minutes later, the Indian rode past as Ike hid in a juniper thicket. Ike turned Ally toward the low hills again. Dark Wolf shouldn't be hard to track. So far, everything was working out like he'd hoped. Maybe the toughest part was behind him.

****

Sue rode in the middle of the braves. Dark Wolf led, flanked by a warrior on either side, with two more behind her. Daylight was finding it hard to penetrate the dense forest as they weaved upward in the dark green realm. As the land grew steeper, they switched to single file. The calendar said early summer, but a cool briskness still dominated the shade of the forest. Sue pulled a small blanket from her saddlebag and threw it around her shoulders even as the Indians continued to ride in thin deerskin vests.

She kept looking back to make sure Ike hadn't followed her. She was both relieved and scared when she didn't see him. Sue wanted to see Kiska before she died, yet was unsure how smart that was. She didn't try to speak to Dark Wolf as they traveled. She didn't know how much English he knew, but likely he wouldn't answer anyway. If camp was still in the same high valley as it was four years ago, the trek would take nearly two days, even with the Indians' thorough knowledge of the land.

The first night they camped in a high meadow along a fast-running stream that pitched headlong down the face of the mountain. This was Ute hunting ground, and they were at ease as they sat cross-legged around a small fire with stars popping out in a clear dark canvas above. Sue fished her biscuits out along with some homemade jam she'd bought at O'Toole's. She forgot to pack coffee. The braves ignored her as she sat outside their fire circle. Whatever they were cooking in that clay bowl smelled delicious. She curled up in her bedroll after her meager meal and watched lazy curls of gray smoke disappear in the pitch-black sky. She'd always appreciated the beauty of the Colorado mountains, but tonight the high night sky seemed to have an exclamation point to it.

The sing-song Ute language drifting from the camp fire soon lulled her to sleep. In the morning, she awoke to the quiet bustle of the Indians as they broke camp. There was a certain rhythm to their actions, as they worked with each other. No one looked at or spoke to her. A quick bite of biscuit and jerky, a freezing cold drink of stream water and she was in the saddle again. Frosty breath hung in the air behind them as they rode west.

****

Ike spurred Ally toward the hills. Dark Wolf and his posse had a good head start, and it would take time to catch up. When he left the Park floor and reached the cover of the forest, Ike breathed a sigh of relief as he searched the ground around him. Soft soil made for deep tracks which meant he wouldn't have any trouble trailing the small party. He nudged Ally, and she moved steadily on the rising slope. No sense tiring her out this early in the trek, so he slowed. He kept an eye on the trail behind as well. Wouldn't do to have the brave that Buster fooled sneak up on him. If Ike reached the Ute camp, the Indian who'd failed to block him would be disgraced and perhaps killed by Dark Wolf. The warrior would have nothing to lose by killing Ike; in fact, that was likely the only way he could redeem himself.

The weather held, and Ike camped that night underneath a sheltered granite promontory overlooking a broad mountain valley. In the distance, a whitish plume of faint smoke rose from the valley floor as a night wind carried a smoky smell his way. He was getting closer. There would be no fire or warm dinner tonight.

In the morning, Ike limbered up his stiff leg and studied the valley below. Toward the upper end, he spied the small group as they broke camp in the distance. Sue's faint light blue dress stood out from the Indians' earthen-colored clothing in the dawn light. Breakfast would be cold as well, but Ike had mornings when there wasn't any food, cold or hot. He scanned the surrounding countryside to the west, looking for the route Dark Wolf might take today. He gazed through the binoculars he'd inherited from Rob. A pass in the distance looked like the likeliest candidate. He'd ride that direction in a winding semi-circle to avoid detection. Dark Wolf probably wouldn't be looking for him, so he hoped the Indians would be traveling at a somewhat leisurely pace.

Ike swung up on Ally as best he could and took a long look behind. There was a slight quiver in his stomach as he thought he saw movement in the trees. Then a large black crow rose from the pines and swooped low into the valley. He turned away and laid the reins on the right side of Ally's neck. She started due west, on a line Ike estimated would bring him and the Indians together sometime in the afternoon. The sun's warmth was just a hope this early in the morning, but the rays lifted his spirits regardless. Riding the ridge wasn't easy, but the narrow flattop was better than riding along the sloping face of the hillsides. Ally moved steadily, a trait Ike had admired from the first time he'd ridden her during the War. She was one of his life's anchors.

By noon, the ridge had taken him north and out of sight of Sue. He'd have to navigate back toward her by dead reckoning from here on. He looked back again.

Nothing.

****

Toward the end of the second day, Sue saw the first faint images of the Ute wikiups spread out in a wide valley ahead. The location looked to be the same as when she'd been here before. The village was backdropped by high peaks sliced by a gray cloud bank doing a good job of hiding the sun. The day's ride had been chilly and nearly nonstop. She rested once on her own for a few minutes, which forced the braves to stop and do the same, but they were soon in the saddle again. Their stamina amazed her.

As they approached the outskirts of the village, flashes of her time here raced through Sue's head. She scanned the camp. Everything still seemed to be as she remembered it. The chief's wikiup, the cone-shaped tipis, the arena where Buster and Ike had both been beaten, the low hills in the distance where Kiska ministered to Sue's gunshot wound and saved her life.

Villagers gathered on both sides of the entourage as the riders entered camp. The women mostly eyed Sue, while the men laughed and pointed at the braves riding with her. She guessed it was because five

286

warriors were bringing one woman in. Everyone fell silent as Rain Water strode out of his tent toward them.

From Rain Water's stately gait, Sue guessed the old chief, Black Tail Deer, had passed away. Rain Water wouldn't be using Black Tail Deer's wikiup if he weren't the chief now. Dark Wolf dismounted and stepped back slightly as the Indian approached. Rain Water stood ramrod straight with a grim expression in front of Sue. He wore a fringed leather shirt decorated with beadwork, shells, and elk teeth. She dismounted. "I am sorry Chief Black Tail Deer is no longer with us. You are now the mighty chief of the Ute nation."

Rain Water ignored her remark but eyed her sharply. "It has been many moons." He turned and glared at Dark Wolf.

Sue sensed that Rain Water suspected Dark Wolf told her he was now chief. She nodded and bowed slightly. "This is now Rain Water's tribe. May you live a long life."

The chief returned Sue's nod. "There." He pointed off to the side and stared at her for a moment. "Go now." He motioned to several braves and mounted his pony.

She didn't know what he meant by that, but she looked where Rain Water indicated. It was a tipi near his. Sue moved toward it, and a woman swept a deerskin covering aside. She was immediately struck by the pungent herbal aroma and dankness that bathed the air inside. Decorative rugs covered most of the bare ground. It was dark, but there was enough light for Sue to see Kiska lying off to one side. A woman sat on the ground near her clothed in an animal hide dress. Rain Water's wife—also Kiska's sister. Sue sat silently near her friend. Kiska's eyes were closed, but her sister prodded her gently. Sue couldn't remember the sister's name. She'd spent much of her time in this same tent in a fog, nursed by Kiska.

Snow Owl—that was it.

The village shaman sat cross-legged nearby, mixing a sour-smelling potion in a small pottery bowl. He raised Kiska's head and spooned a small portion of the liquid into her mouth. She gagged a little, then the medicine man laid her head down, and she seemed to drift off again. Snow Owl shook Kiska's shoulder gently and spoke in hushed Ute.

Kiska's eyes fluttered open, and she slowly turned her head in the direction her sister pointed. When she made eye contact with Sue, tears wound down Kiska's cheeks and dripped onto the woven mat she lay on. Sue tried to keep her composure, but couldn't. She forced a smile, then cupped a hand to her mouth. Her muffled crying gave way to sobbing, and she put a hand on her friend's shoulder. She took hold of Kiska's limp hand, and the two friends let their emotions speak to their deep friendship. Snow Owl and the medicine man drew back and left the tent without a sound.

As Sue sat with Kiska, she talked about the time they'd spent together those years ago. About how Kiska had hovered over her as if she were her own child. How she'd spoon fed Sue when she couldn't feed herself. The one-sided conversation was Sue's way of saying goodbye to the woman who had saved her life. Shown her the quiet dignity of the Utes. She spoke to Kiska long into the evening, when Kiska lapsed into an even deeper sleep.

****

As he rode, Ike continually looked to his left for a trace of the small party. All manner of large rocks, pines, and scrub oak served to mask his vision, but occasionally the view cleared and he could see into the valley. He hoped he was still heading in the right direction, when a bloodcurdling scream followed by a glancing blow knocked him off Ally.

Ike tumbled to the ground with the Indian he'd tricked on top of him. They scrambled to their feet, and the brave brandished a tomahawk in one fist. Ike's quick reflexes were the only thing keeping him alive as the manic Indian swung the sharp blade again and again. He dodged the lunges as they faced off not more than three feet apart. Suddenly, the Indian sprang, and Ike stumbled and fell to the ground. The brave was on him in a second, the hatchet raised high above his head.

There was a whooshing sound as the Indian swung the ax. A loud 'whump' and the Indian suddenly flew off him. Ike heard a groan and staggered to his feet. The brave lay moaning not four feet away, having taken a glancing kick to the head from Ally. Ike leaned over and examined the dazed warrior's skull. Blood flowed freely into his thick black hair. Ike felt around the cut gingerly, but couldn't tell if Ally had cracked the warrior's skull. He took his favorite green bandana off and tied it around the Indian's head. Just then, he heard a familiar voice.

"You just can't stay out of trouble, now, can you?" He turned to see Buster riding out of the pines behind him.

"Didn't you lay another Indian out a few years back?" He had the start of a smile on his face.

Ike protested. "It wasn't me this time. Ally's the

culprit here." He walked over and stroked her neck, then looked back at the semi-conscious Indian. "That one was about to do me in when Ally took over. I'm just glad her aim is good, or that would've been me lyin' there 'stead of him."

"Did he get you?"

"Yeah, but I ducked at the last second, and he only grazed me high on the back. I'm okay; Lorraine's punched me on the arm harder than that." He flexed his arm and they both smiled.

Buster checked his friend's back. "He clipped you more'n you think. There's lots of blood on the backside of this shirt." Buster poured water on the gash and bound a flap of skin with what was left of Ike's shirt. "That'll hold 'til we get back to the ranch. You're gonna be sore for sure."

Ike laid a hand on Buster's shoulder. "Thanks, but you know I ain't goin' back yet."

"Wish you would. Let's mount up and ride back to your family."

"Can't. Not yet. Part of my family's still dead ahead."

Buster said, "What about this Indian? Looks like he's hurt pretty good."

Ike nodded. "Ah, he'll live, he's young and tough." He reached a hand out to the brave. The Indian pushed it away and struggled to a wobbly stand. Ike rubbed a hand through his hair, wondering what to do with him. "Reckon he'll just come with me."

"That's what you did last time, ain't it? Brought a couple wounded braves into the Ute village and Rain Water didn't take it very well."

"Maybe he's got a short memory."

"He'll just slow you down, Ike. Leave him here with me. That way you can ride as fast as you want."

Ike considered. "That might work." He picked the tomahawk up. "By the way, Buster, what're you doin' here?"

"Aw, I couldn't let you have all the fun out in these here mountains. Besides, Quincy can take care of the place for a while. He's ready. Lorraine's already bent him to her will, just like the rest of us, and Jessie's taken a bit of a shine to him."

That eased Ike's mind. Right now, he felt torn between the people closest to him, wanting to be home with Lorraine and Jessie but needing to follow Sue. He knew why Buster had come after him, though. "Well, now that you see I can take care of myself, you can just go on back to the ranch."

"I don't know about that. You didn't take care of yourself so good just now, Ally did. But as long as you stay close to her, you should be all right, so I expect I can get back to my life of leisure."

Ike laughed. "Leisure? Since when have you ever taken a break from anything? You don't even know how to spell the word." They shook hands, and Ike stared at his friend for a moment before whispering to Ally, "You heard Buster. You gotta keep takin' care of me. I'm in your hands." He eyed the Indian, who had slumped to a seat on the ground. Buster stood guard. Ike threw the tomahawk to Buster, grabbed Ally's reins, and willed himself into the saddle with a stifled grunt. He nudged Ally off at a walk, striding west along the high ridge that split meadows below starting to green up on either side. Ally stumbled slightly, then regained her footing. The sun was threatening to set soon, and he'd need to find an overnight shelter for both of them.

As he rode, a picture of Sue as a little girl running to him with her arms out blurred his vision.

Chapter Twenty-Nine

Hawkins was packing gear in his room. "Damn McAlister!" He glanced Slade's way. "Get your stuff, you and me are takin' a little trip over to Waverly's place."

"Sounds like you're lettin' McAlister get under your skin. He's just tryin' to rile you into doin' somethin' stupid. That's what that scene in the Wildfire was all about. As long as you keep a cool head, you've got the upper hand."

"I'd like to blow his head off."

"You keep sayin' that, but I don't see you doin' it." Slade was whittling a small piece of wood into a gun. "You're playin' right into his hand. Better figure this out, Hawkins; seems like you got a lot to lose here. Waverly's where your fortune lies, so a smart man would just let McAlister be."

Hawkins didn't respond.

"How long you figure we're gonna be gone?"

"Might be a while." Hawkins gave Slade a sideways look. He wasn't sure about the shootist anymore, and he didn't like the feeling. At the stable, the two men tied their gear on and saddled up.

"Gonna be gone long, Mr. Hawkins?" Red Crawford had come outside and held the reins of both mounts.

"No business of yours, old man." He scanned the

rundown stable and surroundings. "Besides, looks like you got more to worry about around here than what I'm doin'." Hawkins wheeled his horse and started down Main Street at a trot. They passed a fair number of staring Cottonwood citizens as they left.

The ride to Waverly's spread always seemed to take longer than it should. The trip gave Hawkins plenty of time to think as he traveled. How was his plan going to work? Truth was, he didn't really know himself. The railroad wasn't much closer to coming through today than it was six months ago when he first came to town. Some people in the Park, like miners, were getting rich, but he didn't want to wait on the railroad anymore to find his fortune. As he crossed a small stream, it occurred to him the only thing of real value around here other than land was water.

That was it. His mind raced. Water was like gold in these parts. He'd work on controlling some of the streams flowing through the Park when he got back. Right now, Waverly's place was as good as any to hole up until he figured out a plan. Stay out of Cottonwood for a while, where things felt like they were closing in. McAlister would never let up on him, and the sheriff was better than Slade with a gun. Those two were loose ends he'd have to tie up when he got back. Then he'd have a free hand to make his play.

The riders were about halfway to Waverly's when they stopped to water the horses and grab a quick bite. Hawkins mumbled to himself while he sat.

"Why are you doin' this? Ridin' all this way just to nail down somethin' that's already nailed down? You already got the deal done, don't you? Cheatin' the railroad right and left is gonna make you a rich man.

Why are you runnin'? McAlister? Walnutt?"

Hawkins sneered at Slade as he ate. "What's it to you? All you gotta do is keep me healthy and you get paid handsomely."

Slade put his food down. "Hmm. That might be hard to do."

Hawkins jerked his head toward the gunman. "How's that, Slade?"

"You got a bunch of people after your hide back in Cottonwood. Sooner or later, you're gonna have to go back and face 'em."

"I got you to do that for me."

Slade turned toward Hawkins and his eyes narrowed. "Do you?"

Hawkins frowned and furtively slipped the leather loop off his Colt as he reached for a cup of water. That uneasy feeling he'd felt about Slade now clogged his throat. He stood and squared up in front of Slade, waiting for his hired gun to continue. His eyes darted to Slade's holster. The man's hammer was unlooped, too.

Slade rose. He spread his legs slightly apart and worked his hands into a pair of thin leather gloves. "Turns out I ain't who you think I am, Hawkins. Fact is, I'm your judge and jury, and judgment day is today." He quick-drew his pistol and pointed the barrel directly at the railroader's chest.

Hawkins didn't flinch.

"I'm workin' for the railroad right now, too, just like you. Didn't know that, did you? I'm what they call a troubleshooter. They call on me when they want to make sure things are workin' like they ought to, so when you sent the company the message you needed a gun hand, they didn't have to look very far. They've used me before. I'm not here to protect you. I'm here to spy on you, you dolt. Only requirement for my line of work is to be good with a gun, which I am." He cocked the Colt.

"The railroad knows all about your deal with Waverly, too, because I just might have mentioned it to them. Turns out it's hard to hide a secret that big in a place this small." He kept the pistol trained on Hawkins. "By the way, the railroad wanted me to tell you you're fired. So you're in for a surprise when we get to Waverly's. He already knows you don't have standing to make deals anymore, and he's not the kind of man that's gonna forget how you threatened him before."

Hawkins didn't react. He kept his eyes on Slade as if he hadn't heard anything the man said.

Slade motioned with his sidearm. "Drop your belt and step away."

Hawkins raised his tin cup and took a sip of cool water. "Don't think I'm gonna do that. Guess you're just gonna have to shoot me."

"You got it wrong if you don't think I will." A small smile appeared on Slade's face as he pulled the trigger.

The only sound was the echo of the hammer hitting the back of an empty cylinder.

Hawkins smiled. He leisurely drew his pistol while Slade eyed his Colt. "Guess you should have checked your gun before you made your move. You got a lot of empty chambers there. Now it's your turn, Slade. Drop the gun and your belt, slow and easy. And keep your other hand in the air and away from that extra cylinder you carry in your pocket. I couldn't unload that."

Slade stood with a flinty look about him. "That's somethin' I'd do, Hawkins. Nice touch."

Hawkins motioned toward Slade's gun again. "Drop it, now! You know I'll shoot."

Slade twirled the gun around his finger and let it drop to the ground. "Ain't much good with no bullets. Just a hunk of metal."

"Now the belt. Easy does it."

Slade slid a hand to his buckle and undid it. He bent over to drop the gun belt to the ground. In one quick motion, he snaked a hand into his boot, palmed a short knife, and flicked it at Hawkins, who fired as he threw. Both men went down. Only one moved.

Hawkins groaned as he lay on the ground. The knife stuck gruesomely out of his left side, just above his waist. He grabbed the handle and after two quick breaths, yanked it out. He gasped as blood poured from the wound, and he pressed a hand against it. He nearly fainted but managed to crawl over to Slade, whose eyes were open, but whose heart was still. The only mark on him was a ragged red hole in his cheek ringed with black.

What to do with the body? People saw him leave Cottonwood with Slade. He wanted to leave it here for the animals because he wasn't sure he could drag the corpse anywhere just now. Once they found out about Slade, the townspeople would likely also pin Rob's death on him for good measure. Hang him for sure. Probably raise a posse to hunt him, which meant leaving South Park for parts unknown. He eased himself to the ground, dipped his bandana in the flowing stream, and pressed it to his bloody side.

No! Wait. There was no one else around, no one to

challenge what he'd just done. No witnesses. That's it. He'd tell Waverly that Slade hurled a knife at him, and he was lucky to be able to defend himself. That's what it was. Self-defense, and none's the wiser. Sure. In the meantime, best to stay shy of town until he thought out all the details of exactly how it happened. Pain from the knife wound had sharpened his senses, and he began to see a way out of this.

It was Slade all along who was going to kill him and take his place in the deal with Waverly. No one else but Slade knew about Hawkins' arrangement with Waverly, and that secret had died with him. Hawkins had been too clever, too alert, too smart to fall for the façade of Slade as a gunman. He'd coaxed Slade into bragging about how he was going to be Waverly's partner and kill him. That's when Slade hit him with the knife and he went down. As Slade stood over him, laughing, Hawkins had leg whipped him to the ground, and they fought over Hawkins' gun. He'd gotten hold of it just when Slade leaped at him full force. He'd had no choice but to shoot. He'd tried to hit him in a place that didn't kill him, but there wasn't time to aim. What's more, Slade confessed to killing Rob just before he died. So now Hawkins was really off the hook. All he had to do was sell that story to the sheriff and the town.

As he thought about the fantasy he'd just created, he ripped one of Slade's shirt sleeves off and wound it tightly over the bloody bandana at his side.

It was only right to bring the body back out of the countryside for a fit burial, even if the man had double-crossed him. Waverly would understand; after all, it was self-defense. He spent the next half hour laboring to get Slade up on his horse, first pushing the body up a few inches at a time, then gasping for breath before lifting again. Sweat poured off him. The ride to Waverly's took much longer than it would have otherwise, and Hawkins arrived well after nightfall.

The wranglers in the bunkhouse scrambled when they heard horses outside in the dark. Waverly lumbered out of the house at the commotion. Cowboys surrounded Hawkins as he led the horse with Slade's body on it in. Rifles stared him in the face in the dim light. Waverly shouted, "Identify yourself."

Hawkins held one shaky hand high. "It's Hawkins, Waverly. I've got a two-timing, no-good double dealer here who's breathed his last. I'm on my last legs, too. Someone help me down." Waverly motioned to his men, and arms pulled Hawkins off his horse. They carried him into the house but deposited him in the entryway at Waverly's command.

"Don't want him bleedin' all over my rugs. Better he bleeds right here." He bent over a pale Hawkins. "You don't look so good. Might be you'll end up the same way as that fella outside you shot."

Hawkins groaned. "Help me, Waverly, I think I'm dying."

"That you might be, Hawkins. Ain't got no doctor here, just my cook. He knows somethin' about stitchin' people up, but looks like you need more than that. Reckon we might not get to put our plan into action."

"Whaddya mean?" Hawkins feared Waverly had indeed heard he'd been fired.

"I mean you might not last through the night. If that's the case—" Those were the last words Hawkins heard until the next day.

When he woke, he was in the guest bedroom he'd stayed in before. A small Mexican man was leaving with a pan of some sort. He croaked, "What's going on? Who are you? How long have I been out?"

The man turned toward him. "*No habla inglés, senõr.*" After the man left, Hawkins heard him tell someone outside, 'the gringo is awake.'

Waverly walked in smoking a big cigar. "So, looks like you're gonna live, which is more than I can say about the banker you brought in with you."

"He weren't no banker, Waverly, he was my hired gun. Slade. You met him before."

"Hah! Doesn't appear he was very good at his job."

"He made the mistake of trying to double cross me, and after he knifed me, I shot him. Self-defense, pure and simple."

"That sounds like it might be simple, but doesn't sound pure to me. Why would he chuck a knife at you if he had a gun? Didn't see one on him, but gun hands usually have guns."

Hawkins' stomach fluttered. He hadn't considered that when he made up his story. He hesitated, then said, "Because I had the drop on him. I knew he was going to double cross me, I just didn't know when. He'd already killed the sheriff in Cottonwood, and I knew he wouldn't stop at killing me either."

Waverly lifted an eyebrow. "It doesn't matter to me none, but my guess is you're gonna have to convince the law about that, and it might matter to them. Maybe you ought to spend more time comin' up with a better story."

Hawkins shifted on the bed with a slight groan. "What did you do with Slade's body?"

"Nothin' yet. Guess we'll bury him today."

"Sounds like a good idea." The sooner the man was in the earth the better. He still needed to know if what Slade said on the trail was true, if Slade really told Waverly the railroad fired him. "Did you ever get a chance to talk with him?"

"Why would I have done that?"

"Well, I just thought you might have. You know, he was a gentleman before he became a gunman." He made it almost sound like he liked Slade. More important, it sounded like Slade never told Waverly anything about him and the railroad. He was apt to be in the clear.

"So, we're still good for our deal, right?" He wanted confirmation Slade really hadn't said anything.

Waverly said, "Any reason we wouldn't be?"

"Nope."

"Well, you're welcome to stay here for a couple days and heal. I'll give you some good advice, though. I'm not sure what really went on between you and Slade, and frankly I don't care, but if something should happen to me—if I should die in my sleep or get killed in some accident—I want you to know you're a dead man. I've told my men to skewer you on a branding iron in case I stop breathin' from any cause, understand? Have I made myself clear?" His eyes narrowed.

"Yes, you have." It didn't matter what this blowhard said now, he was scot-free. Railroad job or not, it was past time to take dead aim at McAlister. When he was ready, he'd head back to Cottonwood and tie up those loose ends once and for all.

Chapter Thirty

Ike hadn't decided what he was going to do when he caught up to Sue and Dark Wolf. Riding into the village would likely mean sure death, but staying outside didn't seem like a good plan either. Not much he could do if Sue ran into trouble, and he wouldn't be near enough to help her. But then, not much he could do to safeguard her if he was dead either. His need to protect her had gotten him into a box he didn't know how to get out of. He hadn't thought this through very well, but he figured the only thing to do was to somehow be in camp and near her. Keep her close.

He rode along the top of the ridgeline until about noon. He entered a thickly-forested path bordered with pines that took him on a winding arc first away from, then back in the direction of the small troupe escorting Sue. This was taking longer than he hoped. As he crested another ridge, his heart rose in his throat. Below, Sue was entering the Indian village escorted by the five braves.

Damn!

He wouldn't be able to catch up with her now. He watched her ride in, surrounded on all sides by villagers. The sun had just disappeared behind the summits to the west, and dinner fires were popping up from the large encampment of tent sites. That reminded him he hadn't eaten anything since Buster left. He dismounted and let Ally graze while he broke out some cold jerky and a hard-boiled egg. He filled his hat in a little stream wandering down the foothills. A quick gulp, and he passed the water on to Ally. He broke out some grain and let her eat her fill while he figured out his next move.

As stars twinkled to life overhead, Ike resigned himself to sleeping on the low ridge tonight and getting into camp somehow tomorrow. He untied his thin cotton bedroll and laid on a collection of needles pine trees had courteously strewn about to soften his sleep. Ally also lay under the trees, which gave scant protection from the wind and chill of a Colorado mountain summer night.

****

Sue sniffed the potion in the bowl that sat near Kiska's head. She gagged and brushed at the odor in the air. Kiska's eyelids flickered, and she stared blankly upward. Sue couldn't tell if her eyes were focused or not. She looked at Snow Owl and pointed to various parts of her own body until the woman nodded when Sue touched a hand to her stomach. Then the woman shook her head. Kiska lay slightly curled up on the rug, her eyes slowly closing.

Mixed emotions flooded through Sue. She was glad to see Kiska, but the woman who had nursed her back to health now laying dying in front of her. It wasn't right. Her mind spun. Who would take care of her friend's little girl and boy? She thought of the gauntlet of braves who had pummeled Buster nearly to death. She pictured the central arena where Rain Water bested Ike and she pleaded for his life. She recalled Rain Water's unexpected gesture in allowing her to leave after expelling Buster and Ike from the village. Memories flooded her mind, but there weren't any she wished to dwell on except Kiska's caring touch.

As Kiska slept, Sue rose from her place beside her and pushed out of the tent into the cool evening air. Stretching her legs felt good. She drew her arms across her chest to ward off a chill and scanned her surroundings. Her family seemed very far away.

****

In the morning, a wolf's lonely howl brought Ike upright from a light sleep. He swept his blanket aside and surveyed his surroundings. The sun had not yet peeked over the ramparts to the east, but the pale blue sky was already painted with faint pink clouds. He and Ally were on a heavily-forested ridge which dropped off steeply on one side. He gazed into the valley where Sue and the Ute village were. Smoke from breakfast campfires rose in the distance and hung over the Indian village like a thick morning fog. He fished out another hard-boiled egg, a couple of stale biscuits, and an apple from his saddlebag. A quick swig from his canteen was a big enough drink. A decaying pine log in the small clearing made for a makeshift seat. Ally fed on tender grasses nearby.

Plenty of time to plan his next move. He needed it. There didn't seem to be any way to get into the Ute village without losing his life, yet he was still convinced that's where he needed to be to protect her. Somehow.

He was used to hard times—he'd had plenty in his life—but right now, things seemed especially tough, and he had no control over how they were going to turn out. That was the worst part; not being able to manage what was going to happen. He heaved the apple core into the trees. At least some animal would find it useful and make a meal of it. That was more than he could say about his own usefulness right now.

"Why do you sit and stare at nothing?"

Ike whirled to the voice behind him. Rain Water! Ike sprang off the log as well as his worn body would let him. The brave was no more than ten feet away, but he hadn't heard him approaching. The warrior was on foot, his horse a short distance away, also nibbling on new green grasses. "Rain Water! I...am surprised." It wasn't what he wanted to say, but then he didn't really have a good response.

The Indian brandished no weapons and stood in stately silence dressed in simple deerskins, arms folded in front of him.

When Rain Water didn't respond, Ike labored to think of something to say. The young chief was the last person he expected to see on the trail. Why was he here?

Before Ike could utter anything else, Rain Water spoke. "Why do you follow? I said no."

Ike stammered a reply. "I want to protect my sister."

Rain Water stared silently, then an icy, "From what?"

Wouldn't be good to say 'from you', so Ike searched for something else to say. "I need to be with her." The words didn't begin to convey the depth of feeling that lay underneath them.

"No, you do not."

It appeared Rain Water had come to stop him from following Sue, but Ike hadn't come this far to turn back now. He spread his feet slightly and stared at the Indian, whose eyes bored into his. What was he going to do now? Had the chief come to fight him again? A clash that hadn't gone well for Ike.

Rain Water sat on the same lichen-covered log at a short distance.

Ike swung his left leg over the trunk with his right out to the side and lowered himself to a seat. "You speak English very well."

"I learned from your friend over many years."

"Buster?"

"He stayed in our camp many times. Good teacher." He looked at Ike's extended leg. "Leg still bad." It wasn't a question.

"Yes, it—" and he stopped, not able to think of anything else to say. His mind churned with questions until one popped out. "Why are you here? Why do you sit with me?"

The Indian straightened. "I knew you would follow. I do not want to have to kill you."

Ike hesitated. He didn't know what he was expecting to hear, but that wasn't it. He waited, his mind spinning with the reality of such an unexpected, unlikely meeting with an Indian chief. He finally formed another question. "So you would still kill me if I entered your camp?"

"Yes."

There was no mistaking Rain Water's brutal honesty. Ike's mind reeled. Had Rain Water come from his village just to intercept him and save his life? He couldn't get his head around the unlikeliness of it. "Are you here to stop me?"

"If you continue to my village."

Ike considered. Going into camp meant certain death, and he could see how his being there might also put Sue in danger. Rain Water's sudden visit had changed whatever plan he had. Ike still couldn't believe he was sitting near the man who would have killed him several years ago, except for Sue's pleas. He stared in the direction of the village. He dropped his gaze toward the ground, unsure what to do or say next.

Rain Water broke the silence. "Your sister is safe in my village."

Ike's gaze locked onto the chief. Ike had never heard of an Indian doing what Rain Water had just done; riding from his village to stop him instead of killing him. Ike stared silently at the warrior for a long time, then nodded. He wanted to shake the young chief's hand, but that was not their custom. He hesitated for a moment, then whistled for Ally. She walked over slowly and Ike drew his rifle from its scabbard and offered it to Rain Water. The Indian looked past the rifle and nodded at Ally.

Ike was dumbstruck. He couldn't part with his warhorse, even to save his own life. He shook his head.

Rain Water stood impassively. "Your horse is lame."

Ike whirled toward her. She was standing with one leg slightly bent, and owing to his focus on Sue, he hadn't even noticed. He ran a hand along the injured leg feeling her tendon. It seemed intact. He lifted the hoof to search for stones, but there weren't any. There was a dark spot on the sole, where a stone probably had been. Definitely bruised. He stood and ran a hand along Ally's neck, almost forgetting Rain Water was there. His heart thumped, and he rubbed both hands over his face. He turned to his surprise visitor. "I couldn't ride her into your camp even if I wanted to."

"I will lead her there. You go back."

"I can't leave her. She's…" He stopped, not able to put his feelings into words. His heart pounded and the wound on his back throbbed.

"Go home, Ike Mc-Alister."

"What about Ally?" He pursed his lips hard. Even in the cool morning, sweat trickled down his back.

"I will take care of her, but she may never run again." Rain Water raised an arm, and a brave rode toward them out of the pines. Rain Water spoke to him in Ute. The warrior dismounted and brought the saddleless pony to Ike, then retreated to Rain Water's side. How many more braves were hidden in the forest?

Ike stood speechless. It was all too much for him to take in. He shook his head.

"I won't just leave her. She's part of me."

Rain Water stood silently.

Ike fumbled for something more to say. Couldn't he just walk into camp with her? He stared at the stoic Indian. Rain Water still stood mute. Ike's shoulders slumped, and he turned to Ally. He stroked the white blaze on her head again and again, pressed his face against her nose, and whispered to her. She nickered and bobbed her head. Tears dripped down his face and mingled with the early morning dew. The best thing for Ally would be to go with Rain Water, and he knew it. He drew both arms around her neck and held her tight for a long time. Gently he released her and stepped back.

"It is not far to my village. She will be able to walk there." Rain Water turned to the brave, who reached out for Ally's reins. Ike held fast for a moment, then slowly released his grip. The brave gestured at him then started Ally slowly down the face of the ridge. Soon they both disappeared. The chief nodded toward Ike, mounted up, and faded from view on the same path.

He was alone.

Ally was gone.

Chapter Thirty-One

Questions swirled in Hawkins' head as he rode toward Cottonwood from Waverly's ranch. He didn't know if what Slade said about him being fired was true, but at least he knew Slade hadn't told Waverly anything. He'd find out soon enough if he still worked for the railroad, or if Slade had poisoned that well with his bosses. There were several ways he could play this, all with an uncertain outcome.

If Slade was lying and hadn't told the railroad what he was up to, then he was in the clear. Slade just had an unfortunate accident on the trail, and they'd had to bury him at Waverly's ranch. No one was going to dig him up to see what killed him. He'd pass it off as a fall from his horse as they went down a steep ravine. The man hit his head and never regained consciousness, and Waverly wasn't one to get involved if asked.

But if Slade was telling the truth, then Hawkins was riding straight into trouble.

He slipped into town at night. If anyone did notice a rider that late, they probably couldn't be sure it was him in the dim light. He needed some time to figure the lay of the land. No doubt the new sheriff would be by as soon as he heard he was back. Or maybe he'd turn the tables on the lawman and pay Walnutt a visit at the jail. Sure. That way it would look like he wasn't trying to hide anything. Tell him about Slade's unfortunate accident, and that he feared McAlister was still after him. That's it. He'd tell the sheriff to keep McAlister away from him. That would give him time to plan how he was going to take him down. He'd craft a scheme and let it ripen over a good night's sleep; that is, if he still had a room at the new boarding house.

He stabled his dun at Red's and headed for the inn. Although it was late, the front door was never locked, so he snuck in and crept along the hallway to the back. He drew his Colt and pushed the door to his room open. The three amigos Slade told him about were still there. Two were sleeping on the floor. He kicked them and tumbled the other one off the single bed.

"All of you, get out! Now."

To persuade them, he motioned toward the door with his gun. When they'd dragged themselves out into the hall, he told them to close the door quietly and stand guard. Then reconsidered. He might as well announce his presence; McAlister was going to know he was back soon enough. He opened the door again and slammed it shut. The sound reverberated through the building.

****

In the morning, he walked down the middle of Main Street to the sheriff's office. He jiggled the tricky latch until the door gave way. Walnutt was at his desk, sipping a cup of coffee and looking over some flyers. He glanced up as Hawkins entered, then stood quickly. He fingered his gun.

Hawkins stood at the edge of the desk and pointed a finger. "Sheriff, I want you to keep Ike McAlister away from me. He's—"

The sheriff stopped him. "Where have you been? And where is your sidekick Slade?"

"You never mind him. He's dead on the trail to the west. Tried to kill me but I was too smart. He wounded me but couldn't finish me off." He raised his shirt to show Walnutt the wound. "Before he died, he confessed to killing Rob McAlister, so you can close that case now. And I'm warning you, keep McAlister away. He threatened me, and I won't have it. You were there. In the saloon. He knocked me out of my chair and drew down on me. Now I got proof I didn't kill his brother, 'cause the murderer is already moldering in his grave." His speech was a good way to put the focus on McAlister and take it off him. Besides, reminding the sheriff that McAlister had threatened him was a nice touch. "Do your job, Sheriff, or this could get out of hand." He turned and stormed out of the one-story building with a smile on his face. He'd laid some good groundwork for what he planned next.

Bushwhacking both loose ends.

****

Sue hovered over Kiska as her friend slept. She pressed on Kiska's hand, but there was no response. The woman's breathing had changed in the last hour. More and more, it was coming in fits and starts, her chest moving shallowly with an ominous rattle at every breath. Sue studied Snow Owl, who sat near her sister staring straight ahead.

Snow Owl rose from her cross-legged squat. "Time has come. Stay." She swept the flap aside and stole soundlessly out of the tipi.

Ten minutes later, she returned with the shaman. He flung white powder in the air and bent as he danced around Kiska. The fine particles had a bitter smell like burnt almonds. Sue guessed the rhythmic incantations were the Utes' way of blessing Kiska's passage into the afterlife. During the solemn ceremony, Sue thought she saw Kiska's eyes flutter slightly, but couldn't be sure. The shaman's gestures started low at Kiska's level, but rose, and his hands reached toward the sky as he finished his ceremony. Without speaking a word, he turned and left.

Sue held Kiska's limp hand. She placed two fingers on her friend's wrist and waited, then burst into tears and bent over the still form. Snow Owl gently took hold of Sue's shoulders and pulled her back.

"Kiska journeys. Alone." She placed a decorative blanket over her sister and drew it up around her neck, then left the tipi. Sue stared at her friend. She couldn't remember ever feeling so alone, but she had wept enough. She wiped tears from her eyes and admired the peaceful, kind face before her. Soon, the shaman and several braves entered the tent and wrapped Kiska in a decorative blanket. They removed her from the dwelling, and Sue was alone again. She stood and took a lingering look around. The only reminder left of Kiska was the heady aroma that still pervaded the tipi. She would remember Kiska and that scent forever. She pushed the covering aside and went outside. The crisp evening air chilled her wet cheeks.

As she gazed at the star-laden sky, her thoughts turned to Ike. Big brothers were sometimes a worry. She bowed slightly to Rain Water, who stood like a statue outside the tipi for a moment, then turned away without speaking. She called after him. "I will leave in the morning." Uncertainty clouded her thoughts as she walked back to Kiska's tent. Would Rain Water really let her leave?

In the morning, Sue stirred at first light. She had a helper now, a squaw who stood with food as she blinked awake. A flat flour pancake rolled and filled with something warm. She breathed in an aroma of cooked venison. As she took the flatbread, she realized how hungry she was. She couldn't remember the last time she'd eaten. The woman watched her closely, motioning with her hands to eat. Sue nodded, but after a few mouthfuls, she carried the food outside.

Sue turned to one of the sentries and made a drinking motion with her hands. The sentry nodded quickly, which surprised her. But it wasn't her the guard was responding to. He looked past her. She turned and saw Snow Owl standing near with a vessel of water which she held out to Sue. Nodding to one of the guards, the woman silently turned and walked straight for Rain Water's wikiup.

Snow Owl eventually came out of the dwelling, followed by Rain Water. He was dressed in full ceremonial regalia, with a tall headdress and twin tails of decorative feathers draped down his back. He wore the same multi-colored breastplate she'd seen before and gripped his ornately painted lance. His very presence commanded respect. Snow Owl bowed as he passed her, and the entire encampment converged on their chief. Sue was at the center of a large gathering of Utes.

Rain Water struck the ground with his lance and all murmuring stopped. The silence was deafening. An eagle screeched overhead as it carved holes in the clear blue sky. The chief stood like a statue staring into the distance. His gaze dropped to Sue.

"You are a worthy friend, Sue Mc-Alister. You are

welcome in my camp." He gazed at the sky and swept an arm in a wide arc, then turned and disappeared into his tall home. A brave led Sue's horse to her, along with a small pouch of provisions.

****

Buster was there when Ike rode in on the paint. He reacted with fleeting raised eyebrows.

Buster looked the pony over and in a low voice, said, "I'm guessin' Rain Water kept Ally and gave you this pony, along with your life." He put a hand up. "No need to answer and don't fret. Ally will be well taken care of. My guess is they'll keep a rope on her until she's used to her surroundings, then they'll let her run with their string. They'll treat her right."

Ike knew Buster was trying to soften the blow, but it wasn't working. He didn't respond to what Buster said and drew in a big breath. "Ally's lame. I don't know if she'll ever be right again." He turned away so he wouldn't have to say more.

Lorraine stood nearby. She was more direct. "Ike, thank the Lord you're all right. She hugged her husband tightly then stood back and eyed him up and down. "You look a lot worse for wear though." She glanced at his shoulder wound. "What did they do to you?" She paused. "And tell me about Ally."

He pursed his lips hard because he didn't trust himself to answer. He left the question dangling in the air as he returned her kiss and went inside. He was home, but a big part of his heart was still in Rain Water's village.

Several hours later Sue rode into the ranch as well. Over the last couple of days, three braves accompanied her in silence all the way to the Park basin. Not that she was in the mood to talk much anyway. Kiska's death had seared her. At the edge of the Park, the Indians turned back without a word and Sue continued, not stopping until she reached the ranch.

The McAlister reunion should have been a happy occasion, but there was too much pain in their midst for that.

Chapter Thirty-Two

Lorraine had been keeping a close eye on her husband since he returned from the Ute village. Ally had been one of the family. Not just for Ike, but her and Buster too. She noticed he stayed away from the stable where Buster put the paint up. She recognized his melancholy, although he tried to hide it by throwing himself into his work. But watching over him was easier said than done as she was nearly nine months along. She was reluctant to go into town for supplies by herself anymore, so she asked Ike and he'd agreed to let Quincy go with her. Buster would have gone, but Ike needed him to help work the herd.

In the short time Quincy had been at the ranch, Lorraine noticed he had transformed from a sulking malcontent to a willing worker. Somehow, the kidnapping had a positive impact on him. She had him spend as much time around Ike as he would allow. Buster seemed to take an interest in him as well. Quincy confessed to her that for the first time, he felt like he was part of a family.

The next morning Lorraine caught up with him in the barn. "Bert, can you take me into town?" Lorraine held a piece of paper with a list of supplies scribbled on it.

He brightened. "Sure thing, Miss Lorraine!" He looked at Ike, and Ike nodded. She'd never asked him to go anywhere with her before, and he rushed for the stable to ready the wagon.

Ike stood in front of the ranch house to see them off. As Quincy snapped the reins, Ike held onto his daughter's hand until he almost pulled her off the wagon.

They rolled away from the ranch, and Quincy looked back with a big smile on his face. He turned to Lorraine. "As long long as we're in town, uh, is there anything you need at The Sew Pretty?"

"No, there's not." Lorraine glanced at Quincy sideways, the way she did when she was slightly annoyed. Now why would he ask about The Sew Pretty? She waved him on, and he snapped the reins, still with that wide smile. She said, "Not worried about Hawkins?"

She saw him blanch for just a second. "No. I'm sick and tired of bein' sick and tired, and I'm tired of bein' scared of him." His grin was replaced with a firm set of his jaw.

When they got to town, Lorraine had Quincy stop in front of the mercantile. He took a quick glance around before going in. Inside, O'Toole escorted Lorraine and Jessie around the store as they checked items off on her list. She noticed Quincy was staring out the front window at The Sew Pretty across the street.

"Bert, what are you doing?"

The young man nearly jumped. "Uh, I'm just looking. Outside."

"I can see that, but you're starin' at somethin' pretty hard. Out with it."

"I ain't lookin' at nothin' in particular, Miss

Lorraine."

"You're sure workin' hard starin' at nothin'." She played a hunch. "Have you ever met her?"

Without thinking, Quincy blurted, "Sure, I used to see her in the Wildfire," then he clammed up as his face reddened and he said, "Who?"

"Ah ha! It's Hannah, ain't it?"

"Hannah who?"

"You know Hannah who, Bert. Quit dodgin'."

"Yes, ma'am." He worked his hat in his hands.

"How'd you know she worked there? At The Sew Pretty."

Quincy blushed. "I hear things here and there."

"Well, I'm gonna be a while here gettin' all my provisions. Ned will take care of me while you're gone."

"Gone? Where am I goin'?"

"The Sew Pretty. Go on over there and say hi to her."

"You mean in the shop? While she's workin'? Right now?"

"Right now. Go on and go. She won't bite. I'll be right here when you get back."

The young man rubbed the back of his neck and started across the street, stealing a look back as he went. When he got to the shop door, he hesitated. He looked back again, and Lorraine made a shooing motion at him. He disappeared inside ever so slowly.

After she'd gotten everything on the list, Lorraine was signing her account at the counter when Quincy rushed back in with a whoosh. His face was red and his breathing came in short gulps, but there was more than a hint of a smile on his face.

"Why are you back so soon?" Lorraine put both hands on her hips and narrowed her eyes at him.

"Why, I spent plenty of time over there, ma'am. She was just busy."

"Did you talk to her?"

"Sure, I wandered around the shop a while, then she asked me if I needed help and I said no, then yes, then I didn't know what to say so I just stared at her and she said she knew who I was, that I worked for Hawkins and I told her I didn't anymore." He stopped and took several quick breaths.

"Slow down, cowhand. What's this about Hawkins?"

"She asked me if I knew Hawkins was back in town, and I said I didn't and said I'da told you or Ike or Buster if I knew he was back, but I didn't 'cause I don't have nothin' to do with him no more."

"Okay, take a breath. I'm about ready to go home; why don't you help Mr. O'Toole get everything into the wagon?" There were mostly foodstuffs, but she had also bought ammunition for a pistol she wasn't going to mention to Ike. She kept it hidden against her skirt as Quincy helped load the rest of the supplies.

Back at the ranch, Ike was returning from downrange when Lorraine, Jessie, and Quincy arrived in the wagon. He hurried off his pony to help his wife down. "Everything go okay?"

"Sure thing. Bert did just fine. I think there's another reason he likes goin' into town, though. Seems like he might be sweet on that Hannah girl that's workin' at The Sew Pretty now."

Quincy was unloading the supplies nearby and kept his head down as he worked. Lorraine's voice apparently more than carried to him, as he snuck a glance to see if Ike or Buster heard that.

"You mean that little gal that used to work at the saloon? The one that Rob…" Ike's voice trailed off.

Lorraine nodded and drew an arm through Quincy's. "Don't you worry about her past, Bert. Who knows? You might be part of her future."

He blushed and heaved a sack of flour over his shoulder that hid his face.

"Well, I hear Sue likes her, so there must be something to her." Ike was trying to soften his words.

When the unloading was done, Quincy drove the wagon to the barn and unhitched the work horse. Buster was inside feeding his mount and rubbing her down. "Looks like a good day's work, son. How was it?"

"Fine, Buster." He glanced at Ike, who was arm in arm with Lorraine as they walked into the house. "Sometimes I don't know what to make of Mr. Ike, though."

"Don't mind him. He's just a little off his feed, what with trekkin' after his sister, losin' his horse, and his wife about to deliver."

"I reckon."

In the house, Ike caught Jessie up in mid-rush and twirled her about his head while she giggled. Lorraine sat heavily at the table and asked him to do the same.

"What's up, honey?"

Lorraine twisted a curl of hair, a telltale sign. "Trouble. When I was in Ned's store, he pulled me aside and told me rumor had it Hawkins was back and gunnin' for you."

"That don't surprise me. Has he seen him?"

"Not sure, but O'Toole said Hawkins' sorry

excuses for surveyors have been blabberin' in the Wildfire about how he's gonna get you."

"Maybe I'll ride into town tomorrow and visit Hugh."

Lorraine pulled him close and kissed him. "You just make sure you stay away from him."

"The sheriff?" He knew what she meant.

"Not the sheriff. Hawkins, you joker." She gave him a light punch on the arm.

Ike smiled, but frowned inside. He had a feeling the staying-away part was about over. Justice for his brother's killer was overdue.

****

Hawkins walked to his ruined office and tried to make it habitable, but he never was much for sprucing things up. So far, no one had challenged his right to be there, so maybe he hadn't been fired after all. As he scanned Main Street through the broken window, he saw the sheriff walking his way.

Hugh Walnutt pushed the uncooperative door open and strode into the ruined office. "Hawkins, I am here to tell you to clear out. Much as I would like to, I do not have enough evidence yet to pin Rob McAlister's murder on you. I have been in touch with the railroad though, and they tell me you no longer work for them so you are to vacate this building, such as it is. They are sending someone here via coach to take charge of railroad operations." He started to turn away, but stopped. "One last thing; you are not to leave town until I say you can." He fingered his gun belt. "Understand?"

Hawkins stood mute, shaken by the news. So he really was fired. Damn!

"I said, understand?"

A distracted nod from Hawkins, and the sheriff left.

Now what? He didn't have a job and was under suspicion of murder. Slade was telling the truth about tipping off the railroad about his deal with Waverly, so it wouldn't take them and the sheriff long to find out what really happened to Slade. The shock of Walnutt's news spurred him to action.

McAlister. He walked out of the small office to the stable where Red was hammering away. Without a word, Hawkins retrieved his horse, swung up, and rode west toward the McAlister spread. He traveled off the main path as much as possible.

Just before the ranch, he angled to the left and started a gradual climb up the hills behind the ranch house. Below, McAlister's wife was tending her garden, but there was nothing to be gained by involving her so he held his fire. He didn't see McAlister or his sidekick. He'd know soon enough if they were around.

He drew his rifle, shuffled across the forested face of the rise, and crouched behind a small rock outcropping. He'd been waiting for this for a long time. A faint conversation drifted his way. Quincy came out of the ranch house headed toward the barn.

Hawkins took careful aim and fired.

The young man flew backward and hit the ground while Hawkins scurried away to his horse. Soon, he was clip-clopping down the road toward town. Even though he'd missed killing McAlister, Hawkins felt a surge of satisfaction knowing he'd squared things with Quincy.

Chapter Thirty-Three

When Ike and Buster returned from working their cattle that afternoon, Lorraine wasn't on the front porch as usual. Ike had taken to leaving Quincy at the ranch house with her while he and Buster were gone. He hurried inside to find Lorraine leaning over a prone Quincy, who lay groaning on Jessie's small bed. "Buster, grab a rifle and keep an eye out. What happened, honey?"

"It was Hawkins. Up in the hills behind the house. When Quincy went out to the barn, he got shot. I know it was Hawkins. I ran outside and couldn't see him clearly, but it was a man who mounted up and scurried away."

Ike eyed Quincy's bare shoulder, blood still oozing from the perfectly-round entrance wound. Lorraine was sweating from the exertion of helping Quincy back into the house. "You go and rest, dear. Please. I've been around enough war wounds to help dress this one. Likely he won't die, 'cause he's young and strong and it got him high up and not right in the chest. Please sit over there and let me doctor him."

Ike yelled to Buster. "Go get the doc." He hesitated. "No, wait. We all need to leave. It's not safe anymore with Hawkins on the loose. We'll stand a better chance in town with Hugh's gun, too." He nodded to Buster. "Get the wagon ready and bring the horses."

With the wagon in front, Ike hefted Quincy outside and placed him gently in the bed. He helped Lorraine in as well. "The herd can fend for itself for a while. Buster, close up the house and drive the wagon." He boosted Jessie into the wagon bed next to her mother and mounted the paint.

Buster tied his horse to the wagon and climbed up to the bouncy seat.

"I'll ride scout; get goin', Buster."

The small troupe started for Cottonwood at a swift pace. The road was filled with shallow ruts from recent rains, and the ride jolted the occupants. Quincy's groans suddenly took a back seat to Lorraine's shrieks. Jessie sat with her back to a corner of the wagon bed, staring wide-eyed. She wasn't crying, but her bottom lip trembled.

Lorraine shouted. "You better get us to town quick, Buster, because this baby is on its way! I don't know if I can hold off 'til we get there." The stress of rescuing Quincy and the jostling of the wagon had taken its toll. She screamed at Ike, "Go get the doc, and hurry!"

Ike hesitated. "I'm not gonna leave you with Hawkins about."

Lorraine yelled, "I don't give a damn about Hawkins right now. If he shows up, he can help deliver this baby! Now go!"

Ike jerked a thumb at Buster who scrambled off the wagon and swung up on his horse and galloped away.

When Buster returned with the doctor, Ike helped him into the wagon bed and jumped in. The doctor gave a cursory glance at a semi-conscious Quincy, then turned his attention to Lorraine. She had Ike's arm in a vice grip and was screaming.

Doc Early laid his hand on her stomach for a moment, then begged her. "Don't push anymore right now, Lorraine. Okay?"

In between several quick breaths, she yelled, "Why not?"

Early didn't answer. He continued with a hand to her stomach and didn't look up. "Just give me a minute without pushing, please." He turned to Ike. "Help me hold her still."

Ike's face drained of all color. "What's the matter, Doc?"

He didn't answer right away. For several minutes, he massaged her stomach hard with both hands. "The baby's not in proper position, and I'm trying to move it."

Ike kept his hands on Lorraine's arms. "Does that mean what I think it does?" He'd turned calves inside his cows but had never seen the same done with a pregnant woman.

Doc kept working. "Yes." Every push and press of his hands seemed to send Lorraine to new levels of pain. Minutes more passed as the doctor worked feverishly. Finally, when Lorraine's screams seemed like they couldn't be any louder, he said, "Now push, Lorraine. Push quickly."

Lorraine grunted. Once, twice.

The third time, Doc declared, "We have a baby! A boy!"

Lorraine's screaming turned into sobs of joy.

After wrapping the infant and checking Lorraine's vitals, Doc shook Ike's hand.

The new father sat dazed, yet dazzled, one hand

holding the little bundle that was his son, the other holding his wife's hand. So much had happened since noon it was hard to take it all in.

Buster kept an eye out as Doc ministered to Quincy. "The entrance and exit wounds are clean, so the shooter must have used a smaller caliber rifle. Who shot him, anyway?"

Without looking over, Ike said, "Hawkins. You seen him around?"

"Can't say as I have, but I've heard he's back in town." The doctor dressed Quincy's shoulder then turned to Ike. "I think he'll be okay, but he's not out of the woods yet. Keep changing that bandage the next few days and let me know if it starts getting redder around the wound. That wouldn't be good. Pour some whiskey on it."

Doc Early cleaned the wagon bed up a bit and motioned for Ike to get off. He took him aside. "I'm sure you already know this, but word around town is Hawkins is laying for you. You stay alert, got it? I don't want to be staring at your lifeless face anytime soon. You need to stay alive long enough to be staring at mine. Your new son needs a father. So does your family."

Ike's eyebrows arched. "Son? You did say son, right?"

"Yes, but I already told you that. You must be as addled as Quincy is right now." The young man had drifted off to sleep after all the poking and prodding he'd endured. Doc looked at the unconscious youth, then back at Ike. "Hawkins is a deadly enemy, so don't you forget it." He started to pack up his instruments. "I'll be over in a couple of days to see both my patients.

And congratulations!"

Ike stuck his hand out. "Thanks again, Doc."

He started to climb back up in the wagon when Early said, "You may not remember because you were in such a lather, Ike, but Buster nearly kidnapped me out here, so I'll be needing a ride back to town."

Ike said, "Well, now that you mention it, we're goin' to town too. Not stayin' at the ranch for a while; gonna hole up at Sue's. Likely safer than at the ranch house, sittin' out there all by itself."

Doc grunted. "Sounds like a good idea. By the way, where'd you get that horse, and where's Ally?"

Ike scuffed at the ground and pursed his lips. He was a mess of mixed emotions just now. "Long story." He broke eye contact.

Buster interrupted. "I'll tie my horse off and drive the wagon, Ike. You stay in the wagon bed and between us, we'll get everyone to Sue's safe, okay?" He helped the doctor into the wagon before Ike could respond. Buster left unsaid what the three men were thinking—Hawkins was still out there somewhere looking for a chance to waylay Ike.

When they got to the boarding house, Sue was in a tizzy, overwhelmed by the prospect of protecting the entire McAlister clan now converged under her roof. After she'd gotten Lorraine, Jessie, and the baby settled in, she had the men bring Quincy to one of the back rooms. Sue kicked an unhappy boarder out, but she wasn't brooking an argument from anyone when it came to her family. Ike brought the professor up to date on Hawkins' latest handiwork. "One of us needs to be on guard at all times. No need to be roamin' around outside when it's dark, either. If I were him, that's when I'd strike."

Walnutt and Buster nodded

Sue said, "The day's slipping away, so it's a good idea to put that staying-inside-at-night plan in place right now. I've got dinner started, but with the crowd we got here, I'll just throw in some more potatoes and carrots."

Ike said, "Not for me. I'm gonna be upstairs with Lorraine and the baby."

"Any idea what you're gonna call him?" Buster wore a smile as he asked it.

"I'll leave that up to the one who did all the work. The only thing I know is it won't be Jessie. One of them's enough." Happiness flickered in his eyes for a moment, then was gone as he headed toward the stairs. Hawkins had made a mistake gunning for him at his house. With his family inside. Ike couldn't abide that.

Chapter Thirty-Four

Hawkins' plan was playing out. For the last several nights, he'd been skulking around town as the stars came out. He focused on the comings and goings of The Sew Pretty. With no customers this late, the shop usually closed about now. He stayed hidden as he watched Margaret's hired lady lock the front door behind her, then head straight for Sue's boarding house. It had taken him some time, but he remembered where he'd seen her before. The Wildfire. Didn't remember her name though. She looked different then. Rouged up some. He could hardly tell she was the same woman.

He'd use her to lure Ike out of the boarding house. Hawkins knew Ike was holed up there ever since he'd shot Quincy. He figured the boy was still alive because the undertaker hadn't been working on a new coffin lately. There was no sense in trying to knock McAlister off there, it was too fortified. The only person besides the saloon girl who left the house during the day was the sheriff, and Hawkins knew he couldn't take him straight up. Besides, he already had a plan in place for Walnutt.

Hawkins considered but dismissed the idea of backshooting Ike. Even he wasn't that low. He'd shoot him face to face. Handling Slade was different. He couldn't have outdrawn the gun hand so he'd tipped the scales in his favor. Besides, the imposter was a man who needed killing.

Tonight he'd settle with McAlister. He gazed into the shop as dusk descended. Margaret and the woman were getting ready to lock up. He rushed in with his pistol drawn and saw the surprised looks on their faces by the light of an oil lamp.

"Stay where you are, and don't twitch. If either of you scream, a gun going off will be the last sound you hear." Margaret looked pale in the dim light, while the young woman stood motionless. "Here's how this is gonna play out. I'm taking you"—he pointed to Hannah—"hostage. You, on the other hand,"—he waved his gun at Margaret—"are gonna hurry to the boarding house and tell McAlister I'm waitin' for him." He squinted at Margaret. "If you don't come back with him, the saloon gal gets it first, then you, and I'll get McAlister anyway. So the only way you come out of this alive is if you do what I say. Now get goin'."

Margaret stared wide-eyed with a blank look on her face.

"Now! Move!"

She nearly jumped. She hurried to the door, then stopped and looked around.

"What're you lookin' for? This gun is the only thing you should be mindful of."

Margaret ignored Hawkins and scanned the room. She dashed to a hat on a wall hook and put it on. "I never leave here without proper attire."

Hawkins was speechless as she headed toward the boarding house. He checked his gun and grabbed Hannah by an arm. He doubled it behind her and with the gun in her back pushed her forward out the door, just short of the street. He held back, staying in shadows cast by the faint moonlight.

Waiting.

****

Ike heard the commotion and hurried down the stairs. Margaret stood in the foyer breathless, with a hand to her chest, crying. She wasn't making any sense, sobbing something about Hawkins and Hannah. "Margaret, settle down and speak clearly."

She took a deep breath. "Hawkins is at The Sew Pretty! He's got Hannah and is holding her until you come there, Ike. He means to kill you, I'm sure, from the look in his eye. He told me he'd kill Hannah if you didn't come."

Ike listened with both thumbs hooked on his gun belt. He drew his Colt and checked the cylinder. Full. He eyed his extra cylinder. The same. Just then, Lorraine shuffled up from behind, one hand to her stomach, the other cradling their newborn son.

"Ike, don't do this. He's trying to lure you into a trap. He'll kill you and probably kill the girl too."

"I'm goin'. This has been a long time comin'. Rob must be avenged, and I'm the one to do it."

She grabbed one of his arms and started crying. "I can't lose you, Ike. I wouldn't know how to carry on without you. Think of your new son and Jessie. Don't leave them without a father and me without you."

Ike hesitated for just a moment, then removed his wife's hand and tied his holster off on his leg. He glanced at Buster and Hugh and his eyes asked them to take care of his family. He pushed the front door open. In a swaying crouch, he skirted Main Street and kept to the wooden sidewalk under the overhang. His limping gait didn't do much to conceal him, and he soon heard

Hawkins' voice in the distance.

"Ah, McAlister. I figured you wouldn't come, what with your family and all. I hear it's bigger now, a new son, right?"

Ike squinted in the direction of The Sew Pretty. How did the bastard know that?

Hawkins' raspy voice sounded like a file being drawn across a steel edge. "I have a suggestion for you. If you haven't already named the boy, you should name him after yourself, so your name will carry on after you're gone, which is gonna be real soon now."

He couldn't quite make Hawkins out yet but knew the killer had Hannah. They weren't more than thirty feet apart. "Let the girl go, Hawkins, or do you need to hide behind a woman when you do your shootin'?" That should bring him out in the open.

"Never needed no woman ever in my life, not like you. That's why you're weak, McAlister, you figure you got too much to lose. Makes you hesitate for just a second, and that's something I never do."

Ike could dimly see Hawkins coming out of the darkness into the street, with the woman in front of him. He had a gun to her head. Hawkins tried to push her away, but she grabbed his shirt and held on.

Her voice rang out in the still air. "You don't even know who I am, do you? Don't do this, Father. You don't have to do this. You can put the gun down and just walk away."

Hawkins turned toward the woman. "What do you mean, Father? Who are you?"

Ike had a clear shot at Rob's murderer now, but something stayed his hand. For some time, he'd had a nagging unease in the back of his mind, and it finally took center stage. He'd had enough of killing. Shooting Hawkins wouldn't bring Rob back. Let the sheriff have him.

Hannah said, "You didn't have any idea you had a daughter, did you? You probably don't even remember my momma. No, of course you don't. The only person you ever cared about was you. She told me about you."

"Your momma?" He paused and stared at his hostage. "Who's your momma?"

She slapped him a glancing blow to his cheek. "That's for not even remembering her. She was the best friend I had. She always said the worst mistake of her life was getting involved with you. You didn't even stick around, just left and hightailed it west, you bastard!"

With a hand to his cheek, he said, "Why should I remember? I can get any woman I want, and I have." It was an infuriating boast.

Hannah yelled, "Does Ohio ring a bell?"

Hawkins thought for a moment. "You mean that little gal back in Cincinnati? Her? That was so long ago I don't even remember her name."

Hannah swung at him again but he blocked her arm. "It was Rebecca, and she was worth ten of you."

"What do you mean was?"

"She's gone to a better place; a place you'll never see. It's called Heaven."

"What made her think I'm your father?" He lowered his gun and stood squinting at a child he'd never known.

"She told me your name, and besides, a woman knows these things. And you. You didn't notice any resemblance? What did you think I was doing those times I sidled up to you in the Wildfire—coming on to you?"

Hawkins stood mute.

Ike kept his fingers curled around his gun's stock.

Lorraine, Hugh, and Margaret had come out of the boarding house and stood on the sidewalk watching the drama unfold. Margaret paced a little with a hand to her mouth.

Hawkins turned toward Ike. "This don't change things none. Our business is still our business." He shoved Hannah clear this time and fired in one motion. The bullet whistled by Ike's ear as he barely cleared leather. A shot rang out from behind Ike, and Hawkins stood with a puzzled expression on his face. He dropped his gun, put a hand to his chest, and looked at Ike. His eyes rolled back, his knees buckled, and he sank to the ground and flopped on his back. Hannah fell to a knee beside him and put pressure on the bloody chest wound. Sucking noises accompanied every breath and blood trickled from the edge of his mouth. His lips moved with faint mumbles.

Hannah said, "Oh no! No! I wanted you to suffer, but I didn't want this. I should have told you who I was earlier. I could have saved you. Damn you!" She turned to the gathering crowd. "Someone get the doctor!"

Ike strode toward Hawkins, gun held high. He bent over the dying man with the pistol aimed square at his head. "Why'd you kill my brother?"

Hawkins stared upward, eyes wide, but was able to stutter, "I didn't…kill…your brother."

Just then, Margaret ran toward Ike screaming hysterically. "It was me! I killed him, Ike! I killed Rob! I swear I didn't mean to. Lord have mercy on my soul!"

She slipped into little chirps and looked skyward.

It was too much for Ike to make sense of. "What are you talking about, Margaret?" He pointed at Hawkins. "He killed him."

On the ground, Hawkins slowly shook his head, and his breathing grew labored. He looked at Hannah. "I'm...sorry I didn't...I didn't—" With a shuddering gasp, he breathed his last.

She bent over her father and sobbed on his still chest.

Ike stood stunned and stared at Margaret. "You killed him? You killed Rob? That don't make no sense. You loved him, didn't you?"

Margaret started walking in a small circle. "Well yes, of course I loved him, and he loved me. I know he did, but he never really said but yes he did he just wasn't the type to prattle on about such things and then when he took up with that saloon girl why I just couldn't let that happen. What would people think?" She looked up and raised her arms to the sky as if she were in a play and the stars were her audience. "I waited for him behind the saloon where I knew he'd be during his evening rounds, and when I asked him to hug me, I just grabbed his gun and then all of a sudden he was on the ground staring up at me with the most peaceful look on his face. I asked him what happened and told him I loved him, and he didn't say anything back, but I know he loved me too."

Lorraine slapped Margaret, and Margaret dropped to the ground in a heap.

Ike stood with shoulders slumped in the middle of the street.

Hugh said to no one in particular, "So that's why

Margaret's been actin' so strange lately. Murder is a secret she could not stomach. I have heard guilt can tear people up from the inside out, and I guess that is what it did to her."

Ike shook his head as if trying to clear his mind. Hawkins wasn't the killer. All this time.

Lorraine hobbled as well as she could to her husband and wrapped her arms around him. She leaned her head against his pounding chest. "It's all right now, Ike. Your family is safe, and your folks would be as proud of you as I am. We'll go home in the morning. We have a wonderful addition to the McAlister clan to tend to. I heard what Hawkins said about naming the baby after you, and I like the idea. Ike junior. We can call him Sonny. That has a good sound to it." A big smile adorned her pretty, but exhausted, face.

****

That night the weary families fell into deep sleeps, some on beds, some on blankets on the floor of the boarding house, all watched over by a wide-awake Buster. In the morning, Lorraine brought baby Ike down to Sue and Hugh for a last goodbye.

Ike exchanged a firm handshake with his brother-in-law. "I want to thank you for shootin' Hawkins. Don't know as I could have gotten my shot off before he fired again."

Hugh's eyes widened. "I didn't shoot him, Ike. Lorraine did. I thought you knew that."

Ike's heart skipped a beat, and his ears rang. A vision of Lorraine in danger again flashed through his head. His wife was an incredible woman. She'd just given birth, then killed a man who had Ike in his sights. He stared at her, then drew her, the baby, and Jessie to

337

him in a long embrace. The thought of losing his family almost drove him to his knees. Killing Hawkins wasn't worth that risk.

Sue said, "What's gonna happen to Margaret now?"

Hugh shook his head. "Not sure. She is surely not in her right mind, but she did kill Rob, and she'll have to answer for that in some fashion."

Ike gradually released his grip on his family and shook his head. He pursed his lips hard. "Guilt is a hard thing." He thought of the young men he killed during the War. "It always seems to come out somehow, some day. Can't help thinkin' about how I drew down on a man for somethin' he didn't do. Gives a man pause. Don't know as guns are much of a solution to anything, now are they?"

Hugh said, "In your jargon, I reckon not. Tell me something, though. You had the drop on Hawkins and you could have killed him and it would have been justified. Why didn't you?"

Ike considered. "I don't know. I just couldn't shoot the man. Maybe I'll make sense of it someday." He smiled at Lorraine holding their new baby boy and stroked Jessie's hair while she held onto his jeans.

Hugh nodded. "Maybe so." He glanced at Ike's family as they gathered around the wagon. "Next time you come to town, stop by, all right?"

"Will do." Ike leaned over and kissed his sister on the cheek. "Thanks for bein' the best sister a man could have."

She hugged him hard. "I know you've been weighed down tryin' to be both ma and pa to me and Rob ever since our folks were killed. Maybe now you can lay that burden down."

Ike's eyes misted. "Maybe I can." He cleared his throat. "Maybe I will." He wrapped an arm around his wife and helped his family into the wagon bed. Buster snapped the reins, and they were off. Quincy would stay at the boarding house to heal more before coming back to the ranch.

When they reached home, Ike lifted Jessie out first, then the baby and helped Lorraine off the wagon. As they headed into the house, Buster grabbed the horses' reins and walked them toward the barn.

Ike was getting Lorraine settled in with the baby when Buster burst into the house grinning from ear to ear.

"Guess who's back!"

A word about the author

Mike Torreano has a military back
student of history and the American
love with Zane Grey's novels about the
in the fifth grade, when his teacher made
read a book and write a report every week.

Mike recently had a short story set durin
Yukon gold rush days published in an anthology, a
he's written for magazines and small newspapers. An
experienced editor, he's taught University English and
Journalism. He's a member of Colorado Springs Fiction
Writers, Pikes Peak Writers, The Historical Novel
Society, Rocky Mountain Fiction Writers, and Western
Writers of America. He brings his readers back in time
with him as he recreates American life and times in the
late nineteenth century.

He lives in Colorado Springs, Colorado, with his
wife, Anne.

The Renewal is the sequel to *The Reckoning*,
released by The Wild Rose Press in 2016.

miketorreano.com